It's a Wrap

IT'S A WRAP

❀

H.H. Fuller

Writers Club Press
San Jose New York Lincoln Shanghai

It's a Wrap

Writers Club Press
an imprint of iUniverse, Inc.

For information address:
iUniverse, Inc.
5220 S. 16th St., Suite 200
Lincoln, NE 68512
www.iuniverse.com

Author's photo by Martha MacLeish Fuller

ISBN: 0-595-24607-9

Printed in the United States of America

For Martha, patron and muse; lover and wife

ACKNOWLEDGMENTS

꧁

I would like to express my gratitude to the teachers who pulled me out of the crowd and gave me permission to write: the late Ken Delwiche, Taylor Stoehr and Alan Pike. Al Gowan, whose writers' group occasionally dwindled to two, but never died, provided stamina when my own was running out.

For the brothers and sisters of IATSE Local 481 and IATSE Local 644; and our business agent Rosy White, my intense gratitude for many wonderful years behind the lens.

Forty Ways to Beat the Reaper on the Kancamagus Highway, ©1986 Martha MacLeish Fuller, and *Lightning on the Clam Flats at Squidneck,* ©1986 Martha MacLeish Fuller, quoted with the permission of the author.

CHAPTER 1

❀

"*T*its and ass?" I almost dropped the side cover of the video camera I was tweaking.

"Generic T and A, baby," said Brendan Schwartz, pushing the glasses up his nose. As a television producer, he invoked his connection to the medium by announcing much of his conversation as if the story were already finished, sitting in its tape transport, and available to the general public after the commercial break.

"So," I said, "you want these generic tits and no-name asses to have a wide olive green stripe surrounded by thin black stripes across them, and universal price coding marks?"

"The piece, Bartholomew," he said, shoving his hands into the pockets of his chinos, looking like a professor abandoning his notes to speak *ex cathedra*, "is to be entitled *Banned in Boston*. Your assignment, should you choose to accept it…"

Aha, I thought, the self-destructing-tape-recorded voice in *Mission Impossible*.

"…is to requisition the use of this beast," he gestured theatrically at the almost reassembled Ikegami HL79E on the bench, "take Nick Rodini to drive and run tape, and proceed directly to the area euphemistically known as the Adult Entertainment Zone…"

…and Sergeant Phil Esterhaus on *Hill Street Blues*.

"...there to discreetly record ladies displaying and/or selling their bodies."

"I'll stay in the van and shoot out the window."

"And hey," he said as he left, "try to get a van that doesn't have CHANNEL 8, THE BIG ONE plastered all over it."

Nick must have heard the news right after I did, because he soon materialized with two large cups of coffee. He swallowed the last of a jelly doughnut, which had left a trail of granulated sugar from his paunch to the upper buttons of his sports shirt, and balanced the coffee cups as he pirouetted near the vehicle key board and snatched the keys under the unofficial label of 'Narc Mobile'. Then, and only then, did he set down the keys and coffee perilously close to the camera, and brush off the sugar.

"I was down in the cafeteria when I got the word from Brendan, another dangerous deed for the dirty duo." Nick went over to the equipment shelves and started to pull out a recorder and some accessories. "Should we wait five minutes to see if Brendan changes his mind?"

"What," I said, "and miss all the fun?" Brendan had mastered a decisive manner, but he could change his mind with the same assertiveness.

I hoisted up the camera onto my right shoulder, and grabbed a battered gray canvas bag. Nick ducked under the carrying strap of the video recorder and grunted as he slid his Adidas gym bag full of cables, microphones and tools off the counter. One hand came free, and he used it to resume the balancing act with the two cups of coffee. We headed out past the production manager's office, waving and getting a good-bye wave from him, though his glasses went white with the glare from his ceiling lighting, and his ear, shoulder and mouth were tied up with a telephone. Nick and I made a quixotic pair as we trundled down the corridors of ecru. Nick would have agreed that I was taller than he was and apparently spaced out, though I don't know if he would have appreciated being cast in the role of Sancho Panza.

We made a stop at Brendan's office to pick up the blank tapes for the shoot. The front desk was occupied by Cheryl, an intern from Boston University who was serving as his associate producer. Cheryl appeared to have read a dress-for-success article judging by the dark gray worsted suit she wore. It had been summer outdoors when I arrived at the station forty-five minutes ago, but Channel 8 was determinedly air-conditioned, and Cheryl didn't work in the field.

"Let's see," she said. "You're going out to get some B-roll for *Banned in Boston.*" B-roll is a news film term for anything that isn't a talking head (an interview or a reporter speaking to the camera).

"B-roll? We're going after starring stuff. You won't need any talking heads to tell *this* story," I chided her.

She shoved three cassettes across the desk at me and a clipboard with a pen. "Just sign it next to the three—Bart…Lane, right?"

I nodded, signed and shoved the cassettes into my gray bag. Cheryl said, "Have a good one," and we headed down more ecru corridors, these broken up with large backlit transparencies, depicting the local on-air personalities of the station, including the anchorwoman who gained ten points in the Nielsens for Channel 8's newscasts by closing each show with a wink and saying, "Have a good one."

We made it out of the station without encountering Brendan and new, revised plans. The Narc Mobile was a van of the archetypal nondescript color known as 'wimp green.' Nick and I took a few minutes to wire up the machines for shooting and driving. Nick pushed the driver's seat as far back as he possibly could, leaving room for me to shoot past him. We positioned the recorder and spare cassettes between the seats so that either of us could easily reload the machine. We performed certain other mystic electronic rites that eased the camera's tiny mind, buckled our seatbelts, and headed for Boston.

To leave the station, you first have to wave at the guard, an older man who looks as if he should be sitting at a stage door. Then you go for about half a block between two lots full of new Chevrolets on the left and Dodges on the right. This brings you to Route One, where you stop until there's a break in the traffic.

"So," Nick said, "one more day of work for you before the end of this month, and you'll have to join the union. Once you do that, you'll be at the top of the freelancer's list and you'll even be able to get a staff job."

"I'd really like that," I said, meaning it. My soul could be moved to a contented yawn by the thought of not having to find, or wait for, each day's work. I loved to shoot documentaries. I was holding my breath—only one day after today—somebody would figure it out and screw me out of a job again. "I bet Brendan and the production manager are watching the days too, though."

There was a break in the traffic behind a clattering old station wagon spewing a large cloud of blue smoke. The rear tires of the van smoked, too, as Nick put his pedal to the metal and fishtailed into the northbound lanes of Route One, heading for Boston. I knew what my next duty would be, so I pulled out my trusty Swiss Army Knife and cut notches out of the tops of Nick's coffee (regular with extra cream and sugar) and mine (black, no sugar).

Nick accepted his cup and had a sip as we cruised past the seemingly endless line of new and used car dealers that made up Norwood's *Auto Mile*. I was thinking of how nice it would be to have a staff job and the freedom to contemplate going into serious debt at some car dealer's.

"Here we are again, doing B-roll," I said. "Do you think they'll bring me in to shoot the rest of the story? Some incisive interviews beautifully lit?"

"I don't think so. Brendan did his interviews last week, mainly with a Harvard Law School professor. I was on the shoot. Just this gray-haired guy talking about how prostitution is a victimless crime and all that."

"I can just picture the station manager doing an editorial after the news. 'I think it is high time we welcomed these outcast girls—er—women back into society and recognized the—uh—benefits they have long provided our community.' Have you ever seen a station manager who could speak well in public?"

"They don't have to speak well—announcers do that. All they have to do is fire guys before someone fires them."

"Ah, station politics. Any heads on the chopping block that I should know about?"

"Well...I heard that everybody loved that news series you shot on people getting evicted for condominium conversions."

"*You* know I shot it, *I* know I shot it, a bunch of interview subjects, half of whom are now homeless and don't count in the Nielsens, know I shot it, but I think the producers make it a point to forget who shot it. Most of them have the loyalty of alley cats."

"It's a little better than that," Nick said, pausing to wipe a bump-caused spill from his dark-stubbled chin with the back of his hand. His eyes darted around in apparent paranoia, but he was merely seeing if it was safe to take the exit ramp onto Route 128. "Maybe they'll have something for you to shoot tomorrow, when we get back from this dog-and-pony show. I ran into the shop steward in the cafeteria yesterday, and he was glad to see your number getting up there. Good clean footage that's easy to cut makes everyone happy, especially the engineers. The editors? The editors are split. Some of 'em want the overtime, some of 'em like to leave the station at five sharp, but down deep they all prefer easy edits to impossible ones. You're doing okay."

Nick floored the accelerator again, pulled out of the slow (10 mph over the speed limit) lane, through the middle lane and into the fast lane (25 mph over the speed limit) to careen through the left hand exit into the northbound lanes of the Southeast Expressway. It was all a bit of a warm-up for encountering the largest concentration of Boston drivers in the world.

"I hope—you're right about—the job," I said, my words getting shaken up by the potholes and bumps we were meeting at seventy miles per hour. We were slicing through Milton now, though not fast enough for the painter's pickup truck that was tearing past in the breakdown lane with a tarpaulin billowing out behind it. Nor were we fast enough for the black Mercedes coming up in the fast lane, its driver simultaneously flashing his headlights and talking on a cellular phone.

We made our way through Dorchester, speeding through the basements of triple-deckers long gone, and under the doorsteps of some that still stood. Boston's skyline looked almost as beautiful as it did on the Channel 8 billboard that rose near Morrissey Boulevard. "Yessirree, Channel 8, Boston," Nick intoned, losing his North End accent to sound like an announcer from that mythical land where people speak well and without ethnic or regional taint. "We've only been driving twenty minutes and we ain't even there yet. I guess they think that nobody would watch us if we were Channel 8, Norwood."

We stopped talking as we got closer to the heart of the metropolis. Potholes and cracks gave way to a road surface that frequently was simply not there. The van's chassis slammed and shuddered over nests of reinforcing rods that had had the concrete pounded off them. I thought I could see daylight through some of the holes, but that had to be an illusion because there was never any daylight under the expressway.

We exited at South Station, curving suddenly through well-trimmed green grass, put there, of course, after they tore down a neighborhood to build the exit. Nick cranked the van onto Kneeland Street and through an arch welcoming us to Chinatown. We moved along narrow streets past noodle companies, shop windows hung with ducks dead, ducks drying, and ducks roasted. Groups of men, clad in short sleeved shirts with collars open and dark slacks, broke off Asiatic conversations to stare at us. This happened with increasing frequency, block after block, until I had to say something. "Jesus, I feel like I'm going up the river in *Apocalypse Now*."

"They're waiting for vans to pick them up and take them to all the suburban Chinese restaurants they work at. They're waiters, most of 'em, just off the boat. When they see *this* Italian, they know that this ain't no Chinese restaurant."

Suddenly, a Chinese supermarket gave way to a fabric wholesaler, and a right hand turn pivoted us around a greasy spoon with a Coke sign, next to an adult bookstore. "Welcome to the Combat Zone, or the Adult Entertainment Area, as its city councilor likes to call it. Please check the area around your seat for any wallet you might have brought on board," Nick intoned, doing an excellent Miss America-finalist-turned-flight attendant.

"Let me guess," I said. "Excellent nose, lean around the throat, southern but not military…I'd say post-Vietnam with just a hint of the *me* decade. I have it—American Airlines '82."

"Take your pick of prizes," Nick said softly, nodding toward the street and rolling down the window.

I had envisioned flaunted hips parading down the street, photographed from fore and aft. Nick reached behind his seat and quietly retrieved his microphone. He held it above his lap, pointing up and out of the window. A long directional microphone in its blatantly suggestive phallic windscreen; it looked more suited to a Greek comedy than our twentieth century television documentary. I cradled the camera in my right arm, tilted up the viewfinder until I could look down into it, played with the aperture (which I always preferred to use in its manual mode) until I was peering down at a miniature black and white moving image of high quality. The sun was high and behind us, yielding vivid images and keeping us in the shadows. I focused on two women walking side by side, cropping out their weary faces. One of them wore a tight-fitting pair of designer jeans and a ribbed turquoise tank top. The other was wearing a tight knit dress, mostly white, but with a broad olive green stripe, bordered by thin black stripes, right across her swinging pelvis. I kept them in focus until they turned to exit frame left. Sure enough, the jeans were branded *Chic*, pronounced 'chick'.

"Stop tape," I said *sotto voce*, "let's take it around a couple of corners and find a 'no parking' zone."

"Damn, Bart, I thought were supposed to be shooting meat for sale. One of those broads was dressed up like a can of vegetables. I mean no-name corn." He cranked the van around a couple of corners, his body and arms working as if he were driving a big rig. "We're in luck," Nick said as he gently braked to a stop, letting a tow truck haul its recalcitrant burden of a large, late-model Mercury away from the curb and into traffic. He shamelessly backed the van into the forcibly vacated spot. "How's the view?"

It was good. A wide frame occasionally broken up by the street traffic showed a variety of women waiting. Was there a special girl in your high school who either ignored or spit at you because you didn't have a large motorcycle, and because you did weird stuff like studying? She was there; still wearing the same smudged white nylon windbreaker. Her eyes had changed, though, communicating nothing but a darting hardness. Another hooker had decided to go for the child molester market, figuring that a Black Watch plaid jumper, the universal uniform of Catholic elementary school girls, would attract the right kind of attention. The long sleeves made the outfit less convincing. The close-up showing the wrinkles around her eyes and too much pancake makeup was frightening. She was focusing large Keane eyes on successive passers by. She wouldn't notice the van.

Dirty white windbreaker got the first bite. He was a medium height; round-faced guy wearing glasses with clear plastic rims. His baggy gray pants and plaid flannel shirt, buttoned-right-up-to-the-top, made me think that his mother bought all of his clothes. I started out with a wide shot, which I was pretty certain they'd never allow on the air without black bars across the eyes. I gently zoomed in to a loose medium shot—feet to shoulders. Gray pants shifted from foot to foot. Dirty white jacket reached out to set a hand on his hip. Her other hand began to gesture palm up. Gray pants scuffed his right foot as if to dig a little hole in the sidewalk. The feet started to turn the body away from the encounter. Dirty white windbreaker moved her hand appraisingly over a wallet bulge to grab a gray buttock. The shoulders under the plaid shirt slumped. I zoomed in closer. A hand covered with flashy rings joined a hairy hand with chewed nails. I followed focus as the two walked away to the right, punctuated by passing cars and trucks.

"This is getting expliciter and expliciter," sighed Nick. "Those TV movies that are supposed to 'address the problem' of teenage runaways who become whores always make the women look so attractive, and they're not. I don't see any Cheryl Ladds or Molly Ringwalds here. And of course they get started by some millionaire who looks like Fernando Lamas. Can we get out of here? Now?"

"Let's cruise around and see what else there is to see. We haven't even run off a whole roll yet."

"You really are a tennis player, aren't you?"

"Yeah," I replied, "but what does that have to do with anything?" I held on to the camera as Nick squealed us into traffic.

"It's just that you can never stop, like you can't just win a game by one point. You have to make that shot and then just one more after that to really put 'em away."

"Thanks for the psychoanalysis." It wasn't a bad analogy; I just wanted to give Channel Eight my best shot right now. "How about just doing one more setup then we'll take a break? Maybe we can find a place near Downtown Crossing or someplace to lock up the van and grab some lunch. I should probably call Brendan to tell him what we got and see what he'd like for the rest of his day."

"That would be great," Nick said as he cautiously navigated around a double-parked beer truck. "If it's near a toy store, I got a bambino with a birthday coming up."

"Ricky?"

"Yeah, he's gonna be three. I hope Doctor Brazelton is right and we'll see the last of the 'terrible twos.'"

We turned onto a one-way street. "Pull up on the left by that alley," I suggested.

There was a fair amount of pedestrian traffic passing. It was scrutinized by the dark beady eyes of a possible professional whose blatantly stockinged legs extended up to a pair of patent leather hot pants. She was chewing gum and pulled a hand mirror out of her large bag to check her face and eyelashes, and to bat lightly at her teased black hair with a flattened hand. She checked the beauty mark near her thin-lipped mouth to see that it didn't look too much like leftover breakfast. She seemed to like the effect of chewing gum, though she switched the mastication from bovine to canine. She put the mirror back in her bag just in time to greet a man who walked up to her and gave her a distracted kiss. She did a little bump and grind, as she stretched the hot pants up to extract a wad of cash from the top of one of her black fishnet stockings. He must have been her pimp, but he wasn't a dashing black man with an easy-going gaze, wearing a full-length leather trenchcoat and a wide-brimmed hat. He was a scrawny, dirty-looking white guy with a lipless slash of a mouth and piercing gray eyes topped by a greased back mane of dishwater-colored hair. A tattoo that said 'Lurleen' was indelibly splotched on his biceps; visible because the sleeves had been fashionably ripped from his once-white T-shirt. He took the cash and produced from his pocket a folded-up knife. He gently massaged her neck and face with the handle. His face broke into a horrible sneer as he pressed the button that snapped the blade open and placed its gleaming point under her chin. Without moving her head, she reached down, worked the bottom of her hot pants up, and pulled another bunch of bills from the top of her other stocking. He closed the knife and gave her a resounding slap across the face. Then, his face returning slowly to a sadistic, lipless grin, he pocketed the knife and cash and produced a crumpled piece of paper, which, after a furtive glance around, he proceeded to explain to her. I couldn't help but wonder if it was a whole life insurance policy, group health plan, or a hotel room to meet a client in. This was unbelievable, like he was putting on a show for us, or maybe a car full of the people he worked for.

His eyes darted around again, he pocketed the cash, gave her a pat on the ass worthy of an NFL halfback, and exited frame left. I held on the wide shot as she began to look for customers and wandered out of frame right.

Nick set his microphone on his lap and whispered, "Victimless crime, my ass. Let's get the fuck out of here."

He leaned forward to shift the van out of 'park'. A hand came around him from the left side of the window and slammed him back into the seat. It was followed by a pair of piercing gray eyes, the slash of a mouth we had just seen in action, and the six-inch business end of a switchblade headed right for Nick's throat.

CHAPTER 2

❀

*M*oving only his wide open eyes, Nick looked down at the knife blade that was reaching in under his chin and the blue-veined hand that was grasping the collar of his shirt. I looked from the knife to the pimp, whose wide-open eyes had rested on me.

"Gimme the film, or your friend gets whacked."

I've always hoped that I'd have something decisive to say at a time like this, but 'Pandering's not enough, you're going for murder one,' or any remark that prolonged or, God forbid, deepened Nick's agony wouldn't have rung true. I set the camera on the floor, holding it against the seat with my calves, and swung slowly around to work on the tape deck between the seats. I stared into those hypnotic eyes while I did this. He didn't have a knife at *my* throat; he couldn't feel *my* heart beating through the outside of a fist wrapped around a handful of *my* tennis shirt. I pressed the eject button and the machine whirred and clinked as it unthreaded itself; a small elevator, now operating on a horizontal plane, wheezed a compartment with our cassette in it out the side. I reached past it, creating the appropriate clatter and clanks, and withdrew my hand from between the seats with a cassette in it. I held it black side up, so we wouldn't get into a discussion about whether or not I had rewound it. The tape was now where the attacker would have to let go of something to grab it. I saw the instant of indecision; his hands were already full.

His eyes and the set of his sneer said 'You better not try anything stupid, sucker.' He released Nick's collar and grabbed the tape away from me. "Now!" I barely whispered in Nick's ear. I grabbed the shift lever and put the van into gear. Nick leaned away from his window and jammed the knife hand away from his throat with an adrenaline-fueled left forearm. He wrenched the steering wheel to the right with his other hand and hit the gas. The knife clattered into the van as we squealed into traffic in front of a bakery truck.

"The bastard got me." I looked over at Nick and saw blood on his shirt and the windowsill. It was flowing copiously from a slash on his throat.

"Pull over."

"No way! That fucker wanted to eighty-six me! We gotta get the hell outta here." His arms and feet continued to work frantically. The Pussycat Lounge and the Art Cinema were careening past as Nick plunged the van along an erratic path back to the expressway. I started to work my way out of the seat. "First things first," Nick spat. "Shift me out of first into something more useful. Jesus, I'm losing a lot of blood here!"

I reached down to lay the camera gently on its side, climbed over the tape deck and around the seat, to where I could check out Nick's wound. Red blood pulsed out of a two-inch gash across the side of his throat. Leaving the bloodstained weapon alongside the seat, I wriggled my Swiss Army Knife out of my pocket and cut a couple of strips off the bottom of my shirt. I rolled one into a loose wad and tried to stop the bleeding. It didn't help much, but I bound it into place. I remembered a bad joke from Boy Scout first aid training about where to put the tourniquet for a neck wound. "Think about getting us to a hospital," I said.

"Whatsamatta you? You got something against a little *paisan'* blood? We go to a hospital and they not only steal the show, they break into the van and steal the camera and the deck. There's some alcohol in my bag. You clean and patch, I'll drive."

"Nobody stole the show. I gave him roll number two and we were still on roll number one."

"You aced him, baby. Point and match to—Bart," he said with a sudden drowsiness. He was starting to fade.

"Now pull over and let me drive. You're running on adrenaline."

His foot was starting to slip off the gas pedal. I climbed back up next to him and managed to stop the vehicle. To a symphony of car horns, I wrestled him into the passenger seat and fastened a seatbelt around him. I wriggled back around into the driver's seat, turned on the emergency flashers, and lit out across the financial district for Massachusetts General Hospital with the horn blaring. I ran stoplights, fish-tailed around corners and sent pedestrians running for cover. I was hoping to get stopped for speeding so that Nick could get a police escort. I stole a glance at him as I spun onto Cambridge Street. His head lolled and occasionally bounced as we hit a pothole, but he wasn't waking up. Office workers carrying their late-morning coffee out of The Steaming Kettle scattered out of my path. Still no police.

Fortunately, television news and documentary work had put me in more hospitals than my own personal health requirements. I knew the way to the emergency room. I almost rolled the van as I skidded onto Blossom Street and kept leaning on the horn. I pulled up behind an ambulance that was in the process of being restocked with a clean gurney. I jumped out and shouted, "Neck wound! Arterial bleeding!"

The emergency medical technicians had obviously been busy and were probably looking forward to a coffee break, but they spun the gurney around to the side of the van and delicately extracted a very limp Nick.

"I'm getting a weak pulse," said the taller of the two. They wheeled him into the hospital rattling off abbreviated directions and descriptions to the doctors and nurses inside.

I pulled the truck to one side, locked it, armed the alarm, and made my way into the emergency room. Fortunately, it hadn't been too busy when Nick arrived. I found the area where he was being worked over by a team of scrub-suited doctors and nurses. I heard snippets of conversation. Frightening words like 'trauma' and 'severe blood loss' were punctuated by the beeping of a heart monitor. Eventually, I heard words like 'stabilizing' and 'fighter'. When one of the medics stepped back from the table and pulled his mask off, I figured it was safe to ask questions.

"How's he doing? I brought him in."

"We got to him just in time. He'll make it. I don't imagine that he was cooking and cut himself."

"No, he was slashed while he was in the driver's seat. He wanted to get back to the station with the story we're working on. I have the weapon and I'll fill in the reports. I've got to call his wife first. Tell me what to say."

I reached Patti Rodini at her office. She worked at a computer company on Route 128. "Rodini, management data," she answered.

"Patti, this is Bart Lane. I'm a cameraman who works with Nick..."

"Hi, Bart. What are you calling me for?"

"It's Nick. We were out taping an assignment and he was injured."

"Oh, my God..."

"He's going to make it."

"He's *going to make it?* What the hell has happened to my husband?"

"He got a knife wound. He lost a lot of blood. I got him to the emergency room at Mass. General."

"Oh, Jesus..."

"The doctor says he's going to be fine. He'll be resting quietly in a hospital room by the time you get here."

"This is awful. Thank you, Bart. It must have been brutal for you, too. Did he pass out?"

"Yeah."

"He must have, because he hates hospitals."

"I'm sorry to be the bearer of bad news, Patti. Please call me if there is anything else I can do."

I rang off, dropped another dime, and called Bob Riley, the production manager. I explained the situation. He told me to cooperate with the police, but to get back to the station with the tape as soon as possible.

A Boston cop was waiting at the emergency desk when I got off the phone. He was a beefy old officer who seemed more interested in filling out his report than getting me to reconstruct events. We went out to the van, and his response to the blood around the front seats was the first thing I heard him say that hadn't been learned by rote. "Shit," he said. "What a mess." He collected the knife in a plastic bag. "Did you get a picture of the guy who did this?"

"Definitely. I even have a shot of him holding this knife."

"I'll take the tape, then."

"It won't do you much good. I don't think you have a player in this format at the police station. Let me bring it back and we'll make you a copy you can play. Is VHS okay?"

"I guess that'll do the job."

I gave him Brendan's name and number and he gave me a card that had his name and number on it. I was lucky to get away with the van and the tape.

Since it was barely past noon, traffic was picking up on the expressway when I wheeled up onto it. It was lonely without anybody to talk to, but I didn't feel like listening to the radio, either. As I drifted along at the legal speed, letting everyone pass me, I thought about what Nick had said. I didn't think I was *that* competitive, I was just in a situation where I had to fight for every day's work and win or starve. I drifted past the Keystone complex, wondering what it was they had manufactured there before they turned out the workers, maybe moving the jobs to Taiwan in the process, and transformed it into an elderly housing complex.

I wanted a job—*this* job. My father had always told me that well-shined shoes, a firm handshake and "look 'em right in the eye" would propel me on the path to prosperity. Of course he and my mother had me in 1947—conferring upon me a card-carrying charter membership in the baby boom. Our generation was changing things, just the way a swallowed pig changes the shape of a python. There was, however, a waiting list for jobs, and no matter what you picked, there would be several people with MA, MS, or Ph.D. degrees just ahead of you.

A wave from the Channel Eight guard snapped me back. The poor man had been only expecting a wave and all the blood on what remained of my shirt was more than he had bargained for. He stared, pushing his peaked cap back on his liver-spotted, bald dome, before waving me in and reaching for the phone. I passed the visitors' parking spots, the undesignated staff spots, where I noticed that nobody had tried to steal my battered Beetle, and pulled into a spot that said 'Production Vehicles Only.'

I carried the camera, deck and two remaining tapes, reflecting that I could be barred from the premises for not wearing a whole shirt. I entered the back door, where pressing a buzzer got you the once over from whoever was in the mailroom at the time. If you're young, chunky and black and are reading *The Biography of Malcolm X*, what can you say to a bloodied white guy? "I'm sorry, the Bicentennial was ten years ago. We are not casting the Spirit of '76 again until the next century. Did you get the story?"

"Yup," I raised a fist clenched around a videocassette. I didn't say anything else because I didn't want to plug Nick's near death into the station's rumor mill.

"Right on, Bro!" He returned the salute with a raised fist.

Between there and Brendan's office, there were a few people who popped their heads out of offices at my approach, perhaps nodding if I happened to catch their eyes. Brendan was in; Cheryl was not, when I got to his office. At the sight of me, his feet came off the desk and he almost started to tighten up his necktie.

"Generic T & A per your P.O.," I announced laconically, plunking the cassette onto his desk.

Brendan signed the tapes back in, made some notations with a sharpie on the one we had used and looked around. "We're missing one, here."

"I used it to try to prevent Nick's throat from being slit."

"Bart, why don't you check in the gear with Riley, and see if there are any forms to fill out, etcetera, etcetera."

I left Brendan to his confusion, hauling the gear back to the equipment room. Bob Riley was just hanging up the phone as I passed his office. "Who won?" he asked. "Why don't you eighty-six the equipment and then drop by? Security says we got some serious blanks to fill in."

I set all the gear on the counter. I pried a battery off the camera and popped one out of the tape deck. I plugged them into the appropriate chargers, and retrieved the unused batteries from our bags and put them on the shelf for charged batteries. The camera and deck had a little blood on them. I didn't want to hear Nick go on about people who get *marinara* sauce all over everything, so I ripped another chunk off my shirt and rubbed the units down with some cleaner. My Rod Laver tennis shirt was now appropriate wear for the weight room at Walpole State Prison.

Bob Riley had a round table in the middle of his office. I took a seat opposite him and he picked up some forms and spun away from his desk to face me over the table. "How's Nick doing?" he asked, looking at me over his glasses.

"He was critical when I got him to the Mass. General emergency room. I didn't leave until he was stabilized. He lost a lot of blood, but he's going to be okay. I called his wife. She's probably there by now."

"That's the supervisor's job. You're in no shape to break the news to her."

Nor have I been carefully trained with the precise words which will head off any litigation against Channel Eight, hereafter referred to as 'the company'. "Nick and I go way back. I know Patti and his kids. I felt that it was my duty."

Riley took off his glasses, revealing smaller eyes than I associated with him. He wearily rubbed them. "Yeah, well, you probably saved me a painful call."

"Before I forget, here are the keys to the narc mobile. It's locked up, a little bloody around the driver's window, and," I put the policeman's card on his desk, "the police will want a VHS dupe of the relevant roll. I told this guy that they didn't have the playback for this exotic professional format and he was nice enough to let me keep the footage."

"All I heard was that we had a bloody mess on our hands. The head of security will probably be down here soon. What happened out there?"

I recounted our adventure, finishing just in time to stand up and be introduced to six feet, three inches of crewcut and beige suit. On grip-crushing Tim Smith, security coordinator, the suit looked like a U.S.Marine uniform, and I, at around six feet and one eighty-five, felt simultaneously puny and flabby, even though my stomach wasn't hiding my belt buckle.

I told the tale again, expanding on the fact that we had pictures of the slasher, though not in the act of slashing, and his prints had to be right there on the knife. "In fact," I concluded, "Nick may have done some serious damage to the guy's wrist. He's probably in an emergency room right now, too. I hope it's not Mass. General."

"I'll call Brendan and get him to run the tape up to engineering for a dupe," Bob added.

"Get the forms filled out. I'd better run this up a flagpole at legal and see who salutes. There are some real gray areas here. We're actually only missing a videocassette, and there's some *civilian*," he sneered, "who's out some cutlery and possible use of a hand. We'll get back to you. Bob knows how to reach you, right?"

I shook the second crunching out of my right hand and settled down to the paperwork, borrowing Bob's phonebook to get a street address for the incident and checking with him to be sure someone else could fill in Nick's workman's compensation and health insurance details. "Anything else I can shoot for you today?" I asked as I shoved the forms across the table to Bob.

"I think you've had enough excitement for one day. Take the afternoon off."

"See you tomorrow?" I tried to keep it light, not desperate, not hungry. All I needed was one more day of work out of the next twelve and I might never have to search for work again. I'd be in the union, and next in line for a staff job. Yes, I could imagine shooting every day.

Bob did me the courtesy of spinning around to check the color coded production chart that hung on the wall over his desk. "Nothing that I know about. We'll see you soon."

I thought I had adequate credentials to be somewhat of a conquering hero. Why was I feeling like something to be scraped off the carpet and put out with the trash?

I went through the empty mailroom to the back door. I unlocked my Beetle and popped the hood release. Maybe I had a T-shirt or something. The blood didn't bother me as much as the fact that it looked like spilled ketchup. Then again, ketchup stains were unpleasant because they looked like blood. No spare shirt in the trunk in the front of my car. Nowhere to go but home.

I'd had enough of the Southeast Expressway, so I went against most commuters, going north on 128 and taking the Mass. Pike to the Back Bay exit. A few more turns and lights brought me to an ungentrified brownstone in the South End. There was actually a parking spot right in front so I used it. The distinctive sound of a

Volkswagen Beetle's exhaust and the slam of its door caused a screaming Asiatic horde to come coursing out of the front door and down the front steps. The six Kinh kids were always glad to see me.

When Nguy Kinh, his wife and family moved in, there had been a lot of deferential bowing—or maybe it was their getting out of the way of this large Occidental. One hot summer night, I knocked at the open door of their apartment with two ice cold six-packs of Singha beer. It took a while, but I eventually pieced together the fact that Nguy had been a lawyer in Saigon, and that they had been boat people. He was now a cook in a Vietnamese restaurant and studying English. Since then, we'd become friends as well as neighbors.

Initially, I think that Rottenberg, the landlord, moved them in so that I'd move out of the second floor and Miss Dorothea Halloran, a retired librarian, would vacate the third. With us gone, he could easily pitch out the Kinhs and convert the building into condominiums. He hadn't realized that Miss Halloran had also been a union organizer and that her younger brother was a city councilor. I knew her as a proper *éminence grise* whose well-preserved figure was covered with an overcoat and veiled hat in all seasons. Plotting strategy against the Mephistophelean Rottenberg, a hint of sterner stuff emerged in her lace-curtained parlor as she produced Port to sip and computer printouts of all of Rottenberg's Boston holdings *and* the tenants therein. She also found out, through a zoning application, that he was trying to break loose a chunk of Kinh's apartment for a Bank of New England cash machine. Occasionally I tried to sidestep the assault of facts and tactics to find a way to ask how time and the tides had left her so alone.

It was too early to think about eating dinner, but not too soon to plan something. I took off the remains of my shirt and threw it into the trash bucket. Since it had clearly died in the line of duty, I saluted it, and turned my attention to the old roundtop Norge Refrigerator. There were a few bottles of Rolling Rock, so I pried the top off of one and drank it as I continued my perusal. There was a plastic bag with a couple of fried pork chops in it. Some Boston lettuce had become impatient and died, so I heaved the slime-filled bag into the trash, like the first handful of dirt in the grave of my shirt. The beer was certainly still good, and another day of waiting would neither hurt nor improve a jar of stir-fried zucchini. I went over to the cupboard to see if there was any inspiration in the form of a *paella* kit or instant *fetuccini*. There was a promising box behind a jar of popping corn. Christ on a bicycle, it was chamomile tea.

I could picture Corinne coming home after a day of work. The jingle and scrape of keys at the front door; staccato footsteps and the crunch of a large grocery bag of organic fruits, vegetables, brown rice and some exotic staple like chamomile tea. I sniffed it, but I couldn't detect anything of her scent.

We had met about five years earlier. She was fresh out of film school; a production assistant on a very low budget feature. I was the Director of Photography, or cameraman, a position which spelled dominant male to her. Shooting any feature except, perhaps, for an eight-to-five studio job, makes you part of a large family. Ten to twenty hours a day of enforced collaborative creativity and drudgery create bonds that make sibling relationships look arbitrary and pale by comparison. With the mercurial father figure of the director making us work double time just to keep up with his changes of mind, Corinne and I were like galley slaves who shared a bench before we became buddies. We were buddies before we became lovers.

I thought I knew her before she moved in with me. I thought that someone whose appearance and attitudes mirrored my own late-sixties consciousness had been around enough, at twenty-three, to have seen what life had to offer and made her choices. I should have seen it coming.

It seemed like a good idea when she was offered the job of assistant to the agency producer at Kondazian and Lively. *Do* some time at a large, successful ad agency. *Learn* to separate people from sizeable sums of money. It could only help our future, where she would produce and I would shoot and maybe direct beautiful movies. She did; she learned.

It was only a year before her boss left the agency. It was in the trade magazines that came to cover our coffee table. It was in the *Boston Globe's* business section. He was starting a "boutique-style" production company that would specialize in "the best television commercials".

We went to the opening of his loft studio. The look was commercial archaeology with a five-cent Coke machine, standing open, a Ford gumball machine, and even a slot machine. Corinne looked dashing in a scoop necked royal purple velvet evening gown. High heeled shoes and a French braid completed her regal appearance. I wore my old faithful blue blazer with its pocket full of business cards. There was, in addition to ice cold six-and-one-half-ounce bottles of Coke, wine, cheese, popcorn and an open bar. A videocassette player supplied a large screen television with our host's favorite spots from his tenure at K&L. Corinne was now the agency producer.

We were just getting used to the increased cashflow in our place. She didn't yet feel comfortable enough with her authority to get me some good commercials to shoot, but there'd be time for that. We could do just about anything we wanted to except stay in bed on a weekday morning. Then, K&L was bought up by Higginbottom, Satori, Simmons and Boyle of New York City. Corinne was offered a promotion into the home office. She took it.

There were visits back and forth. I became a regular rider on Amtrak's *Merchant's Limited*; she became a Frequent Flyer on the Eastern Shuttle. Part of us reveled in the luxury of choosing between weekends in New England or Manhattan. Then we missed a couple of weekends because I was off shooting a documentary on a Zen monastery near Carmel, California. Despite frequent letters and long distance phone calls, it wasn't easy for us to get back together.

When we finally did, it was at a bistro on West 57th we had frequented in the past. I got there first, stowing my overnight bag under our usual table for two. When she first came in the door, I hoped it wasn't her. My California girl had transformed herself into David Bowie, complete with stubble on the back of her graceful neck. Our food was barely touched. It came out that everything I had offered or had hoped to offer couldn't compete with her career. It would be very inconvenient for me to spend the night because she had to spend Saturday preparing for a Sunday supermarket shoot.

We were history.

I pitched the chamomile tea into the garbage on top of the Boston lettuce and my shirt.

It wasn't as hard to wake up alone as it had been to climb into an empty bed. Wandering through Back Bay, I had found something to eat and a lot to drink. I hadn't found anybody to pass the time with. I wasn't enough of a regular anywhere to be remembered by a bartender. There wasn't any point in asking *any*body, 'How about those Sox?' It was too early in the season for 'em to blow it. Now my head had a slight ache; my mouth felt like it had been invaded by a work detail armed with library paste and blow dryers. My eyelids lacked the muscle power to open.

The phone rang. The answering machine had been so determinedly empty yesterday that it never occurred to me to leave it on while I slept. I rolled out of bed and went to take the call on the kitchen phone. It was near a large calendar (for checking my availability) and a scratchpad for taking notes. I hoped that the open curtains and streaming sunlight wouldn't present my nakedness too dramatically to any neighbors who just happened to be looking at my window. I grabbed the phone before it could deliver any more shattering rings. "Hello?"

"Bart? Brendan."

"Brendan? Bart."

"Loved your Combat Zone stuff, big guy. You lined up all of the W's."

I don't know why 'lined up W's' made me think of gas station men's room wall drawings of women on their backs, but they did.

"I mean," his voice continued,"you have the 'who', the 'what', the 'where', the 'when', and that payoff scene, if that's not the 'why', I've never seen one."

"Thanks, I mean that's great. It sounds like you have enough picture to tell them what you're going to tell them, tell them, and tell them what you told them. I'm glad you like our work."

"I started editing the piece yesterday and it cuts like warm butter. I think we're talking Emmy Awards and Peabody Prizes here."

"That's great to hear. It couldn't happen to a more deserving producer. Let's go out real soon and do it again."

Brendan's good news voice shifted to his 'new input' or bad news voice. "Unfortunately, we have a bit of a problem there. Tim Smith, Mr. Security, rang me up with some disturbing news. It seems that there is a car full of heavy hitters parked on the entrance road checking out who's coming, who's going. I don't think they're counting traffic for the billboard guys."

CHAPTER 3

❀

"**D**oes the station have any means of protecting endangered freelancers?" I could be shaved, dressed, and on my way to the safe house of their choosing in seconds.

"Tim felt I should warn you and we agreed that it would be good if you didn't drop by until we get this thing on the air. They usually stop trying to kill a story once we've aired it."

"What about Nick? Are they after him?"

"He's under police guard at Mass. General, right now. When he comes back we'll put him in the control room or the studio—something in-house."

As opposed to something *out*house for me. "Thanks for the info, Brendan. Can you give me a description of the car and maybe a plate number? If they're after my ass, I'd like to know all I can about them."

"Let me put you on hold for a minute while I get to Security on that." Channel Eight had musical hold. Not some local radio station that might interrupt with *its* news and commercials, and not Muzak; my wait was performed to *Television's Greatest Hits*. I had to sit through all of the theme from *Leave it to Beaver* and the stirring introduction to *National News at Seven* before Brendan got back to me. "Okay, Hombre, get out your pens and pencils. It's a current generation Buick, large four-door sedan, navy blue—I think GM actually calls it midnight—and its plate number is eight six ee em."

"Eighty-six 'em? I'm being shadowed by a hit man with a vanity plate and a vestigial sense of humor?"

"Sorry 'bout that. I'll be getting in touch with you when this thing blows over. We'll have to have a conversation."

Weren't we just *having* a conversation? I hung up the phone. The digital wall clock in the kitchen startled me as it clicked into ten thirty-one A.M., *sans serif* time. I was naked, unemployed, and now a target for some unfriendly people who suspected that I had done them dirt. If Brendan was any indication, I wasn't currently qualified to have a conversation. I hoped that there was still some coffee in the cupboard.

While the water was coming to a boil, I went into the bathroom and scraped my face with a razor, reminding myself to buy some new blades. Brushing my shaggy dishwater brown hair into a semblance of order, I stared at my face in the mirror. I wasn't doing too badly considering that the big four-oh was right around the corner. My nose refused to turn into a beak in spite of all of the beatings I had obtained for it in my formative years. My chin was tastefully under-stated. I pondered disguise as I exited to the bedroom and started pulling on some clothes.

Back in the kitchen, I turned off the teakettle just as it started to scream and set up a coffeepot. Today I was self-employed; between films; on HQ duty.

First, I typed up an invoice for Channel 8 so that the prospect of incoming funds would soften the blow of paying bills. Checks to Commonwealth Gas, Boston Edison and New England Telephone were next. Even with paying Rottenberg's rent for July, I could go shopping with impunity.

It wasn't a Monday morning or a Friday afternoon, so it was a good time to call up some production managers and hear, anew, the usual excuses. I mean, what could be a nicer time to shoot your commercial than late June in New England? The summer-beachy stuff had already been shot during winter and spring in Florida, the Bahamas or the Virgin Islands. During the actual summer, there were never enough decision-makers around to agree to do a commercial. A crucial member of the team was always on vacation.

Nevertheless, I dutifully dialed away. The receptionist at the first place I called said that the party I wished to talk to did not respond to a page. She asked me to repeat my name and spell it for the message she was taking. How hard can Bart Lane be? The second production house had the person I wanted to talk to on the other line. Would I like to hold? After spending long enough on hold to read articles headlined *HSS&B, MARSCOM VEEPEES INK PACT,* and *UPSWING SEEN FOR NY PROD. SCENE,* in *Backstage,* I was about to launch into *INDO-US CO-PRODUCTION: MYSORE KARMA TO LENS IN NE,* when the switchboard person came back on the line to tell me that Ms. Gerandazian was still on the other line. Other numbers yielded one out sick, two on vacation, enough staff meetings to plan D-Day and a couple of client meetings. I felt that my luck was turning when Pete Pickle of Peter Pickle Productions answered his own phone. Eureka!

"Hi, Bart, listen, I've got someone on call waiting. Could I call you when I'm done?"

A different kind of limbo. When you get past the busy signals, hold, the unanswered ring and the multitude of alternatives to sitting and waiting for your call, to the very party you are trying to reach, shouldn't you be rewarded with a few minutes of telephonic contact? Now, because of his civilized request and his high-tech phone service, I had the opportunity to cease my telephonic activity while waiting for the ring which would probably never come. Hey! Pickle! Shouldn't we sign a contract or something before I agree to stand around and do nothing at your request?

I gave him ten minutes while I turned on the radio, switched from WGBH (because it was too late to wake up with Vivaldi) to WBCN (rock and irreverence tailored to baby-boomers) and made up my shopping list to the accompaniment of Led Zeppelin and The Electric Light Orchestra.

I tried Pete again and got his answering machine. "Peter Pickle picked a peck of prize pix. Can you say that? After the beep?"

I turned on *my* answering machine. My messages had run the gamut from exercises in audio brilliance to the 'I'm sorry I can't come to the phone right now' variety. One harried associate producer had left the message, "You *can't come* to the *phone*? What are you *doing*? Are you in the *john*? Have you got someone in the *bedroom* with you? *What the hell is going on over there*?" I had tried to find out what she was on at the time, and whether it had been supplied by a client of hers, or a competitor of mine. I drew a blank there, too.

What was going on was that I was trying to leave a message that didn't say, "Attention burglars, the premises are empty. Everyone is gone. Since I'm a professional who makes his living with a lot of expensive equipment, there's a chance that it will be lying around, yours for the taking. Be sure to mess the place up so that the insurance company will believe my claim."

I locked the door several times behind me and headed down the stairs. The Kinh kids were not in evidence. The street was dazzlingly sunny, the brick sidewalks pink and warm. I made my way to Tremont Street. Large murals on the side walls of buildings exposed by urban renewal and arson depicted the struggles of large-shouldered and small-hipped Hispanics and sunglasses-and-*dashiki*-wearing Blacks in their heroic efforts to forge *community*. The graffiti that seemed to be magnetically attracted to every other vertical plane were absent on these works of art. Ah, to be an artist with community clout.

There was a *bodega* that I liked to buy what I could at. *Se habla Español* was about the only legible sign on the front windows, most of the other signs being rendered unreadable by the bleaching of the sun and the iron grating that covered the windows most of the time. Inside, the combined smells of old meat, sawdust and cumin dominated. Señora Muñoz, short and cuddly of build, with large dark eyes and black hair in a pencil-bound bun, presided over the cash register. She smiled when I said, "Buenas dias," and returned the greeting elaborately, as if she were my tutor. She was.

Whether or not there were any customers, Señor Muñoz was always scurrying back and forth behind the old porcelain and glass meat counter. A paunch represented his success, but he always ran a worried hand through his graying ducktail as he asked me what I wanted. Maybe relatively large *gringos* weren't noted for paying for what they took where he came from. Maybe he was wondering when he'd have to start making quiche and pasta salad in order to remain solvent in this changing neighborhood. Maybe the building's owner was going to evict him and install a cash machine and a retail condominium. I requested a couple of pounds of *chorizos*.

Señora Muñoz's *adios* floated after me as I left the store with my purchases. There was a genuine greasy spoon next door where I got a cup of coffee to go. I took my coffee and groceries to a vest pocket park in the shade of the Hispanic mural. It's good not to be so busy that you don't have time to stop and smell the ailanthus. It was reassuring to note that I wasn't being followed by a large midnight blue Buick, Massachusetts plate 86 EM.

The late afternoon sun blasted through my window into a vastly cleaner abode. I had initially taken the 'young visual artist' approach to decorating the place. Walls of bold colors with a select few of stark white; a Grateful Dead poster here; a few matted photographs of my own taking there. Corinne tempered my design with Navajo wall hangings, Japanese prints, and paisley curtains, to say nothing of the potted plants in macramé hangers. I was never moved to an orgy of tearing down and throwing out—it still felt more comfortable than it had before she had moved in.

What I really needed was a lobster for dinner. I was not in poverty; I was not in the chips; but I was in New England. My part of the South End doesn't run to lobsters in stores or on menus. An expedition into the heart of the city was called for.

Within walking distance, there are places that will do a lobster thermidor or some other pricey variant, but for that craving that just wants the basic boiled beast with butter, and not much atmosphere, reflected in the reasonable tab, I like Dini's, near Boston Common. If your waitress was ever a student, she'd never let on.

I took a shower and changed into white ducks, a chambray work shirt, and Topsiders. I left and locked the apartment, but headed up to pay a visit to Miss Halloran. Boston Rule Number One: Don't just call a cop, call your councilman. When she opened the door to my knock and invited me in, I was greeted by a scene of unexpected domesticity. Captain Ryan, whom I had only ever seen as a boatered and blazered old gent paying a social call with a bouquet of flowers, could clearly be seen working away in the kitchen, chopping onions very deftly. A shock of white hair hung almost into his clear blue eyes as he beamed and nodded a greeting at me. His sleeves were rolled up, necktie loosened, and he was wearing an apron that looked like it was his. Dorothea, likewise, had shed the Miss Halloran, and was wearing a Hawaiian print muumuu with an orchid in an abundance of wild silver hair that couldn't be imagined under the hats she usually wore.

"Bart, how nice of you to drop by! What brings you here?"

Lives, apparently happy ones, going on under my very nose.

"Good evening to you both," I managed through a grin that was wider than my circumstances warranted. "I'm going out for the evening and just wanted you to know that if you heard loud noises coming from my apartment, it would not be me. The people who might break in are professionals. Call the police, but don't try anything else with them."

"Oh, Bart, what have you gone and done now? More unpopular stories about popular people?"

"Please—uh—put us in the picture," said Boston Police Department Captain Ryan, Retired, wiping his hands on a tea towel as he joined the conversation.

I recounted my adventures of the day before, including all of the details that had since come to light. Dorothea and Captain Ryan were fascinated by the tale, but appalled at Channel 8's behavior.

"It's hardly fair, their hanging you out to dry like this," said Dorothea with well-honed indignation. I was flattered to feel it directed in my behalf.

"I'll call Patrick Horan at District D. He always likes to give the lads in patrol cars something to look for," the captain said thoughtfully. "You should be safe in *this* neighborhood, for a change, but watch your step. Some very big fish might not want this fellow arrested or tried. He may know names."

We said our farewells and I headed down the oak-wainscoted stairway to the first floor. The front door was open, letting in the evening's cool breezes. Nguy Kinh squatted on the front steps; drinking a can of Miller's and watching his brood at play on the sidewalk.

I sat down beside him, not having the bone structure for a good Oriental squat. "Hi, Nguy. Listen, if anyone shows up looking for me, especially if they're in a dark blue Buick, pretend that you don't understand English at all."

Nguy started to stammer, choke and gag in rapid and varying succession. After about thirty seconds, and just before I gave him a healing slap on the back, he stopped abruptly and said, "Like that?"

"Perfect. Thank you very much. I owe you some more Singha beer." I got up, brushed off the seat of my pants, and strode purposefully through the city to dinner.

Dini's will usually be like you remembered it. I was shown to a banquette that faced the door even though I hadn't told them that I was a hunted man. Their available wines included an acceptable

French Chardonnay that was available in half bottles. I ordered that, which the waitress confirmed by asking, "Numbah foah?" After a brief internal struggle between the clambake approach or dinner out, I opted for the latter, ordering an appetizer of raw littleneck clams and a boiled one and a quarter pound lobster with French fries and a side of salad with the house Italian dressing. My experienced waitress read my selections back to me, shoved her pencil into her blond bouffant, and made her way to the kitchen to carry out my fondest desires.

Perhaps an apology is in order to all the marine life that died in order to feed me so well. I needed to sensuously slurp the chilled clams from their shells. It was therapeutic to rend the lobster limb from limb, crack its shells, and consume its flesh. The weight I had specified, though costing more than a mere chicken lobster, provided additional meat in the body cavity. More mayhem; more food.

I finished off with Boston Cream Pie, coffee and cognac. I didn't have to worry about driving, after all. It was about nine o'clock when I finally paid what I owed, left something for my long-suffering server, and reluctantly extracted myself from the shelter of my banquette.

The sidewalks were abandoned and giving up the last of the afternoon's heat. They took me past a few small shops and a lot of office buildings, but this was not an area that might attract pedestrians at this hour of the night. The street, in direct contrast, was so jammed that I felt alone on a stage in front of a packed house. Tremont Street was a snarling, foul-breathed knot of traffic. Was there a particular type of person who habitually drove around the city at this hour? Did they drive big-ticket European imports? A few did. Was there any preference for Japanese cars? Not a marked one. A battered Toyota station wagon emitted a large, dense cloud of burning oil as it lurched forward. 'Save the Whales—Boycott Japanese Goods' proclaimed its bumper sticker. Detroit was represented by taxicabs, a few station wagons with out-of-state plates and OOPS.

A large, midnight blue Buick.

Mass. plate eight six ee em.

A face I never wanted to see again spotted me from the passenger seat just as my mind had leisurely arrived at the conclusion that I was in deep shit. He swung his right hand around to point at me, but he couldn't stop it in time, being unused to having the weight of a plaster cast on that particular appendage. He clouted the driver who briefly lost control and bumped the Ohio station wagon in front of him. Two large shadows tried to get out of the back seat, but they only succeeded in bumping their doors futilely against the cars on either side of them. I took off, my adrenaline finally connecting. I ran against the flow of traffic, running like drunks drive—fast.

At least it felt pretty fast. My Topsiders gripped the pavement and—thank God—my feet. I was getting a rougher ride than my New Balance running shoes would have given me, but the cornering was pretty good as I spun the corner onto School Street. Brookstone's—down on the left—perhaps I could buy a pocket sized teargas canister. Closed. Coming up on The Parker House. Maybe I could get away from everything. Rent a room; buy a newspaper at the cigar stand and hide behind it in the lobby. I stopped short. I remembered an interview I had shot with the manager of that place for *Hotel Headaches*, a special Brendan had done for pre-primetime broadcast in an attempt to hold onto the *National News* audience for the eight o'clock premiere of a series set in a large metropolitan hotel. The manager, requesting anonymity, had appeared in silhouette against a background of the Boston skyline. Remembering what he had said about the senior bellboys "in *some* hotels" I didn't go in. He had said that there was always someone in the Mob's pocket. He couldn't even *consider* changing linen services without getting a visit from some very threatening people. He thought that it might be the doormen or the bellboys, but he didn't really want to know. I could have gone in the front door, and nobody would have stopped me, but I might have left the way he depicted the profits leaving; in a laundry hamper, in a dumpster, or perhaps like the towels in a guest's luggage.

Brendan got an Emmy for that show and nobody got sued. We had done a lot of tight shots that avoided faces, and some explicit reenactment by Brendan in a variety of rented generic uniforms.

Behind me, Tremont Street traffic was crawling. They'd probably try to follow me by heading down Bosworth. I sprinted back the way I had come, remembering cross-body blocks, clothes-lining, and some other good football stuff. I stopped just short of the corner and peered around. The sidewalk had only a strolling couple on it. In a screech of rubber, the rear end of something large and dark blue was slewing onto Bosworth Street.

I didn't know how long Downtown Crossing would tie up my pursuers with the stores closed. With broken-field running techniques that I'd only had a chance to use in my dreams, I crossed Tremont through the heavy traffic and charged up Beacon Street. Up was the operative word, since this was the small portion of that street which climbed the hill of the same name. There was an open cocktail lounge and a bar. If I tried to hide in one of them, I just might get too close to someone who'd stick a needle in me and then help me out like a passed-out drinking buddy.

The Athenaeum loomed up on my left. Large bronze doors, stout enough for a fortress, were swung open. They looked more promising than trying to hide behind the street level balustrade, so I pushed my way through the studded, red leather-covered inner doors and found myself all alone in a dim cavernous chamber that perfectly suited the classic stone facade of the building. I caught my breath under the stern gaze of Daniel Webster and Justice Marshall. There was a pair of paned doors that revealed a sign-in desk and reading room behind them. I approached them and a buzzer sounded. I entered.

A smiling youngish man, whose greased crewcut, ringed ear and skinny tie were clearly all the punkiness he was allowed during working hours, gently inquired, "May I help you?"

I pulled out my wallet, quickly flipped it open to my photo-bearing driver's license and just as quickly closed and pocketed it as I said, "Bart Lane, Channel Eight."

"You'll want the second floor. Do you know the way?"

"No." I hadn't expected to *be* expected, but I thought I might as well go for it.

"Through the next set of doors, to the right, and you'll see the elevator."

"Thank you very much." It all had the ring of a distinctly good idea.

The elevator was a closed, intimate antique. Pressing the 'up' button woke it from a sojourn on some other floor, but it arrived quietly, precisely, and opened its door with the utmost discretion.

It must have made a little more noise when it opened for me on the second floor. My immediate impression was of a room full of well-dressed people sitting entranced amidst walls full of books under the sightless gaze of two ranks of marble busts. The elevator door disturbed their reverie and they simultaneously sat up and began to applaud gently. 'Hear, hear,' and 'Bravo' were heard, but no whistling or stamping of feet.

Facing the assemblage was a woman on a raised dais. She looked very interesting from behind, which was my first view. Chestnut brown sausage curls cascaded over her bare shoulder blades. Her backless gown of ivory plunged to reveal perfection—the small of a lightly bronzed back—stopping its well-planned dive just short of offering up that particular décolletage for public inspection. My second, or third, or fourth thought about her was that she had dressed herself to balance the Venus, with arms, that wasn't quite looking at her from the other end of the room.

I stayed as near to the side of the hall as I could, making my way back to find an empty seat. A poster on an easel revealed that this was a poetry reading and book signing for Elisabeth Hemphill, poet. The celebrated volume was entitled *By Motor Through Five States and Eight Lifetimes.*

I found a seat near a worried-looking man in the back row. He stopped rearranging his few red hairs over the top of his head under the guise of mopping his brow long enough to pull a seersucker jacket off the chair next to him and indicate its vacancy. I looked at the poet just as she set down her glass of water and took her nicely-set blue eyes off me. "Now I'd like to read *Forty Ways to Beat the Reaper on the Kancamagus Highway.*" The front of her gown was as chaste as the rear was risqué. I don't think, however, that your average vestal virgin could speak as well as this woman could. Her voice didn't have the nervous timbre that mine would if I had to talk to more than a dozen people at once. It was the kind of voice that, if you heard it over the phone, would make you not want to meet the speaker face to face and ruin your fantasies.

Her reading and words were wrapping up the audience again, and me with it. Not since I had heard Archibald MacLeish's *Memorial Rain*, delivered by my aging thespian of a sophomore English professor at Williams, had I been so entranced by a poem. I couldn't help but notice that the audience, not apparently one to be moved by such things, was being wound up like the engine she was shifting down into second gear for a hairpin turn to the right. They were following her along clifftops and through rock cuts. They stopped on a dime for:

> "Peter Brown,
> Thirty-four,
> Wife, three kids,
> Trucker of sofas
> Portland to Burlington
> Running late

Out of time
Out of room
Into space.
Gravity won.

She resumed the journey carrying the whole room with her to the dénouement.

Again, silence. Her eyes embraced the audience. "Thank you." Her words again released the audience to a round of applause that threatened the busts of the founding fathers on their pedestals. At that moment, she was approached by the man who had admitted me downstairs. He whispered in her ear, his eyes darting until they fixed on me. Her eyes fixed on me as she smiled and nodded. Bart Lane, the inquiring cameraman, strikes again.

I was sipping Champagne punch and eating a caviar-topped hors d'oeuvre, feeling like I was in a naked-in-the-streets dream, having no tie and jacket, and wondering how I personally might survive another day when Ms. Hemphill excused herself from a conversation with a vaguely familiar gentleman with a walrus mustache and approached me.

"Channel Eight," she said, extending a jeweled right hand. "Just in time, too. I was going to call the fourth estate and give it or them a piece of my mind. Do you know what the fifth estate is?"

"No, I don't."

"Well, neither do I, but if none of you folks showed up, I was going to have my agent give it a call. Your name is…?"

"Bart Lane." I extended a hand to shake. She shook it once but didn't let it go.

"That makes more sense than what I thought I heard up there. Isn't Park Lane a kind of car?"

"Either that or the address of some nice London hotels."

"Much better. I'm Elisabeth, with an 's', not Bess, Bet, Beth, Betsy, Betty, Liz, Lizzie or Liza."

"What about lissome? I think that could apply." Oh, God, why did I say that?

Warm and lovely laugh lines appeared at the corners of her eyes. She brought her other hand into play. "Elisabeth," she said with the straightest face she could manage, "with an 's.'" I hoped that my handshake was proving firm and interesting. "So, where's your big rig?"

"My *what*?"

"I subject, you news person. Lights? Camera? More TV persons?"

"Back at the station, hiding, and convalescing, respectively."

"I don't do this kind of reading every day, you know. If this wasn't a photo opportunity, it was at least a couple of sound bites."

"I'm the cameraman and I'd give anything to be shooting tonight. I'd like to tell you that I'm researching a documentary." Why was I spilling my guts to this person? "Maybe I am, but the main thing I'm doing right now is running for my life."

"Jesus," she looked daggers at someone across the room. "I finally think I'm getting some good P.R. from my agent and it turns out to be a damned fugitive."

"Don't forget 'blacklisted.'"

"You're right, 'damned blacklisted fugitive' scans better." She took my hand again, in both of her hands, and drew herself close to me. My captive hand was forced into a softness not shared with the gathered literati. "Could you do me a favor? I have got to get over there and sign some books. I'd be very grateful if you could keep me supplied with the alcoholic punch and some of those caviar thingummies."

"I'd love to. I have no place else to be."

"One more thing—don't leave."

"Excuse me Ms. Hemphill, but…"

"That's Elisabeth with an 's.' Listen, I have to think."

"*I'm* a sitting duck here and *you* have to think?"

"Yes," she pronounced with a finality that ended my personal audience with her. Maybe it was a good idea. Left to my own devices, I was hurtling toward a mid-life crisis I might not survive. I didn't leave. I fetched and shuttled food and beverage for the poet, feeling useful, for a change. When the line began to dwindle, I thought I'd buy a copy and get it signed. I moved in behind a couple that was discussing one of the poems they had heard. They couldn't agree whether the dominant influence was Rilke or Rimbaud. I couldn't help but wonder if a claim for Whitman by one would have evoked Wilbur in the other.

When I finally got my turn at the table, the lady behind it retrieved her tortoise shell glasses from the end of a pearl chain around her neck and checked a list next to the cash box. "A press copy for Mr. Lane of Channel Eight," she said in a croaking, but cute, voice. "Hang on to your money, dearie," she added confidentially.

I was still at the end of the line when I ended up facing the poet. "Could I sign this later?" Without waiting for an answer, she capped her pen, stood up, took my arm and steered me over to the beverage table. "Get us another round and wait right here." She crossed the room, moving easily through the thinned crowd, and spoke a few words to the worried man I had been sitting next to. With her high heels on, she was approximately my height. A noble thing in a woman, I thought.

"It's all taken care of," she said when she returned, reaching out a hand for her champagne. "Let's finish these slowly and then move on."

I sipped and, as ordered, stayed near Elisabeth while she shook more hands and accepted more compliments. For the most part I felt like a grinning fence post, but occasionally, she remembered a name and the handshakes and introductions included me.

"I believe, Bartholomew, that it is time to split this scene," she whispered softly in my ear as the last well-wishers moved on. We said goodnight to the people who were apparently running the show, and took the elevator down to the first floor. At the desk where I had checked in, the same attendant set out Elisabeth's silk shawl and a briefcase-sized bag.

"Everybody coming out *loved* the reading. They almost all had books and they couldn't stop *talking* about the poems."

"Thank you, Richard," she said as I helped her on with her shawl and hoisted her bag off the desk. Under the guise of clinging to my left arm, she hauled me out past the safety of the door and through the echoing sanctuary of the foyer.

A black limousine glistened in the gaslights of the street outside. A liveried chauffeur opened the door for us. I forgot to check the street for pursuers and followed Elisabeth's example in settling back in the plush appointments as the door was discreetly closed. I found myself enveloped for the first time in her scent as she leaned over and whispered in my ear, "They do this for best-selling authors and the odd marginal poet."

CHAPTER 4

❁

E lisabeth reached to the side of the seat to press an intercom button. "Could you please give us some skyline and Charles River?"

"A pleasure, ma'am," came the slightly electronic reply as the car
pulled smoothly away from the curb. "The bar is stocked per your
request. You'll be returning to your residence?"

"Yes, and thank you, James." She flipped off the intercom and
leaned forward. She opened a cabinet, removed a cassette, and set it
to play on the console that faced us. *Ode to Joy* filled the air. The
driver was gently floating along streets that I had bumped and jerked
my way through many times, but the pavement always stayed
beneath my wheels before.

"A beverage, sir?" Elisabeth was inspecting the bar and refrigerator. In keeping with all of the grape that I had been drinking, I
ordered a Remy Martin with Perrier. She made two and settled us in
with our drinks as James took us onto Storrow Drive and brought
his machine up to whisking speed.

"Now, who and/or what are you running from?"

"At the worst, the Mob. At the least, a pimp who has his wrist in a
cast and feels I'm to blame." I told the story again. I have to admit
that I was getting really good at it. I'd replayed it to myself; too, trying to see if there was something I could have handled better. "To the
owners and managers, a TV station is a well polished entity that

practically prints money. They like to run their hands over it and feel its smoothness. If something pops up, they examine it and are forced to do something about it. I popped up. If I were in the union, they'd have to protect me. I'm not, so they can drop me without ruffling the feathers of the guys who are running the transmitters and keeping them on the air."

"Well, it can't be all bad, can it?" She clicked her glass with mine.

"It certainly chased me into an interesting place this evening. I have never seen a reading quite as powerful as yours."

She regarded me over her glass as she took a sip; probably considering whether or not my experience went beyond badly read Robert Frost in high school. "Thank you. I imagine you were busy checking the entrances and exits."

I looked at her. The lights of the passing city sparkled in her eyes. I pulled my right arm from between us and put it around her shoulders. "Seriously—maybe I was particularly susceptible to *Forty Ways to Beat the Reaper* because of…my particular circumstances, but seeing you up there put entrances and exits out of my mind." She moved closer and I found her mouth with mine. Her lips were deliciously firm and obviously on the same quest. She kept her eyes open as we kissed. So did I, pursuing the biggest close-up I could get.

The driver continued his low-level flight, swooping us over the Larz Anderson Bridge and parading us down Memorial Drive. After a few minutes, I stopped staring into her eyes and took a sip of my drink. "I've never moved through this scenery in quite this way before." Self, I added silently. Why do you babble at times like this? "I'm grateful and honored to be a part of your victory celebration." I looked back into eyes that hadn't stopped trying to look into mine. The passing sycamores slapped their shadows across her face. A full moon hovering over the John Hancock Tower tried to distract me. "Serious gratitude," I added.

She buried her face in my chest and kept it there until the car slowed for its turn onto Charles Street. She gave me a quick kiss and took my glass. She leaned forward, stowed the glassware in a rack and opened the refrigerator. A bottle of Dom Perignon joined my as yet unautographed book of poetry in her bag.

"Ooh, now you're going to have to carry this upstairs for me," she said, laughing, answering several awkward questions before they were asked and steamrollering any stammering I might have committed. The chauffeur materialized to open the door. I stepped out first and turned to help Elisabeth out onto the cobblestone sidewalk. "Thank you for a lovely ride, James. I guess we're all done with you for now." She shook his hand.

I shook it, too and added, "Incredible driving."

James stood by his vehicle until Elisabeth had unlocked the oak door with small barred windows and I had held it open for her. A small walnut-paneled lobby contained two front doors to apartments, a fire door with an illuminated exit sign above it and an open elevator. She led me into the elevator and pressed the button for the eighth floor. Our shared cage engaged with a jerk and laboriously hauled us upward. The noise wasn't conducive to conversation. The cable noise stopped; the door's noise revealed every lever and counterweight of its construction as it opened.

Keying open the door on the left, the poet said, "Why don't you just carry that straight back and leave it in the kitchen?" I made my way down a corridor into a living room that greeted me with a view of the Charles and Cambridge through French doors. An old sofa, covered with a dark striped bedspread, commanded the best indoor point of view. A floor lamp and end tables completed the vision of the sofa as a busy island. To the right, a butcher-block counter separated a natural maple table from a battery of black and stainless steel restaurant equipment. I set the bag on the counter just as Elisabeth entered under full sail. "The bathroom is the second door on the right."

"Thanks, how could you tell?" I wandered back up the corridor. An open door revealed her study. Filled brick and board bookcases covered the side walls. A door turned into a desk held a shrouded typewriter and a confusion of paper. The desk was against a wall that afforded a view up the river through a window and also contained a couple of framed prints and a bulletin board that looked as if it might pull the wall down from the sheer weight of the paper and pushpins it contained. The bathroom was one of those old tiled creations that you could take for granted unless you had ever tried to fix up a bathroom. The lights, when I had found the switch, caused the room to come alive in a riot of color. Where most rooms like this had the upper walls painted some dead or dying institutional tone, my hostess had papered the walls with posters for poetry readings and covered the result with shellac. I was moved to shut the door and sit down. Notices for readings by Rexroth, Patchen, Ammons, MacLeish, Wilbur and Hemphill gave me something to read. Then I washed my face, dried it on a hand towel from the Ritz-Carlton, and realized that the mirror I was looking at was, of course, on the medicine cabinet. I brushed my hair and tried to smooth out my eyebrows while I contemplated looking behind the mirror. Would I find a circular, plastic birth control pill dispenser? A diaphragm case? Empty or full? What if there was a can of shaving cream? Did I want to swing my reflection aside just to come face-to-face with a bottle of Old Spice? It wasn't taste, chivalry or discretion that stayed my hand. I had been standing in one place for too long. Tonight, and for the foreseeable future, I was the hunted, not the hunter.

Entering the living room, I saw that a transformation had taken place. Magazines weekly, monthly and quarterly had been shoved aside on the coffee table to make room for two candles in silver candlesticks to light the scene which included the champagne in an ice bucket, two champagne flutes, and Elisabeth standing at the opened French doors. I went up to stand beside her. "How are you doing?" I asked. "You have got to be exhausted from that reading."

"I'm doing better than I was." She wrapped her arms around my neck and I wrapped mine around her waist. The kiss just about made us lose our balance. I had seen priests fulfill the dreams of a lifetime by kissing the Pope's ring, reeling back with the jolt. I felt as though I understood them better now, though, in my case, it may have been fear and exhaustion.

"Why don't you open that champagne? I'll put some music on." She went over to a dimly visible wall, filled, like most of her walls, with bricks, boards and books, and attacked a shelf full of records. I set myself to duel with the foil, wire and cork. The cork popped and I began to fill the glasses just as the music of Dire Straits began to flow softly into the room.

"I'd like to propose a toast," said Elisabeth as she joined me and accepted a brimming flute. "To getting away from the sons of bitches that are chasing you." We drank to that and she led me around the coffee table to the couch.

I sipped away as she sat down. Her silhouette revealed an aquiline nose mirrored in the graceful curve of jaw to her chin. She reached up and slowly drew ivory combs from her hair. The curls tumbled forward over her shoulders, giving her a beautiful softness. She fidgeted with a curl, let it tumble to her breast and turned to face me, hiking her bare feet onto the couch between us. I started to lean over her knees to tell her how incredibly beautiful she was and to try to put something on her; a hand, lips…anything, when I heard the sound of the elevator stopping and its door cranking open. I froze in panic. "Are you expecting anyone? Does someone else live here?"

"Relax, Bart. It's the people in the other apartment. But we *do* have to talk."

I swallowed. There *had* to be some bad news in all of this. She reached out a hand and laid it on one of mine. She broke the silence. "In my personal mythology, there is nothing I'd be prouder of than picking you out of a crowd, bringing you back to my casbah, and having you any way either of us can imagine. Eight years ago, four years ago, you'd check out my medicine cabinet, figure out whether I'm on birth control or not, and we'd be where I want to be right now. But that's not enough any more. AIDS and death are out there and I don't know you. Who are you?"

"I was born in Berea, Ohio, in 1947, and grew up there."

"Sounds like a disease."

"Sounds like the head bad guy in a James Bond flick, too. But it was more like a disease. Flat farmland, as far as the eye could see, until you came to Lake Erie, which was a dead, poisonous mass for most of my childhood. The Cuyahoga River, over in Cleveland, started burning once.

"Mom was a high school teacher and Dad was an engineer on the New York Central. He ran the *Twentieth Century Limited* out of Cleveland. He loved his job, especially before World War II, when they were trying to go faster and faster and had steam locomotives. His stretch was a speedway; few curves, no hills to speak of, and he was a star runner.

"The *Century* was the main artery between New York and Chicago and he had a keen sense of having a finger on the pulse of it. Whenever he was deadheading…"

"Deadheading?"

"Riding the train back from a run. You work out and deadhead back or vice-versa. Anyway, he always kept a suit, clean shirt, and tie in his bag. He'd clean up and ride home in the club car. He said that there were more movers and shakers in that club car than anywhere else. He had cards printed up that said 'Harrison Lane, Engineer, The Twentieth Century Limited'. To them, *he* was a celebrity. Eisenhower wanted to be an engineer when he was growing up, and so did a lot of other folks who had to settle for drudge work like Secretary of State, president of some university, head of an oil company, etcetera. Once he and Mom started having kids he began to discuss colleges in the club car. I got applications from more places than I'd ever heard of. Most of the forms were marked 'recommendations complete.' That's probably how I got into Williams."

"Didn't you want to be an engineer like your father?"

"I think that both my brothers and I wanted to do that, but Dad wouldn't hear of it. We had a pretty cosmopolitan existence for a family that lived in a farmhouse. All railroad men had passes—free tickets—and Dad used to use his to take us to New York or Chicago for shows. The last time we did that was for *Camelot*. The train was slow, cold and dirty. Dad would have apologized, but he could see that we were all sharing his pain. 'Oil companies,' he said, 'automobiles, business machines, pick any field you want, but don't pick railroads.' With his sense of history he realized that the railroads had had their day.

"At Williams, I played tennis and majored in geology. I tried to get involved with ladies from Smith and Mount Holyoke, but it never worked completely out. Anyway, one of my friends said that since we'd probably spend the rest of our lives drinking beer and watching movies, we might as well take a film course. It was just an interesting class until I took a peek through a movie camera. It was more like crawling through the viewfinder into another world, one you could frame, structure and create. I fell in love. It was an absolutely thrilling way to reinterpret and frame the world and its horror and glory.

"By the second semester, I had conned film and geology professors into letting me do a film on geology as a dissertation. I became a night person, editing around the clock, driven, like the architects and fine artsies. This, incidentally, is divine champagne."

"Mm, it is." She confirmed the judgment with a sip. "What did you do about Viet Nam?"

"I opposed it when I was at college. I used to get the protesters to buy me film so I could shoot the demonstrations and 'actions' and I'd ship the film off to some place in San Francisco that was 'documenting the struggle.'

"My choices were to go to Canada, go to jail, or be drafted. I enlisted in the Army Signal Corps. The most fun about that was hearing my Army recruiter call up the draft board and tell them to fuck off, where I was concerned. I thought I'd have the chance to work with movie cameras, film what was really going on over there and maybe make some connections for a career, but it didn't work out that way."

"What happened?"

I nearly rushed a swallow of the champagne. I was not at all used to being the center of anyone's attention. "I got in the Signal Corps as promised, but I ended up at Fort Devens, right outside of Boston, fixing typewriters. Somebody found out that I could play tennis and so I got a lot of that in, too, giving lessons to officers and their wives, and having the right kind of game with the commandant from time to time. I mean I couldn't hammer him as much as I wanted to, but I didn't want to be an easy match for him either. I fell in love with Boston, but wandering around with my shiny black shoes and GI hair, I felt that there was a wall that I couldn't get past. As soon as I got discharged, I moved in."

Elisabeth split the last of the Dom Perignon between our two glasses and settled in next to me. "How have you remained single for the, what, fifteen years that you've been here?"

"After an all male college and the Army, Boston and Cambridge were much better."

"What?"

"Okay, they were like an unimaginable sexual smorgasbörd. It didn't stop me from trying to get tied down. Three women left me because their women's groups didn't approve of our relationship. One of them, to the best of my knowledge, turned out to share my appetite for female bodies, so she's the only homosexual I could have caught something from but that was more than eight years ago. I experimented with most drugs except for those requiring needles. Then I had a long relationship that turned out to be interfering with career plans; hers."

"That must bring us well into the eighties," Elisabeth said, bottoming out her glass and setting it on the coffee table. "What a fine bottle it was. I wonder how much of what was in that punch?"

"Your turn," I said. "If all this drinking has affected you like it has me, we have a lot of eloquent diction left, but not much else. I know that you're gorgeous, successful in a field where it's just about unheard of, and I find myself hoping that you come to this meeting alone, though I wouldn't wish loneliness on anyone. For instance, I don't know what it feels like to do *this*," I ran my hand down the full length of her bare back. "And I didn't look in your medicine cabinet."

"I know. The hinge screeches something awful. I would have heard. I was born here, in Wellesley, and my family moved to San Francisco when I was about ten. I had grandparents here, though, so I stayed in touch. My father is a vice-president, legal, and he's been that for several companies. Anyway, I hated it when we were going to move from Boston, and I remember the whole family went to dinner at Durgin Park. Do you know that nifty little alley near there that looks so eighteenth century?"

"Yeah, I call it East India Alley."

"That's the one. Well we had eaten our last lobster at Durgin Park, and I'm pretty sure I remember this but it became—you know—one of those stories your parents tell that embarrasses the hell out of you so there's no chance of forgetting anyway?"

"Yes, I followed that. Just so you know."

"Thanks, that was very nice of you. Anyway I ran ahead of the family, and I guess I got out of sight of them. When they found me they were in utter panic and I was in the alley saying, 'Good-bye alley. These people are taking me away but I'll be back!'"

"And?"

"My grandfather was a lawyer, a partner in one of those big firms. He was like a self-appointed Godfather to me. I'd go out to visit him and my grandmother in the summers, and when I was old enough, I got summer jobs at the inn near their summer place. We were close. He was probably one of your Dad's passengers. Anyway, I applied to every place in or near Boston I could think of and I got into Radcliffe. I'm a Cliffie and I'm proud even if my diploma does say Harvard. On my first Saturday I slipped out of some silly reception at Pennypacker, my dorm, and took subways and trolleys to get down to Haymarket. I fought my way through a crowd of people who all wanted to sell me lettuce, tomatoes and melons, 'fresh from the farm'. Then I waded through a bunch of rotting vegetables and empty produce cartons from the goddamn Napa Valley. Then I found *my* special alley. I stood there for a while. It was the way I remembered it. Then I yelled at the top of my lungs, "Alley, I'm back!"

"So, you graduated last year and got all this fame and stuff instantly, right? Turn around, I want to rub your back." I kicked off my Topsiders, got my feet up on the couch, and let her settle back between my knees. The lady had some serious knots around the base of that perfect neck.

"Mm," she purred. "You should be so lucky. My vintage is 'fifty-one. Radcliffe puts it at 'seventy-two. I spent most of my senior year sneaking out to play with a rock band and its leader. Did you ever hear of *The Buzz*?"

"Definitely. They had *Do Me Now* on the charts just about the time I was moving in to this town. I can't really say I've heard of them since."

"I wrote the lyrics for that one. My grandfather would call me up every few weeks and ask me how or what I was doing. 'Well, dear Grandfather, I'm playing tambourine with a rock and roll band, writing some words for their songs, and counting the days until I can move in with the band leader.' It would be a nightmare to your average rock-ribbed bastion of Boston Society, but that dear old man's response was to send me some contracts to have all parties sign. The royalties started to roll in before I graduated.

"So, the single was doing well, and it was time for the band to go on tour. I was packed and ready. Graduate and hit the road making *money*. What could be finer? Well, at graduation, my mother informed me that she was going into the hospital for removal of an ovarian cyst. She didn't ask, but I really wanted to go back to San Francisco to be with her. Dennis Prean, my lover and the leader of the group, appeared to understand even if it did make him almost ill to talk about it. They could get away with not having a tambourine player for the first few dates. I think it was really important to spend that time with Mom.

"The operation was a success, the cyst was benign, and I did get to know Mom a lot better. I was feeling drained, but pretty good when I flew into Philadelphia to join up with the tour. I got to the Sheraton and asked for Dennis' room number and a key. I rode the elevator up to room six-thirteen. I stopped outside the door. Damn if I didn't hear Dennis through the door. I recognized the words, because I had heard them previously, just before I slept with him for the first time."

"That must have been painful," I said, still kneading the area between her neck and shoulders. I had cased out the collar of her gown—two hooks—but suddenly it wasn't a good time to undo them, even for medicinal purposes.

"I wanted to cry. I could tell where he was in the process. He probably didn't even have her T-shirt off yet. I could stop it before it started. Then I realized that I didn't want to! Who wants to spend a life or even a minute with someone who has turned out to be nearly two hundred pounds of treacherous slime? I turned into an actress, going over my lines while I waited for my cue. Sounds wicked, doesn't it?"

"Sounds like fun, to me." I had my eye on those hooks, but, at the moment, it seemed like they'd bite back.

"It was. Can you believe it? I waited as his spiel continued. I heard the slow progress of his hand on the zipper of her Levi's, and the faster rip of his zipper. I slipped the key into the lock and touched up my prose. He was in. BAM! I was in. 'You are an undependable, unoriginal one trick pony,' I said, shriveling him. 'You just lost the best thing that ever happened to you: me. I can see that you're already auditioning a tambourine player. Enjoy the *Do Me Now* tour, because I don't think you have what it takes to get another.' The groupie he had found wasn't even cute. One of those lumpy teenage bodies with something resembling pubic hair all over her head. I marched out and left the key at the desk. I took myself out to dinner and caught a train to Boston. The tour finished on the West Coast, and *The Buzz* never quite made it onto the charts again."

"Do you mind if I unhook this thing?" I was definitely being more of a helpful drunk than a seducer. "You've got some major knots I've got to deal with, ma'am."

She pulled her hair over one shoulder and leaned her head forward. "Can you figure it out by candlelight?" I did and she let the front fall, though it didn't get too far since she had her knees drawn up in front of her.

"So, we're back in the 'seventies and you have revealed your advanced age to me and I'm still here," I kissed her back, and then started to massage down the sides of it. "What could you possibly do for an encore?"

"I got a job at a publishing company as an editorial assistant. I worked at that for quite a few years. I was approached by numerous young lawyers, most of them male, who had come across my name at Hemphill, Thwaite and Hennessey, or seen me there. The worst of those was a charmer who had clerked for my grandfather and dated me while he was starting out at another firm. He took me out to dinner and couldn't stop talking about his clients. They were poor unfortunate souls accused of shooting people, putting concrete boots on them and dropping them into Boston Harbor and generally enforcing for the Mob. I asked him if the stories could wait until after the sautéed sweetbreads, possibly past dessert, but it didn't do any good. Finally he said, 'The things that those people do to each other…' and I said, 'Yeah, and the things that their lawyers do for them.' I went to the ladies room and never came back.

"To make a long story short, I'm single, as you find me. I have not exchanged anything with intravenous drug users since possibly Dennis, and I was never able to lure any gay males into my bed. I did spend a lot of time holding the hand of a friend, book jacket designer, who was dying of AIDS at the time. One month he was there, talking about dipping into his bank account to get a color television for the hospice, and the next month he was gone. I met his parents toward the end. They were racked with guilt and wondered what they had done wrong. I told them I had tried 'straighten him out', too. All four of us ended up in a big tearful hug. It was such a wrench to lose him like that. After the funeral, I had my blood tested for AIDS. I went through hell waiting for the result. It was negative. I had a few more gay friends but they're all gone." She turned around and threw her arms around me, driving me down onto the couch. We lay there for a few minutes. Then she started to undo the buttons on my shirt. "Oh, Mister Lane?"

"Yes?"

"Have you had a vacation lately?"

"Well, I don't work every week. I used to visit my folks in Berea, but they moved to Florida, and I don't think my VW can handle the trip."

"So you haven't really. You need a vacation. I like the hair on your chest, by the way. May I take you on my vacation, starting tomorrow?"

"Well, I have to...."

"Get run over, shot, kidnapped or rejected by clients? You can't even go out for groceries."

"But it's so close with Channel Eight."

"It doesn't sound like they're going to do you any favors."

"Just one more day...and I've got some calls in with producers."

"How many of them call back with jobs?"

This maddening woman was making sense, but it didn't mean that I had to like it. "I just feel like I have to take care of some stuff that..."

She grabbed one of my hands. "Bart, if you mean 'no,' stop dithering and just say 'no.'"

"No!"

"Very well…" She started to lean away from me.

"I mean I don't want to say no. You're right." She was, too. "Yes, I'd love to go on vacation with you."

"Excuse me, that means we have to get up in a few hours. Don't go away." My vision was dulling; I don't know what I was telling myself to do to keep my eyes open. In the candlelight, I saw her step out of her gown and deftly pitch it at one of the chairs by the kitchen table. She moved like a comet through the candlelight, leaving me rapt at her contrail. Silvery stockings over lean ankles, well-turned calves playing the tones of their shapes with celestial accompaniment. I was convinced that if I could turn the shape of her into notes and hum them I could see her with my eyes closed. The grace notes of garters flowing around laced bikini briefed hips. New measure at garter belt, full rest over blank stare of navel in field of flat tummy. Undersides of breasts catching the candlelight to form two whole notes leading to upward run of neck; chin, nose, eye, eye in 4/4 time, taking us to the closing cadenza of hair.

I started to play it over to myself. There was a key to the universe in all this, I was certain. I was lifting my dream baton to bring out those critical whole notes when I conducted a clank. A pried open eye told me it was an alarm clock being set down on the coffee table. Candles were blown out. A luscious warm body crawled on top of me. I dreamt of trying to climb into a too high bed with Elisabeth, stymied by slipping rugs, unreliable ladders, and finally the ringing of a doorbell.

I have never woken up feeling better after a short night on a couch after too much to drink. I felt warm and wonderful. Elisabeth moved in and out of my slowly-widening field of view, packing boat bags and boxes and looking like a lioness setting up a hunt. I felt like a lion who had eaten too much unearned Thompson's Gazelle. Following her into the kitchen area with my eyes, I saw a shirt like mine hung over a chair and a pair of white ducks. I was nearly naked under a flannel sheet. What a hostess! I scratched partly because of an itch and partly to see if I still had my underpants on. I did. I hoped that I was wearing a bold, primary-colored pair. I looked, I was. This was no time to be caught in dull and possibly discolored white briefs.

"There's a new toothbrush in the medicine cabinet, help yourself to the towels on the door rack." She smiled at me, pulled out a chair and sat at the table, leaning her chin on a hand and waiting for me to make the next move. I smiled and got up. "I knew your body *felt* great. It *looks* great, too."

I gave in to a yawn and stretched—a little something in return for the spectacle I had been treated to the night before. "Thank you very much. Did you spend the night in my arms?"

"Mm hmm," her eyebrows arched provocatively as she took a sip from a stoneware mug.

"Damn, I always thought I was too much of a prickly claustrophobic for that. That's unbelievable."

I splashed some cold water in my face to wake up, initiated a new plastic razor on my face, and took a shower. I admired the acoustics of the tiled bath, but kept my rendition of *You've Lost That Lovin' Feelin'* to a low volume. I sang the part of the lower Righteous Brother badly, for one thing, and the words had nothing to do with my feelings or situation. I returned to the kitchen to find a steaming mug of coffee near my clothes. Elisabeth was no less stunning in cut-off jeans and a T-shirt that said 'Quahog Heights Athletic Association'. "Do you think we can sneak past your place so you can grab some stuff?" She closed the refrigerator door and the lid of an ice chest.

"Definitely. Getting up at this hour of the morning is too much like work for the clowns who are chasing me."

"I allowed an extra half hour for us to detour to your place. Is that enough if we're leaving town on the Southeast?"

"I think so. Where are we going?"

"Someplace you've never heard of: Squidneck Island."

"What can I do to help?"

"Throw your sheet and pillowcase into the laundry hamper in the bathroom, finish your coffee, and start hauling this stuff out to the elevator."

Several trips through the wedged open front door revealed that we were taking a box of new mystery books, a case of Rolling Rock (How did this lady know?), a densely packed ice chest full of perishables, two boxes and a boat bag of non perishables, two laundry bags of linens and beach towels and a large suitcase full of clothes.

Elisabeth joined me on the last trip through, locked the door and pressed the button for the elevator. We worked like stevedores loading everything into and out of the elevator. "Do you want to haul this out onto the sidewalk while I fetch the car?"

I looked. I figured that through the opened front door I wouldn't have to get out of sight of any of this stuff while moving it all. A large portion of film and television work is moving stuff in and out of cars, vans, trucks and buildings while surrounded by people who are just dying to steal it. "No problem, just wedge the door open, if you know how, and I'll meet you on the sidewalk as soon as you can rustle up some driving iron."

She carried a couple of bags with her, using one of them to sandbag the door open, just like an experienced grip on a film crew would. Grips, though, don't usually toss their hips with such insouciance and wink back over their shoulder.

I was standing there just about ready to check out a John D. MacDonald thriller in the book box when I heard something like the snarl of an expensive Italian road machine. I looked up to see Elisabeth whip an orange Saab into the loading zone. It looked nearly brand new, but I recognized it as a model they stopped making quite a few years ago.

I let Elisabeth pack the trunk. Almost everything fit there, leaving a couple of items to slide onto the back seat. "I like your car," I said as I buckled myself into the passenger seat. Under her feet and hands it coursed onto the empty streets.

"It's my new car. I bought it new fourteen years ago."

I gave directions as she plunged the car down narrow streets, left taxicabs far behind at stoplights, and very shortly pulled up in front of my abode. "Why don't you lock the door behind me, keep a look-out, and circle the block to the left if you see any large, lurking sedans. Do I have fifteen minutes?"

"Yeah," mouthed my partner in crime. "Any bozo up to N.G. shows up and I'll give him the slip on the QT…"

I scurried in and rushed around packing. In the clothes department, I packed everything from my abbreviated Speedo swimsuit to a blazer that would get me past the door of any restaurant. I opened up my case full of Nikons and lenses and added a couple of light meters and accessories. I hauled it to the refrigerator and threw in some rolls of film: black and white for art, Kodachrome for scenic shots and color negative for the fun of it. While I was at the fridge, I filled a shopping bag with things that might survive the ride and be hard to get on an island, like green peppercorns. A yogurt container seemed lighter than its neighbors. Ah, yes, Corinne's stash of Maui Wowee, Panama Red and Chihuahua Laughing Tobacco. I wondered whether I should bring it or not then said to myself, 'Ding dong, the bitch is gone.' I stuffed it in my suitcase. My Head graphite racquet was in the side of a sport bag that I stuffed mercilessly with shoes and socks. I was pretty well ready to roll.

I checked my watch. I had six minutes left. I pulled out my black book and looked up Nick's number. I might catch Patti before she left for the hospital or work. I dialed and started to write notes for

Miss Halloran and the Kinhs. "Patti," I said when she answered, "This is Bart. I'm sorry about the shape I returned Nick in."

"He's okay, thanks to your first aid and fast driving. I'm sorry to hear that Channel Eight isn't giving you any protection, though."

"So am I. How's Nick doing?"

"He's still at the hospital, but he's out of intensive care and they'll be letting him out in a few days."

"I'm leaving town on vacation because I guess it's not safe for me here. When I find a phone number I can be reached at, I'll let you know."

She wished me luck and we hung up. I made it through the door with my treasures in one trip, locked the door, and set it all down. I ran up to slip an explanatory note under Miss Halloran's door. 'Sleep tight, you wild Irish rogues,' I thought. Downstairs, with my bags, I slipped a note with a set of keys under the door for Nguy. He liked to water the rain forest that Corinne had left hanging in the front windows.

At about three minutes before our deadline, I risked a peek through the curtains of the front window. Elisabeth and her orange car were nowhere in sight. A big, blue Buick seemed to be waiting for me.

CHAPTER 5

❁

*D*amn. I hate to bother people early in the morning unless they're on my crew. I backed away from the window and quietly let myself out of the apartment. I climbed the stairs to Miss Halloran's as quickly and quietly as I could, but eventually, there was nothing to do but knock on the door.

"Who is it?" came Miss Halloran's measured tones. Several deadbolts were thrown and the door opened as far as a brass-plated chain would allow. "Oh Bart. What *is* the matter?" She closed the door to undo the chain and threw it open to face me in a pink quilted robe.

"I'm afraid that the mobsters who are after me are parked outside. Is Captain…er could you…I was just about to leave town. Should I call the police?"

"Do calm down and come in. I'll have Captain Ryan call someone." She gestured me to her couch and triple-locked the door. She went to her bedroom and was soon followed into the kitchen by a sleepy Captain Ryan whom I could hear dialing the phone. Miss Halloran rejoined me in the living room. "Now, what is this about leaving town? It sounds like a worthy plan."

I explained the previous night's pursuit and that someone was probably waiting around the corner to take me to an island. "I don't have a lot of time to wait for the police because we have to catch a ferry someplace," I concluded.

"I don't know how soon they'll get here."

"I have an idea. Do you have a spare overcoat and possibly a veiled hat that you were going to give to Goodwill?"

"I think I can find something. Are you going to sneak past them?"

"I'm going to try."

She headed for a hall closet to rummage in, and Captain joined me. "I've called Patrick Horan about your friends outside. They're just changing shifts so their response might not be as rapid as we'd like."

"Here you are, Bart," Dorothea emerged with a worn black coat and a veiled hat that had seen better days. "Don't worry about returning them."

"Thanks, Miss Halloran and Captain Ryan. I'm sorry I had to bother you so early in the morning."

"Oh, that's all right," said the Captain. "I imagine that anyone who might fret about my keeping company with Miss Halloran, here, is long dead."

"Aloysius Ryan, I'll thank you to keep a civil tongue in your head," snapped the lady in question.

"Except, of course, for my rivals," he added with a twinkle in his eye.

I was a bit over the deadline as I headed back to my apartment. I threw on the coat and hat, and wasn't totally convinced by the senior citizen that I perceived in the bedroom mirror. I dredged one of Corrinne's granny dresses out of the closet, found some old wool socks and—eureka—my Army boots. An umbrella that didn't advertise our local public television station and some paper shopping bags, even if they were from an upscale food emporium, completed the outfit. Stuffing everything I wanted to travel with into the bags, I arrived at the conclusion that my tennis racquet couldn't be fit into or adapted to my new persona. I tried secreting it in the bags, under the dress and in a number of interesting places but it just didn't work. That much I would have to leave behind. Hoping that the goons in the Buick wouldn't hold yuppie grocery bags against a poor old bag lady, I let myself out of the apartment and, with a deep breath, out of the building.

"It's those Kennedys," I said loudly to myself and anyone who would listen to this lonely old deinstitutionalized psychotic. "Every time I want to pick up my social security check, they tell me that Teddy Kennedy says I can't have it. Why I've known all of those boys since they were wet behind the ears," I stole a glance at blue Buick. Quinn and the mobsters were reading the *Herald*, drinking coffee, and watching my building. "Now it's just down to Teddy and some new ones," I mumbled as I made my way down the sidewalk. "Medicaid wants to send me to a state hospital but I know what they are—they're loony bins and nut houses; laughing academies and drool schools." I punctuated this diatribe by hitting the umbrella against anything I could find; trashcans, lampposts and the sidewalk. "Once they get me there, the Kennedys and their kind will have me where…"

I turned a corner to see Elisabeth waiting in her car, the engine running. Coming up the street behind her, a police cruiser turned off its flashing blue light as it approached my street. "Go get those commie drug pushers!" I yelled in my best old woman voice. "They're ruining the neighborhood!"

I made my way to the car and tapped gently on the windshield with the umbrella. Elisabeth rolled her eyes and threw open the passenger door. "I'm sorry, I'm not driving bag people today," she said.

"Well, I'm sorry, too, because I ain't walkin' to no goddam island." I slid my load into the back seat and scrambled into the front.

"I'm glad you don't have to be told to buckle your seat belt." She let out the clutch and set out adroitly for the highway.

I ducked down below the level of the window. "What's happening in front of my place?"

"You tell me. Two cop cars are pulled in on either side of the gas guzzler that seemed to be interested in your house."

"Well, my blood is flowing better than it was a couple of minutes ago. I didn't know what happened to you until I saw the blue car."

"Hey, if there are bandits in the area, I figure that I'd rather be watching than watched." She accelerated up the ramp for the Southeast and began to look for a hole to occupy in the full highway. She spotted some air behind a bakery truck and fit the car into it.

"Lady, you drive one hell of a fine getaway car."

"Feel free to change out of that horrid outfit," she replied.

According to its schedule, the *Squidneck II* leaves from the dock behind a seafood cannery in Warren, Rhode Island, at six, eight and ten AM and four, six and eight PM on summer Fridays. We were trying to catch the 'ten boat', but the dock was empty. We unloaded our cargo near where Elisabeth said the gangplank would land. "I think I have time to grab something of a breakfasty nature before we have to leave. Hungry?" she whispered in my ear.

"Sure, I'll have a large black coffee and something unmessy to eat." She confirmed my order with a kiss through the window and drove off. The rear bumper, which I hadn't seen before, had a sticker that proclaimed, 'BMW—Breakfast of Champions.' She had certainly fed it a few on our trip down.

I watched the lobstermen unloading their catch. Seagulls persisted in adopting picturesque stances on pilings. In the distance, over water that sat like glass, clamdiggers plied their long tongs in an unending wrestle with the bottom of the bay. I wanted to take a picture, but I didn't want to unpack my camera case, so I just sat and drank it in.

A couple of other cars drove up and disgorged coolers, cases of beer, toolboxes, stacks of lumber, bundles of pipe, and suitcases. The owners nodded kindly at me and left to park their cars. The whine of a marine diesel faded up to dominate the air and I looked out to see the *Squidneck II* plowing up the bay. It rocked in its own wake and seemed to pirouette in place to enable a deckhand to grab a bow line off a piling. It swung an opening near its bow very close to where I was sitting. Some of the people who were, by now, waiting with me bestirred themselves and helped the deckhand drag off the gangplank. Then we all started to carry our stuff on board. I looked up from setting one load into the bow to see someone picking up my camera case. 'Hey, wait, you can't do that!' I almost yelled, but I didn't. The perpetrator, a burly gray haired man with a weathered face, also grabbed one of Elisabeth's boat bags; he carried the load up the gangplank and set it with the other things I had hauled on. We finished on ours and, wordlessly, proceeded to load everything else off the dock.

I was hovering around our freight when I saw Elisabeth sauntering in past the cannery. The red bandanna she had tied around her head should have tempered the spectacle, but it didn't. Less than twelve hours ago I had been running for my life. I guess I must have caught it, but like a dog who has finally captured a car, I don't know if I had any idea of what to do with it. I must have been staring because she made eye contact with me and lifted up a brown paper bag, giving it a little shake.

She came down the gangplank exchanging greetings with the other passengers, did a brief inventory of our pile of stuff and said, "Let's go get some good seats. You can buy your ticket once they've cast off."

I followed her back into the cabin and up a companionway. We emerged onto the upper deck and sat down on a bench near the bow. "How long is the boat ride?"

"I guess it's about forty-five minutes to an hour." She extracted a cup of coffee and a greasy, paper-wrapped bundle and handed them to me. "I got you a Portuguese muffin."

My faded cutoffs picked up a few grease stains as I unwrapped this new delicacy. It was like a fried English muffin only larger. It had a crispy side, a pleasantly doughy texture, and a slight sweetness. My first bite caused melted butter to run down my chin. While I tried to find a napkin without opening my mouth to ask for it, Elisabeth was cutting out a drinking hole in the lid of my coffee with her Swiss Army knife. "Most professional," I said, after I had swallowed. "I didn't know that they made a poet's model."

"Special order; this," she used the scissors to cut the lid of her coffee cup, "is for the removal of dangling participles." She folded it in and undid the large blade, "I mince words with this, and you have to know about the muse summoner (bottle opener), genie liberator (corkscrew) and don't forget the special attachment for opening envelopes with rejection slips within."

"What about envelopes with royalty checks in them?"

"That's what the Good Lord gave us teeth for, isn't it?"

I showed her my cameraman's model with its film snipper, for removing the evidence of the worst mistakes; lighting gel slasher, wrap-time beer opener, client earwax extractor, tiny screw picker-upper (for when you're just getting slightly screwed), fine print reader, and, when all else fails, the wrist slasher. "That Swiss Army, they think of everything."

"Oops," she said, looking at the wheel house, "cover your ears." I did, and the ship's horn shook me nevertheless as it signalled our departure. "You might want to get your ticket now. Get a round trip for Squidneck."

I went down to where I had seen a ticket window. The deckhand selling tickets looked like a late nineteen fifties publicity photo of teen idol Paul Anka which had been embellished with pencilled-on Greek fisherman's hat, moustache, and smoldering Camel. "Round trip for Squidneck," I stated.

"Three-fifty," he took my money and slid the ticket and change across the small counter to me. "Ever been there before?"

"No."

"Didn't *think* I'd seen you." He looked past me at the next customer in line.

I climbed back up and rejoined Elisabeth. She pointed out a small empty boatyard where they had just built an America's Cup contender. "I mean Australia's Cup." My brief visual tour of the bay included an acceptable shore diner, a couple of places to buy fresh lobsters, and a yacht club. "I normally come down here on a Saturday boat which is a lot more crowded, but also contains more folks I know. Since this is Friday, the water isn't paved with sails."

It was a beautiful Kodachrome day with a clear blue sky and a slight chop on the water once we cleared Warren Harbor. We both sat and watched the world go by until Elisabeth pointed out a long green island. "Squidneck," she said. A row of small cottages was stretched along the shore of the island, catching the light perfectly. Hills rose up behind them and a few cars, trucks, bicycles and pedestrians could be seen making their way along a shore road to the dock.

The ferry's engine sang in reverse, ropes were thrown and caught or missed by a crowd thronging the dock. Greetings and waving hands filled the air. Many hands picked up the gangplank and lifted it into place. "Riverboat time on the levee," said Elisabeth. We made our way down through a friendly crowd, chatting and shuffling its way to the gangplank. Elisabeth grabbed a bag and pulled a well-perforated commuter ticket out of her back pocket. "I'll get on the dock and you can hand our stuff across."

She held out her ticket for the deckhand to punch and disappeared up onto the dock. Moments later, she reappeared next to a stack of full milk crates. By now, I wasn't at all surprised by the strength with which she plucked everything out of my grasp and set it behind her. I was, however, captivated by the older woman in well-fitting jeans and gray t-shirt who was manhandling the milk crates onto a hand truck with a well practiced fluidity. She spun around to reveal the longest silver ponytail I had ever seen. "Jessica," said a grinning Elisabeth when our eyes met on the next pass.

"Is that how you women age out here?"

She gave me a look indicating that she could have replied to that remark, but if I was lucky, she might forget that I had ever made it.

I finished up with my end of the unloading and the deckhand revealed the smallest hint of a smile as he took my ticket. "Welcome to Squidneck," Elisabeth said when I got to our stack of earthly possessions. "I'll go get something to haul this stuff in, if you don't mind waiting here with it." She made her way up the dock, pausing to shake hands, chat, or hug some of the people she encountered.

I helped slide the gangplank back onto the ferry, a potbellied older man in gym shorts and a feed cap cast off the ferry's lines and waved goodbye to it. The horn sounded, and I found myself alone on the dock. The hazy island air gave the dock, general store and parking lot the look of another era. The average vehicle seemed to be about thirty years old. So was the mammoth GMC pickup truck whose back end was bearing down on me.

It stopped right at our pile and Elisabeth climbed out. "I declare, Miz Scarlett, you are into motorsport in the biggest way," I said over the unmuffled idle of the engine. I swung down the tailgate and we loaded it up.

I climbed into the passenger seat and she growled the truck off the dock and through the parking lot. She waved at a policeman who waved back. "Constable John Perkins," she said. "Meets every ferry, knows who's on and who's off the island. His job description must read 'impersonate three police officers at all times, provide crime computer services without visible electronic support, and be a good neighbor.' Do you think we should tell him that you're on the run?"

"I think that they picked up all those guys who were trying to get me this morning."

"Bart, I come from a long line of lawyers. If the guy with the knife isn't out on bail, his friends will be."

"You're right," but before I had said it Elisabeth had pulled the truck over. She got out and ran back to where the constable was directing traffic and generally waving at everyone. They had a brief conversation. She pointed at me and he checked me out from that distance. I normally wouldn't have liked a policeman to be that interested in me, but I was glad to be acknowledged by the strong but friendly gaze of Constable Perkins.

"He's going to keep an eye out," said Elisabeth as she climbed back in and started out of the lot. Moving ponderously in the truck down the shore road between the row of small cottages and the sparkling bay, I felt like I was in a long telephoto shot. I also felt that I was in a magic place. "You're really good to move stuff with. Some people never get the general idea," she said.

"So are you," I said, marveling at her truck handling. "This is a major vehicle."

"Grandfather again. The prospect of only being able to move a half ton of friends and family at a time dismayed him, and so—*voilà*—a three-quarter ton pickup." She downshifted and cranked into a right turn. The truck began to labor up a hill. "Now we're on the cross-island highway." The truck maintained a speed of fifteen miles per hour. "Squidneck is about seven miles long and two miles across." We seemed to be going between neglected farmland, lightly peppered with the rusting hulks of ancient abandoned automobiles, and forest. A small building with a bell tower sat in a clearing. "That's one of the last one-room schoolhouses in the country."

The truck changed its tune as it began to drift down a hill. Blue water sparkled through a break in the trees ahead. The road appeared to end on an old stone pier. "Boston Landing," she said as we emerged into the daylight. We were suddenly in the midst of large porched and turreted Victorian summer homes. "The New York to Boston packet boats used to stop here. The Grand Hotel was down to the right of the dock until the hurricane of 'thirty eight blew it away." She spun the wheel to the left and headed onto a gravel road that ran between two ranks of the grand old houses. A middle-aged couple reading *The New York Times* and sipping mugs of coffee waved, and Elisabeth waved back. "Well, the Dodges know you're here. They're old friends of the grandparents. I'll take you by for a formal introduction later."

I briefly wondered what she would introduce me as but I was jolted out of such thoughts as the gravel road turned into wagon tracks, approaching the water and rounding a stand of cedar. "Hemp Hill," Elisabeth said.

I was stunned into silence. On a promontory overlooking the bay stood a large gambrel-roofed structure. Silvered shingles covered it from top to bottom. It abounded in diamond-paned French windows and doors; each flanked by white shutters. The fieldstone foundation extended out to form a covered veranda off the north side. The second floor had two balconies that I could see. One ran across the west end of the gambrel, facing the water off one side of the point, and the other perched atop the veranda, extending out from a dormer on the second floor, offering a view of the water off the other side of the point. "So, is this my chance to meet these grandparents I've heard so much about?"

"You'll certainly find out a whole lot about how they spent their summers, but I'm sorry to say they've both died."

"I'm sorry I brought it up."

"No problem. I was with them on weekends and over the summers for a long time." She turned the truck around and backed it up to the door at the end of the house. "Let's unload and get some beer cooling. Then, I'll give you the fifty-cent tour."

She unlocked the door. My first impression was of a long corridor of dark stained matchwood wainscoting with off white beaverboard above that. The dark strips of wood that held the beaverboard to the walls and ceiling yielded a Tudor effect. Photographs of groups and seascapes hung in their thin black frames. A slash of diamond-shadowed light punctuated the wood floor half way down the corridor.

"Let's get the perishables to the fridge," she said. I loaded myself down with a few bags and grabbed one end of the cooler. She took the other and led me down to the lighted patch. I followed her to the right where a large open staircase faced a wall of windows two stories high. I almost regretted carrying so much as she led me up the stairs.

"Hey, don't we want to stash this stuff before you haul me up to your room?" I hoped my breathlessness didn't show.

"You'll see." We rounded the second bend in the staircase and slowly revealed to me was a large kitchen, dining and living room area. There weren't many walls on this floor. We passed a counter and set everything on the floor in front of a large refrigerator.

Elisabeth opened it. "Beer, wine, coffee, iced tea, beer?"

"Beer, please."

"Open one for me." She handed me a couple of Rolling Rocks out of the fridge. "Anyway," she said, transferring food deftly to the refrigerator, "Grandfather stumbled across this island while he was evaluating someone's estate. He fell in love with it instantly. The day after he first saw it, he and my grandmother were back, wearing work clothes, hiking and asking around until they found this plot.

"Can you imagine bringing everything but the fieldstones over from the mainland on a smaller ferry than the *Squidneck II*? Even though carpenters were putting it up, my dad and uncle thought that a trip to Squidneck was as bad as being exiled to Siberia; strictly downhill from Louisburg Square. Then, when my cousins and I entered the scene, I think our mothers got worn out trying to keep us behaving 'for the grans' and not drowning. I could never get enough of the place, though, so my grandparents left it, 'and all that pertains thereto,' to me. Come on."

I followed her across the kitchen which was outfitted, like the one she had in Boston, with restaurant equipment. There were no upper cabinets but racks of slatted shelves hung down from the wooden ceiling on slender supports. "They were inspired by my kitchen in Boston, so I became their kitchen designer."

"Kind of a haiku *de haute cuisine*," I interjected.

"You're the first person to get it" she looked at me as if maybe there were more than had initially met her eye, and threw open the

French doors and went out on the deck. Below us, the waters of the bay lapped at a small beach and the high rocks that surrounded it. Seagulls wheeled, and one of them dropped a clam on the rocks to crack it open. Cormorants stood on rocks barely exposed by the low tide, looking like the crooks of so many drowned shepherds. She led me back indoors and showed me the living room. Comfortable, well-worn pine furniture clustered around a fieldstone fireplace in the corner. A window seat at the far end was the main interruption in two walls of books. I was led through the near end of it to the stairwell and down. "This is my room," she said as she opened a door near our remaining luggage. A double mattress and spring sat on the floor, I didn't see much more before she opened the room across the hall. "Why don't you throw your stuff in here?" I did, noting the sizable dresser and tarnished brass bed. "Down here is the bathroom," she had entered a small corridor opposite the stairwell, "there's another one upstairs in the master bedroom." The corridor also contained a bench with boots, shoes and sandals of all descriptions clustered beneath it and coat pegs glutted with oilskins, waders, and even a Sou'wester. "I guess they felt that they had to have a mudroom. Check this out." She opened the door across the hall from the bathroom. "The potting room. Look at this; a coffee maker, sink, bar, refrigerator; everything just in case they wanted to have coffee or drinkies out on the veranda. You know those little catalogs that show up in the mail? For anything and everything?"

"I've seen 'em around."

"Well, after they retired down here, they must have had a ball ordering anything and everything."

"At least I now know how Bean's, Brookstone's and Land's End can afford to send those catalogs to me."

She led me back to the corridor and to the left. "This is the bunk room, made to put up masses of grandchildren." Six beds were stacked in the room, looking just like summer camp. "It was a very big deal when I graduated from this room and got my own, some time around puberty. This," she opened another door, "was always called the parents' room. They'd get awakened by any ruckus first, before the noise would spread upstairs to disturb the grandparents. I suppose it didn't help their love of the place any." She took my empty beer bottle. "Get your trunks on. Let's go swimming and get lunch."

"Not so fast," I said. "I have a couple of questions." I folded her in my arms and we kissed. Last night's electricity was neither a delusion nor a one-time phenomenon. Minutes passed.

When we finally came up for air, she took a deep breath and said, "The phone is in the kitchen. We'll sort out the long distance calls next month."

"Thanks." Next month? I went upstairs to phone Patti, both questions answered. It was unbelievable that it was only eleven-thirty in the morning.

I dialed Patti's office and after a few forays up the phone tree ended up speaking to her.

"Where are you now?" she asked.

"In the middle of nowhere and in the middle of everywhere." I gave her the phone number at Hemp Hill. "If Nick wants to reach me, he can call me here. If either of you need anything, I can be up there by nine o'clock the following day."

"Sounds like you should stay hidden. Incidentally, Brendan Schwartz called to tell me that *Banned in Boston* is coming together very nicely. It should be on next Wednesday night, right after the news. Hey, enjoy your vacation. You're lucky to get a summer rental on such short notice."

We hung up and I made my way back to my room. I took a minute to stow all my stuff in the bureau and closet. I stared at the couple of swimsuits I had brought. I was in the grips of a priapism I hadn't experienced since spring afternoons in high school, sitting next to a cheerleader whose charms were more appropriate to the Rigid Tool calendar at Malkowski's Mobil station. I decided on the minimal

Speedo. I undressed and wrestled it on; when it came to visual foreplay I decided that I could attempt to give it as well as I could take it.

I emerged from the room to find Elisabeth awaiting me in the barest of electric purple bikinis. She looked me over appraisingly. "Love your outfit," she said, handing me a bucket full of towels, suntan lotion and beach stuff. We went out the front door and across the lawn to some wooden steps that took us down to the beach. A ribbon of dry sand gave way to a tidal flat dotted with rocks and festooned with seaweed. A small sailboat and rowboat were pulled up on one end of the beach.

"Your suit is beautiful," I said as we spread out a couple of large beach towels, "and a tribute to fabric engineering of the highest order. It must be one of those benefits from NASA research they're always talking about." We stretched out, side by side on our backs, absorbing the warming rays of the midday sun.

Eventually, we took turns greasing each other's backs. She climbed on my back and rubbed the soothing salve from the nape of my neck to the heels of my feet, taking extra care around my suit. When it was my turn, she rolled over and moved her tresses aside. "Would you mind undoing the back?" Her voice was slightly muffled by the towel.

I didn't mind. When I had dutifully worked down to where the suit strap had been, I pursued my mission down her sides, experiencing the delicious softness of the sides of her breasts; the taut narrow of her waist, the elastic around the bottom of her suit, and the backs of graceful legs that proved to be as much of a joy to the hand as they were to the eye.

Lying side by side, we found ourselves staring at each other. "I think that you are the most beautiful woman I have ever seen or heard of. Your hair is spectacular, too."

"You think." She gave me a studied gaze that seemed to evaluate this new juxtaposition: me and thought, and pulled one of the sausage curls around and dangled it. "The curls are softening up from last night. Hang around long enough and you'll see me look like Pocahontas."

"Is that a threat or a promise?"

"You're weird!"

"But tasteful. I'm very possibly tastefully weird." We started to kiss and further explore each other with our hands. It would have gone further but Elisabeth looked out to the bay. "Quahoggers," she said, and indeed, there were a couple of clamdiggers working their tongs a couple of hundred yards away. "Let's check out the water." She fastened the back of her suit and raced into the water with me in hot pursuit. "Farewell, cool curls!" she whooped as she dived into the chop. The cold splash came none too soon for me.

After we had swum and done everything in the water that could be done at high noon in the presence of distant clamdiggers and an apparent shipping lane; after we had clutched like the lovers in *From Here to Eternity* and she had declared her love of otters, because they spend a lot of their days playing and making mud slides; she grabbed my buttocks, drew me close to her and whispered in my ear, "Let's dig up some lunch."

Returning to our towels, she snatched an onion bag from the bucket and led me to the edge of the rocks at the south end of the beach. She squatted on a flat rock and pointed out some mussels, growing in shiny black profusion between the high and low tide lines. Her hair, soaked and hanging to the small of her back, moved up and down as she demonstrated how easy it was to wrench them loose and throw them in the bag. "I just love all of this free food lying about. Would you like some steamers with dinner?"

"Are bears Catholic? Do Polish prelates…"

"There are some good clam beds right here. I'll show you how to find them." Engorgement was a large and clumsy companion who, coming back to haunt me, had to be kept from banging his head on doorways and tripping over the furniture. I followed her as she left the bag of mussels and retrieved the bucket and the gardening tools in it. She headed for the water's edge, near the rocks on the north end of the beach. She picked up some rocks and started to roll them over the sand. "I'm trying to make them spurt and show me where they are," she explained.

"Some clams have all the luck," I said. Within a few minutes, one of the stones caused an unmistakable geyser to occur, shooting about eight inches into the air and diminishing to a trickle.

"We could go after these with our bare hands, but you find yourself literally working your fingers down to the bone," she said as she gently scraped away some stones and eased the trowel into the sand. I could only agree that we were already in the presence of enough that was red and raw. She reached into the hole and withdrew a three-inch clam with a one-inch neck sticking out of it. It squirted again.

I got into it, though I was mortified when I put one of the tines of the little rake through the shell of an otherwise viable clam. "That's why they're called softshell clams," my guide offered. Our bucket began to fill up, and I became better at spotting our camouflaged quarry. Occasionally a small bank of sand would fall into the hole to reveal two or three clams standing upright, caught in the act of being clams. "I think we have a few courses here. You want to rinse them off and cover them with seawater?"

I took the bucket out into a couple of feet of bay and rinsed the clams. Elisabeth stayed on the beach 'replacing the divot' as she called it. Since anyone could clam the shore between the tide lines, she explained, it paid to cover the evidence of a mother lode. She joined me with another half dozen clams that we had missed, and we waded back to the beach together.

Carrying the sea's bounty and all of the other stuff we had brought, we made our way up the stairs and across the lawn to the veranda. "Lay down your burden here, and bring a towel." She stepped over the low stone wall and headed toward the rear of the house, shaking sand out of her towel as she went. I followed her example in every way.

Nestled against the house was a single-storied stone turret. Elisabeth opened a weathered door that sat in its frame like half of a saloon door. It was an outdoor shower, open to the blue sky on top and with a spiral floor plan that took one past a small bench and around into the compartment of running water. I set my towel on the bench and joined Elisabeth as she brought the water to a pleasing temperature. "We're supposed to save water during the hot, dry summer months," she said above the cascade. "No washing of pickup trucks. No watering of lawns."

"Showering with a friend is an emergency measure I can get into," I said, wrapping my arms around her and risking drowning with a kiss that found reciprocity. We savaged each others' mouths, and I worked around to undo the top of her suit. She pulled it away from between us and pitched it toward the bench. Beauty squashed itself against me. I ran a hand up to experience the weight and softness. Her hands began to explore the least destructive way to shed me of my suit, finally settling on pulling the front out and down and slowly moving beautiful thumbs around to the sides to shove everything down as far as she could reach. I began to descend to my knees, licking her neck and running my tongue down into her cleavage. The delicate nipples adorning the point of each upturned breast were sucked into fullness. My tongue continued its quest, exploring her navel while my hands took up station in either side of the electric purple bottom of her bikini. Somewhere a truck was growling. It was coming closer. It stopped nearby. "Oh, shit!" Elisabeth stormed out grabbing the discarded top and a towel. I heard the bulkhead cellar door open. I turned the water to ice cold, rinsed out my suit, turned off the water, dried off, and put my damp suit back on again.

I found her standing in wildly floral muumuu at the door, her head wrapped in a towel. She was talking to a freckled teenager who wore racing-striped gym shorts and occasionally scratched behind his ears. Behind him stood a former mail truck awkwardly lettered 'Eric's Errands Etc.' She thanked him for dropping by and closed the door on him. "*New York Times* and *Boston Globe* delivered daily, no lawn mowing for the foreseeable future, and *no goddam tip at the end of the summer! It's time for lunch.*"

We fetched the shellfish from the veranda and headed up to the kitchen. She sprinkled some cornmeal on top of the water in the clam bucket and set it aside. "They'll eat that and purge their sand." She went to the refrigerator and pulled out a bottle of white wine. "Prudence Island Vineyards Chardonnay 'eighty-one. It's from one of the other islands on the bay." She deftly deployed a corkscrew and poured the clear, lightly ambered wine into two long-stemmed glasses. She handed me one and we clicked glasses. "To a long and happy summer."

"To say the very least." It was a wonderful dry wine, flinty and complex.

She showed me how to pull the bissus from the mussels and scrub them with a vegetable brush, and busied herself clanging pots, raiding the refrigerator, and chopping with a lethal-looking Chinese cleaver. When the mussels were finally in a pot on the stove, simmering open with just a touch of white jug wine, and some water was heating up for the pasta, Elisabeth produced a hairbrush from a pocket and went out on the deck. I followed her out and watched as she unwrapped the towel from her head. "My favorite blowdryer," she said, turning her face into the sunshine and a warm breeze.

"Need help?"

"Can you do it without wreaking major damage?"

"Try me." It was long, wet, and tangled, but, starting at the roots and using almost as much fingers as brush, I worked well and delicately. The elements were doing their job, and as I finished up, almost bent double to work down past the small of her back, the edges of the long mane had begun to lighten, brighten and dry.

"Have I told you that you have fantastic hands?" she drew herself against me. "I think we have some pots boiling."

Lunch, served in the sun, was more wine, mussels in a white sauce on spaghetti, French bread and fresh fruit. Elisabeth explained how very few people ate mussels, so they were easily found. "I know what I'd *like* to do right after lunch, but I have this feeling that there might be more callers this afternoon."

"Mmh," I said, having just bitten the tip off a pear.

"I'll show you the island."

A few minutes later, we were chugging down the road in the truck. The inn where she had worked was a cedar-shingled affair with a large deck sprouting *Cinzano* umbrellas. A lawn ran down to complex of docks and a white sand beach. "The crowd is thin right now. Tomorrow it will be packed." She drove on.

It turned out that there was no downtown on the island. The general store at the ferry dock was the center of island life and, at boat time, a place to run into practically everybody else and pick up your mail. Elisabeth pointed out some cottages and summer homes where noted contemporaries had summered. By the fourth of July, most of them would be back for a while.

There was also a lot of waving; every time we passed a vehicle going in the opposite direction, a bicyclist, someone on foot, or people lounging in the sun in front of their houses.

She showed me another social center of the island, the dump, though since we were not within its posted hours, it was only a gathering place for scavenging seagulls. I gazed through the fence at piles of automobile parts and rusting major appliances that lined one side of the dump while Elisabeth copied down the summer hours.

On another part of the island, we walked hand in hand on a long sandy beach, chased by waves that signaled the rising tide. Wading, splashing and carrying on like the carefree young lovers I wished we could be. I could dream—at least until the next time somebody tried to kill me.

We drove up a dusty road that led to a blackberry patch and the first insects I'd seen on the island. A plastic bag and some insect repellant from the truck's glove compartment took care of carrying our harvest and kept most of the mosquitoes, greenhead flies and horseflies from harvesting us.

Back at the house, we did some 'beginning of summer' chores like opening windows all over the house, making a trip to the wine cellar to fetch up a bushel of selected bottles, and hauling firewood from a large stack behind the house to the veranda. "No better way to ensure warm evenings than to have a fire all set and ready for the match," my hostess proclaimed. "Do you sail?"

I set the last load of split logs near the fireplace. "I think so. I'm a graduate of the sailing academy at the Charles River Basin."

"The wind isn't great for it right now, but I'll show you some kick-ass sailing real soon. Do you know Lasers?"

"I've seen them shoot past while I was sailing prams. Is *that* what's down at the beach?"

"You guessed it."

We lounged around for awhile. I tried the library in the living room and found something good to read. Elisabeth stretched out on the deck with Agatha Christie. I alternated between reading, watching the bay, and looking at my companion. Mainly, I just lay on one of the Adirondack chairs and felt on top of the world.

"I don't know about you, but I'm going to change for dinner." She snapped her mystery shut, stood, and stretched, looking every bit the lioness she was proving to be. "Steamers, salad, and maybe something else sound good to you?"

"Rumor is that gods don't eat, but if they did, it couldn't be better."

"See you in the kitchen in a half hour or so," she said as she drifted back into the house.

I heard water running in the downstairs bathroom when I returned to my room, so I grabbed some light slacks, a Hawaiian shirt and my shaving kit and headed for the upstairs bathroom. I raided a linen closet outside the master bedroom for a towel and let myself into the suite. Though the bedroom was neat as a pin, it gave the impression that its occupants, too, would soon be returning to change for dinner. A framed portrait on the makeup table showed a silver-haired man with a lean jaw and light, piercing eyes. Near it, brush, comb and hand mirror awaited use, as did powder and perfumes. A bureau displayed another portrait; this of a woman with a gamine's round face, a wide smile, and swept-back gray hair. I heard the water stop downstairs and stopped my surreptitious research.

The upstairs bathroom was probably among the most elegant environs in which I had ever abluted. There was a tiled shower stall and a giant Jacuzzi. A bidet which must have driven the local plumbers into laughing fits rounded out the complement. I emerged feeling like a new man.

Elisabeth wore a flowing lavender dress, with a beautifully low cut front. She was washing lettuce when I joined her. "Can you successfully impersonate a bartender?" she asked when I put my arms around her. I tore myself away to make vodka tonics.

I worked on the clams and melted butter under Elisabeth's tutelage. When everything was ready, we sat down to dine by candlelight overlooking the bay. "Excuse me," I said, producing a joint. "The fair island of Maui sends its greeting of Wowee. Mind if we smoke?"

"Isn't that nice? It's getting so expensive and dangerous that I'd be afraid to ask it of anyone. Please. Thank you."

Dinner passed slowly and ecstatically. Clams came easily from their shells, through the broth and butter and into our savoring mouths. Their nutty flavor and tender texture eclipsed any clam I had ever eaten. The butter running down our chins was caught by fingers which were languorously licked off. The salad was a symphony of crisp romaine, pulchritudinous tomatoes and firm cucumbers. The dishes stayed where they were as we adjourned to the sofa.

Actually, Elisabeth ran around locking all of the doors on the first floor while I poured snifters of brandy. After one sip, the snifters were exiled to the end tables while great and important deeds were again set in motion. It was the first time I had ever helped Elisabeth out of a dress from the front, and the experience was heart-stoppingly beautiful. First, chaste shoulders were revealed and savored, while skilled and slender fingers set to work on my shirt. A hook and a zipper allowed breasts to burgeon out from the nestling confines of the dress. My lips were glued to hers while she slipped the shirt off my arms. The dress came off over wriggled hips and we re-engaged to deal with two pairs of my pants and one of hers.

The phone rang. "Let it ring," I said.

"I think I'd better get it," she said, quickly covering my face, neck and chest with kisses. "Not too many people know I'm here."

I pondered that as I watched her bound for the phone in the kitchen. Bikini panties were invented for that woman.

She reappeared with a strange expression on her face. "It's for you."

Maybe it was Nick calling for Brendan and I'd get my *one more day* of work and the union card. Maybe it was Patti with bad news about Nick. I stepped out of my trousers and gave Elisabeth a hug as I took the phone from her. I resisted the temptation to bite off a piece of the phone and spit it contemptuously to one side. "Bart Lane, here."

"Hello," said a foreign-sounding male voice at the other end. "This is Mohammed calling."

CHAPTER 6

❀

I couldn't help but wonder if this personal calling from the very prophet was why there were so many Moslems and why they were capable of such fanaticism. "What can I do for you, Mr. Moham-med?" I was standing at the kitchen counter in my purple mini-briefs.

"I am with Vishnu Films of Bombay and we are shooting a film in Providence and Newport, Rhode Island, and other extremely pictur-esque American locations. It is entitled *Mysore Karma* and we need a cameraman. We misplaced the one that we were going to work with."

"Misplaced?"

"Oh, I'm very sorry. We misplaced our faith in the fellow and we had to fire him. I was given your name and that of Mr. Entwhistle Kidd by Nick Rodini. Mr. Kidd is available for two weeks, but not after that."

"That's fortunate for you because I'm not available for two weeks." Elisabeth pulled open a drawer near me and pointed out a pencil and paper. Then, moved by the many meanings of drawers, she pulled open mine, kissed her finger, and planted the kiss very specifically.

"Are you familiar with Mr. Kidd?"

I was; Whiz Kidd was a maddeningly mellow and unfortunately ubiquitous competitor who landed a lot of jobs I would have liked to have. "I think that your film will be in very good hands with Mr. Kidd for two weeks." I met Elisabeth's gaze as she shucked the clams we had left uneaten. This involved slipping shriveled black skins off the sleek erectile tissue of each clam, after busting it out of its pair of shells. "I will not be available for two weeks, and after that, I would like very much to work with you. Since I'm just a boat ride away from you, perhaps I could drop by some day." Elisabeth slipped some leftovers into the refrigerator and set off to close all the windows in the house.

"That is very good. I am Mohammed Bismillah with Vishnu Films." He proceeded to spell 'Vishnu'. "We are at the Biltmore in Providence." He gave his phone number. Then he went on to dictate a list of names and numbers for all of the people an American counterpart would be hired to keep you *away* from, including the producer, Shyam Something; and the director, not Satyajit Ray, whom I had heard of, but Indrani Something Else, whom I had not. Elisabeth, now wrapped in a large white bath sheet, was kneeling in front of the fireplace lighting a fire. "I shall be calling you back," concluded Mohammed, and the line went dead.

I unplugged the phone and waved the end of the cord at Elisabeth. "What was that all about?" she called.

Checking my notes I said, "The Mohammed in question is one Mr. Bismillah. He's with a film called *Mysore Karma*...."

"*Mysore Karma*? How can you resist having a look at that?"

I told her what I had learned and that I might get a day or two of work out of it. "If they want to meet me before that, can we combine it with a mainland provisioning run?"

I joined her standing by the fire. "Excuse me," I blurted, "but if you're worried about anything, I do have a certified blood donor's card from Brigham and Women's Hospital."

"Who'd you give blood to, a Brigham or a woman?" she whispered in my ear.

"A Brigham, I swear, and they never called me with the word that my blood was tainted. Oh, uh, I have a birth control device I could use."

"A condominium?"

"Yeah, if your zoning allows it."

"That's unbelievably wonderful of you to offer. I've wondered how to talk about that at a time like this." She planted her lips on mine and gently twisted my arm behind my back. She unbuckled my digital watch and checked it out of the corner of her eye. She pitched it into a dark corner of the room. "June twentieth. No problem."

I undid the towel and tossed it onto the sofa. Her fire-warmed body seemed to press against every inch of me. We knelt together, bringing each other's pants down and we stood, stepping out together and leaving them tangled on the braided rug.

I picked her up and carried her to the couch, setting her down and kneeling to begin consuming her with kisses. Leaving her face a vessel of desire in the flickering firelight, I explored the little depressions at the base of her neck; celebrated the rise of her breasts and brought a hand to bear on her tight, glowing chestnut curls while I enjoyed every square millimeter of her stomach. By then, one of her hands had me where she wanted me and she pulled me off my knees while she swung a leg between us. Facing me, she brought her legs around me, clamped her feet on the small of my back and pulled me in.

I could have died then and considered my life well spent. That sweet slide into her was the most concentrated moment of pure joy and beauty I had ever experienced.

"Sweet Jesus," she sighed. "I have never…"

I stood, turned us around, and sat with her on my lap. We started to move slowly together. "Elisabeth, just *looking* at you last night was one of the biggest treats I've ever had. I…can't believe…how beautiful you are." I looked at her and began to stroke her hair down her bare back. I reveled in every inch of every strand, lit to flickering perfection, tumbling to her pulsing buttocks. I buried my face between her breasts, and gorged on each in its turn, trying to suffocate. Her fingernails raked slowly down my back, her teeth buried themselves in my shoulder, freeing me only when she threw back her head and locked in orgasm.

"Bart, oh, this…"

I locked my mouth on hers and picked her up. I carried her to the braided rug in front of the fireplace and brought her down gently. Keeping one arm around her, I used the other to bring her hair out from under her and I came down on top of her. We were moving again, and my hands slid along her sweat-glistened body to clutch her heaving ass. In the midst of all this ecstasy a sweet sting started to grow. It crescendoed until we were both locked and rocked by its insistent rhythm. It exploded us into another realm and left two sweaty bodies sharing long, slow kisses on the floor.

"Sir," Elisabeth said when she could speak, "I thought I was experienced. I thought I'd had enough to be convinced that orgasm wasn't a complete myth, but this…"

"I've never been here before, either," was all I could say. Two sweaty, delighted, consumed and exhausted bodies lay on a braided rug in front of a crackling fire on Squidneck Island, and I was more amazed to be one of them than I had ever been to be anything else.

"*Mysore Karma*, eh?" The poet eyed me across the top of an effervescing flute of *Taittinger* and a jacuzzi full of bubbles. "How did he get your name?"

"I guess he found out about me through Nick. Oh, Nick's wife mentioned that *Banned in Boston* will be on the air Wednesday night."

"That should be interesting. Any word on the folks trying to nail you?"

"God, no. If Mohammed doesn't know anything about them, there's a good chance they don't know about him—or me." Or Elisabeth and the island. "I think Patti would have told me if she had heard anything. What Brendan said about laying low 'til this thing blows over is probably the order of the day." The unemployed workaholic was emerging and attempting to dominate my thoughts. "Hey, it was close. I've been freelancing for them for years and this quarter looked good for getting on the staff. There are ten days left in June and I only need to work one of them to get in the union. Listen, I'll try not let it tie me in knots. I'm so…glad to be here with you."

"You, Mr. Lane, are a moving experience." Her knees found my knees under the bubbles. "Why don't you move your cute ass around to my side of the tub so I can pinch it and see if it's for real?"

"Aw, Miss Hemphill, you know that the PTA and the school board have both come out against this particular kind of educational activity." I followed her suggestion.

"It seems to maintain reality fairly well," she said after performing a gentle pinch and leaving her hand there.

I wrapped an arm around her and continued my long marvel at the beauty of her. I dodged the chopstick she had put her hair up with and kissed her on the base of her neck.

"So, about those condoms you're carrying around. Is it any easier to buy them now that safe sex is a broader social concern?"

"Well, outside of getting them with quarters from machines in the men's rooms in truck stops along the Ohio Turnpike, which was easy, it always turns out to be unnerving. Actually, about all I ever got for my high school troubles was the profile of a ring, rising out of my wallet. At the pharmacy in Williamstown, I went in, waited until I thought there was nobody within earshot, and marched right up to the prescription window. The white haired gentleman peered over his half-glasses at me and asked what he could do for me. I was ready: 'One half-dozen Trojans, please,' His voice got a little louder than it probably would have been if he were, say, filling a penicillin prescription for the mayor, 'Regular or reservoir tip? Lubricated or non-lubricated?' 'Uh—regular, lubricated,' I mumbled, trying to bring down the volume. 'Size?' he boomed. I hadn't noticed one of the older faculty wives approaching the counter. 'Medium,' I whispered. 'What a disappointment it must be,' said the old broad in line behind me. I paid and got out."

"And now, in this enlightened era?"

I lifted her into my lap, she swung around to sit sideways and pursue her question with blue eyes that were locked on to mine.

"I passed up my neighborhood pharmacy. They tend to keep them, and everything else, in locked display cases. I made my way to a big CVS. For once in my life, I wanted to deal with an impersonal multinational corporation. I walked down the appropriate aisle and spent five minutes picking the precise texture, shape, quality, quantity and size of my armor as well as the precise moment to take possession of it. I seized my choice and stood in line at a cash register. The machine in question was personned by a heavily mascaraed lady of mid-high school vintage. She wore a flamingo pink frock. Her black hair was forced into an Afro-Mohawk by a silver banana clip. Her accent was South Boston as she pushed the intercom button. "ey, Eileen, whatsa price on el ninety-oh-foah-one-two, Trojans?' Eileen shouted back, 'What size?' "Medium,' boomed the public address system. 'Six ninety-nine,' shouted Eileen."

The laughter was almost floating Elisabeth off my lap. We kissed and sipped more champagne. "And does the covered party…"

"You mean my, uh, penis?"

"Yes, does it have a name?"

"No, it's always too busy rushing off to meetings."

She almost choked on that, spraying me with a mist of the thirty-dollar stuff. "I asked for that," she finally managed to say. "Listen, there's no easy way to say what I want to say,"

"Try me," I said. Uh oh, here comes the bad news, she's figured out that way down deep, I'm shallow.

"Would you move into my bedroom with me?"

I don't think I hid my sigh of relief. "Yes."

"Thank you. Any time you've had enough hot water and bubbly, we can get started."

I imagined that there would be all kinds of qualifications on her part. I mean she had her study and work-space there and poets must not be disturbed. She pulled herself out of the tub and reached a hand to help me. "What if we just move next door?" I inclined my head toward the master bedroom.

"I can't deal with that. It's probably silly, but I feel as if they're still there."

"I know what you mean," I said as we started to towel each other off.

How many gifts could I accept in one day? Wrapped in towels and feeling like half of a Tahitian wedding ceremony, we walked arm in arm around the second floor, carrying the champagne and turning off lights, checking the fire, and finally making it to her room. She led me into the dark and turned on a reading lamp over the bed. I stood for a minute, taking it in.

"I suppose that is rather gauche." She had seen me staring at a large framed photograph of her.

"I love it." Obviously dating from *The Buzz* era of her life, it showed her on-stage and in the spotlight. Purple and red stage lights reflected a thousand times in the sweaty curls that streamed off her head and over her shoulders. Eyes closed, she was singing into an unseen microphone as her tambourine blurred in front of her. Tight bell-bottomed jeans revealed high-heeled boots pounding the stage. "If anyone had ever taken a comparable picture of me, I'd definitely hang it on my bedroom wall."

I was, however, more taken with the live version of my hostess, standing with me; looking around her room and possibly trying to see it with my eyes. I noticed a hurricane lamp on a night table. I lit it. I turned out the light. I pulled the chopstick from the mass of hair coiled on top of her head and helped guide the cascade down her back. She was right; a gentle undulation was all that remained of the sausage curls.

A bed is not the two-dimensional venue for lovemaking that it might initially appear to be. Compared the floor and furnishings of the living room, it might have been, but for us, it wasn't. We did not go gently into that good night. The tempering of our former urgency gave us even more time to experience each other, which is exactly what we did.

It's an accepted convention that people generally look like hell first thing in the morning. I woke from a warm and happy sleep to find Elisabeth propped up on her elbows and grinning at me. She did not look like hell. The lovely tangles which surrounded her appeared to have been arranged by a master of the art. Her eyes were not bleary, but very soft and very interested.

What a way to start the day! An hour later, we were settling down to coffee and fresh blackberries in the kitchen. The bay was filling up with sails blasted into whiteness by the morning sun. "Let's go down to the dock and see who's coming on the ten boat. We can pick up some milk at the general store and I can check the mail."

"Sounds like fun to me. Are you expecting anyone in particular?"

"Some of the summer people I grew up with might be starting to arrive, especially since it's officially the first day of summer. They'll want to be well moved in by the Fourth of July. I think you'd enjoy meeting them."

"Is the Fourth a big weekend here?"

"'Big' is an understatement."

"I haven't had a weekend of solid partying since college. I like it."

"It's funny, isn't it? I mean that this place seems like a luxury, right?"

"You could say that."

"But look at life on the mainland. It has become really transient. Are you in touch with anyone from Berea outside of your parents?"

I thought about that. I was barely in touch with my two older brothers. "Nope."

"No matter where you're settled in out there, it can all change. You can move a few blocks, and you'll never see your neighbors again. If you get transferred to, say, Poughkeepsie, you're leaving behind a whole collection of friends that you'll never have anything to do with again."

I thought about that. I had done a shoot in Cleveland once. There I was, practically in my old back yard. Because of the schedule, my visit there was confined to the offices and factories we were shooting in and our hotel. It was like a dream in which my current friends and I were in my hometown, but segregated in a glass cage from which we could not emerge. "I see what you mean. What are you getting at?"

"I guess I mean that this place is my real home. These people are my friends and neighbors and they always will be. No matter where we get shoved around by our jobs or our spouse's careers, we'll always come back here. Until we die."

"I never thought of it that way." I found it simultaneously warm and eerie, reassuring and frightening. "I'm even more overwhelmed by your inviting me here." She couldn't want an unemployed camera tramp with a price on his head sharing her life, could she?

"I'm trying to figure out how to introduce you to, for instance, the Dodges."

"Well, I'd like to bring a camera down to the dock, so I can be a book jacket photographer."

"That won't hold for more than a couple of days."

"How long am I invited for?"

"Well, the water is warm enough for swimming through September." She eyed me with warm challenge as she sipped her coffee.

That hit me like a ton of bricks. "I would li…I'm…Just…" The urge was there. Let it all go. *Regardez* the nothing which you have left behind and the something to which you have come. "I will try to spend as much of that time with you as I can, but in my professional situation, I can't be sure." I thought that was pretty good, considering I had never attended a law school.

She put a hand on mine, barely suppressing a giggle. "Are you sure you didn't leave Harvard Law out of your résumé? Why don't I introduce you as *a* houseguest? The 'a' implies that there are several others rattling around and you might make a fourth at bridge but not necessarily the hostess."

"I like it. Cut it and print it!"

We visited the Dodges on the way to the dock, ostensibly dropping by to see if they needed anything from the general store. John Dodge was a tall, fit, older man whose liver spots seemed like well-won battle ribbons. He shook my hand warmly and held onto it while he found out where I was from and what I did. Virginia's face exuded Scandinavian warmth and tanned well-being. She quickly appraised me from head to toe and offered coffee.

We drank coffee and I mostly listened as births, deaths, marriages and divorces among people I didn't know were discussed. Just dropping in uninvited and being asked to sit and talk were not normal in most of the country. I began to see what Elisabeth meant by *home* and *community*. To me, they had always meant, respectively, a roof over your head and something to try to organize when somebody wanted to bulldoze your home.

We said our good-byes and accepted blanket invitations to drop by. The shore road was full of vehicles and people on foot as we made our way to the ferry dock. Elisabeth stopped and offered rides until the bed of the truck was filled. We chugged into the lot and everybody disembarked near the store amidst shouted thanks. We found a parking space at the far end of the lot.

I busied myself taking pictures of the pilings and, when it hove into view, the ferry. Elisabeth chatted with a few older couples and introduced me when I was in the vicinity. I had the feeling of being evaluated, but I didn't detect any raised eyebrows. As the ferry unloaded, I started to meet quite a few of Elisabeth's friends who greeted her with hugs and me with handshakes. Of the Arbans, Judy was the lifelong friend and Jon had married into all of this. Judy was shorter than Elisabeth and seemed to have adopted a baggy, utilitarian, possibly suburban appearance. She was glad to meet me—I could tell through her sunglasses—and seemed to be glad to see that her old friend was not alone. Jon smiled at me, and with me, at 'these islanders'. He wore strapped-on glasses, like a basketball player, and a T-shirt that proclaimed something to do with computers.

Don Bachman hadn't arrived on the ferry, he was just hanging out like us. Barefoot, potbellied, and carrying a beer, he smiled down at me as he shook my hand and gave Elisabeth a theatrical kiss. His hair stood out from his head in light brown tangles and his eyes communicated that he had found something to alter his mind with. "For some people, the beach party never ends," Elisabeth whispered as he ambled down the dock grinning, waving and shaking hands.

I met a kaleidoscope of old friends, their spouses and kids. Word was that there was going to be a cosmic beach party on the fourth. It was nice to know that I hadn't missed wild beach parties just because I didn't grow up in Southern California.

"Don't get me wrong," said Elisabeth as we chugged back to Hemp Hill. "Judy is one of my best friends, but it has always been exhausting to be around her."

"How so?"

"Her life has been a series of hurdles. She was worried about going to junior high school, then high school—all summer long I had to listen to her go on and on about how cool everyone was at this high school. Then cheerleading—could she win the competition for that? Do you need a list, or can you imagine a succession of summers, each one absorbed in worrying about the next thing coming up in her life? College, marriage, grad school, career?"

"I get the picture. What is her current crisis?"

"I think it's maternity. Last summer she was agonizing about going off the pill. 'The biological clock is ticking' and, of course, serious doubt about everything she had spent every other summer worrying about."

"Well, I hope that it all works out for her. She seems to be a nice, if somewhat ambitious, person."

"She used to be really attractive, too. I think she felt she had to give up her looks to get ahead at the office. Last summer, she underwent another change. I think she has conceived of the idea that maternity is an uglifying experience, so she is trying to get a head start on it. Am I being unfair? Is she right, if that's what she thinks?"

"I'm not attracted to her, myself, but I don't think you're unfair, and I hope she's wrong, if that's what she thinks."

"Thanks." She stopped the truck in front of the house and turned off the engine. "All campers interested in sailing will report to the shed behind the house in their bathing suits, as soon as possible."

This camper clambered into his trunks and followed instructions. Elisabeth was hauling a sail bag and some aluminum spars out of the shed when I joined her. We carried them all down to the beach and she showed me how to rig the boat. There were even more sailboats on the bay now, and I was glad for an opportunity to be out among them.

Elisabeth ran the show, ordering me aboard while she held the boat facing directly into the wind. "There's no dry way to do this. Pull the sail halfway in."

I did as I was told. She stayed in the water and pulled the boat around until the wind caught the sail. The boat started to rush forward, and she somehow managed to hang on to the tiller and pull herself aboard, dripping wet, beside me.

She tacked it back and forth a few times, and helped me with the timing on the scramble from side to side that turning entailed. "It's so wonderful to sail with someone who knows what they're doing—especially on this." My stomach muscles got a lot of exercise from leaning out to flatten the boat as much as possible. The wind in Narragansett Bay varies in intensity as other boats or features on the land block its passage. We often had to sit up quickly to avoid getting dunked. Elisabeth, in a well-fitting maillot suit of tiger-striped fabric, handled the boat very competently, slipping it around buoys and bouncing it over the wake of larger boats.

"Let's see what we can do with this thing. Coming about downwind. Ready about...and hard alee!" She cranked the tiller at the appropriate moment to spin us on a flat patch between two waves. She set a course with the wind forty-five degrees behind us. I trimmed the sail competently and we both adjusted our placement to make the boat lie perfectly flat. I think we were going faster than the wind. The boat began to emit a groan. "Who says boats are just fiberglass, aluminum and dacron? This boat is happy!"

"I've never heard one having an orgasm before."

We started to move through the ranks of larger boats. More than once, I felt the envious gaze of skippers and crew as they bobbed along, maybe drinking a beer or having their lunch.

We switched places, and I had a turn at the helm. We worked our way north along the island. Elisabeth seemed to approve of my technique, and nestled into my free arm between tacks. Isn't this the way it is supposed to be? Didn't Buckminster Fuller say that the first sea captains had to be lords of the land in order to command the resources to build the ship, provision it, and above all, crew it? What had I done except look for work and run for my life? Elisabeth was definitely the captain and I but a huggable helmsman. "You can sign me up for crew any time," I said into her ear.

"I like the way you tug my tiller," she breathed into mine.

We beached the boat and swam for a while. We seemed to share an approach that yielded both exercise and fooling around. After hauling the sail and spars back to the shed, we took a shower together in the roofless fieldstone carrel. There were no interruptions this time.

When we had dried off and made our way onto the house wrapped in towels, we heard the ring of a telephone. We charged up the stairs, jiggling and giggling, Elisabeth picked up the phone, listened briefly and held it to my ear. There was only the dial tone.

"It must have been Mohammed."

"Sorry you missed the call."

"I'm not. Mohammed can't buy me with promises of Paradise and *houris*. I'm already there, I mean, here."

She wrapped her arms around me and gave me a long, fierce kiss. "Lunch?" she asked when we came up for air.

I didn't at first know why this lady brought so many beach blankets to the picnic we had on the deck. Lunch was chilled white wine, brie, and French bread. After we were done eating, she hung all but one of the blankets over the railings, and shook the crumbs off the one we had been sitting on. "The secret to avoiding tan lines," she pronounced, removing her towel, "is to deal with the *causes* of the problem, and not just the symptoms. Bleach, erasers, correcting ribbon; none of these things work."

Which is how I happened to be lying around naked when my next opportunity came to talk to Mohammed on the phone. Elisabeth had answered the infernal ringing and called me to the phone. "Your prophet, sir," she said, holding her hand over the mouthpiece.

"This is Bart Lane," I said.

"Oh, yes, Mr. Lane, this is Mohammed. We have Mr. Kidd down here and he is working with the director. I asked him about you and he demanded to speak with the producer."

"It seems like an ideal situation for both of us. I'm not available for two weeks, and he's not available after two weeks."

"He has expressed the wish that we use John Younger in his absence."

"John Younger is part of *his* organization." John was Whiz's usual assistant. I was really tempted to say something about the wisdom of sending a focus-*wallah* to do a camera-*wallah*'s job but I refrained.

What I did say was: "I think you should use your organization to make this film, and not Entwhistle Kidd's. When can I meet with you?"

"I am working up the new revised schedule right now. I'll ring you up when I can find an opportune time."

We traded information on the best times for calling each other, said our good-byes, and hung up.

Elisabeth had been looking at a tide chart while I was on the phone. "What's new with Mohammed?"

"Entwhistle 'Whiz' Kidd is trying to get them to use his apprentice, so to speak, instead of me. I leaned on him a little bit, if Mohammeds can be leaned on over the phone. He says he'll be calling back."

"Wonderful," Elisabeth groaned.

"I am not going to spend your vacation or mine waiting for his call."

"Good. Let's go and get some shellfish for the *paella* tonight."

I bent my resolution a little and tried to reach Mohammed at his hotel a couple of times. I was in the kitchen, chopping scallions for the dinner salad a couple of days later, when his call came through. We agreed I would visit the production on Wednesday in Newport. It would involve a ferry ride and getting, somehow, to Hammersmith Farm.

"So," I said across the dinner table that night, "would you like to venture to the mainland metropolis of Newport in a couple of days? Wednesday to be exact?"

Elisabeth finished chewing a mouthful of salad. "Actually, I wouldn't mind hanging around here and working on some stuff I've been thinking about."

"Do you know the bus schedules to get to Newport from Warren?"

"You should probably use my car. It's in the lot across the street from the cannery."

"Thank you, but it's such a gem…"

"That's the right attitude for getting along with him."

"Him?"

"Don Brouhaha."

"Don Brouhaha?" She joined me in the incredulous question, echoing Firesign Theater.

"Anyway, if you're with him, I'll feel that you're safe, and you can bring the cooler along and stock up at a supermarket. Just keep the revs up and Don Brouhaha should keep you out of trouble."

"Listen, I have a confession to make."

"Let's hear it," she said resignedly.

"This chowder is the best I've ever tasted."

"Digging your own clams tends to make it taste that way. Come on, cough it up. Not the chowder; the confession."

"I can cook. I've done time in restaurant kitchens."

"You've been holding out on me!"

"No, no, no, it's not like that. You are just so damned good at it that I didn't want to interrupt the succession of treats that has been dazzling my palate. I was merely wondering if I could provide the dinner for Wednesday night. That's when they're showing *Banned in Boston*, by the way."

"Well, okay. You talked me into it."

"Now you'll have to take me down to the wine cellar so I can research the feast."

I knew why we were getting to bed relatively early for a couple of urban insomniacs. What I couldn't figure is why we also got to sleep earlier. Is it that clean ocean air causes everything in your system to combust more totally so that you burn out more easily? The end result of all of this exercise and sleep is that it was relatively easy to be on the dock and waiting when the eight forty-five AM ferry hove into view that Wednesday.

Elisabeth gave me a good-bye kiss and I hauled the cooler aboard. I climbed up to the upper foredeck and joined the people who lined the rail. I covered my ears in time to preserve them from the horn's blast and waved a farewell to Elisabeth who was waving back at me. I didn't care at all for the sensation of leaving her.

Back on the mainland, I fished the car out of the lot and chuckled to myself as I remembered its name, Don Brouhaha. When I turned into the street, I gave it the healthy tromp on the accelerator that I usually used to get my beetle rolling. The front wheels screamed their vengeance and shot me smartly down the street. "Brouhaha?"

I visited a bank where I was able to use my credit card to get some cash. The large supermarket gave me culture shock after a few days on the Island. I stocked up on all of the items on the list including Tampax. Whether that particular item was a test or a confidence, I was flattered by the errand. Then, I began the special acquisitions for the feast that I would prepare that evening; beef tenderloin, romaine, anchovies, spinach, asparagus and a small block of Parmesan cheese. I knew that I wasn't in the big city, but I thought I might be able to find some fresher oysters and French bread on my subsequent travels. There hadn't been any oysters in Narragansett Bay since the hurricane of 'thirty-eight scoured them away.

I was back at work, selling myself. I felt clean, well-tanned and possibly expensive. David Lee Roth was singing *Just a Gigolo* on the car radio. I was dangerously close to feeling like a yuppie, but I don't use the Y-word on myself. The vacationing hordes tying up the road to Newport were more infuriating than they would have been if I were on vacation, too. I could certainly sympathize with the kids in the back seats of their family cars who wanted to explore the mast-filled waterfront and spend all of their allowances on stuff from Taiwan labeled 'Newport', but I had an appointment with a guy named Mohammed.

All things considered, I felt pretty good about myself as I wheeled the borrowed orange Saab up to the guard shack at Hammersmith Farm. It certainly beat running for my life in the wrong shoes. I was a few decades too late to have been invited there by one of the Bouvier daughters. This was where Jacqueline Onassis and Princess Lee Radziwill had spent their summers, and where one John Kennedy, his smile infectious, perhaps, but not yet famous, had driven his '50 Ford convertible to meet his future parents-in-law. One no longer needed an invitation from the family to visit there, as a parking lot full of cars and tour busses indicated. The gate attendant didn't charge me admission, however, and did give me directions to find the film crew. A large white truck parked along the manicured drive to the main house served as a temporary landmark. Sprawled around it on the grass was a collection of Occidental and Asian folk, apparently 'standing by.' A short, slim California surfer-type caught my eye. Bleached bluejeans, sandals, faded Hawaiian shirt, and a shock of blond hair set him apart.

"Hi, I'm Bart Lane and I'm supposed to be meeting Mohammed Bismillah here." I shook his hand.

He shifted his jaw and casually checked me out. "Uh, I'm Bob Fellowes, the production manager. Mohammed isn't here yet."

"What exactly is Mohammed on this shoot?"

"He's like a production assistant, running around and doing stuff for the producers. He was going to meet you here?"

I suppressed a 'yeah, man' and wondered how a 'gofer' had come to be hiring directors of photography. "He said he would."

"Well, they're out picking up a few shots. They 'picked up' a few goddamn shots at the Roger Williams Zoo, in Providence, and then they went to Belcourt Castle to pick up a few more shots, and they sent us here to stand by. Why don't you get yourself something to drink out of that cooler and, like, meet the crew?" I couldn't tell whether he tossed his head by way of direction or to shake his hair out of his eyes.

Moving through that restful scene, I felt like I was inhabiting a rendering of *Déjeuner sur l'Herbe* done by an Indian protégé of Manet. A young woman with a round, dark face and shoulder-length straight black hair was Birenda. She was introduced as the script girl: the one whose job it is to make sure that everything shot adheres to the script and matches, where it must, everything else. Her face was Indian, but her accent and tight designer jeans said 'New York City.' Vijaya Lal, a slender young man with a long, hawk-nosed face and wavy hair was the assistant director, ostensibly in charge of making sure that everything and everybody necessary was present and functioning properly whenever the movie was being shot. It seemed to me that a lot of critical people were being excluded from 'picking up a few shots.'

Two of the crew were forming a tableau of summer love on the tailgate of the grip truck. Bob Fellowes pointed one of them out as Gene Fender, the second grip (who moved, carried, and set up what he was told to by the key grip). His round, flattened face formed a 'Q' with the unfiltered cigarette dangling out of the corner of his mouth. The arm continued around the waist of Ava Taskardian who leaned back against him, her small dark eyes gazing out of an attractive triangular face into the middle distance. She was the loader, the most junior member of the camera department. If she didn't have any magazines to load with film, she should have been at work clapping the slate at the beginning of each shot. I approached close enough to hear their intimate conversation.

"No, babe. That's a 'slasher,' like *Psycho*. It's not 'slice 'n dice'. You want 'slice 'n dice' you're talking *Texas Chainsaw Massacre*."

"But..." she protested.

"I know, there's some knife stuff in this one but it's not a slasher. Melodrama is more like it."

CHAPTER 7

❀

I thought I'd already seen too many people hanging around Hammersmith considering that the film was being shot somewhere else, but I soon found myself shaking the callused hand of Eric Rose. He was the gaffer, the head electrician and lighting person. I'd never worked with him before, but he was out of Boston and I'd heard of him. "You'll find that there's a lot of 'standing by' on this shoot." He looked at me out of darkly bagged eyes and stroked his beard thoughtfully.

I asked him about the inventory of lights on the truck. Eric rattled off a list that seemed appropriate just as long as the producer and director didn't make outrageous demands.

"Have you met everybody?"

"Not quite."

Eric brought me around and introduced me to Giancarlo, the still photographer, whose gravel-voiced 'far fucking out, man' gave the lie to his adolescent Euro-punk appearance. My doubts about the production's sanity increased as I also met the props person, the sound recordist, and the best boy—Eric's assistant, who was, in fact, a young woman. I finally had to throw political discretion to the winds and ask, "Why on Earth is everybody here if the shoot's at Belcourt?"

"There's undoubtedly a very interesting answer to that question," Eric said softly. "My guess is that the producer probably thought it would be a good idea."

"Who is the producer in question?"

"Shyam. Have you met him?"

"No, I don't believe so."

"You wouldn't forget him if you had. To call the man an evil genius could conceivably be charitable."

"What do you mean by that?"

"Hang around," Eric said expansively, "and find out."

I took out a notebook and started to write down the names of the crew. I wandered around to the back of the grip truck. Ginny, the best boy, wore a Yankees baseball cap. It almost hid the ends of her apparently self-cropped hair. She wrestled with a stand, not yet comfortable with the mechanics of it. Somewhere, I had gotten the idea that these people had been working on this film for a few days. Now, I wasn't so sure. Why have almost everybody *here* when the movie is being made *there*? Was this a movie or a ship of fools helmed by an evil genius?

I ambled over to the cooler, grabbed myself a can of ginger ale and reflected on what had I seen so far. These people needed organization and, in some cases, lessons in how to do their jobs. As a freelancer, I was used to fitting myself into different structures on every job, and doing it quickly.

I was just about to check my notes when a cavalcade of vehicles drove up. A black Cadillac limousine, which was elegant only if you didn't look too closely at it, was followed by a large beige station wagon. I scanned the assortment of people climbing out of the cars to see if anyone looked as if he might be late for an appointment. A short young man with a smooth, round, brown face was darting his dark serious eyes around. I waved when I caught his eye and sauntered over to him.

"Hello, I am Mohammed and you must be Bart Lane. I'm so glad that you found us. Have you been introduced all around?"

"Yes, thank you." I shook his hand. He listed the reasons for the delay and said that the rest of the crew was still at work at Belcourt Castle. "Still picking up a few shots?" I couldn't resist that.

"Oh, yes. We have come to fetch more reflectors. There is Indrani, the director."

Good God, or the Indian equivalent thereof. Indrani was a striking woman who looked as if she had just stepped out of the pages of an illustrated *Kama Sutra*. She was rapidly admonishing Gene and Ginny to break down some reflectors and fit them in the back of the station wagon she had driven up in. Her large brown eyes were ablaze as she hauled sandbags, unimpeded by the formality of the white blazer and skirt that she wore. She was wearing tennis shoes and she was moving fast.

I decided I wouldn't mind colliding with her, so I moved into the path of potential disaster and showed Gene and Ginny how to fold up the grip stands. "You just turn this item upside down," I said, "and you swing these legs around just like you're steering a big eighteen-wheeler out of a parking lot." Smiles broke across their faces as they practiced this elementary procedure. Had these folks been hired because they knew what they were doing?

"Thanks, uh…"

"Bart."

"Yeah, I hope you'll be dropping by again real soon."

I headed back to the station wagon, which was receiving the last of its load. I gave up trying to collide and settled for hovering near Indrani, ready to introduce myself if the opportunity arose and hoping that my occidental, blue-eyed, carnivorous bulk would not prove too offensive. She was talking to an apparent policeman who was really an extra. "Who else are you working for today?"

"I'm supposed to go on to the Universal shoot in Providence. Malick's film."

"I shall talk to him. You will get there in time. In Bombay it is nothing for an actor to be in two different films in two different studios before lunch. There is no conflict."

Mohammed appeared at my elbow. "Perhaps it would be best all around if you could come back to Belcourt Castle with us and speak with Entwhistle Kidd."

The entourage came along just as I got the engine running and I pulled in behind the limousine. It soon became clear that stop signs had no meaning for Madame Director, who was driving the lead car. Elisabeth's car, however, needed only the slightest additional pressure on the accelerator after stopping to lunge back into its rightful place in the scofflaw caravan. We were now entering the sycamore shaded avenues of summer mansions. The vista on the left was abruptly curtailed by a high stone fortification. The lead car turned into an opening; I followed and was treated to a view worthy of the palace at Versailles. Only two things interrupted the incredible spectacle of architecture, gardening and landscaping; the sign pointing to a parking lot and the film crew dominating the front lawn.

Whiz Kidd was hunched over the movie camera. "Oh, hi, Bart," he said and turned his attention to the reflectors that were being unloaded. I recognized Paul Sullivan who appeared to be working as key grip. It was a shame that the rest of the grip department was 'standing by' miles away; he had his hands full and his belly jiggling as he ran from one reflector to the next, training the reflected rays of the sun on a second-story balcony. Receiving this laboriously pieced-together patch of sunlight was, apparently, an Indian actress. If Indrani looked like a Hindu love goddess, with her triangular face and large eyes, Anouk, the leading lady, looked more international with her round face, 'done' shoulder-length hair and only the slightest darkness of skin to make her appear Asian.

Tourists in Bermuda shorts, T-shirts and funny hats made of beer cans continued to come and go through the door directly under the balcony. They took snapshots of the building and each other and seemed oblivious of the filmmaking occurring all around them. The limousine was driven in between the camera and the balcony and a production assistant worked under Whiz's direction to apply black tape over the visible rust holes and sun-reflecting highlights. I wandered over and introduced myself to Scotty Jones, the first assistant cameraman.

"Jesus, not another one," he said as he shook my hand. Scotty looked like an Army sergeant whose personal evolution had progressed through hippiedom. I immediately knew that he was not a kid; he was a professional who took care of cameras and, when he liked them, cameramen; a wiry person with a square face and dark brown hair gathered into a short ponytail by a rubber band.

Shortly, everyone was ready to roll some film and Indrani called the action in a high, clear voice. The action encompassed the balcony from which Anouk's character called to her husband, and the front drive, where he was just about to get into the car. They would meet on the front walk and embrace. This was repeated for three takes. The reason for this particular hug was the exploding of the limousine that would occur just as the husband got to his wife's side in the edited film. The meaningful encounter on the walk was covered in closeup and medium shot, and then it was time to blow up the Cadillac limousine.

Joao, the black Brazilian driver, added the missing hue to the crew's rainbow. He materialized with a collection of Sterno cans, foil roasting pans, rags and lighter fluid. Paul Sullivan, aka Sully, directed the fashioning of a firepot and set it up in front of the camera. When he wasn't asking Whiz to indicate a bottom edge of the framed scene to set the firepot just below, he found time to say, "Bart, I haven't seen you since we spent the night together in a Star Market. This is a long way from supermarket ads, but I'm not sure about which direction it's in."

"How are your wife and kids?" I responded.

"Still one of each, and doing just fine, thanks."

With everything set, the mass of flammables was ignited as the couple stared in horror at the fireball. All of this was done with most of the crew standing by three miles away.

I finally found a moment when Indrani wasn't surrounded by staff, crew and cast pressing her for judgments. I hoped that she didn't have Anglophobia as I walked up to her and stuck out my hand. "Hello, I'm Bart Lane, one of the cameramen Mohammed arranged."

"It's very nice to meet you," she said correctly but distractedly. Her English was impeccable.

I swallowed and only incredible strength of character kept me from reaching up to check the collar of my sky blue Ilie Nastasie tennis shirt. "I hope that I will have the opportunity to work for you."

"That would be very nice," she replied regally. Joao had pulled the limousine up behind her, and she turned and made her exit gracefully into the passenger compartment.

I found Whiz and Scotty talking as Scotty broke down the camera. "Whiz," I said when there was a clear space in the conversation. "Do you think I could drive you back to Hammersmith Farm so that you can brief me on what's going on?"

He mulled it over. With his skinny build, longish black hair and beard, he could mold his long face into an excellent imitation of Christ on the cross. He did this. "Sure, just let me grab my stuff."

"Well," he said as we drove off, "what you got here is your basic melodrama. Boy meets girl in the Indian metropolis of Mysore. You can't show kissing in Indian movies, so she gets pregnant. They get separated. He's from the wrong side of the tracks in Mysore, so her folks send her to a relative over here while he remains in India and embarks on a life of crime. They meet again under strange circumstances. Her folks are, in fact, right about him. He becomes a professional assassin. He comes over to America to perform a contract and who is the victim married to but his old flame. Their little girl turns out to be his daughter.

"This turns everything around and he ends up declaring war on the kingpin who hired him. That justifies all of the fights. If they'd give me a copy of the script, I could tell you whether he lives or dies."

"What's the look? Anything special?"

"Expose the film properly, I guess."

There was a stop sign. I hit the brakes and the car came to a smart stop. Whiz had to throw up his hands to keep from hitting the dashboard. There was nothing coming from either direction so Don Brouhaha chirped tastefully through the intersection slamming Whiz back in his seat.

"I hate to be a bother about the look of this film, but I'd like to know what you're doing so I can match it. I don't imagine I'll see any of it on a screen before I start shooting on the one day when you and John can't make it."

"Yeah, the look…well, they're spending a bundle for the stars and they want to see all of the faces as often as possible."

"Exteriors?"

"You'll be shooting them outdoors," he replied, tiredly.

Another stop sign. Whiz had tightened his seatbelt so the car and I did a number on his stomach. After we got back to thirty miles per hour, about one second after leaving the intersection, I pursued the matter. "Blue skies when available? Always shooting against the sun? Picture postcard or gritty reality?"

"Picture postcard unless something really horrible is happening. This is fantasyland for them. If it doesn't look like the Promised Land, they won't believe it's America."

Whiz was becoming more tractable. When I asked about the people running the show, he delivered a devastating indictment of Shyam. He had obviously had just about enough of the man's skills vis-à-vis the swimming pool arrangements that day. "Shyam's a pathological liar. He'll tell lies when it's easier to tell the truth. He regularly claims to have made preparations that are easier to make than to have to think about, yet they're not made, in spite of his claims to the contrary."

"What about Mohammed?"

"You gotta watch him every minute." He appeared to have recovered from any gratitude he might have felt toward the man who had hired him. "A couple of nights ago, I dropped down to the hotel bar and there he was, having a drink with the package of our exposed film sitting on the next stool. That film was supposed to be on a bus to New York which was leaving right then. I chewed him out good, but I don't know if it sank in."

"Thank you, Whiz." My mind's eye could see us in the orange car in a long shot. We were pulling up to Hammersmith Farm and waving at the guard. The car, I'm sure, looked its formal best as it politely purred along the circular drive. I pulled in behind the limousine.

"What is this thing, anyway?" he asked as he searched for the seat-belt release.

"I don't know, I just borrowed it from a friend." I looked around the dashboard. "I guess it's a Saab. She said something about racing."

"Yeah, well, thanks for the lift." He grabbed his gear out of the back seat and respectfully closed the door behind himself. I found Buffy and asked about Shyam. I was hoping to get a glimpse of the nemesis in person.

"He showed up and left quickly a few minutes ago. That…man," she swallowed her chosen expletive, "is harder to find than page numbers in a women's magazine."

I located Mohammed just as he had bitten into his late lunch so he had to raise a finger and finish chewing his mouthful before he could answer the question he knew I would ask.

"We will require your services as a second camera operator this Friday and as a director of photography this coming Monday."

"That sounds great," even if I was getting the leavings from Whiz's and John's schedules. "I'm looking forward to working for you," I added as I shook his hand.

I escaped with enough time left to make a couple of stops before the six o'clock ferry left for Squidneck. I bought some warm loaves of French bread and fresh oysters. I did all of the loading and parking and still had enough time left to be dazzled by the late afternoon sun on Warren harbor.

"Going back again?" asked the deckhand as he sold me another roundtrip ticket. "How do you like Squidneck?"

"It's great," I replied as he slid my change across the counter.

I liked bobbing along Narragansett Bay on a late afternoon in summer. The sailors who had nearly filled the bay during the day were augmented by the after-work contingent, turning the ferry ride into a boat show of cosmic proportions.

Now the patch of bright water, which had accompanied us along the bay, led the ferry as it turned into the final leg of its run to the island's dock. A silhouette appeared above the sparkle with a distinctive warm aura from the sun's backlighting—Elisabeth. It was nice to get back to the island.

Elisabeth leaned across the gap between the ferry and dock to give me a quick kiss as I was handing her the fruits of my supply run. She could even make olive drab cargo-pocket shorts look provocative.

Once we got the truck back to Hemp Hill, we devoured each other for a few minutes before we hauled everything up to the kitchen. "Might I inquire about what's for dinner?" she inquired before embarking on stowing the provisions.

"Would you rather be surprised now or later?"

"Now, please."

"For the appetizer, Chef Bartholomew informs us that there is a choice between oysters Rockefeller and *huitre au naturel*. Tonight's vegetable is asparagus *Hollandaise* accompanying an entree of *boeuf avec poivre et menthe*."

"You've got to be kidding!" The hug she gave me threatened to set our meal back a couple of hours.

"This is to be followed by a Caesar salad and, of course, we will raid the cellar into depletion for most of the appropriate wines."

"What can I do to help?"

"Tell me your choice on the oysters."

"Raw."

"Would you like to handle the asparagus?"

I scrubbed the oysters and set them to chill. I was glad for the stove's six burners, because we needed them. I soon had croutons working on one, water boiling for a one-minute egg on another, and a skillet standing by on another. Elisabeth would need at least two for the asparagus and its sauce. As seven-thirty approached, I produced a chilled bottle of Möet et Chandon and suggested a break to watch *Banned in Boston*.

Part of me is transported back to the shoot when I watch my work, and another part is busy second-guessing or admiring the editing. I try to keep my mouth shut, but one of the interviews, the one with the Combat Zone's public relations person, wasn't my work and didn't look so great, either, so I had to say, "I just shot the street action." Damn, If I could just do whole shows for those people—or if I could just work my way into a job that I loved…

Brendan had made good choices in the edit. Evocative long shots in which the subjects could not definitely be recognized, and tight shots which conveyed the nature of transactions taking place. He only used black bars across the eyes on the last sequence we shot—the one that showed the knife-wielding pimp at work. "And that, my dear, is the slime that got me chased out of town. Take a good look at him." I didn't know that she would soon be seeing his face without the black bar across it.

"That was beautiful work," Elisabeth said later as I shucked oysters for the first course. We decided to eat them and finish the champagne before cooking the other courses. "To work," she toasted, "I'm glad you found some."

A few moments of candlelight was appropriately augmented by the flavors and textures of raw oysters and champagne. We watched the setting sun work its drama on the western sky. Then we returned to the kitchen for a lengthy flurry of steaming, sauteing, deglazing, grating, saucing and, finally, serving.

"Mmm, I usually don't order *boeuf*, and it's never this good." Elisabeth's eyes sparkled. I was amazed at myself for being able to entrance such a beautiful and brilliant woman for even a moment. "The *Cotes du Rhone* is an inspired choice of red wine. How did you get so good at this?"

"Practice. I've worked on this dish with hamburger and, when I could afford it, chopped sirloin. It's probably a myth, but if I have a certain kind of work coming up the next day, I load up on protein. That way it doesn't make any difference if I get to eat or not."

"The brown sauce sits on the plate like a jewel, and tastes divine."

"Your *Hollandaise*, mademoiselle, surrounds the asparagus like a golden slave bracelet. I'm glad you like your beef rare." We both made it into the clean plate club that evening, polishing every bit of sauce off our plates with crusty French bread.

I turned back into an expensive waiter, tossing together the Caesar salad with a flourish next to her place at the table. In the French tradition, I leered unabashedly at the well pushed-out front of her tank top, and, of course, spilled a tasteful amount of salad there, which had to be removed and fussed over.

After tasting and marveling at the salad and its presentation, Elisabeth inquired, "How did things go with the *Mysore Karma* people today?"

"Good, I met almost everybody except for the producer who's messing everything up and I got a couple of days' work out of 'em"

"Which ones?"

"This Friday and next Monday. Oh, before I forget, here are your car keys." I fished them out and passed them to her. "The car was great. Kept me on schedule."

"Brought you back in one piece."

"Should I get myself up to Boston and grab my car? I feel funny using all your stuff all the time."

"Why don't you take the car Friday, and Monday I'll drop you off wherever they are? I want to pop up to Boston, anyway. As far as 'using all my stuff all the time' I hope you can tell how much you intruded on my space, man, when you used my shucking knife, skillets, saucepan and salad bowl. I mean, I just *know* I'll never get the flour stains off the apron you used." She got up from the table, came around and sat on my lap. She wrapped her arms around me and we shared a long, powerful, garlic kiss. "I think you missed a little *Parmesan* when you…cleaned up your spill."

I licked down to the edge of her tank top. Nothing there but Elisabeth, lightly salted. "I think, mademoiselle, that I shall have to send this garment out to the cleaners. At, of course, the expense of *Maison Bartholomew*." I pulled the bottom of the garment in question free of her combat shorts and up over her head.

"We cannot have the help running around in soiled autograph shirts," she said pulling my shirt off the same way. "We shall get zis sing right out of here."

I guess those must have been genuine Breuer chairs. I don't think that an imitation would stand for the treatment we gave it. That one-piece bent framing wasn't just innovative design; it yielded a lot of bounce.

We ended up, after a lively sojourn in the jacuzzi, washing the dinner dishes wearing bath towels. "Do you mind if we watch the news tonight? I'm curious about the long range weather prospects." I felt silly even mentioning such a banal electronic proposition.

"Well, if you must," she gave my ass a grab that nearly sent a dinner plate sailing. "Just don't make it a habit."

"Oh, never. Only the news, never *Nightline*. Eleven-thirty is too damn late to get serious about national and world affairs."

"Hear, hear. If you don't have an affair going by then, you might just want to hang it up and try again another day."

The Channel Eight news came on. An anchorman I had worked with said, "Charles Street jail overcrowding causes another problem. Early summer heat wave hits hub. We'll have these stories and more news, weather and sports after this..."

Eventually, the news started up. "Overcrowding at Boston's Charles Street Jail again threatened public safety today. According to police, Charles Quinn escaped from a transfer van taking him to Dedham Jail. Quinn, described as a white male, five foot ten, about one hundred and fifty pounds, was being held after apprehension in the assault on a Channel Eight video technician." A black and white jail photo with numbers on it depicted a dirty-looking white guy with a cruel slash of a mouth; the guy who slashed Nick and wanted to do something to me.

"That's the sweetheart I was telling you about," I said.

"The escapee is said to be armed and dangerous," said the anchorman.

CHAPTER 8

❀

The time until my Vishnu debut passed too quickly. By Thursday afternoon, we were winding down, and I would have to leave the island so that I could join up with *Mysore Karma*.

If I was only going to be operating camera the next day as opposed to running the show as director of photography, I had enough equipment with me. I was packing up gear and clothes in the room where I had initially dumped my stuff. I wandered over to our bedroom, where Elisabeth was working away at her desk. The late afternoon sun coming in the window brought out the lighter streaks it had bleached in her hair. She looked like a writer of erotic poetry. She was working fast on something that seemed to be entitled *Lightning on the Clam Flats—Squidneck Island*. I saw the first line: 'We don't speak.'

I don't want to be one of those people that serious work can't be done in the presence of, but I couldn't resist quietly gathering her hair in both hands and lifting it to expose the seldom seen back of her patrician neck. I leaned in and planted a kiss there and the typewriter's chatter abruptly stopped. She deftly spun the swivel chair around and landed me in her lap. "Swivel chair judo isn't purely a defensive weapon, you know."

"Ah," I said and kissed her.

"Anybody home in Providence?"

"Neither Mohammed nor Indrani."

"So, there's no director, and the guy who sorta hired you isn't taking calls and you're gonna go anyway, and leave me all alone on this hint of a job?"

"Clearly not my idea of a good time."

"Bullshit, Bart. You're dying to work and you know it."

"If it was an el cheapo commercial or assembly line training tape, I'd turn it down, but a feature with stars and all…"

"*Somebody's* stars."

"Hey, I could be completely fulfilled by spending my career shooting small but significant documentaries, but that doesn't seem to be an option."

She gave me a dryly inquisitive look that meant I was dithering again. "So, you love it and you know it."

"Okay, I can't wait to sink my teeth into this particular cinematic challenge. I love the learning and the performing. Seven hundred million people, almost none of whom I personally know, will have to live with my mistakes. I can give them better than they're getting and I want to. At times like this, though, if I knew anything else to do for a living, I'd be tempted to do it."

"You're a pretty good muse."

"Well, thank you. I hate to leave on the last ferry, but I think I'd better. I'd sure hate to have to try to get to Providence from here for an early call."

"You mean 'yes'?"

"Yes."

"How long you got to say goodbye, stranger?" she inquired in her best John Wayne voice.

"Long enough."

When I chugged the Hemphill pickup truck down to the pier a half hour later, I was still glowing from our farewell session. Elisabeth's typewriter had been chattering away by the time I got to the front door. If I felt as if I were still bathed in her kisses and caresses, it's because I was. Her scent and sweat still covered me, mingling with my own to make me feel like I was wandering around in a new skin. I had her truck, her car on the mainland, and I was starting to have some of my very own confusion. I mean, with a woman like that, shouldn't I have some visible means of support; some pile of gold with which to whisk her away, cover her with jewels and drape her with silk? I felt like an economic eunuch. I owed her more of a life than I had ever had without her, but I was also beginning to feel smothered. It was nice to have a day of work, but I needed more days than that. Nick was right: one was never enough for a tennis player.

By the time I had done my travelling by truck (hers), ferry (I *did* pay for my ticket), and car (hers), I had worked my feelings around to trying to do the best job I possibly could. She might like me, but if I had some success, maybe I'd be someone she could love, and maybe I'd feel qualified to love her back.

I rolled past the Biltmore's grand entrance and followed signs to a parking garage behind the hotel. I parked the car and made my way down a floor to the front desk. I caught the eye of a stocky young lady. "Hello, has Vishnu Films reserved a room for Bart Lane?"

"Lane, hah," she pored over her reservation register. "Vishnu, oh......no."

"Perhaps you could give me the room number of Mohammed Bismillah."

"I'm sorry, but I can't give out the room numbers of guests. If you're with Vishnu Films, I can give you a room," sounding like a rabbinical scholar stretching a point in the Talmud for a friend.

"That would be lovely," I said in a tone of voice that indicated a deep appreciation of her knowledge of hotel policy and a gratitude for having it used in my behalf.

There didn't seem to be any bellhops in attendance. Perhaps dealing with a non-tipping film crew had taught her to curb the reflex that pounded a bell and shouted 'Front!' My room was newly redecorated. A middle American ideal of pleasantness had overcome all of the luxury with which it might have been built. I threw my bags onto the large chenille-covered bed, fished out some papers, and began to try to locate the producer, director, and Mohammed. There was still no answer in any of their rooms. From the corridor, though, I heard someone speaking in a foreign language which I couldn't even recognize. I opened the door and saw Birenda, the script girl, disappearing into the room across the hall. Usually I didn't have chase people around once I had the job. I took a deep breath and knocked on the door. Another Indian woman opened the door and just stared at me. "Excuse me," I said, breaking the ice, "are you with the film?"

"Oh yes, hello," she replied in lightly accented English.

"I'm one of the cameraman. I just got to town and I haven't been able to reach Mohammed or Vijaya Lal."

"Ah," she replied animatedly, warming to the position of guide and informant. "Our assistant director has just changed his room, and there he is now." She darted into her room and emerged with a list of phone and room numbers for everyone connected with *Mysore Karma*, which she thrust into my hands. I saw the briefest appearance of a mischievous grin before she quickly disappeared. I felt like a big pink volleyball.

Vijaya Lal was walking down the hall in my direction, looking like he was already carrying the burdens of the East and West. I had never seen anyone with such a chiseled, hawk-nosed face looking so utterly defeated. He was probably hoping that this large Anglo-Saxon was not someone he would have to deal with. So much for his quick trip to the Coke machine.

"Vijaya Lal. I'm Bart Lane, the cameraman you met two days ago, and I will be operating the second camera tomorrow."

"Ah," he said gravely, his mind apparently sorting through arrangements made and remade, and what had been delegated to whom. His expression changed. Perhaps he was glad, at times like this, that he was a Hindu and could curse a particular Mohammed without peril to his everlasting soul. "You might not have heard that the plans for the shoot have been changed. We will not be shooting the stunts tomorrow."

"Well, the last words I had with Mohammed were that I'd be here tonight unless I heard otherwise. I haven't received any communication to the contrary. I even tried to reach him before I set out, but I could get no answer from his room."

"The agreement is not always enough with Mohammed. Well," his expression became gently fatalistic; "you're here now."

"So, when is the call time for tomorrow?"

"Seven-thirty at the trucks in the back of the hotel."

"I guess I'll probably see you there unless someone comes up with a better idea," I said, shaking his hand. I thought I'd hang around until I got paid and/or found out about Monday's shoot.

Vijaya was not one for lolling about. He left in one direction; I left in the other. 'Jones, Scotty,' I looked up the assistant cameraman and followed the numbers on the doors down to his room. My knock was answered by, "Come in, the damn thing's open." I did and found the overworked assistant cameraman sitting on the floor in the middle of a circle of open equipment cases. He looked up. "Oh, it's you. Mohammed fuck up yet again?"

"I guess so. He bought himself one too many cameramen."

"Well, it's better than having none, or point oh three shooters like we had at the beginning."

"Listen, Scotty, can I buy you a drink?"

"Sure, if you can wait a few minutes while I figure out what this Coke bottle," he hoisted a fourteen thousand dollar zoom lens in his right hand, "is going to be good for tomorrow."

Down in the recently-created turn-of-the-century saloon on the first floor of the hotel, Scotty took a healthy gulp of his beer and reflected on the shoot so far. "I should have seen it coming when I went to the equipment checkout. Shyam signed me up for this thing, and he was very solicitous of my advice about which cameras and lenses to get. He knew all the brand names and model numbers by the time we were done. The day of the checkout, he kept calling me, telling me that it wouldn't be ready for another hour. When I finally got down to Cineworld, there it was; brand new, latest-generation stuff. When they heard I was from *Mysore Karma*, they gave me the bum's rush, right past the gear and into a back room. There was a collection of sorry shit that they scraped together and borrowed. I'm sure that Shyam is billing the production for the new stuff and pocketing the fucking difference."

"How is he getting away with that?"

"Well, he's the line producer—he's paid to make it happen. He has Edward Lungalang, the executive producer who raised the money, convinced that only he, Shyam, can bring it off. If any of us complain, it's just because we're insubordinate and subject to dismissal."

"Weird," I said. "Usually production people are so damned single-minded about moving it along. What the hell are they up to?"

"Hey, you've met the Hindus, you've met the Moslems. Have you met Shyam yet?"

"No."

"Don't hold your breath waiting. If you hang around, you might catch a glimpse of him tomorrow." He almost swept his beer to the floor with a gesture that dismissed the subject.

I woke up well before the call time because I had to move out of the room that morning. I hauled my bags and kits past the desk, dropping off the key, and headed out the front door. Near the teeming dumpsters in the back alley, Joao, the driver, had the van standing by, so I slipped my bags under one of the seats. A Mister Donut two blocks away provided me with a breakfast of orange juice, chocolate honey-dipped doughnut, and coffee.

The van was still in its place near the dumpster, but Joao was no longer with it. I don't like my stuff being left unattended in a back alley, so I tried the side door to see if it had been left unlocked. It had been, and responded to my tug by rolling open thunderously. The noise caused a figure to pop up in the back seat. It was cinematographer Whiz Kidd. He would have glared at me if he wasn't so busy rubbing the sleep out of his eyes. "Oh, shit," he grumbled.

"Hi, Whiz." I don't know how or why I resisted the temptation to say that it was his worst nightmare speakin', but I did. "I'm sorry that it looks like I won't be able to operate a second camera for you today. That would have been fun."

"They did it again." He rolled his eyes Heavenward. He scratched his beard. He dozed off.

Finally, forty minutes after the announced call time, the doors began to slam shut on the collection of cars and vans that would follow Gene Fender, who was driving the grip truck to the first location of the day. I felt like I was in an Anglo ghetto; the Indians all seemed to prefer riding in the automobiles.

With Ava riding shotgun, Gene set a lumbering pace for the following procession as he negotiated Providence's swelling rush hour. That truck didn't sound very healthy as we noisily and slowly approached Roger Williams Park. Gene led the parade right into a *cul de sac*. There was a great deal of gear gnashing as all of the vehicles tried to turn around with no room for maneuvering. The groaning in the crew van as this happened two more times was almost deafening. Finally, exhausted, our ungainly line drew up near the formal gardens.

Nope. There would definitely be no gunfighting today. Dance was the enterprise *du jour*, complete with a chubby little dance director. He seemed to have the least knowledge of English of anyone, yet he acted exactly like a prissy old English drunk.

I wandered over to where Scotty was setting up a camera with a precise familiarity; maybe he'd be setting up two. It would make sense to me to give this expensive phenomenon multi-camera coverage. I didn't want to interrupt the speedy process of precision components coming out of cases, being checked and then locked onto even more precision components, so I was waiting for a break to ask him what was going on when several more cars pulled up and emptied their loads near us. A tall, well-built man with flashing teeth, blow-dried waves, bright eyes, and strong jaw appeared to dominate the herd.

"That's Ram Reddy, the star," explained Scotty.

Ram Reddy had a brooding gaze that would have quelled a race riot at a Calcutta matinee. He was surrounded by apparently American women. One of them stood out among the other followers by being taller than Ram and probably weighing well over two hundred pounds. She was trying to drape herself all over the star much to their shared amusement.

"And there you see the very lovely Moose. She's a working lady from Providence's red light district, and so are the rest of 'em." Their tight designer jeans on figures that would have fared better in housecoats, heavily made up faces, teased hair and large shoulder bags seemed to bear this out. "Damn Shyam. We had a disco scene, so he rented a strip joint for a morning. Then, for the extras, he cruised the street and got every whore he could find *and* he told them to bring their friends. The man is an asshole, no two ways about it."

Damn it, my life hadn't fully recovered from its last encounter with prostitutes. Of course that was Boston and this was Providence. That was documentary and this was dramatic.

The brightly blossoming flowers and crisscrossing footpaths of the formal garden were all but inundated by reflectors, equipment, the myriad people of filmmaking and, of course, Ram Reddy's claque of camp followers.

George Mukherjee approached me. Another production assistant, he was tall for any race but, being Indian, he tended to slouch around and grin apologetically, peering at the world through thick, horn-rimmed spectacles so that he would appear to be only moderately tall. "Shyam is going to give you a ride back to the hotel in a few minutes."

Finally, I would meet Shyam. Standing near a battered, rusted out Chevrolet, two cars behind the grip truck, was a man who looked like he had been assembled from poorly remembered fragments of the drawings that embellish the advertisements in the back of comic books. Brilliantined hair, a forehead that sloped out to eyes that were simultaneously purposeful and shifty, a large nose that didn't protrude very far in front of a large rack of white teeth, all atop an extremely understated chin. He was almost six feet tall, wore a short sleeved white shirt buttoned up to the collar, and had a prosperous belly. It was hard to believe that this buffoon was capable of the consternation he was causing, but of course Adolf Hitler and Ronald Reagan, two of the most dangerous men of the twentieth century, also seemed like clowns.

Not shaking my hand while introducing himself, Shyam relieved himself of any responsibility for helping with my bags by climbing into the driver's seat of the car. When I tried to open the passenger's door, it wouldn't open until he opened it from the inside.

As soon as the car had recovered from the trauma of starting, Shyam spoke. "There is a shot I would like you to work on." As he swerved and lurched through traffic, he explained that one of the lyrical musical segments would profit from a shot of Sippy, the little girl in the film, riding up in the glass enclosed elevator that ran up the front of the Biltmore. "Can you do this?"

"I can definitely do it, but I need some evidence that I'm on your payroll before I go any further."

"Oh, yes, yes, of course."

When we arrived back at the hotel, Shyam joined me for part of the first trip up and went to his room, ostensibly to tend to some paperwork. I stayed in the glass cage with my luggage, unpacked a director's viewfinder—something that enabled me to see a shot without a camera to look through—and some light meters. I set to work. The elevator resumed its normal rounds, ferrying guests and diners up and down the outside of the building. I finished with my readings and notations of sun direction, lens preference and avail-ability of electricity. I packed up my equipment and took another elevator up to report to Shyam.

"Now, let's just look behind the curtain and see what you have won, Jeannie Hibsinger of Grand Rapids, Michigan," came a voice like Monty Hall's through Shyam's door.

"Please come in, it is not locked," said Shyam from his place on one of the room's twin beds.

My preliminary report had to compete with mellifluous descrip-tions of Drexel living room furniture and Norge major appliances. "Find out if you can get the extra equipment you need and how much it will cost."

I called a friend who lived in Providence who had some lights to rent. He had what I needed, and the price seemed reasonable. I pre-sented Shyam with the alternatives for the shot, based on cost, sun direction, the desired 'look', and requiring the use of at least two crewpeople. The decision to proceed was, of course, beyond him, so we returned to the location.

I grabbed a cup of coffee and wandered over to watch the shoot. Anouk was still running across the gardens with her sari billowing out behind her. The dance director was still blowing his whistle and pounding his stick. Shyam found me near the camera crew and informed me that we would not be making the elevator shot that day.

"The glassed-in elevator at the Biltmore?" Scotty asked as he pulled a piece of highly polished steel out of the camera body and judiciously examined it.

"The very same."

"That's *my* damn shot," Scotty spewed. "I saw that beautiful shot and told 'em about it and they said that I could do it. Shit!"

"It looks to me like it's safe for you for another day," I replied, but I made a note to remember that Scotty was a very enterprising assis-tant who would be looking for a way to do some shooting.

A different whistle shattered the buzz of activity in the garden. Looking around to see who had such incredible through-the-teeth technique, I saw 'The Moose' and four of her companions break away from the knot of groupies around Ram Reddy and run awkwardly toward the roadway. Their efforts at a sprint, defeated by their skin-tight clothing, high heels and large shoulder bags, were laughable. The car they were running toward was funny, too—a red Toyota pimpmobile, but the face in the driver's window sent a chill down my spine that defied the hot summer day—it belonged to Quinn, the escaped knifer. He had just been having a conversation with Shyam; he had moved to Providence, lock, stock and business.

CHAPTER 9

❀

"Excuse me, Scotty," I said as I moved to put him and the camera between the undoubtedly armed fugitive and me. "I've got to try to get the plate number off that Toyota."

"Just a second. Ava!" he shouted.

Ava disengaged herself from a conversation with Gene and came running over. "Get Bart, here, a cup of coffee."

"Black," I added.

"And while you're at it, get the plate number of that pimp's car—the Toyota that the girls are climbing into."

Ava took off at speed. "Hey, what are new loaders for? What's your beef with the boyfriend over there?"

I explained the situation.

"Doing an exposé of prostitution?"

"I *shot* an exposé, but it was just used as B-roll. That piece of garbage had his friends stake out the television station. I almost had a union card. They drove me out of town."

"He started hanging around yesterday, seeing if he could arrange any more extras, I suppose. Well, Bart, it's good to know you. I hope they let you do the damn elevator shot." He extended his hand. I shook it. I hoped that Quinn didn't realize that I was in the neighborhood, or city, or state.

George Mukherjee was huddled over some papers on the hood of one of the cars. His left hand shuffled papers and kept gravity and the wind from removing them. His right hand shuttled between tapping out sums on a calculator, pushing his glasses back up his nose, and sweeping his hair out of his eyes. We haggled a bit, but I came away with a check bigger than Channel Eight would have given me for a day's work, based on my lower camera operator's fee, not my higher director of photography's fee. The Lungalangs, introduced to me as Edward, the executive producer, and his wife, gave me a ride back to the hotel in a new Plymouth. Its vanity plate read 'Lucknow.' He was short, dark and slightly rounded; his face perpetually wore the worried expression of a man who had destroyed too many four-leaf clovers with his rider mower.

I took some dimes into a phone booth off the lobby of the Biltmore and made a couple of calls. First, I called the Providence Police Department and reported the sighting of a fugitive from Massachusetts. I noted the detective sergeant's name and then charged a call to the Boston Police Department. It felt like I had failed to start a manhunt. Relaying all of the information to a detective in Boston, I got the impression that Quinn's escape was a Corrections Department problem, and not a Police Department one. I finally remembered the name of Captain Ryan's friend, and made another call to District D in Boston. After leaving the information with Patrick Horan, it appeared that I'd lit a fire.

I also called Elisabeth. It seemed a miracle that a dime dropped in a phone in Providence and a few numbers recited to an anonymous operator could enable me to talk to that woman on that island. "Hemp Hill," she answered.

"Hi, this is Bart. Have I ever talked to you on the phone before?"

"Only if you were the obscene caller that was plaguing me this past March and April."

"Darn it. I thought I was playing it so cool, so…anonymous."

"You were. You don't even fit the profile. You're all action and not much talk."

"Well, I'm done for the day with these clowns. Anything you need from the mainland?"

"Just something like six feet of voracious lover. You have the truck keys, so you know where to find me."

"It's exciting to talk to you on the phone. I'll be there for dinner. Can I bring a bottle of wine?"

"Yeah, something sultry and sparkling."

I hung up the phone and made my way across the lobby. Did any of these tourists with their bags and kids, any of these impatient businessmen with their briefcases and two-suiters, did any of the bustling subservient staff appreciate the magnitude of what was going on in my life? Here I was getting a foot in the door of some-body's film industry at a high level—getting some action-packed dramatic footage to put on my demo reel.

My paycheck looked more like a personal check than a paycheck, but I took it to a nearby bank and, after showing of myriad identification, cashed it. Laden with cash and luggage, I made my way to Elisabeth's car in the parking garage. It didn't appear to be staked out by the bad guys. Though it would be hard to imagine a connection between a TV documentary in Boston and an Indian epic in Providence, there was at least one—me. I hoped that Quinn would bumble off in one direction and I would stumble off in another.

A liquor boutique in Warren provided me with a chilled bottle of Veuve Clicquot, a champagne that I felt filled Ms Hemphill's mandate. I wrapped it in several layers of the clerk's discarded newspaper—a trick I had learned from track workers on Dad's old line, the New York Central—and stuffed it into my suitcase. It would remain chilled. The late afternoon ferry was filled with commuters, people I hadn't seen hanging around the dock much. The pickup truck was where I had left it, and started right up. I was feeling more and more like an islander as I chugged through the shadows of the late afternoon. Crossing the island, I topped a rise to be dazzled by the sun as it blasted a path of gold across the bay. It was so beautiful that, in a perverse way, it made sense to leave it. How else could I experience these returns?

My strength was ebbing as I hauled my bags and cases to the front door, but it returned when the door opened to reveal Elisabeth. She stood in the doorway, warming in the setting sun like a cat on a living room carpet. Her eyes were on fire. She wore an electric blue evening gown with a neckline that plunged to its tightly gathered waist. Her hair was swept forward over one shoulder, its undulations reflecting the sun's blast in a chromatic scale of hues ranging from hammered copper to glossy black. "Hi, sailor," she said. I still couldn't quite believe she had been waiting for me.

"Mmf," I replied as I locked my mouth to hers in a fierce embrace. I swung my bags past her on either side into the house and lifted her over the threshold, kicking the door shut behind us. "Hello, beautiful," I added when the kiss was done.

"Why don't you get out of those city rags and into something suitable for major feasting?"

"Why don't you take this," I said, pulling the newspaper-wrapped parcel out of my bag, "and shove it someplace cold?"

A sip of Laphroaig single malt Scotch sent the Battle of Culloden resonating around my mouth while Elisabeth created a flurry in the kitchen. It was immediately apparent that oiling, scenting and draping her body were not the only preparations she had made for my return.

The first course was clams casino, served with the Veuve Cliquot by candlelight. When the shells were cleared away, she donned an apron to remove some trays from the oven and do some more preparation. Filet of flounder *Florentine* was duly presented flanked by green beans *amandine* and a twice baked potato. Between exquisite mouthfuls, we caught each other up on our night and day apart.

"You're sure he didn't see you?" Elisabeth asked on hearing of the fugitive pimp's reappearance.

"I don't think so. I kept an eye on him and he didn't seem spooked, or determined to renew a pursuit."

"And you weren't followed."

"I am positive of that. His pimpmobile wouldn't have had much chance against your car, and I was watching. There were freeway entrances and exits that gave me a long time to check for bandits, and I did. I don't believe how paranoid I've gotten."

"It doesn't mean they're not out to get you," she said, her voice full of consolation.

"Thanks, I'll keep that in mind."

We finished the meal with an elegant salad of Boston lettuce and chives. "How would you like your cognac?" inquired my hostess.

"Oh, if you're going to feed me a line like that, I have to say 'in a glass, on the sofa, with you.'"

"And if I don't feed you the line?"

"In a glass, on the sofa, with you."

Our lovemaking constituted a continuous exploration of each other and experimentation with settings provided by Elisabeth, her grandparents, and nature. It turned out that she had a stash of condoms—a gift from a newly AIDS-aware mother in San Francisco. She still couldn't deal with using the king-sized Beautyrest in the grandparents' bedroom, but what's paradise without a Pandora's box? I was tempted to start issuing disclaimers; after all, according to statisticians, I was at least twenty years past my sexual prime. Instead, I felt like a mostly happy anomaly. I knew I wasn't *average*.

I even had a bit of work coming up to brighten my generally lackluster professional life. Channel Eight was no longer a possibility, but I was moving into feature cinematography with stars and a reasonable crew. I could get very involved in that kind of work.

I felt like I was contaminating Elisabeth with my mainland problems when two mornings later, the alarm clock awakened us at seven, but she had insisted on helping me get to Providence. She'd drive me to Boston, so I could pick up my car and take care of a few things. Then, I'd feel better prepared to spend more time on the island.

Over breakfast, I remembered some unfinished business between us. "I hate to be a bother about this, but I remember a certain poet taking *my* copy of *By Motor through Five States and Eight Lifetimes* for the purpose of autograph inscription. You wouldn't have it down here, by any chance, would you?"

"I thought you'd never ask. You don't *have* to be interested in modern poetry."

"I'm interested in you and what you do and I'm looking at a lot of 'standing by' with the folks I'm about to work with. Besides, I've read most of the Agatha Christie in your library."

"What about P.D. James?"

"What about E. Hemphill?"

She excused herself while I cleaned up the breakfast things, and materialized with the requested volume just as I rinsed the last cup. I stuffed the book into my suitcase, and we loaded the truck.

"I feel funny in these city clothes," said Elisabeth looking down at her khaki safari dress. We were waiting on the dock for the ferry. There weren't too many fellow beach bums to rib us.

"You don't look funny," I said, "it's not your sexiest outfit, but you do look great."

Too soon, we were back on the mainland, fortified with takeout coffee and headed for Boston. We could tell when we hit the state line—we were suddenly surrounded by dangerous and negligent drivers.

"Welcome back to Massachusetts," Elisabeth growled.

"Oh, God." I knew that there wasn't a lot of catching up I could do on a Sunday, but the weight of unfinished business began to get oppressive as we approached Boston.

"Do you really like your work?" The orange car snarled out of an entrance ramp and claimed a spot in the fast lane.

"I love it when I'm working. I don't like continually looking for work. I feel like a travelling salesman with nothing to sell."

"That can't be too pleasant. But what I saw of your stuff on TV was great. It didn't look like you merely grabbed whatever you could get, you got the pictures that told as much of the story as Channel Eight could stand to tell. *I* think you have something to sell."

"Thanks. That makes two of us who'd love to see my stuff on Channel Eight. I'll tell you what it's like though. On one day, you feel that you couldn't even get a job sweeping floors in Symphony Hall. The guy who *is* sweeping up there has a real career compared to what I've got. He got his job through his brother-in-law and has a union card, a pension and a health plan. I can't get the job sweeping the floors, but the next day, I have front row center seats, and I'm being *paid* to be there. It's thrilling. One day I can't afford a couple of rounds in some high-toned singles bar. The next day somebody I've only ever seen on the silver screen, and perhaps even an actress I've fantasized about, is grabbing my ass while I try to take a light reading."

"I get the picture. It sounds like an expensive drug."

She didn't need any directions to find my place. She even knew the one way streets. "Well, uh," I said when she pulled up in front of my building.

She leaned over and planted a kiss on my lips. We spent a few moments locked in an embrace, but I have to admit that I was checking the area for a large midnight blue Buick.

"Listen," she said, watching her forefinger trace a pattern on my chest. "Whatever happens, be back for the Fourth of July weekend."

"I should be back before that, I'm just on the shoot for one day."

"Well, there are some things you could do that might make me revise my opinion of you downward."

"I will be…" she stopped my mouth with one finger.

"Miss the Fourth," she said softly, "and you're dogshit."

We said our goodbyes and I got out and pulled my stuff out of the back. "Elisabeth," I said, leaning back toward the car. I realized that I didn't have her Boston phone number—maybe we could do brunch...

She was gone.

I watched her drive away feeling like I had missed a ride on the last liferaft.

What a lonely place my apartment was. There was a stack of mail inside the door, the plants had been watered and the answering machine was flashing at me but it was still an empty apartment.

The mail had some checks, a letter from my parents in Florida, and most of a wastepaper basket full of unsolicited garbage. Mom and Dad were doing fine in Florida. As usual, they were planning their annual escape which involved driving around the northern half of the country. I resolved to call them up and let them know what I was doing.

The answering machine had a few too many blank messages for my comfort; somebody had been checking to see if I was around and they didn't want to leave their name. Brendan's cheery voice said that *Banned in Boston* had received several award nominations and that *this* time, he'd remember to mention my name in his acceptance speech. No invitation to the ceremony, but he said to give him a call. Greenpeace called several times but I knew they were after money.

Since it was Sunday, I called Brendan at his home. He was breezy and noncommittal. "Hey, big guy, long time, no hear."

"You said I should keep a low profile, so I got lost."

"Where have you been?"

"On vacation. Any interesting assignments coming up?"

"Well, Bart. We all want some more of your good work around the station, but with that knifer at large and his heavy friends..."

"You want I should keep a low profile."

"In a nutshell. So, where have you been hiding out?"

"I don't think I'd like to talk about it on the phone. You never know who's listening."

"Well, great to talk to you, Bart. Check in again soon."

Damn, maybe there was an association of aggrieved idiots that I could join and we could start a class action suit. Maybe I should wrap things up and get out of town. I checked the street for lurking mobsters. The coast looked clear.

Three hours later, I had been able to bank some checks and pocket some cash. I paid some bills. I did my laundry facing the laundromat door so I could see anyone who might be coming after me. My only companions were a gaggle of non-English-speaking mothers and their sizeable broods, all loudly enjoying the summer day.

I encountered Nguy Kinh squatting on the steps as I returned with my load of laundry. "Ah, Batterain," he said, rising to extend his hand. "You make it out of town. Why you come back?"

"Yes, I made it out of town. I sneaked back to get some equipment for a job coming up. Don't worry, the job is out of town."

"That's good, people still come around, maybe they looking for you. Don't make another movie about real bad guys, okay?"

"I won't. This is a nice dramatic Indian movie."

"Like cowboys and Indians?" he asked.

"No, from India, the country. Not too far from Viet Nam."

"Ohhhh," he understood. "Are the Indians Hindu or Moslem?"

"Let's see, the guy who hired me is named Mohammed, and the director looks like a classic Indian painting. I don't know, perhaps both."

"Ohhhh, maybe you be safer making movies about *real* bad guys. Maybe this very bad scene."

"I think it will be okay. They're here in America, all working together to make this movie."

"If you say so, Batterain. It sounds very…interesting to me."

"Well," I said, not wanting to spend too much time outdoors in this neighborhood, "thanks for taking care of my plants. They all look very happy. I've got to leave town again."

"I keep it up for a while longer," he said. "Good luck."

I rang Miss Halloran's bell on the way in. She didn't appear to be in her apartment.

I sorted and packed and came down to having two bags of clothes and two of equipment. I hauled it all down to my car and loaded it in. I got in the driver's seat, rolled down the windows to dissipate the intense heat it had collected and turned the key. Nothing happened. I opened the engine compartment and explored the obvious connections; they were fine. I closed it up and tried again with the same result. I remembered that I had been intending to buy a battery, but who could guess what else might be wrong?

I started the process of unloading the car, locking it, and hauling everything up to my apartment. My new plan was to take a taxi to South Station and catch a train to Providence. I was making my last trip down to fetch bags when Miss Halloran came in.

"Bart, I must say it's been awhile since I heard from the likes of you." She was pulling off a pair of white gloves. "Where have you been? Don't tell me now. Why don't you come up for a glass of sherry or something? I want to hear all about it."

It wouldn't do to start exchanging information until I was seated in her parlor with a glass of sherry. She forgave my request for ice and had a cube or two herself.

"I've been on an island off the coast of Rhode Island." I reported after a cooling sip. I recapped my Providence encounter with Quinn. "Maybe they'll catch him this time."

"How did you know about this place in Rhode Island?"

"It belongs to a poet. A...friend of mine."

"Which poet?" The librarian in her was perking up its ears as much as possible under the tightly drawn-back silver hair.

"I don't know if I should tell you." The sherry was almost loosening my tongue, but not quite.

"After your visit of several days ago, I don't imagine us as keeping quite so many secrets from each other." She gave me a conspiratorial smile that finished the job that the sherry had begun.

"It was nice to see that there is a man in your life."

"Thank you, Bart. Now who is this poet who hides fugitives from the Mob?"

"Elisabeth Hemphill."

She got up and perused her bookshelves. She pulled out a volume that didn't look like *By Motor Through Five States and Eight Lifetimes*. She turned it over and looked at the photograph on the jacket. She looked at me and raised her elegant silver eyebrows. "Hiding out literally and literarily?"

I think my blush was threatening to burn away my perfect tan. "Yes, ma'am."

"I think your life must be very interesting right about now. Would you describe yourself as a young man in a great deal of hot water?"

"I think you've hit the nail right on the head."

"But don't you like hot water? I seem to remember the building losing its water pressure from time to time because *somebody* was enjoying the hot water enormously."

What could I say to that?

In my unguarded state, I returned to my apartment and tried to look up Elisabeth's phone number. It was unlisted. Did she exist? Suddenly I felt more alone than I had ever felt and very vulnerable.

I had to leave that place. I called a taxi. By the time I had moved all my relevant possessions down the stairs and into an unusually prompt cab, I was beyond caring whether or not the cab was being driven by the fugitive Quinn. Fortunately, the driver was Haitian, so I only had to worry about making myself understood.

A couple of hours later, I was paying off a Providence cabby and hauling my four bags of clothes and gear into the Biltmore lobby. The doorman opened the door for me, but didn't call a bellhop; these people knew about guys with equipment cases. Again, Vishnu Films hadn't reserved me a room. Again, I managed to talk the desk clerk into giving me one.

When an elevator finally arrived, Mansoor, the sound recordist, exited from it. "Ah, Bart Lane. I am glad that you will finally be shooting with us."

"When is the call for tomorrow?"

"Seven AM at the…garbage containers?"

"Out back by the dumpster?"

"Ah yes, that is the word."

We went our separate ways. My new room was like my old room. I moved in, changed shirts, and found an exhausted Scotty, sitting on his floor surrounded by a jumble of cables and batteries being recharged, running a hand through his hair, apparently wondering what he might have forgotten. He looked like he could have used a few watts of alternating current or, at least, a break.

I suggested dinner.

He agreed, but first he wanted to call his wife. "We got married just before this shoot began," he explained as he put some more batteries on to charge, "and it is definitely taking too damn long."

"I swear that producers don't want anything to do with you unless there's a chance for them to mess up your personal life." Scotty said later, in the dining room. "I mean I talked to Shyam and Edward Lungalang…"

"If Shyam is the producer and money is tight, what does Edward actually do?"

"I think he rounded up the American investors and put up some of the money himself, so he's the executive producer. Anyway, he and Shyam had me on board before they ever put a concrete date on this.

Then they set the date—the day after our wedding. So I'm a married man and I've had one married night with Carolyn—if you can call worrying about this old and battered equipment a night. I'm sure glad we lived together for a couple of years first."

"Well, at least this ought to help finance a honeymoon," I offered.

"Believe it or not, this is better than the way we met. No way to go but up from that."

"What happened?"

"I found myself between apartments, so I decided to take a couple of months off and go to India. This was about three years ago. I was travelling around, riding the trains and generally taking it all in. One of the towns I hit was Amritsar. Ever hear of it?"

"The name sounds familiar." It actually sounded like a brand of institutional foods; cherry pie filling in number ten cans.

"It sounded familiar to me, too, but I didn't know why. When I got off the train, almost everyone was wearing a turban and a lot of the men were wearing knives, too. Sikhs. I wandered around and saw the Golden Temple and I thought that I might as well climb on the next train out—anything that was leaving Punjab, but especially Amritsar."

"Not particularly hospitable?"

"Right. But I saw this nice little place to sit down and eat some curry. It had signs in English, which I needed, and the help wasn't running around in turbans, which I preferred. When I went into the place, I noticed this really foxy American woman. I guess she could have been some kind of European or other, but she just looked American. I could also tell that she didn't want to meet another American. Her look said 'Just what I came here to get away from,' and not 'Hi, there.'"

"Just the kind of friendly face you want to meet."

"Yeah. I mean I certainly wasn't dressed like an ugly American or anything. So I ordered a local beer and a plate of lamb curry and was sitting there looking around. She seemed to be having the vegetarian special. People were going in and out, but we were probaably the only non-Hindus in the place. Then this Sikh comes in—carrying a gym bag. Probably a counterfeit Adidas. I watched him because he was the only Sikh in the place, and I thought I might learn something about Sikh dietary laws."

He took a pull on his Guinness and continued, "I suppose I was wondering if he kept a sweat turban along with his sweat suit. It almost seemed as if he was going to answer my question. He sat at a table by the door, set the bag down at his feet, and started to open it. Maybe he was going to read some Sikh prayer book—grease the wheels for the laws he was about to break. Then his hand came out of the bag wrapped around something black and dangerous looking. I made a dive at the American lady, knocking her to the floor just as she was about to take a bite of her *chapati*. The Sikh opened fire with an Uzi, just raking the place with machinegun fire. I stayed on top of the woman and knocked down some tables to protect us. Then, all of a sudden it was deathly quiet. The Sikh put his gun back in the gym bag—I could hear it being zipped up—and got out of there."

"Brutal. That lady must have been grateful."

"That lady was pissed. She didn't want anything to do with somebody who'd tackle her in a restaurant. By the time I ran into her again, it was on West Forty-Eighth Street. We slowly got to be friends. And that's how I met Carolyn."

"A true-to-life action-packed boy-meets-girl."

"It's funny though. She chewed my ass off at the time; I mean what kind of a paternalistic male chauvinist pig was I, wallowing in Western values? She didn't even stay around long enough to find out that four people had died and seven were wounded. But, if I think back to seeing her for the first time and realize that she's now my wife—it's amazing. If I ever get another moment alone with her I'll know I'm one lucky son of a bitch."

"That's great. I'm glad for you. To change the subject, do you know anything about tomorrow?"

"Perhaps that Moslems hate Hindus more than Sikhs do."

"Scotty, I want to hear something that will either help me get to sleep or mitigate my nightmares."

"Oh, Sorry about that. Seven A.M. at the trucks by the dumpster. More Belcourt Castle—mostly exterior; more Hammersmith Farm."

"How do you like your coffee? I'll bring a cup and ride out with you."

"Regular, thanks." His eyes lit up as he shook my hand. Directors of Photography seldom get coffee for anyone.

Back in my room, I did some calisthenics, took a long, hot shower and stretched out on the bed to watch some of the news and the weather. There was no report of catching a fugitive assailant and extraditing him to Massachusetts. The weatherman said that today had been clear and hot and tomorrow would be the same.

I guess that some people's dreams are rendered in slow motion, others claim that theirs and all others are in black and white, and people who try to sell stuff with created dreams—I among them—assume that there is a sizeable portion of the greater world market area that sees their personal dreamscapes through a gauze filter. I dream of confusion.

What could be more pleasant than dreaming of a dip in Walden Pond? Driving home, my travelling companion, who looks like a Smith girl I never got anywhere with, suggests that we stop in Concord for a frappe. I'm changing out of my suit as we pull up near the Village Green. A huge wasp suddenly manifests itself in the car and my pragmatic companion orders me out so she can deal with it. I exit, clad only in a damp Williams College Athletic Department T-shirt. It's a bright, sunny day. I stand behind the open door as Frieda (I think that's who it was) tries to drive the wasp out with my towel. "It's no good," she says. "I'll have to drive around the block and try to blow it out." She does, and I'm left standing in only a T-shirt in the middle of Concord. I could take it off and tie it around my anal and genital areas, but if I did, I'd be completely naked between the time that I took it off and tied it on. I try pulling it down. That might work for the crowd, but it doesn't help me that much. The shirt starts to shrink. I find a tree to try to change behind, but that will still expose all of me to half of that staid suburb. Frieda drives by and turns right to follow the sign that says 'Boston'. The shirt keeps getting smaller, and now I couldn't get it off if I wanted to. After a dream like that, I usually wake up, close to strangling myself on a tangled bed sheet.

That night, all alone in the Biltmore bed, I dream of Elisabeth. We are driving to the dock. She is wearing a white lacy confection of a gown and I am in white tie and tails. We are unloading the orange car onto the dock; the ferry isn't there yet. It's the middle of a summer day, but it's just us, hauling countless heavy boxes out of the car and stacking them on the dock.

The ferry arrives. The captain and deckhand are dressed almost like Gilbert and Sullivan pirates, with ruffled white shirts, tight black pants and shiny black boots. They put out the gangplank, but they can't help us with the boxes. I can only carry one at a time because I have a raging erection that has become a ceramic penis. If I break *that* it's all over. We manage to carry half of the boxes onto the boat. It is time to leave and the cargo area is full anyway. We stand along the rail and watch our island approach. The dock is empty. I get off when the gangplank is in position. Elisabeth hands me all of the boxes. The captain and deckhand assure us that they'll bring over the rest of the boxes on the next trip. The deckhand pulls up the gangplank. Elisabeth is still on board. She stands along the rail looking at me as the boat pulls away, the wind blowing her gown and hair. The boat heads away from Warren—to the open ocean. I am all alone waving and jumping up and down on the dock. The ferry diminishes and finally disappears in the haze. I hear a distant phone ringing. It's in the general store. I run to find it, to pick it up, to speak into and hear from it and find out what is going on. I wake up to the hotel's operator. It's my six-fifteen wakeup call.

Forty-five minutes later, I was all alone in the dawn's early light, standing by the dumpsters and unable to set down my gear because of the freshly hosed sidewalks. It was a few minutes before seven and there were no Vishnu vehicles in sight. I didn't like it. There I was, alone in an alley, making a large target and immobilized by my load. There was very little traffic passing the end of the alley, but one nondescript old sedan came to a loud stop out there on the street.

I beat a hasty retreat back to the lobby where I found Scotty. I followed him to his station wagon in the parking garage and we drove to the alley. I was grateful for the company and the little old station wagon's armor, however thin it may have been. Once we were joined by more of our motorcade. I sprinted down the street to fetch some coffee.

"Be sure those clowns pay you before you leave, every time," he said between sips.

"I'd heard something like that." I didn't want to engage in sedition against the company that I thought had shown exceptional good sense in hiring me.

"And...cash it immediately. Use the Fleet Bank. I'm not kidding."

The grip truck crept past us momentarily surrounding us in a cloud of blue smoke. We were off to Belcourt Castle, the first location of the day.

Once there, I set Sully and the grips to unloading reflectors and lights; Eric to finding a few dozen amperes of usable electricity for the lighting; and Scotty and Ava to setting up the camera. Vijaya had met our car and walked me through the first setup.

I just finished briefing Scotty when Indrani appeared at my elbow. Her hair was down, her makeup calculated possibly to the last beauty mark and she wore a blue and white striped summer dress. "I must talk to you," she said.

"Fine," I replied.

"Walk this way."

Very few people walk the way she did. I followed her and resisted locking my eyes onto her swaying posterior. She led me into the castle and through its foyer. She began to climb a broad, curving staircase. I tried to remain all business as I did likewise. Halfway up the stairs, she stopped at an Oriental tapestry and pulled it aside. It swung on a hinged frame to reveal a secret door.

Damn. What did this lady have in mind? How long did we have before the crew had set up two cameras, several more reflectors and some lights? Is it nobler to starve the one you might possibly love, or cheat—just a little bit and for a very good cause? Indrani opened the door.

CHAPTER 10

❀

*B*ehind the door behind the tapestry was the kind of warm and cluttered space where people who own castles tend to spend most of their time. Easy chairs in need of upholstery stood by untidy desks where several people worked at palace purchasing, tour arrangements, and all of the things needed to keep a castle running smoothly. Indrani led me to a window overlooking the courtyard and said, "Do you think that this is a good angle to get Ram's walk from the arch to the second door on the left?"

"We'd have to take the leaded-glass window apart if we wanted to follow his move with a pan. If we did it in a wide shot, we'd be throwing away all of the plants and sculpture. This is not a good angle for that nude, for instance."

"This is true, it looks like a blob," she said thoughtfully, "or worse." We returned to ground level.

Shyam's cut rate deal for the use of the castle allowed the flow of sightseers and guided tours to continue unabated. There was no problem blocking the action, deploying the reflectors, or shooting. The only flies in our collective ointment were the tourists who kept drifting into the shot. Giancarlo, the Euro-punk still photographer, was acting as a production assistant, charged with blocking the flow of unaffiliated humanity through the main portal during the actual takes.

"Let us roll camera!" Vijaya would call.

Scotty would turn it on and yell, "Speed!"

Mansoor would turn on his tape recorder and yell, "Speeding!" to indicate that it was up to recording speed.

Ava would stand in front of the camera, recite scene and take, and clap the slate. I would frame up the scene after Ava ducked out of it and say, "Ready."

Indrani would survey the scene and appear to be waiting to snatch one moment out of the passing stream of time and pronounce, "Action!"

...and too many times, on this, my first setup, Giancarlo would stroll absently into the shot and yell, "What?"

Birenda would note the numbers involved, shake her head and stand by to watch it again.

I kept the crew moving, though, and Giancarlo finally absorbed some of the nuances of his job. We finished the main shooting at that location and Indrani glanced at her Rolex. "Oh my God," she exclaimed, "we are on schedule; a little bit ahead, actually. Come, let's do the driving shots."

I asked Scotty for a wide-angle lens on the second camera and used it to drive through the shot with the director. I wasn't too crazy about the way she was struggling with the American muscle-car's four-speed gearbox but she eventually mastered it to her own satisfaction. She took off recklessly, pinning me and the camera to the back of the seat. At the gate, she turned left, using the car's acceleration to cut in front of a motor home from Wisconsin. The shading trees passed in a blur as she put some distance between Belcourt Castle and us. She turned left into a driveway, too close for comfort to an oncoming tour bus. The passengers in the bus all waved fists and were trying to shout but the air conditioning and sealed windows killed the uproar.

"How does this look? You will want to start rolling here."

I took a deep breath. "It looks good. You'll have to make your starts and stops more gently. There's a little bit of hood in the bottom of my frame. How much of it do you want to see?"

"I want to see just enough so that we know what it is. This splendid avenue and the palace gate are the important things."

The ride ended with a guard stopping us at the gate. Indrani leaned out and told the guard, "I want you to step right in front of the car and motion it to stop with both hands." The guard demonstrated a possible action. "That's very good, now let us in, we have to prepare for the shot."

When car and camera were ready, I fetched Indrani. "Your set awaits, ma'am," I said with what I hoped was the most subtle and tasteful of flourishes. This was making *movies*. It was better than I imagined filmmaking to be when I started out. What could be more natural or logical than picking up a camera and going out with a director to make a few shots? Not only did that hardly ever happen, but who could have predicted that it would occur with a director who as an actress had reputedly excited hundreds of millions of one's fellow males?

The first take was flowing like warm honey when I spotted Mohammed in the right side of my frame three-quarters of the way through the first take.

"Please get out of there immediately!' Indrani lashed out.

"I was blocking the traffic," pled the production assistant, attempting to appear as if he were the one being disturbed.

"Traffic looks natural compared to you. See to it that you hide better next time." At the end of the run, she got out of the car to work with the guards and teach them things they never learned at the Pinkerton school. I could see that she was trying to make their visored Anglo-Saxon countenances more frightening than they naturally tended to be.

The tires screeched as she backed into the avenue, narrowly missing a line of station wagons. She zipped the car back to its start position. I hoped that a bunch of tourists hadn't camped in the shot. Car rolled. Camera rolled. Mohammed stayed hidden and whether his job was done by himself or by luck was immaterial. The guards played their parts just right. Indrani called the cut and sighed, "How was that for you?"

"It felt great and looked even better than that," I replied.

"We're still ahead of schedule," she beamed. There was nothing vegetarian in her smile.

Scotty was standing by to receive the camera. Sully and Gene went to work on restoring the car to its previous condition. I felt like a great cinematographer. Didn't I come with grips to the problem?

Buffy dropped by to check out the car. "By the way," she said to us, "anybody remember that lipless asshole who was following the girls around when we were shooting the dance stuff?"

I froze. Scotty piped up, "You mean the guy in the red Toyota pimp mobile?"

"It was definitely red and funny looking. Would you believe he was trying to sign me up? I told him that I had a job and he kept on about 'needing someone like me.' Anyway, the bastard showed up while you were out doing the driving stuff."

Scotty looked up to see that I was speechless and very engaged. "What the hell did he want *this* time?" he asked.

"He wanted our schedule."

"Schedule? This shoot has a schedule?" Sully howled.

"What did you tell him?" I had finally recovered some limited powers of speech.

"I told him that we were all done with his extras and that *nobody* had a schedule for this shoot."

"You did the right thing," said Scotty.

"Well, it wasn't enough for Mr. Wonderful. The son of a bitch pulled out something that looked like a folded switchblade and said that if I wouldn't open my mouth or spread my legs for him, he just might need to cut some more holes in my face or…somewhere else."

I swallowed, perhaps too loudly.

"That fucker's worse than a scumball," said Sully. "What happened next?"

"I told him that half the men on this shoot were Green Berets from Vietnam and that they didn't get their ribbons by threatening girls. The clown tried to give me a look that would scare me but he got his ugly ass the hell out of here!"

"Way to go," said Scotty. He turned to me as Buffy stormed off in a cloud of confirmed indignation. "How are you doing, man?"

I was about to answer him when Vijaya materialized to summon me to the director's car. Indrani was standing by to take me to the next location—Hammersmith Farm. As I attempted not to cringe at her driving, she explained the afternoon's work to me. The next scenes would involve Sippy, a child actress; her riding double; and a horse. Great. Kids and animals.

We paced through rolling pastures that overlooked Newport Harbor. She was walking me through the shots we would make that afternoon. Our methodical laying out of the subsequent shooting was in direct contrast to the production department. Mohammed, Vijaya and Shyam were running around and giving countermanding orders to Buffy, Giancarlo, and Joao about wardrobe, staying out of the way, and fetching things, simultaneously.

In today's scene, the male lead, Ram Reddy, sees the little girl riding. As he stands, rapt in admiration and reflection, she rides into a new stretch of barbed wire and is thrown off the horse. Sippy, playing the little equestrienne, did not know how to ride. Indrani, raised to ride, figured that Sippy could probably sit on a horse and maybe even gallop a little bit. She couldn't begin to comprehend the depths of Sippy's ignorance. This was obviously a kid who had never even ridden a pony at a carnival. Her posterior and the horse's saddle were like oil and water.

The action was set and rehearsed several times, then Scotty was deployed out in the field with the second camera and a telephoto lens to get 'beauty shots' of whatever happened. Ava received a temporary field promotion to become my assistant. That helped move things along, because we never needed to wait for a grip to help move the camera. Her lover, Gene the grip, was standing by to move our gear like he had never stood by before.

After a few more shots, we broke for our lunch of custom ordered sandwiches. An older Indian woman had joined the entourage. Her bright red *tikka* mark was in counterpoint to her wizened face. The conservatism of her complex brown sari was betrayed by the display it yielded of her wrinkled belly.

"Do you know who that is?" I asked Scotty.

He wiped some renegade mustard off his chin.

"That's Indrani's mother-in-law. Indrani's a widow and I don't think the old woman likes her very much. She probably feels that Indrani should have gone up on the funeral pyre with her late husband. Still, who's going to be picky about the company when there's a chance to tour America? I don't think that they're entirely comfortable together. If there wasn't some notion of family obligation, Indrani probably would've left her at the JFK baggage claim."

We soon had our hands full. A line of six reflectors bounced the sun's light onto the action, giving it that Hollywood gloss. Ginny, the best boy, had even come down off the truck, proudly tending one of the large stand-mounted boards. Eric, Sully and Gene tended the other reflectors, leaving one weighted by sandbags.

Indrani paced back and forth between the reflectors and the talent giving orders and observing the results like Napoleon and Josephine rolled up into one. The untended reflector, which had the assignment of bringing out the detail in the horse's tail, seemed to have a mind of its own. No matter how many sandbags were draped around its base, and how tight all the knobs were twisted, it seemed to stray from its duty.

"How can we expect it to stay on the bull's eye when it's pointed at a horse's ass?" Eric asked loudly as he reset it for the tenth time.

We started rolling film. Acting problems plagued the first three takes. Indrani continued striding back and forth. She called action for the fourth time. "Cut, that's perfect!" she called. I took my eye away from the camera to look at her. She was smiling, but behind and above her, the untended reflector was beginning to topple. There was no time to yell. I sprinted for her and pulled her out of the way just as the reflector crashed into the spot where she had been standing. Looking around, which was hard to do because the director was very soft in my arms, I saw the retreating back of her mother-in-law slowly walking toward the parked vehicles.

"Perhaps we need another person in the grip department," I suggested.

"Thank you. Accidents will happen, I suppose." She straightened out her clothes and called for a new setup. We did wide shots until the sky started to turn, and then we did close-ups for as long as we could find patches of blue to stage them in front of. Then, Indrani mouthed the magic words, "It's a wrap."

My crew could wrap quickly—an art readily acquired when there is no time-and-a-half for overtime. Scotty joined Eric, Sully and me as we hung around his car trading business cards and phone numbers. "These buds are for us," he said as he lit a joint and began to pass it around. I found its resinous smell tantalizing as it worked its way around the circle toward me. I was just about to reach out and have some when Vijaya Lal appeared at my elbow. "Excuse me," he said quietly, his solemn face revealing nothing, "Indrani likes the way you work and keep on schedule. She wants you to shoot one more day for us. If you agree, I have instructions to call Mr. Younger and cancel him."

"I'm available," I said as I reached out my hand for the diminishing joint.

"The director would also like you and Eric to scout tomorrow's location with her now."

"I'd love to." I finally got the joint and just passed it on. Better to remain at or near sea level.

We finally got back to the Biltmore at about eight-thirty. I was hungry, I was dirty, and I was a bit proud. I quickly arrived at the decision to give talking to Elisabeth the highest priority. I dialed and let the phone ring for a couple of minutes. Finally it was picked up. "Hemp Hill," she said.

"Hi, it's me."

"Hello, you." Her voice didn't reveal much of a change from her opening remark.

"I thought I'd call to let you know that today was a success."

"You didn't get 'misplaced?'"

"I got extended."

"You got *what*? I thought you were pretty good just the way you were. You said you were a medium and the medium is the massage, at least. I'm sorry, you *work* in a medium and you're much more than that when you're—um—not working."

"They liked my work and they want me to shoot for another day. They bumped John Younger and signed me on."

"That's nice, but have they seen your work yet? I mean don't the pictures have to be developed or something?"

"I think it was my executive style. I kept the crew moving and happy, and I kept to their schedule even though I don't have a copy of it. I think it must be in Sanskrit."

"So you did well. That's good."

"I miss you," I ventured.

"That's also good. I had the distinct pleasure of seeing my gynecologist this morning."

"Oh." *What?*

"It was a long-standing appointment. He had me on the examining table, you know, with my feet in those dreadful little stirrups they have?"

"I think I know what you mean." A few short weeks ago it seemed like there might never be another vagina in my life. Now I was becoming actively involved in the care and feeding of one.

"He had his head down there, examining me under this discreet sheet—they probably put them on you so you can't see them blush or gasp."

Probably. "That must be it," I said.

"Anyway he looked up and over at me and said 'You look really happy down here.' I thought you should know."

"Thanks for sharing that with me."

"I bet you're blushing. I can *hear* you blushing!" So could I. "Should I meet the ten boat at the dock on Wednesday?"

"Yes, please. I really want to see you."

"That's good," she said and hung up.

Oh, good God. Now, outside professionals were becoming involved in our relationship. Hey, at least he approved. As a tipsy civil servant once confided to me—if you can get the consultants to like you, you're safe. The dial tone droned in the background of a confusion of hopes and ideas. How could she possibly love me? How could I not love her?

The next morning I arrived at the dumpsters with my coffee and gear to find out that I had been selected to lead the caravan to the location. I didn't remember how to get there and George Mukherjee wasn't about to try it again.

Scotty and I settled into his car with our coffee to await the outcome. "I got it!" he exclaimed.

"You got what?"

"What's happening on this shoot. We're all flat rated. It doesn't make any difference to them whether they work us eight or twenty-four hours. Shyam probably talked them into paying him by the hour. That bastard is probably getting into double overtime every day."

"It seems like there might be more to it than that," I ventured.

"There *is* something bigger and scarier that that. They have to have heavy insurance for the locations they're using, and if he decides that an insurance claim might be more profitable than the movie, it could get very dangerous around here."

We eventually got to the convent before Indrani and her entourage. I directed a lighting, dolly and camera setup that was completed just as she arrived. "This is not good," was her response. "It will work better if we put the car on the other side of the drive and move the dolly tracks to where the car is now."

"Right," I said to her. We changed everything before the production people were ready to roll.

Shyam and Mohammed finally materialized with about a dozen little girls of elementary school age. They were all dressed in the blue sweaters and plaid skirts that have become, for some unfathomable reason, the standard uniform of Catholic girls' schools. "Damn it Bart," said Sully, leaning on the dolly, "do you realize that we're teaching a sizeable portion of the world's males that the way to get ahead in America is to hang around schoolyards picking up little girls!"

We made several good takes of Ram's character picking up Sippy, as his unknowing daughter, at school. There were spectators; several windows revealed nuns watching the proceedings and some of the girls' parents regarded us intently from the street. The day, which had started out overcast enough to dictate heavy lighting of the scene, deteriorated. Our job got less elegant and more desperate as the moist air finally turned into rain. The close-ups were filmed from under garbage bags and umbrellas. After the last take, we waited for a couple of tense moments until Scotty called, "Gate's clean!" We could wrap out of this location.

Next, Indrani wanted to 'pick up a few shots' for a sequence that Whiz had shot earlier. I talked her and the producers into bringing along the entire crew for this exercise. As we pulled into a 'no parking' zone, the rain was hitting its stride. "Standing by," said Eric as we tried to watch the city through the downpour.

I donned my foul weather gear to brave the elements and call Elisabeth. I huddled under the canopy that the phone company had deemed adequate replacement for a phone booth. The phone rang and rang out there on the island.

I gave up on that and headed into a nearby urban Burger King to get a cup of coffee. Taking up several tables were Indrani, Mohammed, Ram Reddy and everyone but the technical crew. Indrani spotted me. "You must have some food, Bart!"

"Oh, I will, but I'll enjoy it a lot more if I can tell my crew what to do."

"We don't know yet, but we are arriving at a decision."

I brought the crew in. One hamburger later, a decision was arrived at; the crew would have a free hour or so until one o'clock. I walked back to the hotel for a break.

At one o'clock, I found myself all alone near the dumpsters. The truck, vans and cars were there and so was the unremitting rain. Why was I hanging around with the trash again? About the fourth time a short Hispanic man whose smile sported a prominent gold tooth dragged a load of garbage past me, I decided that I had misunderstood the afternoon's plan. Maybe my hanging around alone in an alley next to a dumpster had to do with some arrangements that my knife-wielding nemesis had succeeded in making.

I shuddered as I went back inside the hotel and checked the restaurant. Practically everyone was in various stages of eating large meals. The break had been extended until three, and the day's next location would be a suburban laundromat.

It was a laundromat that fairly shouted, 'laundromat.' It was a long establishment, and most of the action would take place along a line of dryers that stretched seemingly without end. There was also a back room where, at an earlier point in the story, Ram Reddy's character buys a gun.

In spite of the large lighting job demanded by the corridor-like area through which both the camera and action would move, we had the set lit and the dolly ready to roll by the time Ram and Indrani arrived.

Some new American faces had joined the crew; Dick Doherty and his band of merry stuntmen. While everyone waited for Mr. Guli, a man Shyam described as a professional actor from New York who would play the part of the laundromat owner, Dick Doherty busied himself confirming my initial impression that he was a bar brawler. He was a lean, scarred man of average height with curly light brown hair. He started to demonstrate the fight that he had planned for Ram and Mr. Guli, using his assistant, Clyde, who looked like he was still in the Army.

Dick began the fight by pulling Clyde out of the back room through a tacky floral-print curtain. He pinned him up against the wall next to the doorway causing the pay phone there to ring involuntarily. He then waltzed him over to the line of dryers, bouncing him against each dryer in turn, slapping, slamming, slugging and spinning him, trying to extract information from him about an assassination that Ram's character was determined to prevent. Finally, with the victim pinned against the fifteenth Laundromaid Commercial model, Dick pantomimed how the interrogator would punch out the window of the adjacent dryer, gather up a handful of broken glass, stuff it in the unwilling informant's mouth, and begin to slap his face back and forth.

Just after the explicit run-through, Mr. Guli arrived with a few hangers full of clothes. He looked like somebody's uncle who could get stuff wholesale, a pear-shaped man with a big grin. I hoped he knew what he was in for. Soon he and Ram began, under Dick's tutelage, to move through the scene.

Meanwhile, Indrani's mother-in-law had entered the front of the laundromat and was hanging around the counter. I didn't have much time to dwell on it as we started to make the master shot from the dolly, and it took all of my concentration to coach the sweating Sully until he got the dolly's start, speed, and stop correct as he pushed it through several rehearsals. Indrani was walking on the off-camera side of the dolly, along another bank of dryers. Mr. Guli was transported violently out of his office and down the line of dryers for several rehearsals as I practiced following the action and Scotty, in the assistant's catbird seat, perfected the focus pull. Finally, we were ready to shoot it.

I looked up from the camera to catch my breath and saw Indrani's mother-in-law slowly moving in our direction. Two takes passed smoothly, the action getting better each time. The third take was proceeding smoothly when Indrani shrieked with pain.

"What's the matter?" I asked, spinning around to face her on the dolly's seat.

"I seem to have pranged my elbow on an open dryer door."

I looked. Half of the dryer doors, which had been closed throughout the setup and rehearsals, were standing open. One of the dryers was full and running with what looked like a load of brown print saris. Indrani's mother-in-law was walking slowly toward the front of the laundromat. "We will use take two of that shot," Indrani said, rubbing her elbow. "Set up to follow the fight handheld."

Scotty quickly checked the camera, changed lenses and set it on my shoulder. In spite of its weight, it really felt good. I enjoyed adding my choreography to the fighters'. Scotty kept asking me if I wanted to set the camera down between takes. I didn't. Finally, when I set it down after the rehearsals, he seized the opportunity to tape a piece of foam rubber to my shoulder. Wonderful stuff, gaffer tape. At times, it appears to hold the world together; now, it was holding me together. The camera felt even better on my shoulder and two takes later, we had something that Indrani was pleased with. I felt that my life and being were vindicated by carrying the camera through that fight. The natural high, about twelve hours into the day, carried me right through to the breaking of the glass.

"Okay everybody," announced Dick Doherty. "We're gonna be installing the breakaway glass. You gotta sit still or go somewhere else."

I pulled up a camera case and sat near Scotty. The recent brawlers were working like a bomb squad as they slid the breakaway glass into place on the dryer door.

Quiet conversations were brought to a halt as Dick Doherty addressed the crew again. "There's only one sudden move we want to break the glass so, for God's sake, let Ram be the guy who makes it."

Dick gave Mr. Guli a blood capsule to bite at the proper moment so that blood would trickle convincingly out of his mouth. I was on the floor, looking down into the camera's viewfinder. The camera was pointed up for a low angle shot. I had to tilt down from Ram's inspired gaze, starting when he said something that sounded like 'gujudderit.' So that we didn't waste breakaway glass, Indrani would call the cut if the action wasn't right, and I would call the cut if my move didn't work.

Indrani called the cut twice because of Mr. Guli's performance. "Action," she called again. Ram was ranting away in Hindi, slapping Mr. Guli's face back and forth. I was surprised to find myself picking up enough Hindi to cue my moves. Ram peered at the window of the adjacent dryer with an electric flash of inspiration. I panned and tilted down to the dryer, centering the window. It felt good, so I didn't call the cut.

Wham! Ram's fist shot through the window and emerged with a fistful of shards. He wrenched Mr. Guli's mouth open and forced the glass into it, slamming the mouth shut with the heel of his left hand under Guli's chin. Blood started to flow. Ram drew back his right hand for a broad slap across the glass-filled jaw. Guli's eyes bugged with absolute horror as he gave up his pose of ignorance and pleaded for the opportunity to tell all that he knew. "Cut!" called Indrani dramatically. "How was that for you?" she asked me softly as I knelt in a puddle of my own sweat.

"It was pretty good, but maybe I could do better."

She called for a reset. Everyone sat on their hands or left the area. "That lady can really heat up a set," said Scotty. He and I had wandered up to the front of the store to check out the next setup. Indrani's mother-in-law had left or hidden herself well among the clean clothes. I peered out into the rainy night checking for a red Toyota pimp mobile. I hoped that Shyam hadn't booked every hooker in town to wash her dirty drawers as background action. I hoped that the weather would keep Quinn under a rock somewhere.

"Sheeit!" boomed the stuntman's voice. "The son of a bitch broke and it's the last piece!"

"God's will," said Indrani philosophically, eyeing me as if I had better be as good as I said I was. She didn't believe in second takes, anyway.

The dark and rainy night was banished for the shot of Ram entering the laundromat. We made it a sunny summer afternoon. Ram would come in, wait until a family finished leaving its dry-cleaning, then come forward and say the magic words that would turn a cordial and prosperous laundromat owner into a dealer in illegal firearms. Christ, what if Quinn were to get his hands on a gun? I hoped 'God's will' would be on my side.

We filmed the gun deal in the back room of the laundromat. Buffy had turned it into an unbelievably seedy office primarily by buying every periodical of questionable virtue in the hotel newsstand and covering the walls with bare breasted American ladies. I wondered briefly how this would pass Indian censors who objected to kissing. Then I realized that the bared mammaries of primitive cultures are educational like *National Geographic*, and not pornographic like *Hustler* or *Penthouse*. Compared to the Ancient East, we were definitely the primitive culture.

Guli stumbled on his attitude during the first take. Indrani's patience showed a bit of wear as she demonstrated the helpful head-waiterish manner that she had envisioned. The next take went very well until he forgot his line. Indrani impatiently gave it to him, and we started up again. We all breathed a sigh of relief as he made it through his first trouble spot but our relief was premature; he hung up on a subsequent line.

"You must get these lines correctly!" Indrani unleashed her wrath at Guli. "I have a whole crew here, very professional, and they are waiting for you to get these lines correct so that they can go home!" I hoped that I would never become the subject of her unmitigated anger. "Now we will break the scene into little pieces that *even you* can remember so that we can finish this damn scene!"

We finally finished the damn scene. Guli's biggest struggle was to get back enough starch to play the scene correctly. He finally did. It was a wrap.

I overcame my fear of pimpmobiles in the dark and pitched in to help the grips and gaffers take down the lighting and move all of the equipment through the rain and into the truck. If we had been getting overtime, my help wouldn't have been welcome, but we weren't, so it was.

Ginny, the best boy, looked like a drowned rat except that she was shivering as she received equipment on the tailgate of the truck in the pouring rain. Her hair looked more abused than usual, plastered to her skull. She had probably left her Yankees cap in a dry place. I dug a sweatshirt out of my dirty tricks bag and brought it out to her on my next trip. "Funny," she said, exaggerating her New York accent, "you don't look like a Jewish mother."

"Rule number one: dress so that you can be comfortable in the worst place you'll conceivably have to stand for hours."

"I'm quitting this shoot, by the way," she said as she took a folded stand from Gene.

"Find a 'real' job?" I asked.

"Nope. I just don't want to be around people who do what she did."

"Who?"

"Indrani. The way she treated Guli was really awful."

"He was an actor with a part to play." I was thankful for the slicker that was keeping me dry through all this.

"He's no actor—he's a guy Shyam met in the Air India office in New York. He got the *honor* of playing a scene with the Great Ram Reddy," she spat.

"Let me see if I got this right. He put on his best clothes, travelled to Providence and didn't know that he was going to get the shit beat out of him?"

"You got it, man."

An older actor generally knows what he can and cannot do. He has doctors, lawyers, accountants, masseurs and chiropractors to tell him what his limits are. The average late middle-aged guy is about as ready for what Guli had been through as the family station wagon is for the Monaco Grand Prix. Just the act of snapping one's head around to make the punches look real could be disastrous without practice and conditioning.

I thought of the other world I'd be in the next day as I headed in for another load of equipment. Nothing wrong with a cold rainstorm as long as there was a fire going in the fireplace at Hemp Hill. Vijaya Lal found me as I was about to begin a round of aerobic sandbag hauling. "Excuse me, Bart. Indrani has asked me to see if you are available for the rest of the shoot."

It's hard to perk up at news like that after a fifteen-hour day that hasn't ended yet. "How many days are we talking about?"

"The next two days, Wednesday and Thursday, in Providence. Friday, Saturday and Sunday are off for the Fourth of July weekend. Monday is a travel day for the crew. You will travel to New York on Sunday and spend Monday doing pre-production in New York with Bob Fellowes. Then everyone—the full crew—will be there for three days of shooting in New York."

"Where has Bob been, anyway?" I had been looking forward to working with him and, possibly, getting the inside story on what was going on.

"He has been in New York, making arrangements for our shoot there, laying on locations and that sort of thing."

"Let me make a phone call. I think I'll be able to schedule it." I found a pay phone near the front of the laundromat and dialed Elisabeth.

She caught it on the third ring. "Hemp Hill," she said.

"Hello, this is Bart."

"I'm beginning to be able to recognize your voice over the phone. Hello, Bart. Are we still on for tomorrow morning?"

"That's what I'm calling about. I've been asked to shoot the rest of the film. That means that I get Friday, Saturday and part of Sunday off and spend next week in New York City."

"Do you think you'll get off in time to catch the last ferry on Thursday?"

"It's not good. My car is in Boston—dead on the street."

"A dead bug. Maybe you should do something about it before it gets swept up."

"God, Elisabeth, I feel funny about this movie job getting stretched. I mean, it's an opportunity that I can't pass up, but I…"

"You know what you'll be if you miss the Fourth, right?"

"Exactly."

"Well, figure out what a partial Sunday off is. Do we have half of a breakfast in bed? Do we have a fractional swim? You're going to have to help me out on that one."

"I'll see you on the Fourth," I offered.

"Be certain that you do."

I tried to think of something to say, but I must have taken too long. She hung up.

I had just beat Entwhistle Kidd out of a job. I should be celebrating. Instead, Scotty and I were lost in thought as we rode back to the hotel in near silence; neither of us wanted to shout to make ourselves heard above the hammering and splashing of the rain. For better or worse, this whole movie was landing in my lap. Back at the hotel, I helped Scotty haul some of the camera gear up to his room. "Hey," he said once we were riding in the elevator. "I'm glad to see you getting more work on this movie. Whiz Kidd never bought me any coffee."

"Thanks, Scotty."

"I like what you're shooting, too. They'll even like you after they see the dailies. In fact, they probably heard from the editor in New York about yesterday's stuff before they dumped Whiz."

"That makes it nicer. Thanks," I said as the elevator stopped at my floor.

I poured myself a Scotch on the rocks. I looked out at a rain-soaked Providence, its orange glow spread through the sky. I took a shower and stretched out on my bed. I picked up the volume of Elisabeth's poetry and a folded sheet of paper fell out. I unfolded it to find a draft of a poem she had been working on:

Lightning on the Clam Flats—Squidneck Island

We don't speak.
Things are all alike,
A continuum,
Airwatermud
Sticky, bloodwarm.
Nothing moving.
My bucket is empty—
The clams are hiding, buried,
Flesh in shell in mud.

Air stirs, water ripples:
Blue black
monument rising in the west.

Will rain bring out the clams
Like night crawlers?

Will we revive,
Stirred from our lethargy?

Hairs lift on arms and legs,
Skin senses change.

The current runs through us, between us.
The squall line sweeps across the bay.

I was stunned by the poem. I felt addressed. I got up to rummage through the desk drawer for some stationery. I wanted to sort out these feelings and maybe write her a letter. The phone rang; I picked it up halfway through the first ring. I was really losing it.

"Is this Bart Lane?"

"Speaking."

"This is Indrani. Could you please come up to my room?"

She already had me passionately involved with her movie—giving it more that I knew I had. What else could she want or offer?

"Well, I'm not dr…"

"My suite number is Suite sixteen-thirteen—as soon as possible." She hung up on me, too.

CHAPTER 11

❀

*T*en minutes after Indrani's momentous phone call I was knocking on the door of Suite sixteen-thirteen. I thought that my Squidneck tan looked very tropical with the loose white shirt and white trousers I had thrown on.

Indrani had obviously spent some time on herself, too. She answered the door in a light print gown that left no doubt as to the shape of her high, conical breasts. Her straight black Asian hair flowed down her back. "Bart," she said, "so nice of you to be able to come on such short notice." I smelled jasmine as she led me to the couch.

She indicated where I should seat myself. "You must still be thirsty after today's thrashing. Would you care for something to drink?"

"Yes, please. Mango juice, Scotch and soda, anything."

"Which?"

"Oh, the Scotch and soda, please."

I looked around the suite as she busied herself at the cabinet that opened into a wet bar. The couch shared the center of the room with a large coffee table and two overstuffed chairs. A dining or meeting table faced a large window overlooking the harbor and Narragansett Bay. Was I kidding myself, or could I see some lights twinkling on Squidneck in the distance?

Indrani came across the room with our drinks. Hers looked similar to mine, but I didn't know what or if Hindus drank. She handed me mine and sat on the opposite end of the couch. "Cheers," she said, leaning forward to click her glass against mine. "I was very impressed with your handheld work today. Most cameramen would have made the assistant change to a smaller film load. You just picked it up with the thousand-footer on it and went to work. I could tell that you were making it float."

"Thank you. I enjoy doing it."

"Entwhistle Kidd was saying we might need a Steadicam for that shot. What is that?"

"It's a counterbalanced arm that holds the camera away from the operator. The arm is attached to a vest that's a bit like an iron maiden—torture device."

"I see."

"It's also between one and two thousand dollars per day."

"Well, I'm glad that we don't need one. You seem quite—powerful." She moved the slightest bit toward my end of the couch.

"What can you tell me about tomorrow's shoot?"

"Tomorrow is Ram Reddy's big fight scene in the graveyard. I want it to look very sinister." She took a sip of her drink, keeping her large, dark eyes on me.

"Coming up—one sinister graveyard." The Scotch, in addition to the stiff round that I had had in my room, was getting to me. So was Madame Director. Hey, I was just a professional who happened to have the skills she needed; it's not like I rescued her or anything like that.

"You inspire such confidence, Bart, and you're fast. I never saw the crew move the way you have got them moving." Who was moving fast as I held my drink in my corner of the couch? I was turned toward her enough so that I wouldn't get a stiff neck looking at her. She leaned forward as she moved closer still. Light mocha breasts entered the competition for what to look at next. I was lifting up my left arm—to relax comfortably in the circumstances—when the door to the suite burst open.

Indrani's former mother-in-law flew into the room. She saw me and her eyes opened so wide that her *tikka* dot almost disappeared. She unleashed a string of unintelligible—to me—invective. Indrani was immediately on her feet and, it seemed to this English speaker, giving as good as she was getting.

The backtalk was obviously beyond the harridan's personal pale. She stormed over to Indrani with a strong slapping right hand drawn back. Indrani blocked the blow and retreated to one of the suite's bedrooms. I heard the bolt being thrown. The old woman looked at me and stormed into the other bedroom, loudly locking herself in.

There I was, in the middle of a suite that wasn't mine. I looked from one door to the other as I finished my drink. Then, I went over to the door that Indrani had disappeared behind. I knocked. "Are you all right?" I asked.

"Yes," came the muted reply.

"What is call time tomorrow?"

"Seven-thirty at the dumpsters."

"Thank you, it was a very helpful meeting," I added loudly for the benefit of her recent assailant.

I should have learned by now that bad guys *do* get up early, but there I was at the dumpsters again, waiting for anyone else from the film, and the odor of many meals past was making me wonder if I had ever really risen above the rank of resort dishwasher. Just as I was realizing a dumpster was a fairly good way for someone to dispose of an inconvenient body, Scotty finally wheeled his old station wagon into place. I threw my bags in and set a couple of cups of coffee on the dash. The sound of a failing exhaust on an ill-treated American motor accompanied a rolling cloud of blue smoke; Shyam had arrived and was flogging his old car into line. I went over to talk to him.

"Good morning, Shyam. Do you think that you could give us directions to the cemetery, or lead us out there soon, so that we could get a look at it?"

"I would be very pleased to lead you out there personally. I should be free to do this in just a minute."

I rejoined Scotty. "Mr. Shyam has said that he would be very glad to lead us to the location in 'just a minute.' That means, if I'm not mistaken, that he will be driving ahead of us in the motorcade."

"You're learning fast," Scotty said.

That, of course, is exactly what happened. Woodlawn Cemetery was invaded by an unlikely cortege, disrupting the peace with shouts, loudly grumbling trucks, and a distinctly unfunereal crowd.

Soon, our caravan was headed up the hill on a winding, tree shaded road. It wound past monuments and mausolea. It came to a stop where another road crossed it while the production folks, undoubtedly figuring out ways to get lost, caught up. I found myself staring at an expanse of sixty or so small, uniform markers. A large stone erected in the middle of them was inscribed 'The Last Home on Earth for These Unmarried and Widowed Women—The Acushnet Burial Insurance Society.' I was moved to think of Elisabeth and hope she'd do better than that. What was I going to do about it? What would happen if I tried?

We eventually reached our location, an open grave in a relatively clear area. I sent Joao back to guide Gene's truck around the edge of the cemetery to a spot where it would be out of our intended shots.

"Don't forget, we want this to look sinister," said Indrani. She was impeccably dressed in spite of the prospects for a very dirty day.

I put the crew to work on the sinister look and joined the director at the gaping gravesite. "How deep would you like your grave?" she asked me.

I must have paused a beat, wondering if she was in league with Quinn and Shyam.

"For the shot, Bart!"

"Oh, uh, just make it deep enough so the bodies fall out of the shot."

"*You* will be making some shots down there; fights at graveside, bodies falling in, etcetera."

God, I thrive in desperate situations. I looked at the expectant hole in a new light, my brain abuzz with the viewing angles and the closest focus of the lenses I would be using. "I would like it eighteen inches deeper," I pronounced with a satisfying discrimination.

Dick Doherty had expanded his *corps de ballet* for the day's action. Of the new brawlers, Karl was over six and a half feet tall with a beefy build and a round, cherubic face topped with thick, wavy, blow-dried hair; Johnny was black, an inch or two shorter than Karl, and his lantern jaw had been made more threatening by the blacking out of a couple of his front teeth. It was a day for fights; not dialogue.

The ballet would probably come later. Dick was working individually with Karl and Johnny, and it looked as if he were teaching the tango to determinedly foot-shuffling wallflowers. Clyde was standing in for Ram Reddy, but his scrawny build and military hair were poor substitutes for the latter's voluptuous bearing.

We started slow and easy, too. Johnny is digging a grave and runs off to help a comrade in trouble—covered by two cameras. Ram drives up to the scene with Karl holding a knife to his throat. I wouldn't have minded a stunt driver squealing to a stop at my toes, but Ram wasn't a stunt driver. Sully stood behind me with a meaty fist wrapped around my belt in case I had to be evacuated. "You really believe you're going to save my life if that actor misses his mark, don't you, Sully?"

"So do you," he replied.

There were no problems with the fight where Ram is hauled out of the car. There was no visible mother-in-law. If the misadventure of the night before had made it so that the old witch couldn't bear to lay eyes on me, it was worth it.

We were almost finished with the car. All we had to do was use the last piece of Dick Doherty's breakaway glass for the shot where Karl gets out of the back seat, punches out the driver's window, and hauls Ram through it.

The only piece of breakaway glass in New England was lying under a tree, surrounded by sandbags. Giancarlo was taking some production stills of the setting up process. He hoisted one of his two Nikons to his eye. He stepped back to achieve a better composition. "Fuck!" he shouted after he looked down to see what his Gucci-shod foot had done. The irreplaceable glass lay in shards.

"Check it and we'll eat," I said to Scotty after we had finished shooting everything that could be shot without the glass. I left him pulling off the lens and headed toward the food tables near the trucks. I'd been premature about the mother-in-law. Not only was she casting her eternally judgmental gaze over the proceedings; she was ahead of me in the lunch line. The Indian buffet had featured shrimp vindaloo until she helped herself to the last of it. I made do with chicken curry and took my plate over to where Scotty was sitting under a tree.

"That Giancarlo is one fucked-up dude," he said.

"Everybody makes mistakes," I offered.

"You haven't been around here long enough to get a full picture of that junkie. Between the bad ideas and worse diseases, he's an accident looking for a place to happen."

"That bad, eh?"

"Worse. Buffy knows him from Rhode Island School of Design. He's a crackerjack still photographer; develops his film like a surgeon and makes prints like Albrecht Dürer. He's also terminally fucked up. I like to pad my reality with a few chemicals as well as the next stoner, but not with him. Noooo way."

"What's the problem?"

"He's pathologically careless. He's got diplomatic immunity because his old man's something in the Italian Embassy in D.C. and he can't be held or charged with anything, but he *likes* being busted, and he doesn't care who's with him when he is."

"That's awful."

"You're getting the picture."

"Shyam is visiting the set. Any idea what he's up to—besides eating the really good stuff?" I looked over to where he was closing his lantern jaw on an appetizing looking shrimp.

Scotty took a tug on his Coke, looked around, and said, "Probably just feeding his face. There's not a lot to steal at this location."

"What are you saying?"

"I don't know. Did you see the late news on TV last night?"

"No, I missed it." I didn't see any point in mentioning that Indrani had called me away from the TV.

"There's been a robbery at Belcourt Castle. Thieves in the night spirited away about a hundred thousand bucks worth of jewels and antiques."

"Oh, shit." I was just about to expand on that when Indrani materialized in front of us.

"Bart, I have just heard that we will be losing the grave to its long term tenant at three o'clock."

"We'll just have to work fast," I replied after swallowing a mouthful of curry.

"Thank you," she said, and left.

"She believes you," Scotty said. "I can't wait to hear from the editor about the laundromat stuff. You had a really nice look going there."

"Thanks, I enjoy playing with the light in fluorescent locations. Well, I better go have a look at the hole."

The sun was too far overhead to cut with the morning's footage, so we fixed it with a large white silk scrim over the action and some reflectors. I set up a topside shot for Scotty during the first rehearsal. Dick Doherty approached me as I was finishing the briefing. "Ready to go in the hole, big guy?" he asked.

"I guess."

"Karl, let's put him in!" They picked me up like I was a recalcitrant three-year-old and lowered me seven and a half feet into the hole.

"Dick," I said after my landing, "who's going to land in here first, the gorilla?"

Dick rolled his eyes. "Call him Johnny, he likes it better. Yeah, he'll be joining you real soon."

"Listen, Dick," I called, but he was gone. Of course, I had been referring to the character Johnny was playing. Hadn't I? Nice going, self! I had insulted somebody twice my size who was being paid to fall into a hole I presently occupied. I quickly forgot about it as Scotty and Ava lowered the big camera, its battery, a couple of sandbags and a garbage bag to keep the omnipresent dirt out of things. Then it got real quiet up there. Looking around, I saw another piece of heavy plastic bag protruding out of one wall of the grave. I didn't want to think about who or what might be in it so I looked somewhere else. Ants, large ones, appeared to be fighting about which of their number would have first march on this new piece of meat in their midst. I looked back to see them losing ground to a small number of dramatically larger ants. "Hey," I yelled, "the ants are quibbling over who gets me. Let's get this show on the road, in the hole, anywhere!"

Indrani leaned over the edge of the grave above me. "Sorry Bart, Shyam has sent everyone to move their vehicles out of the background of the next...ooh!" Something hit her—hard—and sent her sprawling into the grave on top of me. I hunched over the camera and shielded my eyes. She landed on my back, knocking the wind out of me. I hadn't seen a flash of brown sari, but I knew who had done it.

Indrani was shaken but unhurt. There wasn't enough dirt on her for me to brush off, but she brushed me off fairly well. I marvelled at her dancer's lightness as I gave her a boost up to the surface. Sully and Eric materialized to help her the rest of the way.

Cameras began to roll; I was treated to an incredible low-angle view of Ram's amazing dance at the very crumbling edge of death. In its final moment, Johnny was strangling Ram who was flat on his back, his head hanging into the grave. Ram reached out, found a rock, and skillfully applied it to Johnny's skull. Then, he boosted the body of the man I had called a gorilla into the grave. It all went very well except that I was kicked in the head. A new rule: don't call stuntmen gorillas within their hearing.

When I recovered from the blow, I pulled the camera's tilted view-finder back to where I could look through it. The shot was still there. "Dangerously good for this camera," I yelled. Strong arms propelled me and the camera out of the grave to the cheers of the crew.

We finished up topside after Scotty laid healing hands on the camera. On Indrani's call of action, Ram neatly thrust the trick knife into Karl's stomach and rolled him into the grave where he landed perfectly next to the moribund Johnny; the two of them looking like the last two cigarettes in the pack.

I found a water tap ideally suited to filling small watering cans and used it to rinse the top half of my body. I was interrupted by Dick Doherty. He had used the welding rig in the cemetery's maintenance shop to fashion a new piece of breakaway glass out of the remnants of Giancarlo's misstep. I shook the dirt out of my shirt and put it back on. I noticed Moose and a couple of other prostitutes hiking up the hill ahead of me. I chanced a look behind me and there was the distinctive Toyota pimp mobile with the leering Quinn surveying the action from the driver's window.

"The fucker's back," I said to Scotty a little bit later, as I helped carry some of the gear further up the hill to the next setup. Was this an accident? Why did this piece of human flotsam keep bobbing back into my life?

"The guy who sliced your soundman?"

"Yeah. You got an extra hat in your bag? I gotta work and hide at the same time."

"Try this." He handed me a hat that appeared to promote Stinger missiles. "Apologies in advance for any political anguish it might cause you."

"Thanks, Scotty, but who hasn't wanted a small shoulder-mounted missile from time to time—like now?"

"No problem. We might have larger problems than just your knife artist, though. Check him out now."

I looked down the hill at the gaudy Toyota. I couldn't see in the driver's window because Shyam was blocking it. He and Quinn appeared to be doing business. I hoped that Shyam wasn't describing his new cameraman—fresh from Channel Eight, Boston.

Vijaya walked over from where he had been conferring with Indrani and filled me in on what was to come. Before shooting the breaking glass, Indrani wanted us to film the tumultuous progress of Ram and the two bad guys across the graveyard. She envisioned a broad vista of headstones, grass and trees with brawling and violence intruding vigorously into the composition. I offered her a fairly broad vista.

"It's just not right. It would be so much nicer if we didn't have to avoid the truck and all of that movie equipment scattered about."

I was just about to point out another possible angle which didn't involve moving everything when the head stuntman trotted up. "What's the problem?" he asked.

"The truck and all of the gear cluttered around it are in the background of the best angle for the next shot, and the light is beginning to fade, so we don't have much time to move it," I explained.

"So where do you want it put?"

"About fifty yards to the right, correct, Indrani?"

"That would do very nicely," she replied.

"Let's go, guys!" Dick yelled at the top of his voice. They charged down the hill to the grip truck and, coincidentally, the pimp's car. I watched Quinn's eyes bug out with fear and the unceremonious departure of his car. Shyam strode furiously off in the opposite direction. The stunt army roused a sleeping Gene from his position on the tailgate. He recovered the cap which had been knocked from its position over his eyes and joined the effort. With a mighty thrashing of large bodies, the move of truck and equipment was completed in less than two minutes.

There was one more problem; a middle aged couple was tending the flowers on a grave. Vijaya was dispatched to move them out of the scene. Since Eric and Scotty had set everything up, I racked the zoom lens out to telephoto and watched this minor drama unfold.

I decided that the couple was named Mike and Colleen Moran, and that they had come, as they did every month, to pull weeds and place flowers around the grave of Colleen's parents. They were both well aware that a certain amount of hardware was involved in lowering a casket containing a deceased into the grave without messing up the undertaker's tasteful black suit, but they hadn't known what to make of the large truck accompanied by the New England Patriots front line that came hurrying past, carrying more than enough hardware to simultaneously lower the victims of a major disaster into their final resting places. That was obviously over soon enough and they were back to weeding and watering. Mike was checking a geranium when a shadow fell across it. He looked up to see a thin dark man—Vijaya Lal. Confusion crossed Mike's round Irish face. He had never been one to join the gripes over lunch at work, complaints about people of all kinds of colors, religions and nationalities coming into this country to take jobs away from good, hardworking Americans, but he had probably noticed that there were new types of people showing up. Where was this guy from and what did he want?

I could nearly lipread Vijaya Lal saying, "Excuse me very much, sir. We are shooting a motion picture, and you and your wife are in the background of our shot. Would you be so kind as to move for twenty minutes or so?" I saw Vijaya point right at me. The man I silently referred to as Mike followed his point and got a visible jolt as he saw me behind the device that looked like a cross between a cannon and a TV camera.

They gathered up their watering can and gardening supplies and left, taking care of the large red Ford that was next on Vijaya's list.

The fight was long and far-reaching. Ram was polite enough not to laugh at Clyde, his stunt double, but he was very firm about letting himself in for all the physical abuse that was being dished out. He insisted on it, even to the extent of being hurled to the ground from Karl's outstretched arms. "Always my fans, they are watching," he pronounced gravely. "If it is not me, they can tell a kilometer away."

"He is not kidding," intoned a solemn Vijaya. "His fans will track him down and try to recreate particularly nasty fights."

Ram's character in the fight submitted passively to armed kidnapping, rude removal through the unopened window, being dashed to earth, and absorbing several fierce kicks and punches to sensitive areas of his anatomy. However, when the monster thug, played by Karl, carried him briefly like a baby, an angry streak was ignited in his proud soul, setting off a violent reaction that would eventually turn the fight around.

We used the last rays of daylight to film the breaking glass. Dick's salvage effort wasn't as transparent as the original had been, but it would pass if the editing was tight. I sent Sully into the back seat of the car to shine a large flashlight on Ram's head. Scotty and I both manned cameras as Karl—having obtained the keys by holding a knife at Ram's throat—exited the back seat, punched out the window, and dragged Ram Reddy through it. He held Ram high over his head and threw him down onto a couple of mattresses that had been positioned just off-camera. It was a wrap; Ram's matched brown leather pants and jacket had barely been ruffled by all the violence.

When I got back to the hotel, I just wanted to collapse into a dining room chair and order up a feast. They were used to grubby film people, but I was dirty; covered with a thick layer of Rhode Island and God only knows what else, so I dragged myself up to my room and hosed myself off.

I was too hungry to turn the pursuit of nourishment into a democratic process. I didn't want to track down anyone, wait for everyone else and then vote on where we'd eat; so I tried the hotel's main dining room. A half bottle of white wine with the *escargots* and a half bottle of red with the *tournedos Rossini* had a healing effect on my battered body and made my solitary repast a bit more entertaining.

By the time I finished with dessert, a passable *profiterole*, brandy and coffee, I was determined to return to my room and read some of Elisabeth's poetry. I paid my bill and headed upstairs to do that.

The message light was flashing on my phone when I opened the door. I called the operator to ask for my messages. "Somebody named Indrani called. She wants you to get up to room sixteen-thirteen as soon as you get in." I grabbed a notebook and pen as props for a businesslike manner and headed up to her room.

This time it was a meeting for the whole crew. Tomorrow would start with five AM call. The sunrise was a new shot for us, but the rest of the schedule, the riding, Sippy, Hammersmith Farm and more driving shots, produced a strong sense of *deja vu*. The day would finish up with staging a rainstorm in downtown Providence. Shyam said that all the special equipment was laid on.

Too late to get enough sleep, we were dismissed. I left the room with Buffy. When we were out of earshot of the room, she said, "I'm really, truly going to have to leave town when this shoot is over. I've made arrangements with the police; I've promised things to the Mayor; and Shyam and Mohammed have changed every damn thing. I have shot my political wad, as far as Providence is concerned."

"I guess Ginny had enough, too. Are they going to replace her?"

"I doubt it. They asked me to recommend someone and I refused."

Back in my room, I called Elisabeth. I apologized for waking her up.

"What makes you think you're waking me up?"

"Well, I mean—did I get you out of bed?"

"Wouldn't *you* like to know! You gonna make it for the Fourth, you international shooter, you?"

"Definitely, but…"

"You definitely do have a nice butt, but when's it gonna show up?"

"I have the feeling that they're going to work me past the last boat tomorrow, so it looks like first thing on the Fourth."

"Your butt is cutting it close, and so is that tennis player it hangs around with who's ahead by one point but *needs to get one more!*"

"One more what?" Maybe I had gotten her away from a hot Jacuzzi and a cold nightcap.

"I'm afraid to guess. One more movie? One more little-bitty shot on the Fourth? One more…"

"I'll be there," I said, "if I have to quit this film and steal a rowboat from a park. I'm sorry I interrupted you. What 'one more' thing were you going to say?"

"I don't want to think about it and I'm glad you're going to get away," she admitted—I was hearing some doubt in her voice. We said our goodbyes, but I hung up feeling that I was wearing out my welcome.

I stretched out on the floor, contemplated the ceiling, then did some yoga and calisthenics while I absorbed a television weather report for the next day—possibly cloudy in the morning, clearing off toward noon. I left a four-fifteen wakeup call.

The hotel's new polyester sheets kept me from falling asleep most of the night, so I didn't have any problems waking up. I shaved, dressed and headed into the pre-dawn darkness. I bought coffee and doughnuts and met Scotty at the usual place.

"Jesus," I said, "I forgot to call the police about that pimp."

"Well, who knows what another day will bring?" said Scotty. "Shyam might decide to save a buck on fake guns by renting real ones. We can eighty-six your particular problem and start figuring out what to do about Shyam." A car pulled up behind us. I got out to see who it was behind the glare of the headlights. It was Mohammed. "Good morning, Mohammed."

"Oh, hello, Bart," he reached a hand out the window. I shook it.

"Any word from the film or the editor about Thursday's footage?"

"Everything with the footage is fine."

"Has yesterday's footage been shipped?"

"It has been all taken care of."

I didn't like the sound of that, but I had other fish to fry. "Mohammed, could you lead Scotty and me out to the location right now so that we can begin setting up the shot?"

"That seems like an excellent scheme."

I climbed back in with Scotty and we followed Mohammed's aging Subaru out of the sleeping city. We roared through Barrington, Warren, and Bristol as if we owned the road. We paraded across the Mount Hope Bridge with its faceted gaslights aglow. We zipped past a stranded motorist whose Trans Am had obviously failed him at the crucial moment. "Shit," said Scotty.

"That's Shyam," I said. Mohammed obviously arrived at the same conclusion for his brake lights went on. "Let's get him back on course, Scotty. I'll hold on to your coffee."

Mohammed cranked his car into a hard left turn; entering a farm's driveway and coming to a stop near a shuttered produce stand. Scotty stayed on his tail and angled his car to prevent an escape. I got out and strode up to Mohammed's window. "I saw Shyam, too, but your first priority is to get me to the location. We have a sunrise and they don't wait for anyone."

"Yes, very good. I shall continue to lead," he said with resignation.

The starless sky I had been watching throughout our journey was beginning its slow transformation into a gray day. Indrani had said that the location was the Raytheon slope in Portsmouth. We passed the entrance to the Raytheon plant and Mohammed kept driving. "What the fuck is that halfwit doing now?" I asked.

"You seem to know something about this neck of the woods."

"Yeah, I was vacationing near here when Mohammed called me to follow in the path of this madness."

"Eric and his old lady are renting down here for July—Newport, I think. He can't wait to get back."

"If I'm not back there by tomorrow morning, I won't have the option any longer."

A few miles further on, there was another Raytheon plant. "Oh," I said as we followed him into the parking lot. Mohammed backed up along my side of Scotty's car, gesturing. I rolled down the window.

He gestured to the far end of the parking lot. "I suppose that the slope is down there, at the end of the parking lot." He drove off to retrieve the stranded Shyam.

"God, I hope that they really have permission to be here," I said as Scotty drove across the lot. "This has all the markings of a top secret military research place where they shoot first and ask questions later." There were no other Vishnu vehicles or personnel in the parking lot. I told Scotty what to put on the camera, fished a viewfinder and compass out of my bag, and went to scout out a shot.

'Boy, that could be beautiful,' I thought. 'Boy, they'd be sure to hate it,' I added. A dark silhouette with a peaked cap strode into the scene I was enjoying through my viewfinder. I shifted my footing to change the interloper's place in the scene I was composing. A twig snapped. "Freeze!" shouted the newcomer as he drew a large and lethal-looking handgun and spun in my direction. "Get your hands up and come out of there!"

CHAPTER 12

❀

I complied with the man behind the gun. I slipped a couple of times on the wet grassy slope and hoped that each slip wouldn't be my last. My captor appeared to be a plant guard, one Sergeant Dennehy, in the service of United Security. His gun was a .357 Magnum. "Over to the car," he spat.

Scotty was spread-eagled against one side of the car while a second guard frisked him. "May I speak without getting shot?" I asked as I strode along with my hands up.

"Your friend, here, has said enough already. That's how we found you." Sergeant Dennehy reached into the shadow under the brim of his hat to rub an invisible eye. When I arrived at the car, I was unceremoniously pushed against the side of it opposite Scotty. I rolled my eyes to indicate to Scotty that I thought we'd probably survive the adventure. "Spread 'em," commanded Dennehy as he began to frisk me.

The guard frisking Scotty was a skinny guy whose acne was becoming visible in the gathering light. "I seen dis guy setting up dis fuckin' cannon," he said, trying to impress his superior.

"That's a movie camera. We're out here to film a movie," I gently protested.

"Dat's fuckin' worse around here. Dis is a top secret area, dere. Yer cameras, dere, are a federal offense."

I try to speak very slowly when guns are being waved around. "Listen, there is a movie being shot around here. I am the head cameraman. This is my assistant. Somewhere around here are a producer, a director, an actress or two, and some grips and gaffers." I heard a car driving up behind me. Two doors slammed. A familiar voice said, "Hey, we're not shooting here. Let those guys go." It was Eric. I felt the cold steel of the gun leave my back and turned to see Eric and Sully. "Listen, you guys, the producer sent these people here by mistake. We're all set up across the road, but we need these guys to film the sun rising. We don't have much time."

I could see the disappointment in the eyes of the guards as they holstered their weapons. "I'm sorry about the misunderstanding," I said to Sergeant Dennehy. "You did a very professional job of immobilizing me, but I really have to get back to work."

"Hey, we're right across the road," Sully added helpfully. "Come on over for some coffee. It's from Mister Donut."

"Well, you'd better pack up and get over there, then," said Dennehy. We were gone in seconds.

Everyone else was waiting for us when we finally got to the location across the road. Our vehicles were parked below an embankment surrounding a reservoir. Up on the crest, Indrani was talking to George and Sippy. George was doubling for Ram in this scene and I hoped that the director was telling him to stand up straight; we knew that Ram's fans would be watching this. Sully followed me around carrying the tripod until I had selected a spot for the setup. "Did you know that those sons of bitches wanted a *sunset* shot and couldn't find a west facing vista, or whatever?" he whispered as he busied himself around the tripod.

"These people are so generous with other people's sleep. I guess I had better make it look like a sunset." I stepped over to Scotty's car, rummaged around in a filter case, and handed my selections to Scotty.

Would Ram Reddy, playing the part of an Indian assassin, skip along the skyline with a little girl? That was the action for this scene. Mansoor was earning his rate on this shot by playing music to establish the rhythm of the skipping, using the stereo in Mohammed's Subaru. It was backed up to the embankment and Indian strings and drums blasted out of its open doors.

The sky was incapable of producing either a sunrise or a sunset, according to Indrani. "Please," I said, "look through the viewfinder before you call everything off."

She looked into the viewfinder and through the filters I had specified. "Beautiful, Bart. Come, come," she addressed the crew, "we must shoot this immediately!"

We had the scene in the can after four takes.

Shyam and his apparently fixed Trans Am showed up with a styrofoam-encased breakfast from a nearby McDonald's. What could I say about a day that started off badly enough to make me grateful for a cold Egg McMuffin?

I breakfasted with Sully and Eric. "Where's the grip truck?" I asked between bites.

"Gene and Ava are taking it to Hammersmith Farm for the third setup," said Sully.

I guess that would teach me to take anything for granted. "A lot of fucking good that will do us at Castle Hill."

"A lot of good fucking they'll do until we show up at Hammersmith and knock on the truck. One more reason to carry sound blankets and sandbags," Eric said.

"Sully, do grips do it with sandbags?" I asked.

"Not when there's anybody else to do it with."

I lined up a ride to the ferry with Eric for when we got off the shoot, then set out to see if I could get the grip truck to join us at the next location. I found Vijaya Lal studying his breakfast in the back seat of the Lucknow-mobile. He was glad for any diversion from the possibility of having to eat it. "Vijaya, it seems that some member of the production team," we both rolled our eyes at that, "has sent the grip truck to the third location. I think we'll need it at the second—Castle Hill. Could you send someone to get it over there?"

"I will see to it immediately."

Our caravan made good time through the early morning traffic of Newport. We then made a number of turns that would have sent us inland anywhere but on Rhode Island's convoluted coastline.

We had come to make a tracking shot of Sippy's double riding a horse through the woods, an activity that all Indians would now know was the birthright of any American kid. I would be filming handheld from the rear of the station wagon and would have to try to keep a persistent barbed wire fence out of the bottom of my frame and assorted 'No Trespassing' signs out of the top. That would prove to be the painless part of the shoot.

The wrangler and his daughter showed up in their heavily chromed beige and brown pickup truck, hauling a matching horse trailer. The daughter, a slim dark girl who was a bit taller than Sippy, would serve as the riding double.

Shyam's eyes were shiftier than usual. He looked as if he were ready to sidestep his own shadow. I overheard him briefing Mohammed. "We must wrap up this MOS [from Von Stroheim's German *Mit Out Sound*] shot soon. We have not secured the permission of the management of the inn."

I insinuated myself into the conversation and convinced them to clear things with the inn's proprietor, "He might also be kind enough to let us use his loo," I added, "because we need the forest for filming."

"An excellent plan," beamed Shyam. "George Mukherjee, come here," he shouted, "I need you to run an important errand."

George was dispatched into the inn and returned five minutes later to announce that we could film as long as we didn't block access to the inn.

I wandered through the forest, checking the luminance of areas of light and shadow and finding some peace in escaping to where more things couldn't go wrong. I found a good, clean line for the horse to ride that would be parallel to the road, offer nothing for the horse to stumble over, and have no overhanging branches to snag the rider off the horse.

I marked the run and its start and endpoints in the forest and on the road with gaffer tape and then headed for the area where the horse was waiting with its people and ours. It was responding positively to Indrani's blandishments. The wrangler was on one side of it, having just thrown on a saddle. He pulled the girth strap to tighten up the saddle around the patient chestnut mare and there was a snapping sound. The saddle fell off onto the wrangler and Indrani displayed considerable equestrian competence in calming the startled beast. "Shit," said the wrangler as he dusted himself off.

He walked around to the back of the trailer and peered in. He grimaced and shut the door. He stalked on his high-heeled, hand-tooled boots around to the cab of the truck, opened the door and thrashed around inside. He straightened up, took a deep breath, and strode over to Indrani. "I'm sorry, ma'am. We don't seem to have a replacement girth strap. I'll just run back to the farm and get one." Before anyone could question him about the length of his proposed journey, he unhitched the horse trailer and drove the pickup away.

I read the rear license plate as the truck accelerated away. "Massachusetts," I groaned.

"Outta state," said Eric.

I hiked back through the woods to the inn's parking lot, found the station wagon I would be shooting out of, climbed into the back of it, and fell asleep.

The sound of Eric's Volvo woke me up. I found Sully asleep against a tree, woke him up, and christened him 'dolly-grip-in-charge-of-driving-the-damn-car-back-and-forth-until-we-get-it-right.'

"You better be really smooth, Sully," Scotty said as he stationed himself on the roof of the station wagon. He was lying down and facing backwards so that he could keep his manipulating hands on the camera from above. I was sitting on the tailgate of the car with my belt being gripped by Eric, who had braced himself into the back of the wagon. I would point and shoot and Scotty would change the aperture halfway through the shot.

There was still no horse, so we practiced. Sully found a smooth line for the car to run; Scotty developed cues from the trees for all the stuff he had to do to the lens; and I was having a good time.

"Too bad we don't have the grip truck," Eric said as he settled back with a cigarette.

"It should have been here by now—I asked Vijaya to get it sent over," I said.

"You backed the wrong Indian on that one. I think he's on the outs with Shyam and Mohammed," Sully offered.

"What's the problem?" I asked.

"He knows what he's doing," Eric explained. "They hate it when that happens."

Eventually, the girth strap arrived and everyone was able to stop acting like stranded tourists. Indrani changed the shot I had set up and probably had no choice in the matter since the stunt rider didn't seem to be able to take direction. My revised assignment was to frame up a shot of the empty woods, hold it until the horse came into the shot and *then* start the car rolling so that I would have the opportunity to absorb the impact of the start while Sully tried to catch up with the horse and Scotty hung on for dear life.

"Roll the camera and *action!*" would come Indrani's shrill command.

"Horse in and *roll!*" I would call to signal Sully to start the car moving.

"Shit!" Sully would say, as Indrani's fevered coaching sent him over a bump he had never encountered before.

Scotty didn't fall off for the six takes that we did of that shot. By then, I felt that there was enough for the editor to choose from.

The grip truck, of course, marked our destination at Hammersmith Farm. Gene and Ava were sunning on a bed of sandbags and smoking in a languorous post-coital way.

My notes called for a shot through a section of barbed wire fence of Sippy's double riding the horse through the gate between the upper and lower fields. As she rode toward the camera, a quick shift of focus would show the threat of the barbed wire she was riding toward. The focus would return to the horse and rider, and follow her up to the fence where the horse would recoil from the wire and unceremoniously dump her.

"Look at this shit," Buffy gasped as she labored to string up the fake wire. There was so little of it that a threatening quality was difficult to engineer.

"Let me guess," I ventured. "Shyam was in charge of acquiring the barbed wire." It would have been easy enough to buy some, but of course he hadn't done that. By now, we knew that the production had been billed for a full roll of it but we were surprised to see that he had obviously stayed up one night making fake barbed wire out of thin rope and electrical wire. The end product had been painted a dark rusty gray.

Finally, I set up a beautiful shot that conformed exactly to the director's wishes of the night before. Buffy had cosseted the wire into a very frightening configuration that would fill the frame with menace and the threat of tetanus. The wire would disappear entirely while it was out of focus, and suddenly snap into a composition of leering barbs. We finished that exercise just in time, too, because Sully was exhausted from running back and forth impersonating a horse and rider.

The director was sitting cross-legged on the ground, going over the shot with the wrangler, Sippy, her stunt double, and even the horse, who was hanging her head into the conversation with a bemused expression on her face. I approached the group and waited for the appropriate moment to interrupt.

I leaned over, tapped Indrani on her shoulder, and said, "I believe that we have set up the shot you wanted."

"Thank you, I'll have a look at it," she said as she accepted my proffered hand to rise and brushed the grass off her dress.

"This is beautiful," she said as she watched through the lens. Sully outdid himself in the field of horse impersonation and Scotty pulled focus just right. "There is a problem, though. We cannot do the shot as planned; the gate is locked and cannot be opened."

"Couldn't we send someone to get permission and a key to the gate?" I hadn't seen anyone, in fact, checking the gate.

"No, no, the gate is out. We will pick her up when she is on this side of it. Buffy," she raised her voice, "I want the wires arranged differently. I want to see more wires in the shot."

"Grumble, bitch, complain!" Buffy said when Indrani was out of earshot. "Now, I *know* that Shyam billed the company for a whole bale of barbed wire."

It was like a kid's puzzle from a highway gift shop. Buffy didn't want to cut the stuff, because there was so little of it to begin with. Finally, after a dozen attempts, we arrived at a good arrangement. "Let's go with that," I suggested.

"It's what we had to start with," she said skeptically.

"Not really, it's the mirror image. We had it going up from left to right. It was rising; aspiring; ascending. Now it's going down from left to right—threatening, falling and all that. I bet she'll love it."

"God, Bart, that's impressive bullshit."

"Thanks."

Indrani accepted the barbed wire. Without the gate to start the horse's ride from, it was difficult for the crew to set up a repeatable route so that Scotty could follow the focus and I could work movie magic with the barbed wire.

Birenda seldom spoke to me—getting all the information she required from Scotty and Vijaya. Between takes, I saw her extend a palm toward Vijaya. They had a standing bet of some sort going and he appeared to be losing. Eventually, we and the horse got comfortable and made a shot almost as nice as our first setup had been.

Lunch was being served; a cold buffet that Shyam and Indrani's mother-in-law were first in line for. The wind joined the festivities, too, tearing plates off laps and blowing over paper cups wherever they were set. In spite of the day's tight schedule, an hour was given over to the lunch break. Nobody seemed interested in joining Indrani, her mother-in-law and Shyam on a tour of the mansion. Most of the crew stretched out for a nap.

I found a pay phone attached to the guard shack and called Miss Halloran. "Bart," she greeted me, "it's been so quiet here without your fascinating intrigues."

"I wish they were all behind me. Do you know how I can reach Captain Ryan or his friend at Area D, Patrick Horan?"

She rummaged around for a moment and gave me both numbers. "What seems to be the problem?" she asked.

I explained the situation with Quinn. "It's only a matter of time until he spots me," I added, "and I can't just leave, because the movie people have the phone number on the island." I couldn't give up; I had to stay in the game.

"Well, I'll get off the line so that you can call Captain. It'll give him something to do. He loves that."

I called the number she had given me for him. While it was ringing, I admired the rambling elegance of the main house. I couldn't tell if it had been built all at once, or if additions had been governed by an iron hand that kept the passing decades at bay and continued a clapboard neo-colonial style. The sky had cleared up and the few puffs of cloud gave me a postcard vista. "Ryan, here," said a voice on the other end of the line.

"Hi, this is Bart Lane, Miss Halloran's downstairs neighbor."

"Yes, Bart, is there a problem?"

I brought him up to date. "He's set up in the pimp business here, driving around in a red Toyota, Rhode Island plate number," I consulted my notes, "six-nine-ar-eye-dee-ee. I called this in to the Providence cops, but he's still around. It's just a matter of time until he makes me."

"I'll see if I can't get someone to lean on someone else."

"That's not all," I continued. I had been absent-mindedly staring at the house. Shyam was letting himself out of the front door of the mansion. "Have you heard about the Belcourt Castle robbery a couple of days ago?"

"Oh, yes."

"Well, I think Quinn might be trying to move into that part of the antique and jewelry business." I pulled myself behind the guard shack and continued to watch Shyam. He was striding toward the grip truck.

"Well, Bart, my concern for your safety overrides breaking up a burglary ring right now. If I turn that information over to anyone, they're going to want to leave Quinn out of jail while they work up the evidence to make something bigger stick. That could take weeks, and I don't think you want that."

"You're right. Just get someone to pick the creep up. He's probably working Providence's equivalent of the Combat Zone."

"I'll get on it and stay on it. Thanks, Bart."

"One more thing, Captain Ryan, I was going to come up to Boston some time soon to pick up my mail and try to get my car started. Do you think it's safe?"

"Well, Bart, Patrick's boys chased a couple of suspicious cars out of your neighborhood. It looks like some big people are interested in you. It may have stopped, but the car registrations he ran through the computers turned up a number of shady outfits that we'd never heard of. If you have a choice—stay out of town until this thing is resolved. They hate witnesses—even redundant ones."

"Redundant ones?"

"Well, the video you shot tells it all. I don't think any prosecutor would need you on the stand, but you're a loose end. Stay out of town. Let Dorothea ship you anything you need."

"That leaves me with a car on the street outside the apartment. It might get towed. Is there any way I can deal with that?"

"I'll get 'em to hang a disabled tag on it. That, and whatever influence I have at Area D ought to hold it until we get into snow emergencies. Stop worrying about it."

I thanked him and hung up the phone, but I didn't leave the shelter of the guard shack. I looked to where I had last seen Shyam. He was no longer in evidence unless his were the feet I could see under the grip truck. Shiny, thin shoes and the cuffs of gray slacks made that a near certainty. I couldn't see any of the film crew around; they had probably found a sunnier slope to stretch out on. I made my way through the parking lot and tried to figure out a way to keep out of sight of Shyam. I found one of Vishnu's vans to hide behind.

I could barely make out what he was up to. First, he was kneeling near one of the sandbag compartments which sits under the side of the truck. Then, he was carrying sandbags and stacking them near where Gene had stacked some others. I looked around the parking lot. The elderly guard was out in the middle of it giving directions to someone in a small station wagon. Even if I told him what I thought was going on, that Shyam had stolen some small things out of the mansion and had secreted them on our truck, would it be worthwhile sending one old man up against a panicked Shyam, who might be carrying a concealed weapon?

I waited until Shyam headed for the parking lot, then joined the rest of the crew napping in the sun. Indrani and her mother-in-law were coming from the mansion. There was nothing for it but to get back to work.

Sippy, who had not learned to ride in the several days that had passed since our last visit to Hammersmith, was to fall off the horse.

I was to let her fly out of frame, keeping the horse's head, and not the mattress pile, in the shot. Everything was carefully set and rehearsed—except for the traumatic tumble—and Sippy was diligently working up the courage to ride *and* throw herself off the horse.

Indrani called for the camera to roll. It did. She called for the action to begin. It did. Sippy galloped the horse right up to the pre-arranged spot and yanked on the reins. The horse stopped suddenly and Sippy dove through the air (on camera) and onto the pile of mattresses (off camera). She landed on her recently-filled stomach. The intense pain of the experience drove several years of maturity away and she screamed, wailed, and probably cursed in Hindi.

"Did you get a good shot?" Indrani asked me calmly.

"Very nice," I replied, "but it might be nice to do it again for safety."

Indrani knelt on the ground next to Sippy, whose justifiable tantrum had subsided. No matter what she said to the child, or how she said it, the small dark head would not stop shaking back and forth. All of us on the crew understood. When she felt better, the mattresses were moved and we filmed her rolling around on the ground as if she had just landed. It was a wrap at that location.

I looked around to see Indrani's mother-in-law taking an interest in the horse. She was talking to the wrangler who was holding its head. She seemed to be interested in the saddle blanket.

While we were wrapping, Indrani took the horse for a ride. She declined the wrangler's offer of a helping hand, put her foot in the proper stirrup, swung into the saddle and sat. The horse reared up and dumped her on the ground before she could settle herself. I ran over to drag her away from the threat of wildly thrashing hooves.

The stunt rider and the wrangler got the horse calmed down. Indrani was shaken, but not hurt. "I'm very glad that I know how to fall off one of these, though I don't do it often, I assure you."

Her mother-in-law wasn't in the immediate group as the wrangler undid the girth strap and lifted the saddle off. Then he lifted the blanket off and said, "Here's the little critter that did it." He held up a large burr that had clung to the blanket.

"Indrani," I said quietly. "I think your mother-in-law put the burr under the horse's blanket. Is there any way you can get that woman out of our hair?"

"She is my responsibility. If I abandon her, I will disgrace my family."

"She's trying to kill you. If you want to sacrifice yourself, I can't stop you, but I have to think of the safety of my crew. That's part of my responsibility."

"Thank you, Bart. I'll see if I can't fob her off on the Lungalangs for a tour or something."

"You're welcome. Please keep an eye on that woman if you can't get her out of here. Listen, you're a good director and I enjoy working with you. Surely if this film works out your family will forgive you for doing what you have to do to save your life."

"You're very kind, but you don't understand. I have died in my own family and been reborn into hers. She is a problem that I cannot solve in the obvious way." She rested her hand on my shoulder. "Come, we have driving shots to do."

I wandered over to where Gene was working on the tailgate of the truck, receiving equipment from Eric and Sully. "Gene," I said quietly. "Come with me."

"Yeah, sure, Bart…"

I gave him the silence sign and led him around to the sandbag compartment. I looked around. The Indians were all out of sight, gathering in the parking lot. "Open this compartment."

He unhooked the large, full key ring from his belt and began to try the keys on the lock. "It looks like the lock I keep on it, but it's not opening."

"Are you coming with us to do the driving shots?"

"No, they're sending me back to Providence to pick up the extra lights you ordered."

"O.K. This is what you do." I steered him away from the locked compartment. "If you have nobody leading or following you, take Route Twenty-Four north toward One-Ninety-Five. North of the big bridge on Twenty-Four, there is a police station on the right. Stop there and get them to bust the lock. Anything in there that is not sandbags has probably been stolen from Hammersmith Farm. I am a witness. You got that?"

"Shit, yeah."

He climbed back onto the truck and started storing equipment that had piled up during his absence. I made sure that Sully and Eric would load everything the driving shots required into a van. Mohammed showed up to collect the exposed film from Ava. "Ah, there you are, Gene," he said. "George Mukherjee has taken my car so that he could get back to Providence to arrange his costume for tonight. Could I get a lift from you?"

"Sure," Gene replied, looking slightly overwrought.

"Gene," I said. "Forget about picking me up that extra stuff. We should be able to find a hardware store on the way back."

"Gotcha," he replied, keeping a poker face.

In no time at all, we were pulled over in an expensive new development on Ocean Drive, waiting for Shyam, who was supposed to be there with the Trans Am.

Shyam was not there.

The Lungalangs and Indrani set off in search of Shyam.

A private policeman, charged with keeping Ocean Drive safe for plutocracy, pulled up to the remaining two cars in his four by four. He gave me a hard look through his mirrored sunglasses and said, "This road is private property. You are not allowed to park here."

"Oh," I replied before I had a chance to think it out. "We're not really parking; we're working on a film." Jesus, that could have cooked our goose.

"Well, then, be careful and have yourselves a good shoot." He drove off with a whir of big-treaded sand and rock tires.

Shyam was not so much found as shaken out of the environs. With the Lungalangs and Indrani searching for him, he simply appeared, by himself in the banquet manager's coupe. I put Buffy, Eric and Sully to work on the car, getting it ready for the shot. The cleaning, stripping and rigging went so quickly that I was soon sitting in it, holding a fully prepared camera and waiting for the director to return from the hunt for the elusive Shyam.

She eventually arrived, marched over to the car I was waiting in, and climbed into the driver's seat. Scotty gave me and the camera a last once-over, and did a thumbs-up. "Shyam," she called, "please have everyone follow us to the location for the drive-by shots. Bart?"

"Yes," I replied, wondering if this was when our relationship might begin a new chapter.

"Be ready to roll when I tell you." She started the engine. Gravel spewed and rubber squealed as she accelerated the car off the shoulder and onto the macadam. The acceleration pushed the camera into my face. Through the lens I saw the approach of a curve, bounded on one side by a rock face rising up like a stone wall, and on the other by a sheer drop of one hundred feet to the surf pounded rocks below. "Roll!" she cried as she floored the accelerator. The camera filled the air with the sound of a coffee grinder. The car squealed out of the curve behind some sightseers dawdling along. I started to reach my thumb toward the camera's switch. "Keep rolling!" She up-shifted and swerved the car over the double yellow line and left the mere mortals in her wake. She came back into the right hand lane and promptly downshifted while I used all of my strength to keep the camera from flying through the windshield. The car screamed around another sharp rock-lined corner. Ahead of us lay a beautiful scenic straight-away where loomed large summer homes of the rich and famous. It looked just like my vision of 'shots along Ocean Drive.' "Cut!" called Indrani.

She slowed the car until the straight stretch had run out and we were approaching a curve cut into a rock face. "Roll!" she called as she plunged her foot down on the accelerator and took us around the turn in a four-wheel drift. Four cyclists had been at rest as they pondered the size and majesty of the sea. They scattered. I had no way to check if they survived. "Cut!" She turned to me, inhaling deeply and looking as if she had just enjoyed a bedroom bout with an incredible sexual athlete. "Do you think we have done enough?" she inquired coyly.

Jesus, I thought, she had done too much considering that we had no permission to be there, no police sealing off the road to protect the public from her driving, and no stunt driver to insure that I'd make it back alive. "You're the director, but if we want some passing shots in the same light, I think we had better get to work on them."

Looking, driving, pointing and discussing, we found an appropriate corner guarded by several grand old stone mansions. Scotty found us a few minutes later, carrying most of the crew and equipment in his station wagon. I passed the camera to Scotty and walked off with Indrani. She and I were directing each other; she, telling me what to do with the camera, and me, telling her what to do with the car. Since we were down to a skeleton crew, she would impersonate Ram for the shot. I picked low angles with glaring reflections from the car's windows so she would be almost invisible.

I went back to work with Sully and Scotty on the setup for the shot and Indrani drove off with Eric. In the absence of Walkie-talkies, he would have to stand at a corner of the road and relay hand signals. Then he would have to hide behind a privet hedge.

We did it in two takes. The driver had remained nearly invisible. "How did I look?" she asked after the final take.

"Very, very butch," I answered.

"'Warm and touching,' Vincent Canby, N.Y.Times," said Sully.

"Not unlike an invisible Ram Reddy," piped Scotty.

"Good," said Indrani. "It's a wrap on this location."

"This has been a very fishy day," ventured Eric as Scotty's car carried us across the Mount Hope Bridge.

"This is true," I agreed, enjoying the view of Narragansett Bay. "Near arrest for espionage, God only knows what happened at Hammersmith."

"It's just that almost everything had been designed to leave us stranded in very expensive places," Eric continued, "waiting for all of this stuff Shyam should have taken care of."

"What about the locked gate at Hammersmith?" I asked.

"I tried to get out there to check the lock, and Mohammed headed me off," Buffy complained. "He sent me to use the pay phone to check on the caterer."

"That and the barbed wire were the only things that could hold us up there, unless they wanted to kill someone," Scotty added dryly.

I told them what I thought Shyam was up to and what I had tried to get Gene to do, only to be foiled by Mohammed. "So, tonight is Kennedy Square and Benefit Street," I continued, trying to get back to the movie business.

"Yep," said Eric, "right in the middle of town. Providence folks are so gung-ho about hanging out there that two restaurants in *trailers* set up there every night." He groaned. "We are not looking at a peaceful evening."

"What about Benefit Street?" I asked.

"It's the most expensive-looking area in Providence," piped Buffy, "right next to Brown University with gaslights and the whole bit."

"So we're supposed to go up there in the middle of the night and make a lot of noise?" I asked.

"Or create a major diversion?" Eric contributed.

CHAPTER 13

❀

B uffy shuffled some papers as we arrived at the hotel. "Dinner is in the saloon downstairs, on the company," she reported. "They're breaking the crew into two dinner shifts. Eric and Sully will be rigging the limousine while the rest of us eat. They're also going to be arranging the rainstorm with the firemen."

"So, on our behalf, the Providence Fire Department is going to sponsor a cooling shower on one of the hottest nights of the summer, right in the middle of town?" I asked.

"Yup," she replied. "Lotsa luck."

I arranged a ride to Warren with Eric before he and Sully headed grumblingly for the grip truck. Settling in next to Gene in a booth, I asked him quietly, "Any luck with that locked sandbag compartment?"

"Well, you saw Mohammed riding shotgun. He got me out of the truck just after we picked up the extra lights. I had to run the rental forms right up to Shyam's room, right?"

"Right."

"When I got back to the truck, the compartment was still locked, but the lock looked a little older. It opened with my key. The compartment was empty."

"So Shyam and/or Mohammed have emptied it out and secreted the loot somewhere else," I speculated.

"Well, when I went upstairs, the TV was playing so loudly in Shyam's room that he couldn't hear my knock on the door. I finally had to shove the rental contract under the door." Gene shrugged and continued, "It was either that or wait for the commercial. Maybe he wasn't there."

After I had ordered the most expensive steak on the menu, I excused myself and found a phone. I called Elisabeth collect.

"I have a collect call from Mr. Park Lane, will you accept?" said the operator.

"I don't know," came the measured tones of the woman I was trying to reach.

"Operator," I said, "tell her that I'll promise to behave."

"We can't relay messages until the *char-ges* are *accep-ted*," said the operator.

"Well, tell her I promise to be there to pay for the call tomorrow," I said.

"Well, in that case, I'll accept," said Elisabeth.

"You may *proceed* with your *communication*," sang the operator.

"Hello, it's me," I said.

"Hi, you."

"I will be arriving on the ten boat tomorrow. If I'm not on the ferry, check the water around the dock, because I'll be swimming in from Providence."

"It's a deal," she said.

"I can't wait to see you," I said.

"That's nice," she replied.

I explained that I was still working and we said our good-byes. I had the feeling that she thought I was cutting it a bit close.

The conversation around the dinner table was heavy on sighs and groans. It was over twelve hours since we had begun work.

After dinner, I checked on Eric and Sully. They had installed a basic lighting setup in the aging Cadillac, powered by a trunk full of automobile batteries. I sent them off to their dinner. Gene fetched me the few items I needed to refine the lighting and make things a little more organized.

I stuck my head out a window and spotted George Mukherjee, who would be playing Ram's part as the driver. "George, do you have the keys for this thing?"

"Mohammed should have them, and he's eating dinner. I will fetch them promptly."

It took him about fifteen minutes to round up the keys. The car was a real sweat box by then, so I got out of it and walked a couple of blocks to check the preparations for the rain storm. I heard the unmuffled roar of fire fighting equipment before I saw anything. A large truck was positioned near the area we would be shooting. It reached fifty feet heavenward with a telescoping arm that was crowned with a water spout. The apparatus was directed from the ground by remote control. A few people were watching and the more adventurous of them, kids in gym shorts and running shoes, were darting in and out of the spray.

I joined Eric who was talking to the firemen operating the spray. "How's it going?" I asked.

"They're getting the height right. They claim that they can get any kind of spray we want."

"Let's make sure it looks like a rainstorm, and not some guy shooting a fire hose."

"Roger," Eric said.

I went back to the car by way of the front of the Biltmore. Birenda had mentioned that its marquee would be included in the shot, and since Shyam had probably negotiated its appearance in the film against our room rates, I thought I'd do what I could to make it look good. The marquee was just the right brightness to match the level of our lighting in the limousine.

Back at the car, I was greeted by George, self-consciously wearing a chauffeur's uniform and cap. "Impersonating Ram Reddy yet again?"

"Oh, yes," he replied. "You are not supposed to see the front of my face, are you?"

"Nope, not this close."

"Ah, I am relieved. I am blind as a bat without my spectacles."

Indrani was all business as she breezed into our midst. "Let's get into the car and get started."

"We are all set to include the front of the hotel with all of its lights and brass," I volunteered, trying to break the ice.

"We have already used that in another sequence, so we won't be shooting it tonight. Come, let's get to work." Birenda, standing nearby with her clipboard, rolled her eyes at this latest change in the scenario.

Working like a dutiful squire, Scotty armed me with the camera, buckled a battery belt around me and gently guided me into the center of the back seat. Then, he and Gene wrapped me and the camera in black cloth until only the camera's lens protruded. George started up the car, which didn't seem to be running very smoothly. As he eased the car into traffic, Indrani said, "Bart, I don't want to see George's face in the rear view mirror. George," she called in a louder voice.

"Yes," he replied as he turned the car onto a busier street.

"Take off your glasses!"

Suddenly, I felt grateful to be protected by the black velour blanket in the back seat of a limousine being driven by a blind man through a fake rainstorm in the middle of Providence on a hot summer night. I also missed seeing several things that might have put me off: the snack wagon that had moved in right next to the fire truck; the fireman who, in demonstrating the hose, had shattered a streetlight and an insurance agent's window; and the huge, volatile crowd that was being drawn to all this activity like bugs to a lantern on a summer night.

George was concentrating on following the white line down the middle of the street—there was nothing else he could see without his glasses. He didn't notice that he had almost been hit by a topless Jeep whose owner, infected by the mood of the swelling crowd, was driving back and forth through the torrent of water.

A couple of blocks down the street, Indrani said, "This is far enough, George. Turn the car around. Are you ready, Bart?"

"Mmf," I replied.

"Blink the headlights, George. Eric will get everything ready and wave us through."

Through the lens, I saw a tiny Eric appear in the middle of the street—two blocks away—and wave.

"Drive, George. Take that first right turn after the rain starts." He drove forward through his personal fog to find our custom rainstorm.

"Camera," called Indrani.

"Rolling and…speed," I replied, though I'm sure it came out 'mmf.' Under a stream of sweat, I watched the shot through the camera's flickering viewfinder. The nose of the large black car and the back of George's head framed the shot. The rain hit hard, just like a sudden cloudburst. Eric and the rest of the crew were keeping the crowds well out of the shot. Suddenly, the topless Jeep drove right under the center of the torrent, stopped, and its owner stood up, beating his naked chest to the wild approval of the crowd.

"Cut," said Indrani. "Let's do it again."

Blind George Mukherjee slowly navigated his way through several circles and turnouts that divided Kennedy Square according to some urban planner's traffic scheme. I got out from under the blanket and, for a moment, I was probably the only person in Providence who found the night air cool. A fat lady, clad only in jiggling striped satin shorts and a strained tank top, stepped back to allow our limousine to pass. Near the water cannon, Indrani called for Eric to stand by for another run. Scotty made eye contact with me to check if I needed anything. I didn't. I looked around for a policeman, a customary figure on street shoots; there wasn't one in sight.

Two more trips through the fake rainstorm yielded two good takes. Eric's timing and crowd control were essential to our success. "Okay, very good," Indrani commented briskly after the second take. "Now we need to set up a shot from Eric's corner. I want the widest shot you can give me that shows the car driving into the rain."

George put on his glasses with obvious relief and then shuddered as he contemplated the mobbed square. I set the camera aside and climbed around the car turning out lights. George dropped me and the camera off at our corner—in the middle of the mob.

Scotty was there to take the camera off my hands. He had brought his car right up to the camera position. Sully materialized with garbage bags to cover the equipment and an umbrella for the camera crew so that we could set up as close as possible to the water spout. This would yield the widest wet shot available. "Uh, Bart," Sully said when he had finished covering everything valuable in sight.

"Yeah, Sully," I answered as I lined up the shot through the camera.

"I think that the crowd is turning ugly."

"I'll try to get us out of here quickly."

"Thanks," he said.

I checked my watch—it was eleven PM—eighteen hours into the day. Indrani joined me at the camera and I showed her the shot I had lined up.

"It's very nice, but I would like a pan shot so that we can follow him around the corner."

"There is almost no room to pan with this spray."

"See how wide you can get the spray. Maybe you can move the camera into the str…" she was cut off by the cheering crowd. The jeep driver had come to a full stop under the spout. The firemen had compressed the spray so that a blast of water threatened to flush the beered-up adolescent out of his car. Undaunted, he was standing on the seat, jumping up and down in the torrent and bearing its brunt on his apparently impervious buzzcut skull. Then he sat down in the driver's seat, still blinded by the spray, and started to drive off. Scotty and I started to shift the camera and tripod into the street at the same time that the departing jeep made a quick U-turn, its knobby tires coming up over the curb. The crowd shifted and some of the barely dressed kids began to run out past the camera into the cooling storm, and into our shot.

The first take of George driving the limousine into the cloudburst wasn't usable because the shower takers could not be kept out of the shot. Vijaya tried to coax the urchins out of the street. He would clear them off in one direction and more would flood the scene from another direction. George was weaving the limousine uncertainly back to its start marks. The lessons of the Jeep driver, however, were not lost on more prudent Providence residents who began to drive their sedans and station wagons in under the torrent to wash them.

I heard the siren of a police car. Maybe we'd get some help with this mob. I saw the flashing lights swerve around the limousine where George awaited the call of 'action.' The headlights were weaving back and forth while the flashing blue lights tracked straight toward us. The police were not coming to our rescue—they were in hot pursuit.

I was transfixed by the approaching light show. As the pursued vehicle passed under the surviving streetlight nearest us it revealed itself to be a red Toyota. They were chasing Quinn, the son of a bitch! Sully and Eric pulled me out of the street—I dragged the camera; not out of any heroism, but because it offered some perceived safety. As the budget pimpmobile fled past us, I made fleeting eye contact with the desperate, angry eyes of the knifer. In that instant, I knew that he had recognized me.

"You okay, Bart?" It was Sully.

"Yeah, thanks for saving my life. You, too, Eric."

"Thanks for saving the camera, Bart," said Scotty. "That guy—the one being chased—looked familiar. Was that the slasher?"

"Yeah."

"Did he make you?"

"Without a doubt." I took a deep breath. I raised my voice, "Let's get some crowd control working here!"

"No way," responded Eric, Sully and Buffy in unison.

"You're right." I started to laugh.

"I got a bitchin' production still of the rescue," piped Giancarlo.

I turned and saw a half dozen members of the mob beginning to use Scotty's car as bleachers for the spectacle. "Hey," I bellowed in a voice that had apparently never experienced the benefits of higher education, "get da fuck offa da cah!" The car was immediately cleared and given a wide berth. "Not bad for a Williams man," I added quietly to an appreciative Scotty.

I ordered a lens with a narrower field of view from Scotty and waded through the crowd to try to buy a cup of coffee at the nearest snack wagon. They had sold out of everything.

Using the narrower field of view as a defense against joyriders, carwashers, thrill seekers and the damned jeep, a usable take was made.

"I think we have sufficient coverage of this material to cut with Entwhistle Kidd's rainy footage," said Birenda, studying a clipboard that had miraculously remained dry.

"Vijaya," I called into the crowd.

"Yes, Bart," he emerged from the mob looking like a drowned rat.

"Please inform Madame Director that we have lost this location and tell the crew that it's a wrap here."

"Yes." He raised his voice. "It's a wrap here."

Word from the director arrived simultaneously. It translated into: "Let's get our asses the hell out of here!" Not only had the location become unworkable; the crowd was becoming even uglier.

We packed with incredible speed. It was after midnight and we were beginning our twenty-first hour, but we all knew that the day's work was not yet done. The next stop would be Benefit Street, where we were scheduled to 'pick up some driving shots.'

Scotty swung his car in behind the Lucknow-mobile, the limousine, and the grip truck and we lumbered across Providence. As we crossed the Providence River on a low bridge, we passed the Jeep that had been plaguing us all night long. The driver, still soaked, appeared to be in a state of near nervous and physical collapse as he alternately made attempts to bail out his machine with an oil can and occasionally struggled faintly to erect the Jeep's fabric top. I understood his exhaustion.

The grip truck whined loudly in first gear as the caravan climbed Federal Hill. Most of the windows were dark; it looked like the inhabitants had ended their day hours ago. This was a very expensive neighborhood, illuminated solely by gas lamps.

With loud gear clashings and door slammings, the caravan pulled over. I felt like what we were doing was criminal. These people had a right to sleep undisturbed. In spite of the fact that film companies often seemed to make their own laws, filming high-speed chases, crashes and explosions, there are some unwritten rules of conduct. If we had started shooting in this neighborhood before dusk, and everyone knew who we were and what we were doing, it would be no ethical crime to work all night; we would expect to. Showing up cold at one AM was simply not done.

"Scotty, have one magazine ready with the fast film," I said as I tried to get up the energy to climb out of the car and talk to Indrani and Edward Lungalang, "and get everything else unloaded and ready to ship."

I wandered over to the van. I rolled back the side door and spoke to Vijaya. "What has been planned for this location?"

"She wants to film the limousine driving slowly down this street," said Vijaya.

Birenda rustled some papers and added, "...and she wants to film the limousine driving into three or four alleys. She wants the action covered with POV shots and exteriors."

"Could you show me what she had in mind?" I asked Vijaya.

He dragged himself out of the van.

When we were out of earshot I stopped him. "What's going on, here? I can't be responsible for setting up a circus in the middle of the night."

"Shyam said that the fire department will soon be here with a generator."

"Have you ever heard a fire department generator?"

He shook his head.

"They're very, very loud. Everyone within three blocks of here will be awakened by the noise. Has Shyam arranged anything else here?"

"I seriously doubt it." Vijaya tried to rub his eyes awake.

"Shyam is running some kind of a con, isn't he?"

"I'm afraid that much of the evidence points to this."

It was only getting later. No fire department generator was arriving. Nobody else had gotten out of any of the Vishnu vehicles. "What is Shyam's angle?"

"I don't know all of it, and I hope I never find out," Vijaya said softly. "I came here to do my job, but I think Shyam came to America for an entirely different reason. To us, America—and all of the West—is a young culture. Some Indians look on it as a place where you take what you can—any way you can get it."

"Like pirates and shipping lanes?" I volunteered.

"Like the cowboys and the other Indians."

"Thanks," I said. "I had better go and talk to the director."

An exhausted Indrani and a copiously sweating Edward Lungalang were sitting in the front seat of the Lucknow-mobile. Shyam had secreted himself in the back seat, his eyes darting between Edward and Indrani. It looked like the two of them were dragging Indrani over the coals. A blast of air-conditioning greeted me when Edward rolled down the window. I asked them what they had in mind for the location. Edward quickly, as if to cover up a conversation about something else, outlined the shots that Vijaya had just listed for me.

"We haven't got all night," I said. "What you are describing is a full night's work, and *that* is a night that hasn't been proceeded by a very full day."

"Can you do it?" Edward's dark eyes bored out of his round face.

"I've already put in two and a half days today." I gave Edward the steeliest gaze I could muster. "*I* can do a little bit more, but I don't know about anyone else. I do know that *if* the fire department arrives and starts up the generator, the very influential citizens who live here will have everything shut down before we do take one."

"That's it. It's a wrap," pronounced Edward. From Indrani's side of the seat came a sigh of relief. Shyam was transfixed in the back seat, staring straight ahead; saying nothing. "Send the crew over for their checks," Lungalang added.

I was glad that he came through with a little class. We film technicians give extra points to producers who hang around after a day's work and write checks on the hood of their cars.

I spread the good news. Buffy reached into her canvas carryall and produced a bottle of Wild Turkey. "Take, drink," she intoned ecclesiastically, "this is my bottle."

"Will this movie be made?" Eric asked as rhetorically as he could without letting out too much of the smoke he had just inhaled. The crew was in his room. He passed me the joint.

"It better be," said Scotty. "They rented the truck for a piece of the profits when the film starts to make money. Some small operator in Nashville is going to have to subscribe to the Indian equivalent of *Variety* to find the first nickel from this. Vishnu made a similar deal with Souperfilm Laboratory for the developing."

I coughed on the resinous smoke. "Souperfilm? They're the best in the business."

"You got it." Scotty shook his head in disbelief. "They tried to make a deal with Birenda Avukaderkutty to edit the thing. She told 'em to find another woman."

"She's probably pissed at the way they're treating Vijaya," Buffy put in. "They got him to put the deals together in India—to get Ram Reddy and Anouk—and then be the assistant director over here. He's getting one thousand dollars, period. I think they're trying to get him to quit before he collects that."

We were stunned into silence by that. If this had been a union shoot with overtime, most of us would have cleared that much in the past twenty-four hours.

Gene broke the silence. "Let's have a toast to the man who pulled the plug. Especially since there are a couple of inches left in his bottle of Scotch."

Eric dropped me off near the cannery in Warren with several minutes to spare. I got my stuff on board and spent a few minutes helping haul other people's beer on board. I also kept an eye out for Quinn. I didn't see him, or anybody who looked like his Boston crew.

On the upper deck, I covered my ears for the parting blast of the ferry's horn and settled back to enjoy the perfect, slightly hazy, summer day.

I hadn't realized how much I really needed to be there until I spotted Elisabeth in the waiting crowd on the Squidneck dock. Seeing her face light up as she spotted me caused the fatigue to flow off me in waves. Here was this beautiful, amazing woman and she was waiting for *me*! I disembarked with my bags to a dock full of kissing and hugging, but I seriously doubt that anyone else was having the heavily sensuous experience that I was, as Elisabeth pressed herself against me. "I used every trick in the books to get here," I said. "I feel like the welcome is much warmer than I deserve."

"Yeah," she grinned and picked up half of my bags. "I was just thinking of one of my classmates. She started going with this guy after she was out a couple of years, and soon afterwards, whenever I asked how he was, or how it was with him, she'd go into this bit about their 'working on their relationship.'"

"Uh huh," I swung my bags into the bed of the truck. So did she, with an uncanny sense of which ones should be set down carefully.

"After a few years of that, I asked her the usual question and she answered that they had broken up. They both got bored silly with continuously working on the relationship and never enjoying it."

"And…"

"This," she let out the clutch and truck began to climb out of the parking lot, "is a wild weekend."

I probably should have spent more time reflecting on what had been said and what had not, but I started telling her about the agonies and ecstasies of working on *Mysore Karma* and realized that she should know about the latest development with the knifer. "I have a problem. Last night, the guy who sliced Nick definitely spotted me behind the camera. He also knows one of the producers from supplying hookers as extras. Mohammed knows your phone number, and he is the second most suspicious guy on the shoot."

"Let's update the policeman." She wheeled the truck into a driveway, and turned around. "Well, it's not as if I've ever run for my life before," she said, "but I know that the only information that they'll get from the phone company if they track down my number, is the fact that I'm on the island. They'll have to come over here and ask if they want to get closer than that." She pulled the truck up as Perkins was about to climb into his cop-equipped jeep.

"Howdy, Miss Elisabeth," he touched the visor of his cap, "hi, there," he added, looking across at me.

"John, Bart says that there's still a problem. There is…Bart?"

I brought him up to date and mentioned being spotted by Quinn. "Now he knows I'm with the movie…"

"I'll get the sheet on him from Boston. Anyone else?"

I told him of my suspicions.

"So, we're worried about people who show up looking for Hemphill's, right? Expecting any more house guests, Miss Elisabeth?"

"No," she replied.

"Well, I'll tell Jessica and some of the other people who hang out here about it. If anybody asks for your place, we'll find them before they find you."

"Thank you, John."

"It's a pleasure, Miss Elisabeth. Have a nice Fourth. You, too, Mr...."

"Bart," I said, "Lane."

"You, too, Mr. Lane," he said.

"Miss Elisabeth, eh?" I said when we were once again en route.

"You bet. The grandparents were Mr. and Mrs. Hemphill. My dad will always be Jack. I'll be Miss Elisabeth until either I become Mrs. Something or my peers take over the general store and the constabulary, in which case I'll be Elisabeth. I've said 'Call me Elisabeth' to all those people, but they have a couple of thousand names to keep straight, so I'm Miss Elisabeth."

The perfect day made it hard to concentrate on people who might be trying to kill me. The occasional fireworks were unsettling, but I cavalierly told myself that I'd never hear the bullet that had my name on it. Driving up to Elisabeth's fortress really did vanquish all thoughts of Quinn, Shyam and Mohammed.

After we carried my bags into the house and left them in the bedroom, we became entangled in a provocative embrace. I started pulling the Quahog Heights Athletic Association T-shirt free of her cutoff jeans. She stopped me just as I had gotten one hand onto her bare waist. "We've got to make chowder for the blowout tonight, then maybe you can get some rest on the beach. You must be exhausted!"

"Chowder for how many?"

"About fifty. You remember Don Bachman, the beach bum you met on the dock?"

"Definitely."

"He dropped off about a hundred pounds of quahogs yesterday, so let's get started."

Processing a hundred pounds of large, heavy-shelled clams and making a vat of chowder are more like manufacturing than cooking. Still, with Elisabeth and a few Rolling Rocks, it was fun. I steamed the clams open in large batches and peeled potatoes, and Elisabeth rendered a couple of pounds of fatback and chopped onions and potatoes.

It was as we were adding the flour to the mass of sautéed onions and potatoes that things began to heat up between us. I was working a long wooden spoon with both hands, while Elisabeth held onto the large pot with one hand and sprinkled the flour in with the other. There was a lot of warmth and friction between our bodies. "Don't stop now," she blew into my ear as she emptied the last of the flour into the mass I was stirring. She poured the first quart of clam broth in. It was speedily absorbed but the stirring became easier. The air was filled with steam and the light muskiness of freshly cooked clams.

The second quart began to thin the consistency of the chowder to where I could stir it with one hand. Elisabeth was beautiful when she sweated heavily. I worked my free hand around her waist and started moving it up under her shirt. To have a hand on one of the very breasts that had been doing such interesting things to that QHAA T-shirt was very exciting. She drew more tightly against me, moaning softly until she said, "I…think we can let it simmer with a cover on for a couple of hours…The chowder, that is."

Had it been a week, a month, or a lifetime since we had been so close? I lifted her shirt up over arms and hair stretched toward the beamed ceiling, her bronzed breasts popping proudly into the light of day. We reached the living room couch, almost too far, leaving a trail of clothes. A rivulet of perspiration tried to make a break for it but my tongue caught up with it somewhere south of her collarbone.

She settled back onto the sofa, bringing her hair over her shoulder with one hand and grabbing me with the other. I wallowed on the waves of her as she rode my storm. I was swept past chivalry and courtesy. Fortunately, she was running on the same timetable. We exploded together with a ferocity that spilled us off the sofa and onto the floor.

We lay spent, watching diamond-paned shadows playing across each other until the sizzling of a boiling-over chowder pot from the kitchen reminded us of our culinary responsibilities.

I used a couple of hours of beach time to catch up on my sleep. Elisabeth woke me before I burned and set out a picnic lunch of sandwiches and beer. Whenever my eyes were open, I found myself simply amazed by the beauty of the woman, the place, and the day. I also felt insubstantial; a careening calamity with armed pursuers punctuating my string of failures. I wanted to become part of her life and make her part of mine, but I knew that if I opened my big mouth I'd hear, 'You're really nice, but…' This is what happens to underemployed guys named Bart from Berea who have people trying to kill them. Who was I trying to kid?

The traditional Fourth of July celebration on Squidneck amongst the kids, a group which included us, is a bonfire. Wood is collected for it during spring cleaning, beachcombing, and various construction projects. The pile, which begins to dominate a piece of uninhabited beach, is almost always augmented by an unrepairable quahogger's boat.

Other arrangements occur just as effectively, as if by telepathy. These people probably sorted out who brings what a couple of decades ago. Elisabeth and I arrived, hauling the chowder, some paper bowls, plastic spoons and napkins. Don greeted Elisabeth's truck by passing something to smoke through the window, so we were stoned out of our tiny minds by the time we got our contribution to the food table.

News on Squidneck still travels by the coconut wireless—quickly. I usually have to give a guest lecture at a film school to have so many people milling around wanting to meet me. Elisabeth's fellow kids had all heard about me.

Don took me aside and shoved a beer into my hand. "Hey, man, Constable John told me about your little problem."

"Does everybody…"

"It's cool, man. He knows that I'm either on the dock or the beach somewhere. It sounds like you got into something a little heavy."

I gave a capsule description of my experience with Quinn.

"That would be wicked pisser if that asshole should come around here looking for you. I mean, if you shoot the fucker…"

"Yeah," I said though I had no intention of shooting anyone.

"Some other asshole is going to show up and try to shoot you just for revenge."

I definitely agreed with him there.

"But," his eyes weren't glazed over now, "if you do the son of a bitch with a clam rake. They'll take one look at the body, or even just read in the papers about this huge fuckin' claw that just *did* the dude….you won't have any more problems with those assholes. Hey, it looks like you're good for Elisabeth."

"Oh, thanks…"

"No, man, I mean it. She's glowing, her coat is sleek. She looks happy. Her teeth are—Elisabeth! Get your ass over here so I can check your teeth!" She obliged. "See, her teeth are great. Seriously."

Elisabeth shot me a look that indicated that Don did this kind of thing to his friends. "Don, are you going to dental school now?"

"No, man. That's too much like work. I was just telling Bart that I thought he was good for you. You smile more." He held forth with a monologue that was impossible to interrupt with conversation. When he finally asked me what else I did on the mainland, I probably sounded like a pathological liar with my response. I'd had the kind of year that included everything from the evening news to a special shot for a Hollywood feature. Later, when Elisabeth and I were watching the fire send showers of sparks into the sky, I heard him talking to someone else. "He's okay," came the beery baritone, "I couldn't understand half of what he was telling me, but I could tell he's okay."

"Well, you seem to have impressed our Don, among others," Elisabeth whispered into my ear.

A vaguely familiar woman came up to Elisabeth and me. "The chowder is better than ever!" It wasn't until she opened her mouth that I recognized her as Judy Arban. The sun and some relaxing had transformed her into a fairly ravishing specimen—even—or possibly especially—in a T-shirt and tight shorts. Jon was almost similarly unrecognizable without his glasses. "How does your chowder just get better every year?"

"Well," said my companion demurely, "I did have some help."

"Are you going to tell me that El Hunko, here, cooks, too?"

Heavens, I thought, here I am, a beefcake legend in my own time. "He's been known to scorch the odd filet. To perfection, of course," Elisabeth replied breezily.

"That's not fair," Judy elbowed Jon to underscore her response. "Well, now that you know the recipe for the best chowder, what are you going to do? Hit Conanticut Island?"

"But I don't know the recipe yet. She distracted me just as she was adding the secret ingredients."

"Distraction? Is that what I am?"

We finally moved away from the Arbans while we were all still on speaking terms, though I doubted that Jon would be calling me either for cooking lessons or male bonding activity.

Somebody cranked up Louie, Louie on a ghetto blaster. Genuine baby boomers are incapable of anything but wild gyrations when that anthem fills the air. We danced well together; to that and the hours of music that followed. We began to move down the beach. The burning quahogger's skiff collapsed to a cheer from the crowd.

Up beyond the bonfire's sparks, the incredible star-filled sky reminded me that we were all citizens of the Milky Way. It was the most intense Fourth of July celebration I had ever experienced.

"Distracted, eh?" said Elisabeth. The party was a distant throb; we were pulling the chowder pots out of the truck.

"Well, I wasn't going to spill your recipe to Judy and I didn't want to say, 'Get lost, bitch, you can't have it.'"

"Why don't you get out some more Maui Wowee or Chihuahua Laughing Tobacco when we get this stuff back to the kitchen. I'll show you 'distracted.'" Her eyebrows arched provocatively.

A few minutes later, we were down at her beach. She stuck a bare foot in the water, and it sparkled. "What is that?"

"Phosphorescent jellyfish," she replied. "See where they're hitting the shore?"

The sparkle was everywhere, but you could see the outlines of the organisms if you concentrated. They could be glowing aliens. "You're probably wondering why I've asked you here tonight," she said as she finished unbuttoning her shirt and started pulling mine over my head.

The first embrace of goose bump-covered flesh on a cool summer night is very arousing. Moonlit and naked, we settled into the warm water. We glided, sparkling, into deeper water, swimming and caressing with hands, tongues and hair. We moved like gods light years long, at play among the stars.

CHAPTER 14

❀

*E*lisabeth wanted to drive me up to Providence to catch the train to New York. In spite of a thoroughly fun and exhausting weekend, it seemed easy to catch the nine boat on Sunday morning. I didn't see anyone who looked like Quinn or a hit man coming off the ferry, so we boarded and rode into the sunrise on a nearly empty boat; a very stylish backdrop against which we read the Sunday papers and enjoyed the cruise. I was savoring the peace, because I knew that with Vishnu Films there wouldn't be much of it in my immediate future.

The orange car started up quickly and hurtled us toward Providence. "Why," said Elisabeth when we were under way, "are you going back to that movie? It doesn't seem safe or sane."

"It would be nice to have a piece of a feature to show what I can do. Even if it's in Sanskrit or Hindi, it has some of the best work I've ever done. Then, there's the crew; Scotty, Eric, Sully and Buffy have been working so damn hard on the film that I'd hate to abandon them."

"That's a nice instinct, Bart, but their asses are not on the line. It seems that somebody wants you dead. This is no time for games. You can win this one by getting out while you're still alive."

Unfortunately, it's necessary to go through a piece of Massachusetts in order to get to Providence. A thundering, rusted Chevrolet cut us off in an unsignaled lane change just after we got on to I95 West in Fall River. Fortunately, it gave me a few moments to think.

"Why can't Massachusetts drivers pretend, just a little, to be civilized and competent?" Elisabeth complained as she braked to avoid a collision.

"I had hoped that the worst of them would still be in bed or the emergency ward after last night."

"So, you must be ready for more adventures in the wonderful world of movies."

"I'm ready to hope that there won't be any adventures, just a chance to make some pretty pictures and get paid. I'm starting to think that I'm the only person who can bring this movie off, and I want to. I guess I feel…that I've been such an independent idiot in the past, that I don't have a choice anymore."

"You really have to stop that 'unemployed person' crap," she looked at me and checked the mirror on my side before whipping the car over one lane. "You've been working. The phone has been ringing for you. You seem to be very successful for someone who is not in New York or Hollywood."

"Thanks," but if she only knew of the days and weeks that could go by without a nibble; the overwhelming feeling that you have missed the boat; lost two points in a row in the big game and…

"What do you feel about me?"

Just what I needed when I was trying to psych myself up for the pursuit of fame and fortune miles from her side. I felt grateful. I felt smothered. "Incredibly grateful."

"You're welcome." She set her jaw and concentrated on the road just a little more than the Braga Bridge warranted.

I wanted to sweep this woman off her feet. I wanted to stop being an economic eunuch and try to give her some fraction of what she had given me. "I find you very attractive."

"Are you *trying* to put me off?"

"No. I'm trying to organize my thoughts."

"I like what I've encountered of your thoughts, Bart. You have some very pleasant, interesting and entertaining thoughts. What about your feelings?"

"I'm trying to organize them, too."

"Organized *feelings*? What is this, a game of *Old Maid*? You're shuffling your hand and I get to pick a card—any card?" She pressed down on the accelerator to block a BMW that was trying to pass us on the right at ninety per. "I can't believe your spontaneity."

"My experience hasn't run to group therapy." Oh, Christ, I didn't mean it like that...but it did buy some silence and a chance to look at some of the highway department's expensive forests.

Elisabeth swung the car onto the exit from Route l95 to Route 95. She made about three lane changes on the ramp, leaving almost an even dozen of assorted vehicles in the lurch. Snarling out of the ramp, she and Don Brouhaha found some more punch and placed us immediately in the fast lane. "How's the organizer doing?" She briefly locked her eyes with me and returned to scanning three rear-view mirrors and the road ahead.

"I'm in a muddle."

"Mid-muddle or late muddle?" She spotted the Atwells Avenue sign and swiftly wove the car into the right hand lane for the exit.

"If I were a poet, I couldn't pass up the chance to use 'mid-mud-dle' either. I *do* find you very attractive."

"So you've mentioned. Well, that's better than being nominated for a *Cosmopolitan* makeover—*and*?"

"I feel like you're my best friend." That was true. But what had I experienced of friendship? I once thought Brendan was a friend, but Jesus, the guy sent me out on a dangerous mission, I succeeded, and suddenly 'playing it safe' was the rule of the day for him. Nick and I had shared something thicker than water, even if it *was* his blood, but now he was probably back at work and I was yesterday's news.

"Thank you." She was wheeling the car into Kennedy Square. It was relatively empty. "Does that mean that if you make other good friends you'll be in bed with them and I'll be out in the cold?"

"You, out in the cold?"

"Listen, Bart, I only want to know more about you. I don't cling to a solitary life, I just happen to have one and it works, in a way. It's predictable and leaves me a mind that I can work with, but I'd like to think that I didn't have to end up like Emily Dickinson."

"I know what you mean. I spent so long desperately wanting a relationship that I wonder if I'm capable of one." I didn't know what had become of the promises made to the idea of the perfect woman on cold and lonely nights, I only knew one thing, and that was that I didn't need to wrench my guts out right now. People were trying to kill me; people were trying to hire me. *Mysore Karma* was becoming the most important movie in my life.

"So far," she said wearily, pulling up to a red light, "all I know is…that you're probably the best fuck on the East Coast."

"Oh." She wasn't going to catch me responding to that with a mere 'Thanks.' What a thing to say! What a thing to be! If I could cast my values back to the locker room at Berea High School, that praise would have me sitting on top of the world. Maybe there'd be some kind of a letter for it—a big F with a tasteful gold penis in the lower right corner. Does the East Coast even count in Berea's league? The corridors and locker rooms were filled with boasting and gossip, but the only guys everyone knew were getting it were fathers before they graduated. This award would definitely show *them*. What about a satin jacket of orchidaceous hue? I was becoming seriously overwhelmed. Maybe taste would dictate a lapel pin in the shape of the East Coast—with Florida cranked out erectly. "That's incredible praise."

She was approaching the Biltmore. "Pardon my French, but I don't feel like using the word 'lover.' Maybe you're the best fuck in the United States."

"How would you…know about that?"

"Okay, forget it." She drove the car in under the marquee. A smartly uniformed doorman opened the door for me.

"Er—thanks," I said to him, getting out of the car and reaching into the back seat to pull out my bags. "You mean I'm not…?"

"I mean," she reached over to grab the handle of the open door, "maybe I don't really know. How's that for a thought? Maybe I've got to go out and do some more research! One more thing! Find that goddam Mohammed or whoever and tell him that the Rhode Island phone number for you is obsolete."

"Obsolete?"

"It was a summer rental, you're not there anymore. Let the knifer try to find you in Boston or New York or somewhere I don't have to worry about!"

"That's a…" I started to say. She slammed the door shut. Don Brouhaha left a patch of rubber very near where I stood; holding my bags full of cameras, light meters and summer clothes; watching her disappear around a corner in her fast orange car. "…good idea," I finished. I had forgotten to tell her that they had moved the train station; it was no longer just across the square from the Biltmore.

I tipped the doorman to keep an eye on my bags while I went in to use the house phone. As long as I was at the hotel, I figured that I might as well feed Mohammed this new information and try to find out what the latest arrangements were. My first call was to Edward Lungalang to confirm my travel plans.

"Yes, yes," was his reply when I asked him if the company would reimburse me for airfare and taxis.

"What hotel should I stay at?"

"Oh, by all means you should stay at the New York Sheraton."

"Is that the one near Penn Station?"

"Yes, definitely. We'll see you there. We look forward to a very good shoot in New York with you."

I wasn't having any luck reaching Mohammed or Shyam. I looked up from my phone list in time to see both of them wheeling a borrowed bellboy's cart out of the elevator. They wheeled it to the other side of the fountain and unloaded it, straining at the heavy beer cooler. I waited to see which way they would go. Mohammed had just exited toward the elevators when a gentleman in a dark, rumpled suit approached Shyam. Staying out of Shyam's view, I moved to where I could hear what this seedy-looking man had to say.

"…hotel detective, and I would like to have a look inside your cooler." He bent over and opened it. Inside, I could just make out the gleam of silver—and here I had been thinking he was stealing the beer that we almost never got when we were wrapping. "I'm afraid that what you have here is a cooler full of stolen hotel silver and china."

"What have we here—this is indeed atrocious!" Shyam was trying to justify his guilty blush with indignation.

Hoping that he would be arrested, I retrieved my bags and had the doorman call me a cab.

I settled back in my seat with a Bloody Mary as the express train to New York barreled along the New England shore. Since the Vishnu folks had promised to reimburse airfare, I was travelling first class on the train for approximately the same money.

South of Providence, there were tantalizing glimpses of Narragansett Bay—its blue waters swarming with sails. I thought I had almost spotted Squidneck, but the view was blocked by a forest before I could confirm it to my satisfaction. I hoped that I would get back there some time soon. I hoped that Elisabeth would speak to me. Did I love her? Would that be enough reason for her to love me? Did reason have anything to do with it?

The train returned to the shore in Connecticut. Beyond the train's tall shadow, the sun blasted the rows of houses and gave a warmth and urgency to the summer that was passing.

The shore gave way to the Connecticut suburbs and New York bedroom communities became industrial slums until the train ascended out of the Bronx on the Hell's Gate Bridge to land in Queens. It immediately tunneled under the East River to come to a stop underground, at Pennsylvania Station.

The first-class ride ended, and I hauled my luggage into the crowd that filled the platform and waiting room. I thought I might lighten my load temporarily and leave some of my bags in a luggage locker. They were all occupied. At one locker, a haggard young mother with a hard Appalachian face was taking out some cereal and canned milk to feed her ragged child. At another, a skinny young black man was depositing a heavy overcoat and removing a massive portable stereo. Some of the homeless had found a place to keep their stuff.

Wedging my kits and cases around me as a security measure, I learned by phone that Vishnu Films was unheard of at the reservation desks of every Sheraton in New York. Late afternoon was turning into early evening. I didn't want to join the homeless for the night.

My personnel list—about the only non-Sanskrit printed material that the production company had ever handed out—gave a home number for Scotty. I hated to bother him but I was running out of quarters and options.

"Joneses, Scott speaking," came the voice over the wires.

I identified myself, explained the situation, and asked if he knew anything.

"Bob Fellowes is down here. Do you have his number?"

"No, I guess it's one they left off the list."

"Bob's number is PLaza 4-8936. If you get stranded, you're welcome out here. I heard that they were going to put the crew up at the Broadway. That place is bad news. Why don't you come on out and sleep on our living room sofa."

"I don't think that crashing your delayed honeymoon is the way to develop a long-term friendship with your wife. By the way, where can I cash a Vishnu paycheck around here?"

He gave me the name of the bank and extracted a promise that I would call him if I ended up stranded for the night. I dropped my last quarter on a call to Elisabeth. The phone rang and rang. A loiterer who was dressed appropriately for winter in a Welsh mining town—with the mine closed—eyed my aluminum meter case. I locked it between my feet and the prospective culprit wandered off in search of other prey. There was no answer on Squidneck. At least I got my quarter back.

I tried Bob Fellowes' number. His answering machine greeted me with an original rendition of *Don't Hang Up (Oh, Baby)*.

I waited for the beep and responded to his Coasters ripoff with a bit of vintage George Carlin. "Dis is da toiteent' precinct, dere, and we got a director of photography named Bart Lane checking inta da Broadway Hotel dis PM. You can save us a trip to your place by calling dis 'cking guy."

"Yo, Bart baby," came Bob's voice over the line.

"Screening calls?" I asked. Bart baby? We had met once.

"Not so much that as collecting inspiration for future messages—outgoing and incoming. You gotta leave something snappy—like you just did—or you're dead meat in this town."

"Well right now I'm homeless meat."

"I can dig it. There's a room waiting for you at the Broadway. It's at Seventh and Fifty-fourth. Take a cab. Call me tomorrow and I'll take you around to the locations."

"Will do."

The Broadway had probably been remodeled since Scotty had labeled it bad news. No bellhop, but there was a large, bright busy lobby that boasted a color television and lots of new printed cherry-wood veneer furnishings. The couches and easy chairs spaced around the large room were full of men and women dressed in the uniforms of El Al, Air India and Pan Am. Expensive carry-on luggage abounded.

Once in my room, I gave Scotty a call. I didn't want him and Carolyn waiting around and/or worrying about me. "Listen, Bart, are you sitting down?" he asked after I had given him my room number.

"I am now, what's up?"

"Carolyn was doing some computer work for an insurance company. She looked up Vishnu Films. There's the standard insurance on the production with millions and millions in liability. No problem there, they have to have that to get location permits from the city. Then, there's a policy on Indrani that's larger than the policy on the film. Shyam's is the sole signature for Vishnu Films. This is *not* standard."

"Oops," I said.

"God, I'd love to go back to the days when I thought Shyam was a bumbling idiot."

"We're going to have to keep our eyes open on this one," I philosophized.

"One more thing: I bought Providence papers for the last few days. Remember the chase with your knifer guy and the Providence cops?"

"Oh, boy. I've almost forgotten."

"In the Saturday edition of the Providence *Journal-Bulletin* I found a news item about two Providence police cruisers damaged in an unsuccessful chase Thursday night. It went on to say that the car being pursued, a red Toyota reported stolen from a Providence real estate development firm, was later found abandoned near Davol Square. Nice real estate development."

"Beautiful, he's on the road again. I'd better check with some Boston folks tomorrow."

"Sorry to be the bearer of bad news."

"Thanks for the info, Scotty. At least I got some rest thinking that they'd caught the bastard." We promised to keep each other advised and hung up.

Another night, another town. There were undoubtedly cultural opportunities all around me, but I limited my activities to moving in, finding a Brazilian restaurant for dinner, watching television, doing some calisthenics, and getting a lot of sleep.

The next morning, I awoke, savored the time available to take a shower and eat a big breakfast, and then I called Bob Fellowes.

"And now, from the Fellowes Phone Five, their latest hit—*Street Fightin' Jew!*" rattled off the machine automatically.

> "Well, in a long black coat,
> You know I perambulate the street,
> I give a *klop* in the *kups*
> To all the Pee El Oh's I meet.
> You might wonder who I am,
> I'm just a Hasid name of Sam,
> Well, I'm a street fightin' Jew,
> And I fight for keeps,
> I want to hear from you,
> So baby here's the beeps!"

By the time all of that went by, I was ready with an icebucket. I used it to give my voice that radio announcer's polish and enthused, "Loved the blues zither riff. If you want wider market visibility for this piece, call me, Bart, at the Broadway Hotel—the shack of the stars—room twelve-fifteen."

I picked up Elisabeth's book of poetry and was just about to relax with it when the phone rang. "Hey, great to hear from you again. How about I pick you up in one hour?"

"Sounds good to…"

"Listen, could you do me a favor?"

"Float it past and see if I pick it up," I replied.

"I don't have the Yellow Pages for the boroughs, and we need an ice skating rink in Manhattan, Brooklyn or Queens. Indrani wants Rockefeller Center and she doesn't really believe that it's a restaurant in the summer. The City Skating Club is booked, so that's out. Check it out and I'll pick you up on the Seventh Avenue side of the hotel at—well—find yourself some lunch and we'll make it one-thirty. And—hey—forget about the Bronx. We don't have enough armed cops to do the Bronx."

Right. All I had to do was find an ice rink in July…for a New York production manager with *no Yellow Pages*?

I called, searched and researched. There were no available skating rinks outside of the Bronx. Between locating Yellow Pages for the boroughs and telephoning, I was physically and mentally exhausted by the time I went down to meet Bob.

He materialized at the appointed time in a small blue Mustang with a vanity plate that said DO IT 2. I was given the clients' special VIP tour of the locations that had been arranged, cancelled and rearranged. The laundromat he had found would provide a very good exterior for the fight scenes we had already done as long as we maintained an angle that didn't show where the counter didn't exist. There was a nice view that put the Chrysler Building in the background; it fairly screamed *Manhattan*. There was an exit to the Queens Midtown Tunnel to provide a scenic alternative. It looked good to me.

Grand Central Station was the next stop. Here, a phone booth would be used for Ram's telephoning scene. "Does Indrani want mobs and mobs of people in the shot?" I asked.

"Sure," he said, "why else would she do it in New York?"

Bob pointed out some alternative laundromats on the way to the next location. They all had architectural features that prevented them from looking like the outside of the building where we had filmed Ram stuffing a guy's mouth with broken glass and slapping his face around.

Then, he took me to the Prospect Park Zoo in Brooklyn. He assured me that it was the best zoo available outside of the Bronx with the Central Park Zoo closed for renovation. I believed him.

We did a couple more locations and headed back for the hotel. Bob produced a joint, we got high, listened to the stereo, and stopped worrying about the rush hour traffic that had slowed us to a crawl—at best. I was even visited by the thought that terminal gridlock—that moment when all the cars, trucks and busses block each other into place—would be an incredibly fascinating event to participate in. I mean, here I would be at the very first gridlock *in the world*! It would really be a cosmic spectacle as long as I was in somebody else's car. I felt *so* in touch with the horror and glory of it all.

As Bob pulled up to the Broadway Hotel, I asked him, "Any word from the lab yet—on the Friday and Saturday footage?"

"I haven't heard anything," he replied. "They only call me when there's a problem, so I guess that it's probably good news."

I floated into the nearly empty lobby and asked at the desk if the rest of Vishnu Films had begun to arrive. There was no record of that, so I left my room number for whoever, whenever. Back in my room, I picked up the phone to call some friends who live in New York, but I put the phone back down. There was no way of knowing what I'd be doing or when.

I checked the lobby again, finding only Bob and the guard who would be watching our vehicles overnight. The guard was a sturdily built, amiable, off-duty cop who wore a tight gray gym shirt and carried his .38 Police Special in a gym bag along with what looked like weightlifter's stuff. He and Bob didn't seem to have too much to say to each other. I wondered if I should mention the knife-wielding fugitive I kept running into. I dismissed the thought.

Soon, the crew began to trickle in without ceremony or sudden increase in the noise level. I tracked Eric and Sully to their room to witness their collapse on their beds.

"What is it, a hundred and fifty miles from Providence?" Sully asked rhetorically. "It's a whole fucking day, and if we weren't sharp, we'd still be in some rotten rest area waiting for Shyam to make one more phone call. I mean, seeing that lying son of a bitch trying to keep the whole damn house of cards from falling apart by stopping at every phone…"

"I think he likes to make calls from near highways," interjected Eric. "He's probably pretending he's making the calls from a car phone…"

"And billing the production for the car phone that doesn't exist," concluded Sully.

I produced a fresh bottle of Scotch and we began a reunion party that soon moved up to Buffy's room and ended up descending, *en masse*, on Vijaya Lal and bothering room service for more glasses.

We finally got Vijaya to join us for dinner, but only on the condition that we avoid Indian restaurants. "Please," he begged, "I was gorged at an Indian feast last night and I would like some American food."

I got back to my room shortly before ten to make a few phone calls. "How's the movie business?" said Captain Ryan, whom I had reached at Miss Halloran's.

"Dangerous. Quinn spotted me while he was being chased Thursday night."

"What a disaster! Y'know Providence has nothing out on Quinn, they were chasing him for us. Now they're down two cruisers and mightily pissed at Boston. Patrick Horan at Area D has stopped looking forward to my calls."

"Well, I'm in New York. I'm hoping that Quinn has fled in another direction. Thanks for trying. By the way, if you hear anything about a theft at Hammersmith Farm, maybe I can give you some info that will help crack it."

"Save it for when we get Mr. Quinn back behind bars." He admonished me to take care of myself and stay out of Boston and we rang off.

I called Nguy next. He had just gotten home from the restaurant and felt elevated by receiving a long distance telephone call. "Batterain! So good hear from you."

"Thanks, Nguy. Any suspicious characters trying to track me down?"

"Nobody is trying that for a long time. How is the movie?"

"Very interesting."

"Are the Hindus and Moslems behaving?"

"I'm not sure. Why would someone in a well paid and responsible position betray his employer?"

"There might be some bits of religious resentment there. Remember that Mahatma Gandhi was assassinated by a fellow Hindu *only* because he reluctantly accommodated the Moslem separatists. There might be some—how you say—bad blood?"

"That says it just fine. I didn't think I was working on a holy war. Is that all there is to it?"

"It could be what I heard described as the Calcutta syndrome. That is a…big appetite."

"Big appetite? Eating a lot?"

"Not just food—everything. Grabbing everything you can because tomorrow you might be several stations below the beggars. You might be crawling through the sewers and manure piles looking for something to eat *and* having to fight to keep what you find there. You might be a refugee."

"…and running off with just what you can carry?"

"Exactly."

"How do you know so much about Indian culture?"

"Well, there was a big community of Indians in Saigon. There were merchants, tailors and small businessmen. Some were my clients."

"Well, why would an old woman try to kill her widowed daughter-in-law?"

"Just a minute—a woman is a widow, and her late husband's mother tries to kill her?"

"Right."

"The younger woman has become a member of the household by marrying the son. The old woman might perceive a threat to her control of the household. It the son is dead, his wife has inherited his property. If there is a lot of it, the older woman would want to—how you say—bump her off to get control of it. Maybe there is a large dowry that the mother-in-law wants. That particular kind of murder happens quite often. Is there a mother-in-law hanging around the movie people?"

"I'm afraid so."

"This is a bad dream you had, no?"

"No."

"Good luck, Batterain. You'll need it."

"Thanks, Nguy. It looks like I won't be able to get back home for a while."

"Don't worry. Your flowers will be safe with us."

"Great. Well, good bye."

"Make it *au revoir*, Batterain."

I woke up before the call from the front desk. For breakfast, I tried the quasi-fast food restaurant in the hotel. From the unbearable delay before I got my first cup of coffee to the late bill, breakfast was excruciatingly slow.

I eventually hauled my bags out from under the table and headed out into the dark, gray side street to encounter the first major problem of the day in the parking lot. Someone had promised under grip

Gene that he'd have a Teamster to drive the truck in New York. There wasn't one that day and Gene refused to drive the hulking, erratic grip truck around New York.

I told Gene to unlock the truck because I had a long list of stuff he'd have to fit into the vans. I ran the truck's contents through my internal database and came up with a list of what would be needed in the worst cases all day long. I noticed the Lungalangs leaving the hotel with Indrani's mother-in-law. Mrs. Lungalang seemed to have broken her habitual silence as she chatted with Indrani's nemesis. She herded the older woman into the back seat of the Lucknow-mobile and Edward drove away with them.

Sully set about loading everything necessary into the vans and the U-haul Trailer that Shyam appeared with. Gene was back at work humping sandbags, scrims, silks, reflectors, stands and lights out of the truck. I made sure that Scotty would have the camera depart-ment—wherever it was stuffed—ready for a two-camera shoot. "Some interesting news," Scotty said quietly. "I keep hearing Mohammed and Shyam talking about the exposed film."

"Oh, shit."

"I think our resident penny-pinchers tried to save on shipping by bringing it down with us. Speak of the devil," Scotty nodded his head toward a straining Mohammed.

Mohammed was straining under the burden of several days' worth of exposed film. He was carrying it to Bob Fellowes' car.

"Jesus," Scotty exploded. "One accident, one bust or even a break-in and we'd be up shit creek. Excuse me." He headed over to where Mohammed was giving instructions to Bob. He gave the former a piece of his mind. He admonished the latter to take the film to Souperfilm immediately—stopping only for traffic lights. He stayed on Bob's case until Bob drove off. Then he spun around, high on rage, and headed toward Shyam's car. Shyam escaped in reverse, nearly causing several collisions.

We arrived at the location ahead of the production people. The vans and the tagalong trailer pulled up in front of the laundromat causing the eyes of a black mime in an NYPD uniform to bug out with astonishment as he dexterously directed lines of traffic into the city. I grabbed the New York film permit off the dash and waded through the traffic to show it to him. He looked at it and his eyes drifted skyward in silent prayer.

I stopped by the trailer to go over the shot's requirements with Eric and then set out to find Scotty. It wasn't hard; I heard his strident, enraged voice first.

"This permit says we can be right here, right now," he announced to a female parking cop. "If you want to get in *big* trouble with the *Mayor's Office of Film*, just keep bugging us!"

I caught Eric's eye and signaled him to get the gear unloaded very quickly.

"I'm paid to take all kinds of crap," replied the woman, "but not this much. You can just take that piece of paper and show it to 'em down at the tow yard because that's where you're gonna be!"

I slid myself into the dispute. I thanked Scotty and sent him to set up the camera. I turned to the fuming civil servant. "What seems to be the problem?"

"You can't be here right now because you're blocking every f…blessed commuter from Queens and Long Island."

Out of the corner of my eye, I could see that the trailer was just about empty. "Where should we put the trucks? We certainly don't want to be in your way."

"You can put 'em across the street," she offered helpfully. We did that.

Since the director and the leading man weren't there yet, I worked out everything for the *beautiful New York City shot*, presided over by the Chrysler Building. We fine tuned the shot. Vijaya and Birenda were conferring, just like an assistant director and a continuity person should, but what I overheard was Birenda saying, "…dollars, not your worthless *rupees*, there is no other shot possible that makes any sense."

"Just wait," said Vijaya. "She will change it and you will lose again."

Dick the Stuntman arrived leading a very large Karl. They made straight for me. "Hey, Bart, how ya doin'?" He didn't wait for a reply. "Listen, Karl has to fly out to the West Coast today, so if you can get his stuff done early, it'll be great."

"I'll do what I can," I promised.

Indrani and Ram eventually arrived with an entourage of costume and makeup men. I deferentially showed Indrani what I had in mind for a shot.

"No, it is not right," she pronounced definitively. Behind her, I could see Vijaya putting his hand out to Birenda to collect on the bet. Indrani led me around ninety degrees to the obvious shot—the tight, frontal view that could have been filmed anywhere brick building meets concrete sidewalk.

Ram's action was not merely entering; he had to make his way past the loitering Karl, who might as well have been picking his teeth with a switchblade knife. Ram was also supposed to be carrying a suitcase, and the lack of one caused a diaspora amongst the production people. I left, too—to get a pack of gum from the candy store across the street.

Behind the counter in the little shop and looking out of place among the displays of mentholated cigarette blondes and macho American males was an Indian. "It is a very nice day we are having," he dutifully commented as he gave me my change.

"Do you follow the Indian cinema?" I asked.

"Oh, yes. I am always pausing at the Indian grocery on my way home to rent a tape for my VCR."

"You might want to take a look across the street, then."

He eyed me suspiciously. I could be a stickup man, trying to get him out from behind his counter. He came out of his lair and looked where I was pointing. "Omigod, it's Ram Reddy." I think I made his day.

Back at the location, the suitcase arrived and the shot was quickly made. D. W. Griffith supposedly invented the close-up to save the day rate on one of the two actors in a scene. I talked Indrani into a close-up to prevent having to re-stage a matching traffic jam.

We loaded up and moved on. Bob Fellowes' direction would have helped, but he was noticeably absent while the rest of us were struggling with the location he had set us up with.

Grand Central Station's environs are jammed with people and vehicles all day long. Into this mass our motorcade crawled. The big truck would have been a great wedge and maybe even handy for hiding behind. As it was, we were several lifeboats full of fools, bobbing around in two vans, one sedan, and the U-Haul trailer.

Finally, a beachhead was secured; a pair of phone booths half a block to one side of Grand Central. It wasn't the setting I had agreed on—it subjected us to all of the crowds generated by Vanderbilt's monument without giving us a glimpse of it. I worked a skyscraper into the shot, Eric and Sully set up reflectors to give Ram the glow of stardom, and Vijaya supervised crowd control. Buffy and Ava were joined in cleaning the phone booths by the man whose job it was to clean them, and we eventually made an acceptable master scene. The closeup was a piece of cake.

It was two locations down and three to go and we were still on schedule as we loaded up and headed for Park Avenue. Fortunately, there were enough 'No Parking' signs on Park Avenue so that we could park with the aid of our filming permits. Here Ram's character, the strange Indian hit man in an even stranger foreign land would research his upcoming assassination by checking out the office of his target.

We needed two cameras here, with Scotty operating the second one through a window on the thirty-second floor. Someone had been so enamored with the multi-camera concept that no thought had been given to the fact that the wide shot from above would show a camera and crew at work in the stainless steel and glass environment below. Whoever it was had felt that a large camera, complete with tripod, focus-pulling person and me, in my loud T-shirt, would be invisible while every subtlety and nuance of Ram's dark Asian gaze would be transmitted to the aerial camera.

Shyam drove up as I was trying to sell Indrani a shot I could make from under an overhang. Indrani hated the angle. Shyam reported that Bob would be meeting us with a catered lunch at the next location, and then squealed his car back into traffic before anyone could request an elaboration.

I had Ava and Gene haul the camera over to the curb near the street corner. I set up a shot that was the archetypal crowded sidewalk shot and turned the viewfinder over to Indrani to get her approval. The wind that tall buildings direct around their bases was disrupting Indrani's unfettered tresses to the extent that she couldn't get a proper look at the shot. I chivalrously gathered up her hair and held it behind her while she checked the shot. It felt as silky as it looked. I couldn't tell whether it was the coursing of my creative juices or an overactive imagination, but I felt a current passing between us. She looked at me and her eyes phrased a question. "Very nice, thank you," she said as she took a deep breath that threatened the buttons on her seersucker dress and stepped back from the camera.

Leaving Ava and Gene to mind the setup, the rest of us trooped our burden of equipment into the skyscraper across the street. Walkie-talkies above and below would keep everyone in touch.

The building's security guard must have had his finest hour as he held us up despite our permissions, permits, connections and burden of equipment. We were eventually vouched for by a dark, round, balding Indian man in shirtsleeves and tie. Where Scotty's threats hadn't prevailed, this man's clout did. We were led into an elevator and, after a quick ascent, into the offices of Air India.

Glass cleaner, a precariously stretched tripod, sandbags and a ladder were necessary to get the shot. Since our vans and trailer hadn't appeared anywhere else in the movie, I didn't worry about their presence in the shot. Neither did anyone else.

Back on the street, I noticed that two recent Hispanic arrivals to our shores were on the corner selling T-shirts. I joined them and uncorked enough of my rusty Spanish to borrow one of their large cardboard trays. I inverted it over the camera and me and deployed the walkie-talkie. "Ground base to Eagle, ground base to Eagle, over," I radioed, sounding like someone I saw on TV once.

"Eagle to ground base, I read you," crackled Scotty, having doubtless wasted time watching the same insipid television show.

"Can you see me from up there? Over." I could be succinct when the occasion demanded.

"All I can see is this lady standing next to a box adjacent to some other boxes full of T-shirts. Over."

"Standing by to make some," I responded.

We got it in three takes with very little additional confusion. After Indrani called the wrap, but before she could get back down to ground level, we moved the camera closer to Ram's position and I directed him through a couple of close-ups.

The Lungalangs, having left Indrani's mother-in-law elsewhere, joined the motorcade for the journey to the zoo in Brooklyn. I took a moment to remind Mohammed not to forget Sippy, the all-important child subject of the zoo footage.

We headed out Flatbush Avenue. Part of it was like an unimproved highway on the outskirts of any town, except that I couldn't see any mobile home sales lots. We were making good time until Joao's voice crackled uncharacteristically over the airwaves. "They wanna stop." The lead car pulled over in front of a store, and everyone in it and the next two vehicles headed into the establishment which promised 'Coke, candy cigarettes, and gum.'

Expensive minutes passed. Eventually, everyone and their snacks were fit back into the lead vehicles. Eric radioed them, "Eric to lead vehicle, over," a nice gaffer turning into a trucker before my very eyes. "Thank you for the meal and beverage break. We would have loved some, too."

The road was narrowing and becoming surrounded by taller apartment buildings when the lead vehicle pulled over again. Vijaya's quiet, resigned voice now came over the air. "Someone has forgotten Sippy."

The Lucknow-mobile made a cautious U-turn and headed back to Manhattan across the vast urban expanse that had just been so laboriously covered. "I don't believe these clowns," moaned Eric.

"When we finally get Sippy, do you think she'll need a stunt double to walk past the monkey cages?" piped Sully from his position amidst the stacked reflectors in the rear of the van.

"Indrani's so insistent on the monkeys that Sippy simply has *got* to be *allergic* to 'em," rejoined Buffy.

Prospect Park faces the rest of Brooklyn like a ship with a sharp prow designed, no doubt, to split the waves of traffic which someone once thought would assault it. Our caravan split to the left and instructions, suggestions, and ideas about where to shove the vehicles crackled between the trucks.

There was no Bob to greet us. There was no catering truck and no lunch. I found Indrani to show her the location. The zoo was mercifully almost empty of zoo-goers and the sea lions were sunning themselves in the few rays that filtered through the large canopy of leaves shading the center of the zoo. I led the director through a break in the buildings that surrounded the center to the appropriate monkey cages. They were just beginning to get the sunlight that I was counting on. "Okay, God," I thought, "cue the lights on the…"

"Are these the monkey cages we want to film?" screamed Indrani in horror. "This is terrible; far worse than a maximum security prison!"

"In the ideal world, this is indeed an oppressive setting for cavorting simians. Bob," and I fervently wished he were there to take the heat that was definitely steaming up Indrani's Ray Bans, "assured me that any monkey cage in the greater New York area would be just as bad." My reading of *The Kama Sutra* outlined no proper course of action for showing someone an exhibit of caged mammals that they hated.

She rounded on me, tearing off her sunglasses to reveal eyes that were ablaze with rage. "What can you be thinking of; leading us all this way to film a prison for animals!"

"Bob assured me that it was the best of a bad lot. I'm sure that we can talk the supervisor into letting us remove that layer of wire," I responded. The silver-tongued son of a bitch had, after all, talked *me* into the location.

"Bob this, Bob that—I'm sick of Bob," she lashed. "Where is he with our dinner?"

Eric joined us and suggested, "If you want a more open look, what about the sea lion pond?"

"I want monkeys. The script has monkeys; *we must have our monkeys!*"

I hate to quibble when there is shooting to be done. "While we're waiting for Sippy, why don't we bring in some equipment and set up a shot?" I suggested, "We're here, after all. I'll be bringing up the light level and we can get Mohammed to talk the manager into letting us pull off that wire."

"*If* Sippy gets here! *If, if, if!* There is no point in bringing out all of that stuff until we have our Sippy!" She stalked off, followed by her angry black hair.

I stared at the offending cages for a couple of beats and strode thoughtfully off in the same direction. Ram Reddy was standing near the lion area chatting with Mrs. Lungalang, who probably felt that she had already gotten a good return on her investment in the movie by having an informal chat with such a major star. In the background, Mr. Lungalang looked even more worried than our bleak circumstances dictated.

No Sippy. No meal. No Bob. Our waiting was crowned with hunger and futility. Magic hour is that time of day we cameramen love to use for night because the environment is lit by the setting sun to such a low level that the lights on cars and signs, and those behind windows—invisible in full daylight—shine heartily in the background, but the sky is not black. Magic hour was approaching. Calling it an hour is a misnomer; it is usually more like fifteen minutes to a half-hour. The Vishnu Films schedule called for a magic hour spent in Times Square; a crowded and volatile little shoot. It could be worse. Quinn could join the festivities. Being away from him was at least one good reason to be in New York.

Indrani finally gave up on the zoo. Bob's caterer would find no paying customers in Prospect Park.

It was not a smooth trip back to Manhattan. We stopped once so that Mohammed and George could leave the caravan in search of telephones. "Hey, there's fried chicken!" Sully enthused.

"Read the small print," said the streetwise Scotty.

"Oh, backs and necks."

Mohammed and George eventually reappeared from opposite directions five minutes later. Mohammed was left to intercept Sippy's entourage. The rest of us, under the cloud of an evaporating magic hour, headed for dinner. Scotty established a command post between the front seats of the van and tried to direct everyone to a Greek restaurant in the West Village. The other vehicles weren't very good at following directions, but we finally pulled up in front of a small restaurant festooned with beer and soft drink signs. "Hey, is this the place where all those Greek coffee cups come from?" Sully asked.

There was space for the equipment-bearing vans in front. Inside, there were plenty of tables and an ouzo bar. We all mellowed out considerably.

I have formulated the theory that the difference between cheap and expensive Greek restaurants is that the waiters ignore one in the former and insult one in the latter; this was a cheap one. I finally got the waiter to take our orders and threaded my way over to the booth where Shyam, Indrani and the Lungalangs were sitting. "Hello," I greeted them. "Has anyone lined up the battery-powered lighting I requested for tonight's shoot?"

There were meaningful glances between Edward Lungalang and Shyam. Edward broke the silence. "I'm afraid nothing has been done."

"Will you authorize the expenditure if I can line it up?"

"Yes, yes," replied Edward. "Find it, let me know, etcetera."

I returned to our table, outlined our needs and probable sources to Sully, and gave him a handful of quarters for the pay phone. The Greek salad arrived; more of a Greek tragedy, actually, what with a sweet and sour dressing that had no hint of either feta cheese or tahini. Since it was the first meal in ten hours, I was devouring it, shortcomings and all, when Sully returned.

"I found what we need at Filminc, and they're open, but they never heard of Vishnu," he reported.

"Coming," I mumbled as I wiped salad residue off my chin. I had an account there and had spent an amount on cameras and lenses that would have bought any sane person a Mercedes Benz.

"We're in the lighting department," came the reply, "and we don't have any record of your account."

"Call Barry Mossberg at home." I thought that bringing the owner into the picture might help.

"Can't do, can't do," squawked the phone.

I finally hit on the name of someone in camera sales who was working late that evening. Filminc would remain open for another thirty minutes. Edward produced fifty dollars for the trip and my shish kebab remained untasted.

It took a few minutes to flag a cab, but I got a good one. He made exellent time to Filminc and waited for me without insisting on a deposit.

At Times Square he helped me unload and pointed out some police in the area. I perched on the light case, feeling safe, and started to read an Agatha Christie I dug out of my bag. After a few minutes, I looked up from the tale of upper-class mayhem in England to notice that the police nearest me were engaged in an illegal-left-turn sting operation. About every forty-five seconds, some New Yorker thought that he or she could get away with a left turn onto 42nd Street. "After all," they must have argued to themselves, "it's not rush hour any more." The officers would flag them down with officially suppressed grins. The motorists, to a person, all leaned out of their windows and looked back at the sign they had violated with looks of surprised discovery on their faces. The officers could have checked off the right boxes on the traffic tickets in the dark but they didn't have to, yet.

The sun was leaving and magic hour was drawing near. Lights were beginning to flicker on. A couple of large, familiar silhouettes materialized in front of me; Dick Doherty and the looming Karl.

"Yo," Dick greeted. "Where's the rest of the crew? Can you get 'em to take care of Karl's shot first? He's takin' the redeye out to the coast."

I was getting *déjà vu*. "Didn't I take care of that first thing this morning?" I looked around desperately. No sign of the crew yet. "I've gone to the wall to get this special equipment, the crew and Ram Reddy here in time for the magic hour. I really have to take care of that scene first." Still no caravan, no Vishnu folks. "So, Karl, you working on another movie out there?"

"No," he explained. "I wrote a book and the publisher has it all set up for me to go out there and do the pictures."

"Oh," I was pleasantly surprised to discover this literary side to the stuntman's life. I was looking beyond him, from time to time, trying to spot the arriving crew. I couldn't help but notice a couple of prostitutes working just out of the policemen's view. One who was into black leather had caught my attention, dressed like that on a hot summer evening. She appeared to be handing money over to a guy who looked familiar. He looked up from counting the money she had just handed him. As he glanced around before pocketing it, I caught a look at his face. It had a sneering slash of a mouth. It was Quinn, now a fugitive in two states. I thought I'd stay hidden by Karl. "What's the book about?" I asked.

"Breaking things with my bare hands," he earnestly replied.

We were interrupted by the voice of Eric the gaffer. "Hey, Bart, you're not trying to sell your body, are you? You haven't even been fired yet."

"Naah, I seen dis rube walkin' down da street wit' just da right light fer dis shoot. Since I mugged him, da price was right for Vishnu. Anything you need to know about the battery powered Arri HMI?" The name of the luminaire rolled trippingly off my tongue.

"What, this little hymie?"

"I'd rather you called it an HMI. So set it up, already."

Indrani, Shyam and Edward Lungalang were conferring alongside the Lucknow-mobiles. "I've got the light," I said as I joined them.

"We must get this car shot out of the way first," Indrani pronounced. "Here is the car," she patted the Lucknow-mobile, "here is the action: Ram is sitting in the driver's seat. Karl comes up from the back seat. We must not see him until he rises into the shot. He holds a knife to Ram's throat."

Knife. That reminded me of my nemesis. I looked around. I couldn't see him. Maybe he had to leave the area to collect from some of the girls working the new Javits Convention Center. "We can do the shot right here," I said, trying to move things along. "We can motivate the stopped car with a cutaway of a stoplight…"

"I don't want all of these lights in the background," said Indrani in the middle of Times Square just before magic hour.

I reached into my shoulder bag and drew out something that looked very much like a pistol. It was a light meter. I surveyed an unlit old stone and glass facade a half a block away. "Okay," I told her, "there's just enough light to use that unlit block of offices as a background. With the light I just brought, we can do it quickly and safely."

"I hate that background," she protested. "I want a moving shot and it must cut with the graveyard you shot." She still had the illusion that she had all of the choices in the world.

"Had I but script enough and schedule," I said, but my mind was racing. There were simply not enough minutes to go anywhere else. Magic hour was beginning to blossom as the lights of man commenced to catch up to and surpass the diminishing sun.

"We could go out on the West Side Highway," suggested Dick.

"It's torn up, and the only possible background is New Jersey and New Jersey is a determinedly backlit state at this time of day," my mouth spouted. My mind was racing toward a solution. A moving, lit background that could cut with day; a little piece of the puzzle for the mind that was hurdling over the fact that I would be risking my life and others by filming in a car being driven by a multi-million *rupee* star with a knife at his throat.

I had it! We could make the matching shot in a tunnel. I didn't know if we had what it took to make it safe. I wasn't stopping to think that riding in a car being driven through a tunnel by an actor who had a bright light shining in his eyes and a greater concern for looking good than driving safely might be fatal. I didn't even consider that the replacement cost of the rented equipment would come out of my meager estate. I turned to share my brilliant solution with Indrani.

Right into Quinn and his knife.

CHAPTER 15

Quinn's leering face came to within a foot of mine, then jerked to a stop. Was this the feel of death? I hadn't felt the thrust of his blade, but maybe you didn't always feel a fatal knife wound right away. Surprise and rage filled his face as his right hand, holding the stiletto, came down and was twisted up behind him. A large beefy hand was clamped around his wrist. Karl pulled it up a little harder and said, "I don't think he read the script. He's trying to stab you and you're not even acting in this scene."

"You're dead, you motherfucker," hissed the frustrated assailant. Somebody else was holding him, but he only had eyes for me.

"He looks hungry to me," remarked Dick Doherty. "Feed him some concrete. What is this guy's beef, Bart?"

"I videotaped him threatening one of his girls with a knife. Then he nearly killed my soundman. He escaped from jail. I guess I'm part of the Mob's witness elimination program. Eric?"

"Yo!"

"Why don't you secure this guy with gaffer tape? His right arm might be a little tender where my soundman messed it up. Buffy, could you call the police?"

"What about the ones around the corner?" she asked.

"No good," Scotty said. "They're traffic and this is an escaped felon. Maybe they'll call the right ones for you, though."

"Thanks for saving my life, Karl."

"No problem. I'll just keep a foot on him until the cops come." Karl shifted the foot he was keeping on Quinn's head. One eye came up to regard us with a frightening pure hatred.

"You goddam piece of shit," hissed Quinn. "I'm gonna get out of this, and I'm gonna find you, and I'm gonna cut you up so bad your own mother won't know you. Then I'm gonna get a bunch of my friends and we'll have a circle jerk on your goddam bones. I don't care where I find you—Boston, Providence, …that fuckin' island…"

He was hitting close to home. "Who's going to get you out of this, Charles Quinn?" I asked.

"I got a lawyer, and I got your boss. The fuckin' producer— Shyam. He ain't gonna let no low-rent assholes like you guys mess with me."

"What are you to Shyam? He can get girls anywhere. He's probably already lined up somebody else down here."

"You fuckhead," he spat at me. "I'm helping him out with a special project."

"Karl," I said. "We're not cops and we're not paramedics, but maybe we can help our friend with his right arm. He's having trouble talking." If I hadn't been so tied up with the filming, I would have shit in my pants when I turned around and saw his knife. Now I was being overcome with curiosity—anything that kept me from collapsing would do.

"Gaah!" he screamed as Karl applied some pressure to the sensitive arm. "I'm his fence. Okay? He steals stuff and I find buyers, okay? Now get your hands the fuck off me."

"Yuck," said Karl as he pressed the knifer's face back down to the pavement. "Let's get some gaffer tape on his mouth so that we can get some work done before the cops come." Dick grabbed Quinn's head by the ears and Eric expertly ran several wraps of tape over his sputtering mouth.

"Who is this man and what was he trying to do with that knife?" Indrani joined us and regarded the captive newcomer. I started to explain. I was just about to point out where I had spotted him earlier when I heard the screech of tires. A black Thunderbird was bouncing onto the sidewalk and accelerating toward us. "Run for it!" I shouted, grabbing Indrani and throwing both of us into a doorway. I saw the angry face of Indrani's mother-in-law behind the wheel as the car skimmed past us. Her expression turned to astonishment as the car thumped over the gaffer-taped form of my recent assailant. The bump caused Shyam's lantern-jawed face to rise out of the back seat. He stared back at Quinn's crushed form on the pavement and his expression changed to that of a man who had lost everything as he spotted Indrani and me. The car thumped back into the road and squealed recklessly into traffic.

We were stunned into silence except for Indrani who was sobbing in my arms. She was soft. She was beautiful. She really seemed to need me.

"Looks like you can call those traffic cops now," said Scotty as he checked the crushed body for a pulse and shook his head. "I got the plate number. It was a rented car."

Indrani headed back to one of the vans to talk to the Lungalangs and I stood with the crew, waiting for the police. When they arrived, we gave our statements and got some satisfaction from watching them put out an APB on the car. I made sure they got Captain Horan's name in the Boston Police Department. They promised to check up on the late Quinn up there. Scotty sent them to Indrani and George to get the names of the occupants.

Quinn was eventually manhandled into a body bag and loaded into an ambulance. It drove away with no lights and only the barest of electronic beeps to let it into traffic, leaving only the stench of death. I felt as if a huge weight had been lifted from my shoulders. I tried to feel guilty. That was bullshit. I was in his way; it drove him to do something stupid, and now he was dead. I hoped I could live with that.

Well, there was the movie. I had done some good work and given it more than I knew I had. Maybe it would be easier to finish with Shyam in jail or on the run.

The crew and I were dumbstruck and exhausted. We stared at the lights; magic hour had passed. We stared at Bob Fellowes when he pulled up in his Mustang. We watched him get out and walk over to where Indrani was talking to Ram. We watched Indrani start to rail at him. He raised his hand and managed to stop the torrent long enough to squeeze in a few words that silenced the director completely. We watched him return to his car and drive off, his vanity plate, DO IT 2, soon disappearing into traffic.

"It looks like he's done it to us," said Eric.

I looked where he had been looking. Indrani was huddled in a doorway with Ram, her face buried in her hands, her body racked with sobs. I joined them in what had rapidly become the darkest spot in Times Square. Ram Reddy met me with an anguished gaze that I had never seen him wear in all of the fights and murder attempts I had filmed him performing. "The film has been stolen," he said.

Indrani's face rose from her hands. "All of the film from the last four days. It's a wrap."

My eyes began to sting with tears I couldn't fight. The bottom had fallen out of my life and I was in freefall. "It's some of the best work I've ever done," I finally managed to say quietly to no one in particular. Rage started to rumble up from the bottom of my empty stomach. "Four days?" I said much louder, fixing my glare on an advancing Mohammed. He apparently thought the better of trying to speak to anyone present and retreated.

Indrani stood in the doorway, her dark eyes reflecting none of the neon display that surrounded her. "It's a wrap," she repeated. "I have to get out of here." On slow, unsteady legs, as if she were leaving an abortionist's, she made her way to the car the crew had been setting up. She let herself into the back seat, shut the door, rolled up the window, and sat staring straight ahead.

"It's a wrap," I informed the crew when I had gathered them all together. "The footage from the last four days has been stolen."

"I think I know what happened to Bob and the catered dinner," Scotty ventured.

"Jesus, those damn fuckheads. Well, anyway, here's *your* dinner," Buffy said, handing me a brown paper bag with grease stains on it to indicate cold Greek food.

I thanked her and took the bag. I wandered over to stand with Ram Reddy, who was staring blankly at the twinkling and pulsing neon signs. I was appalled at the waste; not only of the four days' exposed film, but of where I was standing; a place I had busted my ass to get to. The shoot was over. I had failed. The film may have been a third rate piece of shit, but it was *my* third rate piece of shit.

"Ram," I said, "I just want to thank you for the wonderful things you have done that I may be the only person to see. Your dance with death along the edge of that grave was incredibly beautiful. It was the action-packed preview for this film. It was…beautiful. Thank you for the show."

"Thank you, Bart," he said, giving me the full force of his brooding, yet piercing, stare. "You're very kind." We shook hands and his gleaming star quality seemed undiminished as he strode away to join Indrani in the Lucknow-mobile.

Finally, my legs gave out. I barely made it over to one of the vans and let myself in. I sat there; eating cold shish-kebab with my fingers while the crew packed up the equipment and speculated. A brief rest was more healing than the food. I wiped the pungent lamb grease off my hands and got out to check that the rented light was being treated well and to see where it was being packed. The combination of the cold Greek food and the dead Indian film was very depressing. I felt like a lamb on its way to the slaughter; equally at home in shish-kebab or curry.

Back at the hotel, I threaded my way through the throng of neatly uniformed and residually cheerful airline crews and took a crowded elevator up to my floor without even windowshopping the assortment of stewardesses crowded in with me. Sonia Braga could have been wearing the Varig wings I was staring blankly at, and I wouldn't have noticed. I squeezed out at my floor, dragged my weary ass through the pools of light in the corridor, let myself into my room, and collapsed on the bed.

A knock on the door jolted me into motion. It was Scotty. "Hey, big guy, I just called Carolyn and she invited everyone except that damn junkie Giancarlo over to the place for a post-mortem, wake, wrap party, or whatever we think is appropriate."

"That sounds worthwhile." I was still numb. *Four days* worth of work had been hoarded, hauled, bounced around so much that its odds had finally run out and it had been stolen. I shuddered as if someone had just scratched a blackboard. "Scotty, old buddy, I think I have something in my working bag that's designed for emergencies just like this." I delved into the front pouch of the bag and found a joint. "Fire it up, bro…" I said, handing it to Scotty. "I don't know if it's going to give us enough altitude, but anything's better than sitting around in the dumps."

We inhaled and held our breath in silence for a few moments. "What do you think, Scotty; was it Teamsters trying to teach us a lesson or has it been kidnapped for ransom?"

Scotty knitted his brow in thought. "Well, it wasn't too damn hard for whoever did it to follow us around and wait for the opportunity. All that running around with the cans this morning—all someone had to do was follow Bob and wait for the right time to help themselves."

"I thought I had checked out the shipping practice. You would take the magazine off the camera, give it to Ava, who unloaded it, to Mohammed, who would rush it to the bus. When I was a loader, there was always somebody hovering over me to grab the exposed footage and get it to the lab as soon as possible. I don't even have to ask who decided to save a couple of bucks by hauling the stuff down when the unit moved here." After the energy and ecstasy of the shoot, the marijuana was plunging me into one of the deepest despairs of my life. I couldn't have felt my body and soul to be in more mortal danger if I had followed the devil to the ledge outside my fourteenth-story window.

Scotty was staring intently through his wire-rimmed spectacles into middle space. "It's going to be a cold day in hell before fucking Fellowes, the wonderful Mr. Answering Machine, ever works in this town again. It got stolen out of his fucking *trunk*! You never put it in the trunk. That's the easiest damn lock in the whole car to pop. You put it on the seat right next to the driver and you take it straight to the fucking lab. I mean it's so damn stupid that the insurance company's just gonna tell'em to fuck off!"

"Listen, Scotty," I had been eloquently formulating what to say but I had been also rapidly and stonedly digressing and exploring the ramifications so that Scotty was sitting and waiting for what he was supposed to be listening for. "I gotta take a shower and change. I feel like I'm covered with shit."

"Hey, it's not on *your* head. Seriously. You did some great work for these clowns. Listen, I'll go check out Sully and Eric. I'll drop back in a half hour or so."

"Good. Check your watch."

"God, it's moving very slowly. See you in a long time." He let himself out.

I peeled off my dirty clothes and headed for the bathroom. I came back and rummaged around until I came up with *By Motor through Five States and Eight Lifetimes*. I went back to the bathroom, locked the door behind me and sat down. I opened the book. An elegant, flowing hand addressed me on the flyleaf. 'Dear Bart,' it said, talking to me. 'Get your sweet ass back to this island as soon and as whole as possible. Love, Elisabeth.'

'Love?' She wouldn't write 'love' when she meant 'like' or even 'lust for your body.' She meant love. Had I destroyed that with my hesitations?

I read it several times, marveling at how she had taken pen to paper on my behalf. She certainly wasn't signing them like that at the Athenaeum the night we met. I turned a page numbly encountering the printing information, the title page, and the table of contents. This was turning into one of those bad dreams where you're unavoidably detained on the toilet while your ship comes in and departs without you. I got up and hauled myself over to the telephone. I knew the number. I dialed direct even if it meant that Vishnu Films might end up paying for the call. It was ringing. Somewhere the night air was clear, the moon was probably leaving a trail of platinum across Narragansett Bay and in that place, a phone was ringing.

The ringing stopped. The phone was picked up. "Hemp Hill," came the voice that lady radio announcers all over the country would have killed to have; cool but unaggrieved; powerful but not strident. I was digressing again.

"Hi, Elisabeth. This is Bart."

"It's the conquering shooter! Don't tell me. They've extended your contract to cover the India filming."

"No. It looks like I'll be getting back to New England before I thought I would."

"Working real fast?"

"Work has come to a screeching and crying halt because…the exposed film was stolen. Four days' worth. Some of the absolutely best stuff I've ever seen or done. Gone."

"Oh, I wish I could say something cheerful or consoling. I…uh…can't think of anything good to say about it."

"That's okay, Elisabeth, I wouldn't believe it anyway. I don't understand this."

"You really are down, Bart. You weren't this bad when there were people chasing you and trying to kill you. Oh, I'm sorry I brought that up."

"Well, in fact, that may have stopped," I recounted Quinn's demise, "but Elisabeth, I gave this film everything I had. I *prayed* for it. Is it too much to ask to be able to work? I just want to be able to earn a couple of bucks to rub together."

"There's only one buck that matters to me."

"Really?"

"Do you need hard copy on that?"

"No, I just thought that…"

"I want to see you, Bart."

"You don't have to say that just because I'm depressed and at the end of my rope. You want to…see me?"

"You bet your ass."

"I'll be there, but I don't know when. I gotta go now, but…"

"Don't do anything foolish."

"Okay."

"Promise?"

"Yeah, I promise not to do anything foolish."

"Good. Let me know when you're coming home. 'Bye, now."

Home? "'Bye."

I took a shower and spent too much confused time figuring out which clothes to climb into. I probably ended up dressed like someone who was looking for a golf course in Central Park. I stared out the window at the city. All the lights put there by generations of millions of people. The bottomless pit that failure could plummet you to the unimaginable depths of. The top of the heap—something that an unemployed technician was better off not thinking about. There was a knock on the door.

It was Scotty and Eric. "There is a *very heavy* meeting going on in Indrani's suite," Eric reported. "I saw the Lungalangs going in there along with some very upset looking Indians that I've never seen around before. They're probably tearing her to shreds." He headed into the bathroom, emerged with the clean glass and helped himself to my Scotch.

There was a hammering on the door. "Hey, open up! This is a raid and if we have to bust your door, they'll put it on your American Express," came a voice that was unmistakably Sully's. Scotty opened the door and admitted not only Sully, but Ava, Gene and Giancarlo. They were all carrying glasses.

"Well, gang," I said, "you've been a great crew. I'm sorry it had to end like this. Is there any way this movie can be saved?"

"Hey," said Scotty. "You do your job the best way you can, but you might as well try to make book on whether Mohammed or Shyam blows it next. Hell, we could even have point spreads. Who's going to get blamed?"

"They'll try to blame it on Vijaya," piped Sully, "since he's some-one who really knows what he's doing. I heard that they owe him a bundle, too."

I was listening, but I was also replaying the lost footage in my mind. I wanted to save the film; to leave something besides disaster in my wake. "I think," I said when I had sorted a few things out, hoping that I hadn't forgotten what I was going to say, "that the crew should send Indrani a message. Let's tell her that we're with her and that we're anxious to go back, do it all over again, and even make it better."

There was general support for that but Sully had something to add. "It sounds like the supportive message is probably the best thing we can do right now, but there's one big problem. I've found out that when someone is determined to fail, you can never quite save them from themselves."

"What do you mean by that?" I hadn't expected the good-natured heavy hauler to be a voice of dissent.

"She's doing some strange things. She's ignoring Vijaya, for one thing. As far as I can make out, he must have told her that Shyam was best suited to chopping chickens in a tandoori joint and Mohammed was a perpetual refugee. *She* blew the zoo scene long before today. Remember the day at Roger Williams Park, in Providence, when you showed up, Bart, and got sent home after a few wild goose chases?"

"God, yes," I replied.

"They had Ram, Sippy, an extra camera, and they had you. Right next to where Anouk was dancing, there was a zoo with a picture perfect monkey cage; just what she was crying for this afternoon. That's just a couple of days' worth of stuff."

"Well, we've learned what to do by doing it already. Can we help the production folks who aren't in jail to learn from their mistakes, too? If we can help plan…"

"Lotsa luck trying to help 'em plan," said Eric.

Sully and Ava left to fetch more to drink. I turned to Scotty. I rolled my eyes toward Giancarlo who was manipulating his digital watch in a stoned stupor. "I think I'm going to have to beg out of your party. I don't feel lucky enough to travel over some of the most dangerous highways in the world in an altered state of mind tonight."

"I can dig *that*, man. I think I'll hang around. Carolyn isn't making any big plans or anything and I don't really like the idea of ferrying everybody around, either."

Sully and Ava returned with more glasses, ice cubes, some donations to the liquor stock, and Buffy. We planned in the luxury of the vacuum we were in. I got everyone to tune down their war stories while I called Indrani's suite. The phone was not being answered, so I left a message with the hotel operator.

"That was painless," I said as I hung up. I did feel relieved. I felt like I had accomplished something major, if only by proxy. Finding that I still had the somewhat glazed attention of the crew, I kept talking. "Now, exactly how shall I deliver the message?" I paced over to the bureau into which I had unpacked all my clothes in anticipation of a few days' stay in the Big Apple. "I mean," I continued as I began to feel an even greater input from the various substances I had been ingesting, "I can deliver it in basic Californian." I grabbed a Hawaiian shirt out of a drawer. "'We on the crew really want to share this production experience with you, but we really can't relate to where you're coming from.' Or," I stuffed the shirt back into the drawer, opened another and extracted a bush jacket, with shorts to match, "I could give 'em British Colonial." Sully's face was red, his body quaking with suppressed laughter. "Like, 'Now see here, chaps. You've been missing the mark by no small amount as of late. I've been tolerant and very fair, I think you'll have to agree, but things have begun to get out of hand.' If it gets any heavier than that, Buffy will have to dig a swagger stick out of the props department."

"Swagger stick, far fucking out," said Giancarlo. "Swagger stick! Swagger stick!" he started to chant. It caught on and was getting louder. It was passing the point where a neighbor might call the management and approaching the level of a police complaint when the phone rang, quieting the cacophony instantly.

It was Indrani. "Hello, Bart, I am returning your call."

"Hello, Indrani. You certainly got the message quickly. I've been talking with the crew and we wanted to give you our support."

"Yes, Bart. We must talk. Could you please come up to my suite? Room twenty-twenty?"

"I'll be there in five minutes."

"That will be very good, thank you." She hung up.

The crew agreed to move the party to Eric and Sully's room and await my report. I stayed in the clothes I was wearing and mustered as much of my businesslike self as I could.

"Please come in, Bart." The Indrani who greeted me didn't look like she had been torn apart by anybody, unless you counted the slit in her long black skirt or the three buttons that were undone at the top of her billowing silk blouse. Neither did it appear as though I would have to pretend civility to Shyam, Mohammed, or her ex-mother-in-law. "Thank you for saving my life." She briefly rested her head on my shoulder and the scent of patchouli flowed over me. "My former mother-in-law is in jail and I'm not about to post bail. Ditto for Shyam. That is settled. Now, would you like something to drink? Your usual?"

I could get used to this. "Yes please, that would be wonderful."

"Make yourself comfortable while I concoct your drink." She motioned me to the sofa and busied herself at the bar.

"Now, then," she said after handing me my scotch and soda and settling herself on the opposite end of the sofa from me, "what is it that you wanted to tell me?"

"The crew and I wanted to let you know that we really want to help you make this film. We feel your loss very acutely because it's our loss, too. We want you to know that we are behind you and if we have the chance to reshoot, we'll be able to do it faster and better." I actually remembered everything and got it all out.

"Thank you very much." She hiked one of her legs on to the couch in a very graceful manner. Just as smoothly, her skirt slid away to reveal a long, perfectly contoured, light brown leg. "I do not know if the insurance will help us out on this."

"Why not?"

"Because they do not insure against stupidity, per se."

"Is there anything we can say to the producers to keep the film alive?"

"Oh, it is alive, all right." She leaned forward to continue in a conspiratorial vein. I was also receiving a full visual report on what was, and what was not, under her blouse. "You see, there are Indian and American investors in this film. Many of the Americans have strong ties to India, like the Lungalangs. Wealthy Indians cannot take or send very much cash out of India, so they invest in the part of the filming that we will be doing in India. When it starts to make money abroad, through a series of limited partnerships, they have the option to leave the money in an account abroad, or bring it back to India."

"What does this mean for us?"

"It means that much of our shooting will be done in India. We will hire a studio, lay on an army of lighting men and grips, and finish it completely first class."

"So the film will survive?"

She smoothly drew herself closer to me. "The film will thrive." She locked my eyes in her tantalizing gaze. I was getting an inkling of what a cobra feels when it comes up against a mongoose. There was no staring at my melting ice cubes now. "I want you to shoot it." She pressed her right breast against my shoulder. How can something be soft and firm, taut and yielding? Something caused me to spill a bit of my drink.

"Oops," I said.

"Clumsy me!" she exclaimed. "I have dampened your pants. Let me wipe that up!"

"Oh, that's al…" I was too late, she was sailing across the room to fetch a towel from the suite's bathroom. I usually prefer to 'dampen my pants' the old fashioned way, through sheer sexual excitement.

"I'm so sorry," she said as she knelt on the floor and began to sponge off my lap. She officiously mopped up my thighs and began to work higher up on my person. She slowed down in a critical area and looked up at me as if she had been ritually washing my feet. In this important 'hands across the ocean' I hoped that I was making a favorable impression; the reputation of WASP manhood was at stake. "Have you ever seen the sun set over the Indian Ocean?"

"Not yet," I said.

"Consider it," she said, launching the used towel toward the suite's bar and rising to slide onto the couch next to me. "There are almost eight hundred features shot in India each year. Three or four of those should have your name on them, as *Mysore Karma* will."

I took a deep breath. The sweet tang of her perfume was combining with the musky scent of her sweat to create a symphony for my nose. Things were moving fast. I'm not really certain exactly how my arms made their way around her, but they did. Her eyes, which I had so often seen burning with determination and concentration, were looking into mine and prompting my next move. This exotic dynamo from half way around the world wanted me. Her stare shifted slowly downward, followed by long, dark eyelashes, and her head tilted slowly to one side to enable her to move her lips smoothly toward mine. Talk about snatching victory from the jaws of defeat! I thought I was down and out but it flashed across my mind that if I passed up this opportunity, I'd never be entitled to complain about being lonely and unemployed again.

There was a knock on the door. We separated. "I have to get back to the crew," I said, realizing that she hadn't mentioned them, "and let them know that you're not contemplating suicide, and…that the film will survive." We stood up. I untucked my shirt, hoping that its tails would hide my wet pants. I had to do some quick and unabashed rearranging before I could walk straight.

She raised her eyes from watching my efforts with an equally unabashed interest and said, "I will be at the Biltmore in Providence tomorrow night. Let me know of your decision. At any time."

She showed me to the door, which opened to reveal Birenda, bringing a copy of the script notes for the day's shooting. "Thank you very much for the kind words, Bart," she said in parting. Birenda looked back and forth between us, but I'm not sure what she saw. I nodded a greeting and left.

The crew was pleased that Indrani was heartened by their support. I didn't mention India; that was private and pending. Nobody was surprised that stupidity was not insurable, nor were they in a hurry to keep working for Vishnu Films. Scotty summed it up: "Shyam probably got enough money from the investors to insure against stupidity, but then he undoubtedly did the usual; bought a cheaper policy without the stupidity clause and pocketed the difference. It may not be the only time bomb that bastard left ticking"

There was murmured assent. Scotty shook hands all around, saying that he had to leave because he would have a long day returning the camera equipment to all of the rental houses Shyam had scrounged it from. Giancarlo, navigating life uncertainly with the aid of some powerful hashish he had managed to score since arriving in New York, followed Buffy out of the room.

"Gentlemen," said Eric to Sully and me, "I think that this is a time when it is one of life's great bargains to go to some nice place and buy a lot of drinks."

"...and drink them," added Sully, rubbing his ample belly in anticipation.

We trooped off to be dazzled by the lights of the city, and ended up occupying the outdoor bar at Rockefeller Center that only becomes a skating rink when the Creator decrees that winter has begun. We closed the joint.

Back at the Broadway Hotel, Eric noticed music and light seeping through the door of Gene Fender's room. He raised his eyebrows at us and knocked at the door. In about thirty seconds, the door opened to reveal Gene, clad in jeans and with his STP hat on sideways with Ava, wearing a football jersey, clinging to him. "Any fresh news about Vishnu Films?" Eric asked.

"You missed the really big item, eh?" Gene's smoldering Camel bounced up and down in the corner of his mouth as he spoke. "Vijaya took Mohammed out drinking. Mohammed came back with a broken arm. He says that he fell down. You believe that?"

"I bet he had some help falling down," Sully offered.

"Some other folks think so, too. Vijaya is now officially in hiding and Mohammed is trying to put out a warrant for his arrest, charging him with assault and battery."

"At least that's what he said he was going to do as they were taking him to the hospital and everything," added Ava brightly, clearing the hair out of her face with a hand temporarily relieved from the duty of caressing Gene's naked biceps. "I think he's back again, though."

"Thanks for the inside info," I said. "I'm going to try to get some sleep. Tomorrow will probably be a long one, what with trying to get paid and all."

Eric and Sully added their goodnights to the couple and we headed down the corridor. "How are you getting back to that island, Bart?" Eric asked.

"Squidneck? I'll take the train to Providence, maybe catch a bus to Warren." If I was indeed headed that way.

"I've got a better idea. I left my car in Providence and I'm going to join Molly at our summer rental in Newport, so, if you want to help us get the van and grip truck back to Providence, I'll probably be able to give you a ride to the ferry."

"It's a deal," I said as we parted company. I had my future to sort out but I'd have to hit Providence in any case.

The next day dawned slowly on me; there was no film to be shot so why would I want to get out of bed? I wondered how Elisabeth woke up when she was all alone. I wasn't wracked with the large philosophical question of a tree falling in the forest, but did she bound out of bed, unseen, with the sunrise and start doing things to sheets of paper? Did she race naked to the shore to get in a swim before the quahoggers showed up? Did she sleep late without a lover to wake her up? Maybe she merely wandered through the fog until she had managed to assemble her first cup of coffee, just like the rest of us mortals.

As I stared into the bathroom mirror to brush my teeth and scrape a blade over my face, I listed my objectives for the day. First, I had to get paid. Next, I had to find out what the hell was going on. Then, I had to get packed and check out. Following that, I had to get my hands on the rented lighting and get it back to Filminc. Making it back to Providence and maybe Squidneck seemed like the easiest part of the day.

After a breakfast that took too long, I tried to find George Mukherjee. When I knocked on what I thought was the appropriate door, it was opened to reveal Mohammed in a cloud of smoke. The short, round faced man looked cute as a button in his American short-legged pajamas with his arm in a sling. "Hi, Mohammed, I was sorry to hear of your fall."

"I am not of much use with this," he said, gamely raising the slinged member.

"Hey, you do what you can. Would you know where to find George?" I couldn't help but notice that there were a half dozen prosperous-looking Indians in Mohammed's room, smoking heavily. They looked like new faces to me, but I had the feeling that I wouldn't be introduced.

"I have not seen George for a couple of hours. He might be with the Lungalangs in room eight-fourteen."

"Thanks. By the way, that Rhode Island phone number you have for me is just a summer rental that has expired. I'm going back to Boston from here. Do you have that phone number?"

"Oh, yes, I already have it."

"Great. Take care now."

"Good bye," replied Mohammed blankly. He shut the door. I hoped that if someone out there was still trying to kill me, and if Mohammed was in touch with them, the new information I had given him would point any residual heavy hitters away from Squidneck.

Mrs. Lungalang answered the door at my next stop. She acknowledged my greeting with a darting glance of her dark, flashing eyes over her shoulder. George, seated on a bed behind her, nodded in reply and I was admitted. The reason for the guarded greeting became quickly clear when my eyes adjusted to the curtained darkness. There, seated at the head of one of the unmade beds, was Vijaya.

"Hello, George, Mr. Lungalang. Nice to see you, Vijaya." I shook hands all around. As I shook Vijaya's, I added, "I heard about the highly understandable accident."

"Ah," he said, his small, round eyes showing a deference that rarely appeared on his hawklike face. "I would appreciate it if you would not tell anyone where I am."

"My lips are sealed." I pulled out my wallet and handed him a business card. "If you ever decide to hide in Boston, hide at my place."

"I will be getting you a check later this morning, Bart," George said. "Will you be travelling back to Providence with the crew?"

"Yes, I guess I'll be seeing you later in the parking lot." I excused myself and left.

The human and mechanical components of Vishnu Films were scattered over a sizeable portion of the parking lot. Scotty had created an island of order behind the grip truck, checking and shuffling camera parts among a dozen open yellow, white and blue trunks and reclaiming his own gear into a large canvas bag. "Hey, big guy, how's your head today?" he asked.

"A lot better, thanks. Is everything coming out even here?"

"Pretty much so. It took awhile to square things up after our panic wrap last night. I hear Mohammed received some additional reward after I left."

"Yeah, I guess it's mending well." I spotted the rented lighting I had to return. Eric, Sully and Gene were making an inventory of everything in the grip truck. "Back on duty, Eric?" I asked.

"Part of me is, let me know if you see my mind. I think I lost it in this pile of grip truck stuff."

"How can I get the battery light back to the rental house?"

"I'll borrow a truck; it will probably be that one," he said, indicating the van we had spent yesterday in. I loaded the cases into the van and Eric soon materialized with a key. In moments, we were in a traffic jam.

"Damn," said Eric. "I could have gone to work in the fish market right out of high school and ended up just like this. Stuck in traffic on a hot day in a van."

The sparkling, mellow cityscape of the night before had disappeared under millions of desperate feet and competing bodies. Several people were emulating TV commercials, running down the streets, dodging pedestrians and vehicles while wearing suits and carrying briefcases. We eventually attained Filminc, where I returned the rented gear and found out how much to tack onto my bill.

Our trip was so slow that I was afraid we would delay everyone's departure. That was optimistic. Gene and Sully had arranged most of the grip truck's equipment in neat rows, but before we could help load it in, George approached us, clipboard in hand, and asked us to return the rented trailer across town.

"Hook it on," Eric said. "Give me the paperwork."

It took forty minutes get back to the trailer rental place. It was on the first floor of what really should have been an abandoned warehouse. We followed arrows and lines painted on the floor and signs telling us where to leave what. Eric drove the large van and its trailer in the large door and turned right, to an area dedicated to unhooking trailers. He reached into the glove compartment in front of me for the rental agreement. "Oh, shit," he said after a cursory examination. "That sonofabitch has his name down here as *Gandhi!*"

"Beautiful, let's unhook the damn thing."

While we set to work unhitching the trailer and its hitch, I whispered conspiratorially, "See all of those people working behind the counter?"

"Nh huh," grunted Eric as he wrestled with a recalcitrant chain.

"Try to get taken care of by the blonde lady. The short woman with the square face and the box-shaped perm is probably a company clone; you'll never distract her from filling out every little box and making every little check. The guy with the flattop and vacant grin doesn't look bright enough to do the job, so he'll probably have to get someone to show him how. Talk to the blonde. Ask her for directions on how to get out of Manhattan, headed east, for Long Island. Get her so involved that she won't be paying so much attention to the rental agreement."

"Good idea."

"I'll have the truck waiting right near the counter."

Eric did it right. Five times, the young lady bent over the form and five times Eric asked her searching questions, grabbing maps out of the racks on the counter, spreading them all over the paperwork, and finally sneaking every pen on the counter into the slot marked for the return of the keys. His act culminated in making a gesture that indicated that he had left something very important in the van. He strode out of the counter area, climbed into the passenger seat and said, "Let's get the hell out of here." We did.

Back at the parking lot, the crew was in an uproar. Edward Lungalang had taken his wife and the recently reunited Reddys on a trip to Staten Island. He had also taken the checkbook. George had commandeered the Lucknowmobile and taken to the streets in hot pursuit after explaining the situation to the crew and promising paychecks at his family's house outside of Providence.

Eric and I collected our luggage and loaded it into the van. Sully and Giancarlo moved into the back seat, and we were off, even if we did have to keep it slow to avoid losing the grip truck.

Having the big truck following us meant that we would have to travel to the tip of Manhattan on city streets. Our walkie-talkies were back in play as Eric figured out the route and guided Gene in the lumbering grip truck.

Giancarlo offered a lit joint to Eric and me in the front seat. We declined.

"There's our turnoff," I said.

"Where?" said Eric as he drove past it. We wound through the Bronx on a series of secondary roads, now travelling through a totally manmade and abandoned landscape. Finally, we surfaced up a ramp onto a recognizable interstate just in time to pay the toll.

On the Connecticut Turnpike, the toll-booth didn't even seem to be an imposition and the attendant seemed to like the music that was coming over our radio. We paid and were waved through the gate but soon found ourselves in a combination of Breezewood, Pennsylvania, and a concentration camp. Trucks of all sizes were pulled over—hundreds of them—and the marshalling was being run by a cadre of jack-booted, peak-capped, and very tough-looking Connecticut State Troopers.

"We gotta pull over," came Gene's voice over the walkie-talkie.

We pulled over at a location that gave us a view of the grip truck.

"If those fuckers are searching for drugs, man, you gotta cover for me," said Giancarlo.

"No, *you* have to cover for *us*," Eric snapped. "Just keep your damned mouth shut and they'll never know."

The grip truck neded an expensive license to proceed through Connecticut. Giancarlo was hoping to get caught calling the police every name in the books. Gene found one hundred and twenty dollars and paid up. It was drawing close to the afternoon rush hour when the truck was released from the checkpoint and we headed once more down the road.

All we had to do was burn up the highway between here and Providence, get paid, and pick up Eric's car and I could catch the last ferry of the day. The Connecticut Turnpike, however, was not all there. Ever since a section of it had collapsed into the Miantic River, carrying several people to their deaths, repairs and piecemeal rebuilding had led to closings, load restrictions, detours and other things that an inveterate train rider like myself wouldn't know about. The grip truck would have to take a detour and we would meet it again further down the road.

Gene pulled in behind an Intermountain Express eighteen-wheeler and Eric sent a cheerful "So long, good buddy, see you at the first service stop after you rejoin." We left the truck in a line that looked like it contained every rig in the Northeast.

In the van, we all breathed a sigh of relief at being freed, however temporarily, from our cumbersome appendage. The contented silence was broken by a something like a gunshot that came over the walkie-talkie. Gene's stressed voice followed it immediately. "The truck just went bang and stalled."

"Shit," Eric hissed.

I had been reading the Squidneck ferry schedule the way I used to study the Sears catalogue before Christmas. I put it back in my sweaty wallet.

"It's not starting," crackled the radio. "We're in the exit chute for the detour headed uphill. The fucker still doesn't start. There's no way around us."

"Stay with it if you can, we'll get you some help," Eric replied as he put the accelerator to the floor. We found a trooper a long couple of miles later. Eric spent an anticlimactic ten minutes talking to the trooper and peering into the interceptor. Occasionally, the trooper talked into his radio.

"The truck is being towed as we speak," Eric reported, back in the van, "and they're taking it to Interstate Motor Service in Stamford. It'll take a while."

Later, Sully, piloting us through Stamford, exclaimed, "Far out, there's a White Tower!"

"Amazing," said Giancarlo from the back seat. "They still have 'em? I thought that they existed only in fast-food legend! I want a cheap hamburger and it better be greasy!"

"Yeah," said Eric. "Let's head in there and use the phone."

Not only had this White Tower been able to maintain its existence into the nineteen-eighties, it had been able to exist without a phone. Maybe it survived because it had no phone; nobody could call it up and tell it that Burger King and McDonald's had sucked the life out of all the other White Towers.

"Nope," said the man dexterously flipping sizzling patties on the griddle. "There's a phone at the Seven-Eleven next door." With that line, most of his audience and potential clientele evaporated.

Sully had the first use of the phone. "No answer at Interstate."

"Hey, they're out towing Gene," Eric said. He got to the phone next. He dialed, recited some numbers into the phone, waited, and hung up. "There might be some problem getting out of Providence. I couldn't reach the person I left my car with."

"One does what one can," I said as I took my turn at the phone. Somewhere, out across Long Island Sound and up a bit into Narragansett Bay, Elisabeth wasn't answering the phone, either. She had probably gone down to meet the ferry, just in case.

We had to backtrack two exits on the turnpike and ask directions several times to find Interstate Motor Service, a Texaco station gone bad. It was locked up tighter than a rusted oil drum. After a wait, we were joined by the Lucknow-mobile with George Mukherjee at the wheel.

"Gene told me to come here over the radio," he said in greeting. "I imagine that he will be here in five minutes or so."

George was relating in colorful detail how he had tracked down the Lungalangs to retrieve the checkbook, and I was trying to figure out how to ask him for my check and get to the train station when we were startled by the blast of an air horn. A mammoth tow truck was approaching us. Behind it, the grip truck with its nose suspended in the air looked like an afterthought.

After the tow truck driver had worked on the grip truck for a few minutes, he called for someone to try to start it. Gene broke up a petty cash conference with George and climbed into the cab, simultaneously stuffing some bills in his wallet. As I headed for a phone in the garage, I heard the grip truck's engine turn over and start to run.

I tried to call Elisabeth. There was no answer. I felt like I had been abandoned.

"I have to go to the State Police and try to get that unreasonable permit fee returned," George was saying when I emerged from the garage. "It strikes me as a strictly unconstitutional appropriation of Vishnu Films' fundings." He shook his head as he climbed back into the car. "I'm sure I'll find you up along the road, somewhere," he called through the window as he drove off into the darkening early evening.

I didn't want to see him vanish into the sunset. I wanted my check. I wanted to grab my bags, hop on a northbound local at Stamford, change to Amtrak's Boston train at New Haven and sit in the drinking car all the way to Providence. Damn George got away again.

Thanks to the quick repair, courtesy of the tow service, it seemed that we might finally get our show on the road. I climbed into the driver's seat of the van and everyone else boarded their respective vehicles. I had the illusion that, at the wheel, I could get us up to Providence without further incident.

Darkness was arriving as we wheeled into the service area to wait for the grip truck again. This time it had to find a route out of Stamford that wasn't blocked by low bridges. It was a perfect magic hour, but there was nothing to shoot. I sent Sully with the radio to keep a watch for Gene and headed through a parking lot that rang with door-slamming, arrivals, departures and families being herded into and out of station wagons and the Burger King.

I found the pay phones and dialled Squidneck once again. The ringing stopped. "Hemp Hill," said Elisabeth.

"Hi, it's Bart," I said.

"You can call yourself 'me' if you like," she replied.

"Hi, it's me."

"That's better. Where are you? I've met every ferry, picked up my mail, bought a Providence Journal, and enough milk, cream, and butter so that I won't have any excuse to visit Jessica's store for a month."

"In pursuit of my paycheck, I have had to ride in one of the company vans back to Providence. We also got saddled with leading the grip truck which is on its last legs."

"How far did you flog it today?"

"Right now, I'm ten miles east of Stamford." I explained the latest delay. "I guess I'll get there some time tomorrow, but I don't know when. I have to cash the paycheck as soon as I get it and then get to Warren."

"If it's on a noun bank, most of them have branches in Warren," she offered helpfully.

"What's a noun bank?"

"Fleet, Hospital Trust, Old Stone; banks with names like that. Peter Pan runs buses from Providence."

"Peter Pan?"

"Either that or Bonanza, so call me from Jessica's when you get to the island, okay?"

"Fine. Elisabeth?"

"Yes?"

"I miss you."

"Thanks. See you later, Bart." She hung up.

Eventually, we were joined by the grip truck and headed down the highway with me clinging not only to the steering wheel, but to the hope that Providence was only a couple of hours away. On the railroad tracks that paralleled us, a passenger train sped east, its silent, dark, electric locomotive hauling a string of warmly-lit windows. I knew that I was seeing the second to the last Boston train of the day.

Eric interrupted the static-filled rock music that the van's radio produced intermittently. "Listen, Bart, I might not be able to run you down to Warren tonight."

"Oh," I said, punching the accelerator to get us past a station wagon full of rambunctious kids who had been making faces in the glow of the van's headlights. "Wonderful of you to wait until we had left Stamford. I could have caught a train there. I could have caught one in New York and been off this gig ten hours ago. What's the problem?"

"The person in Providence that I parked my car with when we left. I might not be able to get it back tonight."

"What's a fella to do?" The ferry had made its last run of the day anyway, so it was moot as far as I was concerned. I was just leaning on him because I wanted my options. Maybe I loved Elisabeth, but…our silent meditation on getting to Providence and how to get the hell out of there again was interrupted by the honking of a car horn. George Mukherjee was alongside driving the Lucknow-mobile with one hand and waving his walkie-talkie out the window with the other. George led us off the highway to a truckstop and gave everyone directions to his family's house in a suburb of Providence promising that he would have all of our paychecks there. We believed him.

"Also," he added, "if anybody needs to stay in Providence for the night, there is plenty of room at the house."

"Shit," yawned Sully, "there goes charging a room at the Biltmore to Vishnu Films."

"Eight days on the road and I'm *not* going to make it home tonight," I thought in spite of the fact that I *still* didn't care for country and western music.

Dinner left a feeling of well-being that stayed with us across the parking lot full of idling engines and hissing air brakes. We climbed into the van feeling happy and satisfied, and set out to keep leading our white elephant travelling companion. Eric was driving, his face lit by the instrument gauges. Perhaps it was just a tad too quiet. Maybe we were all being pursued by the late Quinn's colleagues. I wondered if I should have moved some sandbags into the van so that we could bomb any pursuers. I was getting tired of myself for thinking that way and had just about fallen asleep when I was wrenched back to the here-and-now by something that felt and sounded like gunshots thudding into the van.

CHAPTER 16

❀

"Krrr..." went the walkie talkie. "It feels like someone's shooting at the truck."

I was wide awake now. I scanned the sides of the highway for telltale muzzle flash. I couldn't see anything.

Gene came over the air again. "I think something just went out on the truck. Could you have a look at my tires?"

"Standing by," returned Eric. "You pass us, and then we'll pass you. Over and out."

I dug up a flashlight and inspected the passing truck. No bullet holes were evident. The process was reversed and I checked out the other side of it. "No problem that I can see," I reported.

"I don't see anything dragging, either," added Sully.

"You check out A-okay, good buddies," broadcast Eric in a drawl that contained more tiredness than Tennessee. "Let's keep the show rolling."

"I gotta pull over and check it out," squawked the infernal black box. The truck pulled over to the shoulder followed by the van. Sully grabbed the flashlight. "Hey, I'm still the key grip, so I might as well grip something."

"Uh, that's lighting," Eric bitched.

Sully got out to help Gene check out the truck.

I had to get out, too. I looked at the light of the waxing moon that was playing on the tall grass of the shore plane. I wanted to take a piss, but there were no nearby bushes to step behind. Since we were near the Connecticut—Rhode Island border, I didn't really want to wade into the tall grass which would be crawling with Lyme Disease ticks or Eastern Equine encephalitis mosquitoes. There was also the passing audience on the interstate to be considered. I disappeared into the shadow of the grip truck and figured that if Ava was going to stumble upon me she'd probably get her feet wet. When I emerged from the truck's shadow, considerably relieved, the piercing headlight and flowing clatter of the night's last train to Providence punctuated my weariness and paranoia.

"Son of a bitch," said Gene, watching Sully check out the outside right rear tire.

"That tire is disintegrating," diagnosed Sully. "Well, there's another tire on this end of the axle. I think we can make it to Mukherjee's house if we keep her down to forty. We'll have to follow it well back to watch out for flying rubber."

We headed on down the road. I was riding shotgun; Eric was driving very slowly and keeping an eye on the crawling truck ahead. "So," I said. "Any luck lining up your car?"

"I did reach her, and she'll be waiting for me," he said tentatively, "but I don't know if I'll be heading down to Newport tonight." He looked at his watch. "Shit, this *morning*."

"So, we're not talking about the lady you're sharing a summer rental with."

"Oh, no, that's Molly, the woman I live with." He nodded encouragingly to himself as he spoke.

"I think I see. You got me out here in the middle of the night, with the last train to Providence long gone, and *you* have decided to have a change of life crisis. Christ, I'm glad you didn't turn into a certified public accountant between locations, but this is pretty weird. Who is this wondrous parking lot attendant, or should I say car-sitter?"

"Her name is Jennifer. Buffy lined her up because she has a parking space at her apartment that she doesn't use. She's an artist and she looks like a model." His voice dropped conspiratorially. "I figured that if I let her use my car, I wouldn't have to pay ten dollars a day to park it. I sure didn't know that we'd be getting in at such a strange hour of the morning."

I risked a look at my watch. It was creeping up on one A.M. We were proceeding at thirty-five miles an hour behind a wreck that had yet to clear the Rhode Island state line. Why should I trouble my weary mind with math when the bottom line would only make me feel more desperate?

Eric continued with what he probably hoped would be the capper to his argument. "I mean I can't just go over there at two A.M. and pick up the car and leave."

Two A.M. in Providence. A restless sleeper in a suite who was offering me an incredible body and, possibly, a career. 'Let me know of your decision—at any time,' she had said. "So what *can* you go over there at two and the morning and do?" I asked.

"I don't know," he replied thoughtfully. "This latest delay makes everything more difficult. I mean I want to see her, and she wants to see me, and she's so damn young and beautiful."

I certainly wasn't getting any help with my choices. "Maybe she's really where it's at for you. Do you really care about her?" Did I really care for the woman who was waiting for me on a small island? What about the one in a suite at the Biltmore?

Eric took a deep breath. "Yeah, I really think I do."

"Do you think she rates more or less than being a small chapter in the long and arduous breakup of Eric and Molly? Where will you be the next night? A quick run down the eastern shore of Narragansett Bay to tell Molly that it's all over?"

"Gee, I don't know," said Eric, suddenly puzzled.

"Well, let's forget completely about the new strains of incurable social diseases; that's right out. What if you go over to…what's her name's…"

"Jennifer's."

"…you go over to what's her name's and you have the most incredible emotional and erotic experience that has ever crossed your being. What then? Do you wake up the next morning and say, 'Jeez, I gotta call Molly and tell her we're through'?"

"No, I don't think so."

"Do you go home all transformed, and try to leave this experience out of your life? Whether or not Molly can tell that you're not telling her something, *you* know that you have started to build a part of your life that you can't share with her. Is *that* what you really need?"

"I really can't decide now."

"Ugh," I grunted. "It's one-thirty A.M., do you know where *you're* going to spend the night?" Silently, I asked myself if I knew where I'd spend the rest of my life.

"Listen, man," came Giancarlo's voice from the rear of the van. "I don't know what your, like, issues are up there, but you guys can crash at my place in Providence. It's real close to the train and bus and stuff."

"Thanks, Giancarlo," I called back. "I don't know if there will be any sleeping time left."

Sully was interested and started to make a reservation for the living room futon.

"Okay," sighed Eric. I risked a glance at him. "We're at Mukherjee's exit. How do we get there?" None of us seemed to remember George's instructions.

I raised the truck on the walkie talkie and ascertained that Gene knew the way. The truck exited, leaving a trail of pieces of tire. We followed it to a quiet residential street. Another right turn brought us onto a dead end drive, where we spotted the Lucknow-mobile.

By now, the grip truck was destroying the night's peace with its throaty exhaust and the clashing gears. Gene was trying to get into the Mukherjees' driveway. The neighbors pretended to remain asleep. I was grateful.

George awaited us at the door to his parents' expensive-looking split-level house. "Please come in," he said. "Help yourselves to some of these beers or whatever from the refrigerator while I make out the checks."

I sat at the dining room table and worked on my bill. I could see that George's appeared to be an All-American home with a few pictures of deities, near deities or gurus hanging on the kitchen wall.

George, peering through the black-rimmed spectacles that had slid down his nose, was dexterously examining bills and and writing checks. I got paid for my days, including the travel day I had just spent, and reimbursed for my train fare, lighting rental, and every meal I had been able to find the receipt for. "Oh, and Bart," he added as he handed me my check, "Indrani left a message for you on our telephone answering machine." He pulled a piece of paper out of his breast pocket and handed it to me.

First, I inspected the check to see what bank it was drawn on. It was Fleet Bank, a good Rhode Island noun bank if ever there was one. I could move that paper in Warren before I caught the ferry, or in Providence, if I found myself there. Then I unfolded the note. In an ornate hand it said, 'Bart Lane to call Indrani at the Biltmore, Suite 1613 regardless of time of arrival.'

Eric was settling with George now. George brought his pen to a rest over a blank check and pushed his glasses up his nose to peer at Eric. "What about twenty-five dollars per person to take Bart and Sullivan to Boston?" he inquired.

"I'm not really sure about that. I don't know," replied the exhausted and perplexed Eric.

I leaned into the conversation and addressed myself to Eric. "Shall we step outside for a minute and get this travel confusion settled?" I queried gently, though rage and confusion might have reared their ugly heads.

"What's the problem now?" I asked, trying simultaneously to talk myself out of collapsing in a suite at the Biltmore and possibly subjecting myself to delights my Ohio upbringing and New England bachelorhood couldn't conceive of.

"I just don't know," the decision was making him sweat in the cool suburban quiet. "I mean…you can stay here, or at Giancarlo's and catch a bus first thing in the morning."

"It *is* practically first thing in the morning right now. I'm tired and confused just like you are. Do you want to call Jennifer and have her leave your keys in the mailbox, or do you want to call Molly, and tell her that she's going to be all alone tonight, and tomorrow night, and the night after…?"

"*Okay, motherfucker.* What is *your* problem?"

Indecision, in a word. Where would *I* spend the night? In a bed at the Biltmore with the director? What about waiting for the first bus to Warren at the Greyhound station, watching beggars and touts and trying to figure out if there is still a price on my head and who knows it? "My problem is that I could have been in a very comfortable bed right now if I hadn't listened to your offer of a lift to Warren. I could have climbed on a train and never seen that goddam grip truck again. I thought I'd help you and Sully get this stuff back to Providence and maybe have a chance to get to know you better. I'm sorry to find out that the woman you live with is as expendable as I am. I'm even sorrier that, in some way, you've made it my business."

"I see," he said.

"I also have an irrational desire to get out of Providence. That guy who was run over by Indrani's mother-in-law and Shyam in New York probably has associates here. They may or may not think that their business with me is done."

"Tell you what," said Eric, "let's get George to leave us at Jennifer's."

"Great. Thanks. I have to make a phone call."

"You *what*?" said Eric as I headed for the phone.

"Good evening," said Indrani's voice on the other end of the line.

"Hello, this is Bart Lane," I chose my words carefully, not wanting everyone in the room to know that I was speaking to the director.

"Where are you now, Bart Lane?"

"I'm at Mukherjees' house. We have just arrived from New York."

"Will I be seeing you shortly?" Her voice sounded soft and vulnerable. I had to remember that she was one hell of an actress before she was a director. She also might just be feeling soft and vulnerable.

"I'm afraid not. I have just received word that another production I'm involved with is starting up pre-production earlier than they planned. Thank you for your lovely offer."

"I'm sorry I won't be seeing you."

"I'm sorry, too. Good night," I said and hung up. I turned away from the phone to encounter Eric, who had obviously been standing near by.

"'Another production?'" he asked, failing to keep a straight face. "What other production?"

"The rest of my life," I said.

"I hope, for your sake, that it has a running time of over ninety minutes."

"So do I."

George loaded Sully, Eric, Giancarlo and me into the Lucknowmobile. Our luggage transformed our journey into a magical clown act with an overstuffed car. He wheeled us past the Biltmore, and I found myself counting up from the ground floor to see if there were any lights burning on the sixteenth floor. There weren't.

At Jennifer's, Eric's keys were in her mailbox. Looking at the Victorian house that contained her apartment, I thought I saw a curtain moved aside in one of the upper windows. After we had loaded everything and ourselves into Eric's Volvo, started it and pulled away, the curtain flowed back to its normal position. I don't think Eric noticed.

I was fading fast. Underexposed slides were projected on my dim brain. East Providence, just off Route 195. A coffee shop full of smoke with me buying Eric a lumberjack's special. Passing the Dunkin' Donuts in Warren. *Nighthawks* '86. An elbow in the ribs. Protesting.

"No, you gotta hear this, man." Eric turned up the radio.

"...acting on a tip from the New York City Police Department. The value of the recovered antiques and silver has been ascertained to be well into the hundreds of thousands of dollars, according to a spokesman for Hammersmith Farm. A new development in Mayor Cianci's trouble with..." Eric turned down the volume.

"How about that?"

"Uh...any word on the perpetrators?"

"To quote the radio, 'Indian nationals are being held on hit and run charges.' I'm glad they're still locked up. Here's the shore. What do I do now?"

I kept giving brief instructions and retreating into sleep.

"It's a couple of hours until the first run, what are you going to do?" We had found the dock and Eric was studying the posted schedule by the light of his car.

"I'll swing my gear on board the ferry and get some sleep up in the bow. Thanks for the lift and have a good summer. Give Molly my best wishes and keep some for yourself. I hope I'll get to work with you again."

"Will do. It was great working with you, too. Bye."

He drove off. The gangplank had been pulled from the ferry, but it was close to the dock. The low tide made it easy to swing my bags over the rail and then clamber aboard after them. I moved my stuff into the bow, found a sweatshirt to put on, and fell asleep curled up with my worldly possessions.

"You got your ticket yet?" Another dark image, the mustachioed deckhand with the Paul Anka face and the smoldering Camel was shaking me awake.

"Ticket? No, but I want to buy one. You're still at the dock, right?"

"Yep," he said, pausing to blow smoke out of his nostrils. "I'll be opening the window in a few minutes. We sail in about half an hour. Glad I found you. The captain hates derelicts, but I know what it's like to end up on the wrong side of the water."

I stretched and wondered why the wheeling, screaming sea gulls that worked the cannery dock hadn't awakened me earlier. "To me, the wrong side of the water is underneath it—with concrete booties."

"You'd have to go to Providence or Boston to get a ride like that. We don't do that. It's unecological and besides, why waste all the lobster bait?"

"Thanks," I said, finally making it up onto my feet. I helped him with the gangplank, mainly to reduce the squealing noise that his doing it single-handedly would produce. Then, I made my luggage shipshape and found a clean T-shirt to put on. I ducked into the men's room and rinsed my face but decided not to shave with the small trickle of cold water available. I coaxed my hair out of its matted, slept-on messiness into the casual untidiness I preferred to be seen in.

"A remodeled person," remarked the deckhand as he sold me a roundtrip ticket to Squidneck.

"Can I use this on the ten boat and store my stuff somewhere until then?"

"Leave it where it is. It won't go anywhere. I'll make sure of that."

I ascertained that I had my paycheck with me and did enough stuffing and consolidating to yield an almost empty canvas bag.

There was no point in visiting an island without bringing provisions, whether ordered or not.

I hit the nearest diner and killed some time with too much coffee and a Portuguese muffin. I found my noun bank and was waiting with my paycheck and all of the identification I could muster when it opened. Thank God and also the relevant Hindu deities that the check was good.

I had promoted myself, in the first few hours since the dawn, from derelict to person with pocketful of money waiting for ship to leave port. In this condition, I visited a liquor store and purchased a few interesting bottles: some Prudence Island Chardonnay, a good vintage of Chateauneuf du Pape, and some Dom Perignon. There are times when it has to be French and sparkling wine, *méthode champenoise*, won't do. In spite of the fact that my hostess had almost every reason not to want to see me again, I hoped that this would be one of those times.

I stayed busy, making friends through outrageous buying at a fish market, a grocery store, and finally a florist's. I felt good enough to find a pay phone and call Captain Ryan in Boston.

"Well, what have ye gone and done now, Bart?" he asked after I identified myself. "Don't ye know that we police appreciate our fugitives? They give us a reason for being and all that."

"I'm so sorry you miss him. Does anyone else?"

"If you're asking if anyone is still after you, I have only heard that his mouthpiece, who claimed to know nothing of his flight, has signed off on this one. If he were trying to sue somebody for incapacitating his boyo without the proper paperwork, it would mean that there's interest in, shall we say, modifying potential testimony. It seems that everyone has had it with the late Mr. Quinn. I think you're off the hook."

I may have been just too relieved to ask all the right questions, but as I sent along best wishes to Miss Halloran and signed off, I started to believe that I had a life.

For a day that went on the clock in quiet desperation on the Connecticut Turnpike, it was beautiful. The midsummer haze looked like a master cinematographer had scrimmed the bay with the most subtle of silken gauzes. The ferry's bow sliced the glassy calm of the bay.

Cormorants grouped themselves with an incredible eye for composition on solitary rocks and pilings, transplanting the scene to Macao with their presence. I leaned on the railing and looked up the bay to Providence. A tiny ribbon of skyline revealed the simplest of details—the tall building that Superman had leapt in a single bound, at least for the TV show.

Looking forward, I could see Squidneck. A row of small cottages squinting in the mid-morning sun under a spine of green. The parking lot with no discernible old GMC three-quarter ton pickup truck—nothing quite so new. A weekday ten boat didn't attract as big a crowd as a weekend one; nevertheless, Jessica was wheeling a handtruck down the dock to collect the newspapers and the full milk crates that were fencing in my belongings on the cargo deck. I thought I recognized Elisabeth's neighbors, the Dodges.

A few minutes later, totally loaded with cargo, I was proffering my ticket with my teeth. The deckhand took it, tore it, and stuck the stub back in my mouth.

I nodded at the Dodges and received a nod in return. Then, Virginia Dodge remembered where she knew me from. Her smiling blue eyes opened up. "Aren't you Elisabeth's young man?" she asked.

I looked around to see if she could possibly be addressing that remark to anyone else. "I'm not sure," I said through teeth that were still clenched around a ticket stub.

"Well, of course, you are."

"Virginia," said John, "perhaps Mr., uh, Lane, would prefer to…"

"Nonsense, John. I bet you'd like a ride to Hemp Hill, wouldn't you?"

I took a deep breath, set down half of my load and removed the stub from my mouth. "Thank you both, call me Bart, and yes, please."

Virginia was looking around the parking lot. "Elisabeth's definitely not here. Does she know you're coming?"

"She might know," I replied, "but she might not really believe it."

"That's good, uh, Bart," said John. "You have to keep them guessing."

"What a terrible thing to say, John," said Virginia. "Are you trying to surprise her, Bart?"

I flailed at a number of replies. "Definitely."

I ended up in the back seat of Dodges' 'fifty-three Ford. Here I was, nearly forty years old and on an island in New England, and the ancient car was taking me back to the Sunday drives of my childhood so strongly that I almost became carsick. As we headed across the island, Virginia turned to address me from the front passenger seat. "I think that if you want to surprise Elisabeth, you should get out at our place…"

"Sounds good," I said.

"And don't slam the car door shut. That third slam will just communicate the fact that something's different."

"Do you do this often?" I said.

"Of course not," said Virginia, "we just notice things."

I wondered what else they might have noticed. I decided not to care because it was such joy to have them on my side. As planned, they pulled up to their house on the side that faced away from Hemp Hill. John got out and slammed his car door shut. I hauled my stuff out of the back seat as fast as I could while Virginia stood by with the passenger door open. Her eyebrows arched as she counted down to zero with her fingers and we slammed our doors in perfect unison. "Good luck," whispered John.

"Goodness has nothing to do with it," I whispered back.

Carrying everything, I went along with the Dodge-inspired sneakiness. I kept off the scrunching gravel, muffling my footsteps in the grass alongside the road. Then I turned a corner and Hemp Hill emerged from its screen of cedars to dominate the near horizon. I couldn't see Elisabeth in any of the windows. I hoped she was there. I wondered for the umpteenth time how she woke up in the morning when I wasn't there.

Under my burdens, I made slow but determined progress across the lawn. I made it to the front door and smartly rapped the brass knocker. I heard footsteps lightly thumping down the stairs. I could see her make the turn into the hall and see me. A quizzical look crossed her face and turned into an uncertain smile. She was as beautiful as I remembered her, wearing a Radcliffe sweatshirt and apparently little else. She opened the door and stopped. "Hi, stranger," she said.

"Honey, I'm home," I said.

"Kind of a cross between *Leave it to Beaver* and Stephen King." She threw her arms around me and I had to set everything down before I could reciprocate. When a long and satisfying kiss had ended, she continued. "You look like someone who has been through hell. Where did you sleep last night?"

"In a van, in a car, and on the deck of the Squidneck II."

"Listen, since you didn't call when the ten boat got in, I figured that I'd take myself on a picnic down at the cove and stop sitting by the phone until the afternoon ferry. Why don't you get into your suit and join me? You can work on your tan and sleep simultaneously."

"Sounds like just what I need. I also need to get some of this luggage into your fridge before it rots."

Maybe I was wrong not to lead with a bouquet of flowers. I'd get to 'em. I left most of my luggage in the hall and followed her up the stairs. I was dazzled by the sway of long, now straight, dark brown hair and its gentle brushing back and forth across her lower back as she mounted the stairs. I was physically and emotionally exhausted but awake enough to catch and appreciate a glimpse of her electric purple bikini under the sweatshirt.

In the kitchen, I kept her busy, handing her filet of salmon, fresh crab meat, beef tenderloins, some sensuous vegetables, fresh raspberries, and finally the Chardonnay and the Champagne, as she filed them in the refrigerator. "This is beautiful," she said.

"No more than you deserve," I replied.

"What did they do, pay you in cash?"

"Nope, just a very perishable check."

"I'll expand my picnic a bit, why don't you get ready for some serious beaching?"

I hauled my bag with its still-hidden load of flowers out of the kitchen, secreted it in a safe place, and went downstairs to change. On the beach, we covered each other with suntan lotion, and I fell into a deep sleep.

She woke me for lunch. We sat on our towels and looked out over the bay as we worked on cold grilled chicken, a Boston lettuce salad, and a delicious, fruity *Sancerre* to wash it down with. After we finished the fruit, I told her about the body count from my adventures: one dead, two jailed, and some valuables already recovered.

"That must have been horrible," she said.

"It was, but it was a relief, too. I couldn't ever picture Quinn getting out of prison without being bent on revenge. I hope that whoever he was connected to won't take it too seriously."

"He certainly seemed to have connections."

"I'll say. You don't just drift into Providence and set up in business almost immediately. Even more so for New York. Hey, maybe some godfather or kingpin of organized crime will figure that they gave Quinn every kind of break and opportunity and he still wound up blowing it all by trying to murder someone."

"That would be nice. Get some more sleep."

I was on my back, I turned my head to look at her and saw her turn her face away from me up to the sun. There was so much I wanted to say to her, but my drowsy state didn't bode well for choosing the right words. I collapsed again.

When Elisabeth woke me up by whispering in my ear, I had recovered enough presence of mind to throw my arms around her and roll her into the sand. "I have to kiss and hug you before I do anything else."

"Neighbors in boats," she said. I looked around to see the Dodges in a skiff bobbing in the afternoon's glittering chop about seventy-five yards offshore. I carried out my threat briefly and rolled off Elisabeth. We both waved. They waved back. We raced into the water and the long cool swim cleared the remaining cobwebs out of my brain.

My refreshed mind was brimming with anticipation as I walked my hostess to the shower. This time, the roar of unmuffled internal combustion interrupted us before the water got warm, before we went to work on each other's suits. "Damn," she said. "Time to pay for the newspapers."

"Just as well," I agonized, "I probably ought to scrape my face with a razor blade before I scrape anyone else."

"Good idea, I was afraid that you'd gone for the *Miami Vice* two-day-growth look. I'm not exactly certain what happens to you people when you find work." She wrapped a towel around her waist and headed around to the side door. I went in, unpacked my toilet kit and some clean clothes and headed toward the upstairs bathroom. I spent a few minutes arranging the flowers where they'd be seen at an opportune time and making other arrangements before hitting the shower. I emerged squeaky clean some time later.

I looked as good as I could in my hotel-laundered white ducks and a loose white shirt, but I was almost rendered speechless by the Elisabeth who inhabited the balcony outside the kitchen. She walked slowly back and forth, like a haunting spirit; the wind billowing the crystal pleats of the white evening gown she wore. As she walked, she was brushing her mythic tresses to dry them in the sun, which beamed its late afternoon warmth at her from one side. In that moment, I began to understand *Gotterdamerung*, not as Wagnerian bombast, but as twilight of the gods.

I couldn't just say 'Drinkies?' under the circumstances, so I filled an ice bucket around the chilled bottle of *Dom Perignon*, put it on a tray with a couple of champagne flutes and carried it out to set it before her on the balcony.

"You have remarkable non-verbal skills," she said as she smiled in agreement with the choices I had made.

"I have to start somewhere," I said as I tackled the foil and wire cage that bound the cork. "Are the contestants all in position? Shall I fire the starting gun?"

She set her hairbrush on the table. "Do," she said.

With a mighty prod from my thumbs, the cork sailed over the railing with a satisfyingly loud report. I guided the bottle as the champagne propelled itself into the flutes. I handed her one and raised the other. "I'd like to propose a toast to you," I said, "the lady who saved my life."

We drank. "I had a hunch about the gratitude," Elisabeth said.

"I feel like I've treated you badly. I'm so sorry I couldn't get out what I was feeling when we went up to Providence."

"Maybe I shouldn't have pushed you, or maybe I should have started earlier. You were starting a new job and dodging people who were trying to kill you. If I think back to the last time I was getting ready for my first day at some office, I wonder why you didn't try to climb out of the car before we even got to Providence."

"Thanks, but you deserve better than a wordless hulk like some grunting D.H. Lawrence male protagonist."

"You're much better than the coal miners, Bart, I'd even be willing to put you right up there; somewhere near the gamekeeper."

"A large part of what I was feeling, and might feel again," I refilled the glasses, "is a confused desperation, like Willy Loman in *Death of a Salesman*. Am I obsolete? Did I make all the wrong choices and have I thrown my life away on them? I sit by the phone and wait for someone to call me up with work and reaffirmation. Instead of those pats on the back, I get the feeling that someone has decreed 'Bart Lane will never work again in this town,' and told everyone but me.

It gets so strong that I wonder what right I have to involve you in my bad trip."

"God!" she exclaimed, almost choking on her champagne. "What a load of sexist bullshit!"

"What do you mean by that? So I'm guilty of holding doors?"

"Why is your employment, or lack thereof, so damn important to you that you'd let it tie you in knots and keep us apart?"

"I guess I think that I want to, or that I ought to, be able to, uh, have some visible means of support before I...

"Before you what? Before you tell me how you feel about *anything*?"

"No. Before I make a claim on you by telling you how I feel about you."

Her eyes sparkled as she pounced. "There! That! How deep does that male chauvinism go? Why should whether or not you can 'support' me—I assume you're talking about money—have anything to do with how you feel about me? Why should I be deprived of feelings that you might have just because you don't have enough money? Should we invite the guy who pronounced that you'd never work again into bed with us?"

"No."

"Am I to be deprived of you just because the rest of the world is giving you a hard time? Why do you think you have to feed, clothe and house me before you can tell me how you feel?"

Cobwebs were getting blasted out of corners in my mind, but Elisabeth wasn't slowing down. "What if you had all the work you thought you needed and met a woman you wanted to marry and she refused because she wasn't making enough money?"

"I guess I'd say she was being ridiculous."

"Bart," she looked into and through my eyes, skewering my soul with her gaze. "You are being ridiculous. Are you person enough to see that?"

Incredible. This was happening to me. I could see what she was saying and, yes, the damage that my well-intentioned male chauvinist piggery had been doing to our developing relationship. I let it go and was overcome with a feeling of relief and well-being. "I fervently hope so," I finally replied.

I could tell without looking that the sun had descended below a line of clouds I had seen near the horizon.

"Listen, Bart. You're trying to make movies in Boston. I never heard of a film industry there, but you're managing to pay your rent, eat, and keep the possibility alive. I think you're doing amazingly well on your own terms."

"I want to show you something," I got up and offered both hands to pull her to her feet. "Bring your glass," I said and led her through the kitchen. We turned right. I opened the door to the master bedroom.

"It's kind of early for the jacuzzi," she said.

I led her past the bathroom door. "You can't…We can't…" I led her into the late grandparents' bedroom. The sun was where I knew it would be, blasting through the French doors and creating a new kind of magic hour. It caused the bed to be alight with the lavender sheets I had generously strewn with purple and white orchids.

Elisabeth froze with amazement. "What have you done? You know how I feel about this room. God, those flowers are beautiful, but this is the grandparents' room and…they're still here."

I set my champagne on the night table, gently removed hers from her grasp, and placed it carefully alongside mine. I put my arms around her. She was trembling. "They're orchids," I said. "I think your grandparents are still here, too, at least I hope so."

"Why?"

"Because I need a witness or two." We stood together in the biggest key light of them all. Her eyes blazed into mine. I swallowed and spoke, "What I feel right now is love for you. I love you. I don't really know how easy or comfortable it's going to be to stop being a solitary person, but I want to try."

"So do I." She embraced me more fiercely than she ever had. "Oh, Bart. If you only knew how I've been waiting to hear you say that."

"Your turn," I said, "How much?"

She moved her arms around my neck and threw her head back. It caused her hair to flow smoothly against my arms.

"I loved the idea of you when you stumbled into that poetry reading looking like a misplaced sea captain. The reality of you was a bit more frightening than that."

"Keep talking, you're doing just fine," I said as I picked her up and lowered her gently onto the bed of orchids. I was starting to feel something I couldn't place at first. I think it was undiluted happiness.

Many myths and fears were shattered that night. Vague sayings of old wives and people who were too young to know what they were talking about, things like 'the first time is the best time,' landed on the floor alongside an uninhabited white, crystal pleated evening gown, a pair of white ducks, a shirt and some deck shoes; dashed, rumpled, stretched, and, in some cases, evaporated.

Cambridge, Massachusetts, 7/22/02

0-595-24607-9